ICE VALLEY

Jill Metcalfe

First published 2021 by Jill Metcalfe
Reprinted 2026 by Jill Metcalfe
jillmetcalfe.com.au/

Produced by Independent Ink

Cover design by Daniela Catucci @ Catucci Design
Edited by Anne-Marie Tripp @ Dettori Publishing Pty Ltd
Internal design by Independent Ink
Typeset in 12/17 pt Adobe Garamond Pro by Post Pre-press Group, Brisbane

Cover image: Jill Metcalfe

A catalogue record for this book is available from the National Library of Australia

ISBN 978-0-6452386-0-0 (paperback)
ISBN 978-0-6452386-1-7 (epub)
ISBN 978-0-6452386-5-5 (kindle)

To Laurie, thank you for believing in me.

To all impacted by Tourettes.

CHAPTER 1

Occasionally I lose things. Recently, I almost lost my mind. I'd pushed myself in what had been my messiest year. I'd finally organised some leave; I'd intended to stay home and hibernate. Then after speaking to Uncle J one morning, I decided to step outside my comfort zone and leave the city instead.

I found the perfect place online – a farm-stay in the Hunter Valley called Ruth's Cottage. It was one of three holiday rental cottages on a working winery. I hoped it was available. With my last-minute decision I didn't like my chances.

On the fourth ring, the owner, David Walton, answered. According to the website he lived in the main house on the property. He did have a cottage he could rent to me for two weeks. He was going to be away for several days, and the other two cottages were vacant, so initially I'd have the place entirely to myself. Kismet, it was called. I felt it was meant to be.

I let my best friend John know where I'd be staying and left him to pass it on to our mutual friends. As yet, I hadn't told Uncle J. I'd phone him after I'd packed the car and was on the road. It was a perfect Sydney winter day, azure sky, sun shining brightly to match my mood. I wanted to share my last-minute decision, knowing he'd be impressed; he loved spontaneity.

Uncle J picked up on the third ring, sounding thrilled. 'Princess, princess, princess. How wonderful to hear from you! I thought our conversation this morning would be the last before I head off tomorrow. Forget to tell me something?'

He was about to head off on a soul-restoring trek around Nepal. That's one of many things we have in common – our love of walking.

Excitedly I said, 'I thought so too, but after talking to you, I realised I needed to get away as well. I've booked a cottage in the Hunter Valley for two weeks. I was lucky to get it, leaving it so …'

Uncle J cut me off. 'The Hunter! Grandma Ella would be pleased.'

I smiled at his instant connection to his mother, my grandmother. I'd give him free rein to interrupt me on this call. Overseas travel always over-stimulated him; well, both of us, really.

Hungry for information, he continued. 'So where are you staying?

'Google Ruth's Cottage, Pokolbin. Click on the third link down.'

Tap, tap, tap; I listened as he typed. 'Uncle J, you're as fast as the wind on a keyboard.'

'There have to be some benefits, princess.'

I smiled again. Another thing we have in common is lightning-fast reflexes; more on that later.

I heard him take a deep breath and with amazement infusing his deep, rich voice, he said, 'Pip, you've been there before; don't you remember?'

'I don't think so, Uncle J, though the cottage did keep drawing me back to it. When have I been there?'

Happy to enlighten me, with child-like enthusiasm he beamed his response. 'You were about seven, maybe eight, and mum – um, Grandma Ella – took you there one school holiday. The cottage was owned by a friend of hers, Ruth – yes, that's it; Ruth Richards. It's where you had your first premonition.'

He'd used the 'p' word; I wasn't pleased. He was heading down the paranormal path again. Not wanting to sour our call, I bit my tongue and said, a little disingenuously, 'Um, that's starting to ring a bell.'

He kept on the same trajectory. 'I hope it's not an alarm bell.'

Yep, he was on a roll. I knew he wouldn't be deflected easily. 'Okay, you win. What premonition?'

'Oh, princess, don't you remember? You, Grandma Ella and Ruth were all having a wonderful time, until she went to pick up her nephew. When Ruth went to collect him, you had a terrible premonition …'

I'd heard enough. In an unnecessarily sarcastic tone I fired back, 'Of course, I have a perfect eight-year-old's memory of that. Really, Uncle J, what memories do you have from when you were eight?'

His response was hurt silence.

In my defence, I was tense with both the topic of conversation and his impending trip. I was also instantly sorry.

Before he had time to respond, I apologised. 'I'm so sorry; that was terse and uncalled for. I'm nervous about you going overseas tomorrow. I'm going to miss you. Also, it's been a while since I've spent time away, on my own.'

He said nothing. Pleadingly I continued. 'Forgive me, please?'

His voice mellowed. 'Princess, princess, princess, of course I do. I'll be able to email you. No, come to think of it, maybe not; maybe I'll text you. No, I hate texting, I'm all thumbs, which I realise is the whole point of texting, but honestly … how can I type the way you like me to, as fast as the wind, and tell you all about my travels? How will I find out what's going on in your life?'

He was on an intractable tangent, nervously prattling on. I bit my lip, and he continued. 'I'll make sure I can find an internet café. Oh no, maybe I shouldn't have booked this trip quite so soon after …'

In obvious distress he stopped, leaving the sentence unfinished and me feeling like a total bitch. I must sound like a child, but, in my defence, it really is confronting when your only living relative decides to trek around Nepal on his own.

As both our moods turned dark, the weather seemed to want to match us. Suddenly and dramatically, it took a turn for the worse. The sun disappeared, and fierce winds and dark threatening clouds replaced the glorious day.

This change in the weather was a gift of sorts, supplying a reason to terminate our call. 'Uncle J, I might need to hang up soon. The weather has gone from perfect to threatening. Remember, I love you more than all the stars in the sky. As soon as you arrive, please text or email me. By the way, the cottage has free Wi-Fi.'

His voice filled with concern. 'Please drive carefully, Philippa. Remember, I love you more than all the stars and all the moons in the universe. I promise I'll e-talk to you soon. Love you.'

As he hung up, my heart squeezed tightly. I soon forgot all about our call as the weather turned very ugly, very quickly. Icy winds hit the windshield, forcing me to turn the demister on. These were apparently courtesy of two storm cells meeting. ABC radio's severe weather report said a cold front had moved north from Tasmania across the east coast, bringing with it bitterly cold, wild weather. I sure knew how to pick a time to go away on my own.

As I reached the Branxton Interchange, the skies opened as the storm reached near cyclonic strength, breathtaking in its ferocity. The windscreen wipers were fighting to keep up.

The drive was both slow and terrifying, the rain so heavy at times and visibility so bad that I could only stay on the road by following the tail-lights of the four-wheel drive in front.

I usually hate following four-wheel drives, but not tonight; those tail-lights were a beacon guiding the way. It gave me comfort to see the family in this car ahead of me, knowing I wasn't alone.

The winds buffeted my car so fiercely and shook my confidence so badly that I nearly turned around and headed back home. Then I thought, *Stuff it, I've come this far.*

After an unpleasant relationship breakup, then months of unrelenting and heart-breaking family stress, I was exhausted physically and emotionally. There was no way in hell I was going to cancel this trip.

The storm made my mind drift into the past, back to my childhood. Information stored deep within the connectomes of my brain came to the surface.

Grandma Ella was there. We were in an unfamiliar garden, a thunderstorm raging around us. I vividly recollected her gently taking my hand and guiding me inside. The house was strange to me, and although we were there together, I was upset and agitated, crying inconsolably.

I was upset not only about the storm, but about feelings of dread I was having, feelings my little eight-year-old brain could not understand or decipher. This flashback, so sudden, so powerful, took my breath away. Then as quickly as it appeared, it went.

My neural pathways had taken me back in time. I knew there was more to remember, but for now I was firmly back in the present, back to reality. Shaking my head to clear it, I put all my concentration into arriving safely at my holiday destination.

I wondered if I would remember the rest of that afternoon,

of whatever had happened all those years ago. Part of me didn't want to revisit a time that had so obviously upset me. The brain is an amazing and complex organ, and sometimes of its own volition it throws up the long-forgotten.

As I drove on in the unrelenting and terrifying storm, my courage was starting to dissipate. Why the hell hadn't I turned back when I'd had the chance? It was too late now, so instead I offered a plea up to Grandma Ella, asking her to be with me, to help me arrive safely, to protect me. I don't mind admitting by this stage I was scared out of my wits.

As I finished my plea, an overwhelming sense of calm came over me. I felt her presence and knew she would guide me safely.

Again I drifted back in time, only this time Grandma Ella and I were warm and safe inside. Grandma had her arms wrapped around my trembling little body. My head rested on her chest as she gently stroked my head to soothe me.

As I calmed down, she asked me what was upsetting me, assuring me that I could tell her anything and she would believe me, she would help me to understand.

With trepidation, I told her that I had a feeling that something bad was going to happen. She listened, gently encouraging me, asking me to explain what my bad feeling was about.

As I remembered this long-past day, I clearly smelled the fresh smell of earth after a storm, and the lavender scent on her clothes, a scent I will always love.

Feeling safe in her arms, I told her that I thought something bad was going to happen but couldn't say what. As I began to cry again, my beautiful, sensitive, and – I was to learn – clairvoyant grandmother explained to me that I didn't need to be afraid, that what I was feeling was called a premonition.

She told me she also had premonitions, and that they were sent as a message only, not to do harm. She said I wasn't to be afraid; she would always help me decipher and understand any messages I received; she would protect me always.

As these memories cascaded from the recesses of my mind, someone behind me in the traffic, growing impatient at my slow pace, sat on their car horn, loud and long. The jarring sound shocked me back into the present. As I shook my head to again clear my mind, I raised my hand in apology and began to move at a faster pace.

As I got back up to speed, my impatient fellow traveller passed speedily, making a rude gesture that I chose to ignore.

Calmer now, I thanked Grandma Ella for getting me through the worst of the storm. As I drove, I felt a warm glow at the recollection of that memory, of her loving care toward me, the gentle way she'd tried to explain something inexplicable on that stormy afternoon so many years ago. For many reasons I had pushed that memory to the back of my mind.

CHAPTER 2

The storm had abated a little, and with rain falling, though less heavily, a thick fog had drifted in to keep it company – Mother Nature was using all her guns.

With an unfamiliar road, steady rain and a heavy fog, by the time I reached the cottage my nerves were frayed. All I wanted to do was find the keys, get inside, have a shower and collapse. When I'd spoken to the owner on the phone earlier, he'd said he would leave an outside light on; he hadn't.

With the wet, windy, freezing weather and no light, finding the keys wasn't easy. Hands shaking, drenched to the bone, I was about to give up when I stumbled across them. Finally, something was going my way.

Door open, I fumbled around in the dark, found the light switch and unpacked the car. I'd packed the retro olive green '60s suitcases Uncle J had given me for my twenty-first. They not only look amazing, they're hard-sided and waterproof.

I'd packed too much, but hey, it's better to pack too much than not enough, right?

I'd put in lots of comfortable and warm clothes, my favourite pairs of black jeans, and tracky dacks for cosy nights in front of the fire. I'd also packed several different-coloured t-shirts, walking shoes, my black leather boots and my favourite Lisa Ho three-quarter-length red wool dress, some jewellery, brightly coloured scarves, a hat and gloves. I'd covered all bases.

I'm not a high-maintenance woman in many ways, but I do love my clothes to reflect the mood I'm in. On this trip, I was in the mood to dress for fun, even if it was fun on my own.

Reading being a lifelong passion, I'd packed my e-book, and my sketching pad and pencils, a travel set of watercolour paints and paper. I'd made sure food-wise I was set for the night, until I would be able to shop locally. I'd packed a crusty French breadstick, butter, pâté, avocado, prosciutto and rockmelon, and a batch of zucchini and tarragon soup I'd taken from the freezer. I'd also put in a bottle of sauvignon blanc and a pinot noir, and, to top it all off, Lindt dark chocolate with caramel and sea salt. After the harrowing trip to get here, I'd earned the feast.

Now I was safely inside, nothing was going to get me out, not until this weather settled. Once I'd packed away the food and put the soup in the microwave to defrost, I had a look around.

As I made my way to the main bedroom to unpack, I saw that the cottage was warm, cosy and inviting. There was an eclectic mix of old furniture and cane pieces, a shelf full of books, and a comfy wingback chair and ottoman right next to the open fireplace which I'd light as soon as I settled. All in all, a very pleasing mix.

I instantly felt relaxed; another thing I felt was familiarity – not the sort that breeds contempt but the sort that makes you feel at home. Uncle J may have been right; I might well have been here before.

I took my bags to the main bedroom, hung up my clothes and put my toiletries in the bathroom. The bathroom was another pleasant surprise. Besides a walk-in shower, it had a wonderful clawfoot bathtub, which sat next to a window that overlooked a private courtyard crammed with ferns and small shrubs.

On the wide windowsills sat candles of all shapes and colours. At the end of the bath hung a glorious old gilt mirror. It was an enticing and inviting room, and I knew I'd take advantage of the time I had to luxuriate in that bath, to relax, unwind and take time to just be.

There was second bedroom with two single beds and its own bathroom. I fleetingly thought how perfect it would be if I could share Ruth's Cottage with my friends. Once I'd settled, maybe I'd text them and invite them up.

The cottage had light gold polished wooden floors, with colourful rugs scattered around, comfortable lounge furniture, and a porch that overlooked a vineyard. It was lowset, and from what I could see through the rain, it seemed the plant-filled porch blended seamlessly into the vineyard beyond.

Someone had put a lot of love and thought into this

charming cottage, and I couldn't help wondering if, as Uncle J had said, Ruth was my grandmother's friend and if I'd met her all those years ago. If you understand magical thinking, that would be called serendipity.

It was secluded and quiet, except of course for the storm, which had picked up again and seemed to have no plans to end soon. We try to control many events in our lives, but Mother Nature is definitely not one of them.

I find that both reassuring and humbling.

As I turned from the window, away from the flickering shadows cast by the storm and past the crackling fire that I'd soon got roaring, I felt content.

As I went to put my soup on the stove, I passed a mirror in the hall. When I caught a glimpse of my reflection, I was momentarily surprised. I saw a brand new me staring back, my mouth agape, my eyes wide with a look of delighted surprise.

I'd wanted to change my life so badly that at lunchtime, in a fit of what can only be described as temporary insanity, I'd walked into a barber's shop and had my long dark hair cut very short. Thirty minutes and twenty dollars later the new-look me had walked out.

The short cut suited me, accentuating my green eyes and cheekbones. I was pleased with the new style. I now looked my age; and best of all I'd finally done what I'd wanted to do for years.

My ex, Zac, would hate it – good. One of many positives post breakup: I could be my own person. If I'm honest, I'd also lost my place to hide – my security blanket, if you like – by cutting off my flowing locks. New hairstyle, new life – well, that was my plan.

I'd been in a toxic relationship with Zac for four years. Initially we'd had fun, but after a while he'd begun to try to control me, telling me how to wear my hair, how to dress, and he'd sure as hell put me down.

Nothing I'd done had ever been good enough. I'd felt I needed him to survive, so I'd put up with his behaviour. The truth was, it had been the other way around.

Inadequate people put down their partners, both to keep them and to make themselves feel better. My only excuse for putting up with his cruel and controlling behaviour was, well, when you know you're different, you accept the unacceptable.

As my soup gently simmered on the stove, it smelled delicious. While it was heating, I decided to have a shower to warm up. It worked, and afterward I felt like a new woman, in more ways than one.

I was exhausted, and pleased that I'd brought the soup, bread, butter and wine. I was starting to relax when I felt a chill down my spine. I got up to check for a draught – there wasn't one. I put it down to a rough day.

For distraction while the soup heated, I plonked myself in the chair in front of the fire, put my feet up on the ottoman, began to sip the wine I'd poured, then took out my e-book and read.

Lost in reading, I hadn't noticed that the storm had died down. With no storm noise, I realised how very quiet it was. My mind was used to being bombarded with city noise, so I gave in, turned my iPod onto shuffle and listened to my favourite music – loud. After all, who else was going to hear it?

I soon relaxed under the influence of good music, the intoxicating smell of food heating, the fire hissing and my glass of pinot noir. Red wine goes well with fires and wet and windy winter nights, though if I'm honest, I prefer a sauvignon blanc. Tonight I was playing to a script, so red it was.

As I added wood to the fire, my soup slowly bubbling on the stove, the fresh scent of zucchini and tarragon mixed with the aroma of freshly cut bread permeated the room. I was feeling no pain, relaxing nicely and definitely back in control after my unsettling drive up.

After dinner, I sat in front of the fireplace. The storm had picked up yet again, but this time it didn't bother me. While I relaxed, I felt pleased I'd also packed my sketch pads and pencils. Once I'd unwound enough for my brain to slip into alpha mode, I'd pull them out.

As I was sitting there, mesmerised by the flames, I heard a loud thump. I turned down the music, hoping it was the wind. It came again, only this time it was a heavy thud on the front door, which I barely heard over my own heartbeat as my sympathetic nervous system prepared me for fight or flight.

I stood and cautiously walked to the window next to the door. I gingerly pulled the curtain aside to look out; there was no one. I sighed, thinking it must have been the wind in the trees or an object being flung around in the storm.

Relieved, I walked back to my chair and sat. Then I heard a louder, more persistent thumping, this time on the lower part of the door. As I turned, then bent down to listen, the thump became more insistent, more urgent. So did my frayed nerves.

With trembling hands, I reached for the key and went to take a quick peek outside. Mother Nature helped me with that decision: as I turned the knob, the door flew open, forced inward by the wind.

As I struggled against the air pressure to shut the door, rain drenching me again, I felt something wet brush my leg, and saw a fleeting shape dart inside.

I locked the door, checking it three times to satisfy the OCD side of my personality. Whatever was inside with me now was in for the night.

I grabbed a towel to dry myself off and another to throw over my uninvited guest. At least the thumping had stopped. Now I had to search the cottage and find my unwelcome visitor. I hoped to hell it wasn't a wild one.

CHAPTER 3

I don't know if you know much about OCD, but as I said, I'd definitely locked the door, checking it three times, a slave to my obsessions. The rational side of my mind was telling me to unlock it in case I needed to expel my guest quickly. Naturally the irrational side won, and I started my search of the cottage with the door firmly locked.

I knew from where I'd felt it brush my leg that it was small. I began to search the cottage; if and when I found it, I'd then decide what to do. Hopefully it was cute and fluffy and more scared of me than I was of it.

After searching the entire cottage, I found nothing. Finally, I put it down to my imagination. OCD and a vivid imagination can sometimes go hand in hand.

It had been some day, and as I settled back in the chair, I must have drifted off to sleep. When I woke, the mystery of my uninvited guest was solved.

Sitting in front of the fire, its back to me and grooming

itself, was a very bedraggled-looking cat, so wet that I couldn't make out its colour.

I still had the towels sitting on my lap, and thought I'd cautiously introduce myself; if that went well, I might even try to dry it off.

Not wanting to scare my uninvited guest, I very slowly stood, towel in hand, and in a gentle and reassuring voice said, 'Hi there, little one; bit wet, I see.'

In an exaggerated startle response, it jumped high into the air, wet fur standing up all along its back and tail fluffed to three times its normal size.

My response matched the cat's, and after I'd screamed and jumped nearly as high, I said, 'Oh shit … you frightened the crap out of me, you little creep!'

We were off to a great start. When the animal finally stopped backing up, it began to spit and hiss at me.

Great – I'd let in the Hannibal Lecter of cats. Either that or this cat was especially fearful of humans. Either way, I was screwed. My response to his response definitely hadn't helped matters.

After my heart and pulse had settled down, I took the higher moral road – yeah, right, like cats see it that way – and began to coo what I hoped were soothing words.

Hannibal wasn't having a bar of it, and began to yowl. That yowl told me in no uncertain terms, cat to human, that I was in its territory and it was not happy.

I had to find a way to settle him down, and I remembered there was some smoked salmon left in the fridge. As I moved slowly toward the kitchen, Hannibal came at me, spitting and hissing. I grabbed a cushion from the lounge and put it between my legs and its snarling face, and in a less-than-soothing voice I spat back, 'Well, charming. I was going to get you some food, but not if you don't want it.'

For some reason my tone seemed to settle the cat, so I continued my retreat to the kitchen, took out what remained of the salmon and put the plate on the floor.

I was fast running out of options if this didn't work. My next plan was to head for the bedroom and lock myself in.

My feisty feline companion gave another yowl for good measure, letting me know he couldn't be bought that easily.

I wasn't an instant hit; the salmon, however, was. Keeping a close eye on my movements, intermittently growling, the cat moved in a low, slow slink to the plate.

When he finally reached the food, it was heartbreaking to see how hungry he was. As I watched him scoff, I racked my brains for anything else I might be able to feed him.

I remembered I'd packed a tin of tuna. To reassure the cat – it's astounding how we humans think animals can understand our jabbering – I stood, protective cushion in place, and asked, 'I've got some tuna, if you'd like it?'

Ignoring my inane comment, the cat sat in front of the fire, licking his paws, at the same time keeping an eye on my moves. Sensing I was going to the food place, he graciously let me pass.

I opened the tin of tuna and put a small amount into a bowl. If Hannibal was still here in the morning, he would obviously need breakfast. As I went back into the room, he gave me a half-hearted hiss for good measure, and once I'd placed the tuna next to the empty plate, he again wolfed it down.

Realising he probably needed water as well, I cautiously stood, leaving my cushion behind, and filled a bowl from the sink tap. As I was filling it, the saying 'dogs have masters, cats have slaves' came to mind.

Know your place.

When the bowl was full, I giggled, realising I'd reached new heights of humility in trying to satisfy this one. Either that or I'd have to stand my ground. Again – yeah, right.

By the time I re-entered the room, the tuna was gone, and I thought I heard a faint purr. Taking this as a good sign, I put the water bowl nearby. My reward was a half-hearted hiss. This cat definitely did not like humans, and it had me wondering why.

To take back some control of the situation, I cautiously took a towel from the lounge, bent down next to this now softly purring cat and said, 'You look so wet. Do you mind if I dry you off?'

Seriously – 'Do you mind?' I actually said those words. It seems the cat didn't mind, as he condescendingly allowed me to do just that.

As I dried him off, I realised he wasn't a wild cat after all. He had a collar on. As carefully as I could, I slowly turned it around and read the name. He was definitely a he; his name was Albert.

Once his coat was dry, I could see that Albert was a ginger tabby with beautiful even markings. I also saw that Albert had the most amazingly penetrating green eyes. He was captivating, all things considered.

After drying him off, the truce was over. To let me know my place, he hissed and scratched me.

Disappointed, to say the least, my response to him was, 'Oh, you little mongrel, that hurt. You make it difficult to like you; has anyone told you that?'

As I said this, I backed up, making my way to my toiletries bag for some tea tree oil. I dabbed some on the scratch, and by the time I made my way back Albert had made himself very comfortable in the chair I'd set up directly in front of the fire.

I'd had enough, and as gracefully as a defeated human could, I said, 'Well, looks like you've made yourself at home. I'm off to bed. Please feel free to see yourself out before I get up, if you know the way. Otherwise, I'll see you in the morning.'

Albert's response was to yawn and turn his back on me.

Round one: Albert.

I have a grudging respect for the feline species. The Egyptian culture revered and held cats in high esteem and, well, I guess I kind of understand their reverential attitude.

Besides, he reminded me of one of Grandma Ella's cats. I loved that cat, and so did Grandma Ella. Perhaps that had some bearing on my tolerance – perhaps?

As I prepared for bed, plugging in my mobile and e-book to recharge them, I could hear the storm had started up again in earnest. Branches of nearby trees groaned under the force of the wind. Bushes outside my bedroom window were scratching on the glass. I hoped I'd sleep with all the noise and fury.

Sleep for me can sometimes be problematic. In part that's down to genes, but more on that later, when you get to know me better.

Tonight, though, my head had no sooner hit the pillow than I was fast asleep. It had been some day.

My sleep was full of vivid and wild dreams. I'm one of those people who dream in colour and always remember their dreams.

Over the years, encouraged by my grandmother, I've kept dream diaries. I had one with me, and as I lay there during the night, occasionally woken by the storm still raging outside, I knew I would have some very obscure and hard to fathom dreams to enter into my diary by morning.

When I woke, according to the bedside clock it was 11 a.m. It's unusual for me to sleep that long. I wasn't alone, and for an instant I thought of Zac. As I sleepily rolled over, I saw that Albert had joined me on the bed and was snuggled into the crook of my legs.

Trying not to disturb him, I gently stretched and slowly went to pat him, thinking I'd won some sort of truce or reward.

Nah – wrong again. When Albert realised where he was and who he was in bed with, he jumped up high, hissed, leaped off the bed, skittered sideways and arched his back in a territorial manner.

Instead of feeling justifiably hurt, I raised my eyebrows, stretched, yawned and casually said to the ungracious Albert, 'Well, good morning to you, too. Glad to see a meal and a good night's sleep have improved your disposition.'

Albert ignored me, ran to the front door and started scratching to get out. I decided to make him wait and have my shower first.

As I looked out the bedroom window, I could see that the weather had improved dramatically. There were lots of leaves and small branches down, but it was a perfect, crisp winter's day. The haze, a violet-hued misty fog, still hugged the ground, so I grabbed my camera and snapped a few shots before it dissipated. After my shower and some breakfast, I'd go outside and explore.

Why do things always seem better in the morning? I felt positively refreshed and energised by my night's sleep, even though it had been full of misty and unfathomable dreams. After my shower, I planned to write my dreams into my diary, before I forgot them entirely.

I do my best thinking in the shower, and while the glorious hot water cascaded over my head and down my back and shoulders, it eased away the aches and pains in my tense muscles. It felt odd, that first time shampooing my now short hair; odd and liberating.

As I showered, I thought about Albert.

When I'd booked, the owner, David Walton, hadn't mentioned a cat. I wondered if he was now feral, abandoned or belonged to a neighbour.

Whatever the case, he seemed very hungry and very thin. That infuriated me. If he did belong to someone, why weren't they feeding him properly? If he was abandoned and now feral, how hard did he have to work to survive?

Albert's story was starting to intrigue and touch me, and suddenly I felt childish and cruel to have not fed him or let him out before my shower.

As I was drying myself, I heard my mobile ping. I hoped it was Uncle J texting me. When I opened it, I felt instant relief when I read, *'Hello, pumpkin, about to board after stopover in Singapore. Interesting first leg, nice stewards, very understanding and accommodating – bless them. How's the Hunter? Hope your drive up was uneventful? Remember the cottage? Text when I arrive. Love you more than all the stars. Uncle J xx.'*

Elated to hear from him, I immediately texted back, saying, *'So glad to hear they're looking after you. Trip up was a bit wild weather-wise. Glorious today though. The cottage does seem famil-iar. I had an uninvited visitor last night – a soaking wet ginger tabby just like Grandma Ella's Meggs. Remember him? Please keep in touch. Stay safe. I love you more. Pip xx.'*

CHAPTER 4

After my shower, I threw on my ripped black jeans, a t-shirt and a big pullover. I put on a little make-up and, to compliment my new short haircut, a pair of large hoop earrings. I was content with what I saw in the mirror. I'd become very tired of the way my long hair had seemed to drag me down. It probably wasn't the weight of the hair as much as the way my life had been. My new style made me feel much lighter in so many ways.

By the time I'd finished, Albert had given up scratching at the door, but if looks could kill I'd be dead. Opening the door for him to go outside and seeing in the light of day how thin he was felt heartbreaking.

I wasn't sure of cat protocol, but I guessed that when he'd finished relieving himself, breakfast would be the right move. Heading toward the kitchen, looking back over my shoulder, I casually said, 'Is tuna okay again for breakfast?'

Albert was no fool; he knew the kitchen was where the food

came from, so after relieving himself he grudgingly followed me in. When I opened the refrigerator door, he gave me a fleeting leg cuddle. Things were looking up; maybe I wouldn't need the cushion for protection this morning.

Whether he was abandoned or feral, I understood why he'd stooped to giving a human a leg cuddle. As a reward, I emptied the entire can of tuna into the bowl. Who knew where his next meal would come from?

Albert ate his meal with as much dignity as a hungry cat could muster, then he walked over to the door, looked disdainfully over his shoulder at me, then jumped up and touched the door handle. I swear to you he did. I felt sure then that he'd done this 'open the door' routine before. I wasn't sure who with, but lesson number one of a hundred ways to make a human feel small and inferior had just taken place.

Without delay I unlocked the door and let him out again. He instantly disappeared into the bushes, and I was sure that was going to be the last I saw of him. A little part of me felt deflated. I'm not a masochist, fond of pain and humiliation, but I do love a challenge, and he was company.

What can I say – company is company. Now that I lived on my own, I missed talking to someone on a daily basis. Notice I didn't say I missed talking to Zac; just company.

I wanted to explore the property, but with two glorious weeks stretching ahead, there was plenty of time for that. After a quick breakfast and a piping hot coffee, I drove down to the local shops at Pokolbin to stock up on groceries.

On the drive, I was staggered to see the number of trees that had been blown over. I was very lucky that one of the larger trees near the cottage hadn't fallen on the roof during the night.

I stocked up on all my favourite things, and, I'm not ashamed to admit, even bought some cat food just in case my antisocial feline friend returned.

After I'd shopped, I found a coffee shop open and sat for a time, looking at the town. It seemed almost deserted, which surprised me.

As I walked back to my car, I was disturbed and saddened to see several young people hanging around who were quite obviously affected by some very serious drug.

I tried to push this from my mind – I'd come up here to escape the failings of city life, not confront them.

Back at the cottage, I put away what I'd bought, put on my walking boots, and packed water, a protein bar, my sketch-pad, pencils, and my camera into my backpack, and set off to explore the vineyard.

Exercise is an extremely important part of my life. It's beneficial for both my body and my mind. I was delighted to stumble across a small dam on the property. It was a secluded and enchanting spot and I kept it in the back of my mind as a place to return to.

After an hour of exploring, I was hungry, and headed back to the cottage for lunch. There was no sign of Albert. I was surprised at how disappointed and deflated I felt.

I spent the afternoon engrossed in the novel I was reading. Before long I realised the sun was disappearing. I wasn't ready for dinner, so I set about getting the fire going. There is something very empowering about getting a fire roaring – perhaps it goes back to prehistoric times, a feeling buried within us all.

Once I had it well established, I ran a deep, relaxing bath. As the light was fading fast, I lit all the candles that sat on the windowsills and all around the bath, including in front of the mirror that hung low and directly at eye level at the end of the tub.

I set my iPod up, then opted for total silence instead, except for the noise of the flickering fire just outside the door and an occasional sputter from the candles in the room. I also burned some lavender in my oil burner.

When I finished setting it up, the room looked inviting and safe, a true magical space. I lay my dressing-gown on the Bentwood chair next to the bath, and slowly lowered myself in. It was heaven, and with each exhalation, I soon felt the stored tension in my body start to melt away. I store a lot of tension in my young body, but more on that later.

I hadn't noticed how tense my muscles were from the past several months. I made myself a promise then and there that for the next two weeks I'd luxuriate in this bath as often as I could – daily, if possible.

As I lay there, my 'monkey brain' was still chattering away at me. I didn't want to listen to any chatter tonight; I wanted total peace and total relaxation. To help achieve this I took some deep breaths, and went through a relaxation exercise starting at my scalp, working all the way down my body to my toes.

After the first time through this process, the chatter slowed a little. Not to be defeated, I did it again, again and again, concentrating on my breathing; finally, it worked.

I closed my eyes to help block out any visual distractions my overactive mind could latch onto, and when I opened them again, I looked into the now misty mirror hanging at the end of the bath. I smiled at myself and said, 'You made it, Pip; time to concentrate on you.'

I must have drifted off, a combination of the velvety hot Radox and the smell of lavender. As I opened my eyes, I became mesmerised by the gently flickering candlelight reflected in the mirror. It was intoxicating to watch, but as it flickered, I saw a fleeting image of someone who looked like Grandma Ella within the mirror.

Surprised, to say the least, I squeezed my eyes tight and rubbed them. When I opened them again, she was gone. I concluded I'd been daydreaming, or that the lavender scent had made me think of her. The smell of lavender always conjured up thoughts of Grandma Ella.

In that fleeting image, I had felt there was a shadow behind her. It was too indistinct to make out. Seeing her, though, made my heart swell with a longing to really have her here with me; it was bittersweet, that shadowy glimpse of her. I think of her most days, even now, and miss her all the time. She is always in my heart.

As I lay there soaking in the tub, I had a flash, a memory of my visit to Ruth's Cottage all those years ago. I remembered listening to my grandmother and Ruth talk about the ancient art of mirror scrying.

They shared how they'd each adapted their own version of scrying to help them access messages or visions. I then felt that the vision I'd seen in the mirror, Ruth's mirror, may well have been my grandmother, and perhaps the shadowy figure behind her was Ruth.

Blissfully relaxed, I shut my eyes, put the washer over my face, and tried to clear my memory of that fleeting image. But even as I relaxed further, I couldn't help but wonder what message they had meant to bring me.

When I took the washer from my eyes and looked back into the mirror, all I saw was my own reflection. I laughed to myself, stood and pulled the plug, deciding I'd had enough relaxation and reflections for one night.

My mind has a tendency to jump; thinking of reflections reminded me that I had my favourite book with me: *Reflections* by Hermann Hesse. If nothing else, my fleeting glimpse of Ella reminded me to take it out and read it yet again.

As I dried myself off, something inside the cottage made a very loud and jarring crash. I was momentarily startled until I realised that perhaps Hannibal – I mean, Albert – had returned. I hoped so, anyway.

After I slipped on my dressing-gown, I cautiously made my way into the living room. Sure enough, Albert had jumped in through the partly opened kitchen window, knocking over a jug in his haste to get inside where it was warm and where food was available. I'm not naive enough to think I was part of the reason for his return.

I felt relieved to see it was him, despite his disdainful and aggressive behaviour toward me the previous night. In fact, I was inexplicably pleased to see him. Albert had done nothing to endear himself to me, yet I was delighted he was back.

Round two: Albert.

I knew he'd be hungry – aren't cats always? – so, looking directly at him, eyes narrowed in a non-dominant gesture, I asked, 'So, had a good day Albert? Would you like something to eat?'

Of course I wasn't expecting any response, but he did condescend to give me a very quick dart between my ankles and a chirruping response. I took this as a gesture of truce, if not a show of affection. Like all good cat slaves, I set about preparing his food.

After he'd eaten, I fully expected him to jump outside again the way he'd come in, but Albert, full of surprises, took himself over to the rug in front of the fire, plonked himself down and promptly began to groom. Yet again I felt he knew this cottage well.

Now that the master had been served and sated, I cooked my own meal. I wasn't in the mood for anything too elaborate, so I settled on a smoked salmon and fetta omelette with dill and slices of avocado and cherry tomatoes on the side. It hit the spot, and before long I joined Albert in front of the fire.

I read for a few hours, then I heard a ping on my phone; it had to be either John or Uncle J. It was Uncle J again, and it read, *'Princess, I've arrived. What an awesomely amazing place. My brain is in overdrive – you can imagine!!! Lovely people, good feelings about the place. Glad I made this trip. Going to try and stay awake. How are things with you? Love you more. Uncle J.'*

I was relieved he'd arrived safely and that, so far, he seemed genuinely pleased he'd made the trip. When you get to know more about Uncle J, you'll understand both my concern and my relief.

Straight away I texted him back. *'So great to hear you've arrived safely. Glad the people are lovely. They will love you, I know. I'm doing well here … relaxing!!! Oh, and Albert the cat is back … so I've got company. Cottage has a claw bath, which I plan to use often to relax. Was so relaxed last night, thought I saw Grandma in the mirror at the foot of the bath. Love you lots, P.'*

I knew this update would grab his interest, and half regretted adding the last bit, but it was out there now. He didn't disappoint, responding with, *'How wonderful, unintentional mirror scrying. Ella loved scrying. Unusual to get such a fast result, though; must be the stored energy of being there with her. You really are so like her, Pip. Have to fly. Hope to find a real keyboard soon. I'll take lots of photos to show you. All my love, Uncle J.'*

I was proud that Uncle J thought I was like my grandmother. I'd always known I was more like her and Uncle J than like my parents. I'd always fit more comfortably with them both.

Next I texted John, Phoebe and Annie – my three best friends – to let them know I'd settled in well and that there was plenty of room if they wanted to get away. It would be difficult for Phoebe and Annie, as they both had young children, but John and his partner Max might make it up if their busy social life had an opening.

After I'd sent the texts, I prepared myself for bed. Just as I was about to turn out the lights, I remembered Albert. I went to see if he was still around, and found him curled up on his favourite armchair – he'd claimed my chair back. I gently covered him over with a throw, switched off the lamps and went to bed.

As I said, I can have difficulty sleeping from time to time – it comes with the genes I've inherited. Soon I'll tell you about those genes. I share that genetic lottery with Uncle J.

Sleep didn't come straight away, so I pulled my old, battered and yellowed copy of *Reflections* out, to hopefully read myself to sleep. That did the trick, and in no time, I was in holiday mode and sound asleep.

The next morning, I woke fully expecting Albert to be asleep on the end of the bed. He wasn't. One thing cats aren't is predictable. That's one of the many things I love about them.

I showered, pulled on my clothes, and made myself a piping hot pot of tea, some toast and marmalade, and a bowl of muesli with yoghurt.

I had no concrete plans, and I felt relaxed enough to try some sketching, so after I'd cleaned up, I packed my backpack and headed out the door.

CHAPTER 5

Looking for a place to sit and sketch, in the distance vineyard I saw a little ginger shape. For some reason, this scrawny, unlikeable ginger cat had got under my skin. There was also the challenge of trying to win him over, so I headed his way.

He was standing staring at the rose bush that stood at the head of the third row of grapevines. As I walked toward him, he turned my way, looking at me intensely. As I approached, he began to dig frenetically at the dirt around the base of the rose bush.

Fancy that, I thought. *A rose scented litter tray.*

I don't know much about vineyards or why they plant rose bushes at the head of each vine. I'd have to google that. I felt sure the owner wouldn't be pleased if Albert clawed his rose bush out, though.

When I reached him, hands on my hips, I said sternly, 'Albert, stop that, you naughty boy. Find somewhere else to poo.'

Albert's response was a very nasty and long growl, as he continued to claw at the red clay volcanic soil around the base of the rose bush, scattering it everywhere. I knew then I only had one option, to walk away, and I did.

I went up a hill, and found a picturesque spot to sit, under the shade of a glorious old mango tree. The tree looked as if it had been there forever. I tried to forget my grumpy little ginger friend's behaviour, hoping he hadn't done too much damage to the rose bush.

Before long, I'd slipped into a relaxed alpha mode, the mode I do my best sketches in. I was pleasantly surprised with my sketches of the surrounding vineyard. It had been a long time since I'd been relaxed enough to draw at all, let alone well.

After a few glorious hours making pictures, I headed back to the cottage to grab something to eat. After the unpleasant scene with Albert in excavation mode, I wasn't quite as disappointed this time when he was nowhere to be found.

After lunch, I went for a long walk around the property. If I'm honest, by this stage of the day I was looking again to see if I could find Albert, but if cats don't want to be found you won't find them.

I stumbled across the other two cottages that were for rent. I could see, even from the outside, why they weren't being rented at present. They needed some attention, seeming forlorn and abandoned.

Before long, I found myself at the main house. I knew I shouldn't be here with the owner away, but I was concerned about Albert and wanted to make sure he was safe.

Knowing the house was empty, I tried to peer in through the windows, in case Albert had found a way inside. All the windows had closed shutters. It seemed there was no way he could get inside.

Being near this house made me feel uncomfortable and it wasn't just that I had no right to be here. I wanted to leave, so after calling Albert for a few minutes, I headed back to Ruth's Cottage, where I felt safe and content.

For some unfathomable reason, the main house had left me feeling very unwelcome. I feel that mainly with people, but sometimes with places as well.

Some places, like Ruth's Cottage, feel welcoming, warm and inviting – like going home – as if Ruth had left her lovely warm energy there.

The townhouse I'd recently bought, for instance, made me fall in love with it the moment I walked into the courtyard. The positive energy I felt straight away definitely came from the woman I'd bought the place from. She'd left her positive and creative energy behind for me to enjoy.

Once back inside the cottage, I felt safe and at home, and I set about cooking myself a meal of lentil patties. As I cooked, I fretted about where Albert could be. I had just finished my meal and was enjoying a glass of wine in front of the fire, when my little feline friend jumped up on the outside windowsill and frightened the living daylights out of me.

Despite his noisy reappearance, which made me spill my glass of wine everywhere, he was a welcome sight. I stood and slid open the window a bit, allowing him to gracefully slink inside.

We were turning into the odd couple, Albert and I. Somehow, improbably, we had a special connection.

In a mock stern voice, finger wagging, I scolded him. 'Where the hell have you been? I've been looking everywhere for you.'

Naturally there was no response apart from a very brisk and, I like to imagine, apologetic leg cuddle. Not to be put off by this transparent display of affection – it was dinnertime – I continued chastising him. 'Don't think you can crawl back that easily. I suppose you've been causing havoc digging up rose bushes all over the place? I'll wipe this wine up then get you something to eat. You must be hungry after all your excavation work.'

Seriously, when I looked down at him, I swear he was smiling one of those inscrutable cat grins.

I wasn't in the mood to be placated that easily, and huffing off to the kitchen I added, 'You've made me spill red wine over my favourite top. Stop scaring the living daylights out of me, okay?'

I'm not proud of my petulance, but I'm only human. At that moment, I wished for and wanted to know exactly what Albert was thinking, and I would have done anything to get a response from him. Unrealistic, I know; he wasn't Koko the gorilla.

After dinner, I grabbed a book on gardening from one of the shelves. The book tag told me it had belonged to Ruth Richards.

As I looked at the photos of stunning gardens – the book was called *The Vision of Edna Walling* – I smiled to myself as I realised that Ruth must have been a keen gardener. She was the likely reason why the garden around the cottage was a stunning riot of winter colour and fragrance.

Someone had lovingly and thoughtfully planted jonquils, lavender, violets, snowdrops and pansies. Maidenhair ferns were also strategically dotted throughout the garden. It exuded a feeling of warmth and it smelt divine; I knew I would enjoy every moment sitting in it during my time here.

As I was flipping through this book, something fell out onto the floor: two photos. From what was written on the back of each, I knew one was of Ruth and her husband Thomas – such a good-looking couple – while the other was a photo of Ruth and a woman named Muriel.

Uncle J was right: seeing these photos, I now had a vague memory of meeting her all those years ago – thirty years ago, in fact – when I was eight and visiting with Grandma Ella.

CHAPTER 6

I'd been at Ruth's Cottage for ten days; Walton was due home in two. Albert and I had slipped into a love-hate relationship. One day he'd be affectionate, the next distant and surly. I took the affection when I could, and ignored the less endearing side of his nature.

He'd been down to that same rose bush several times. Some days he'd scratch away, other days he'd lie at the foot of the bush. I soon knew it was a special space for him, and left him alone with his thoughts.

I was keen to continue exploring the property while I still had it to myself, and drawn by God-knows-what I headed back to the main house. I wanted to see if it still held that same unwelcoming feeling, now that I was in a much more relaxed mood. I was intrigued, and my curiosity enticed me back.

As I approached the house again, I could feel that same foreboding. It didn't have the charm of Ruth's Cottage, that's for sure. The paintwork on the veranda around the house was peeling in places, while the decking badly needed oiling, all of which was a shame; it would have been a gracious home in its time. You could tell the garden had once been magnificent. Although someone had recently half-heartedly worked on it, it didn't have the same appeal as the cottage garden.

I always have my camera with me, and never go anywhere without it, so I snapped a few photos to show Uncle J. I'd also taken photos of the cottage, its garden and the surrounding vineyards to show him. The contrast between these photos was staggering to see.

My shots could never compare to any he was taking of the beauty and majesty of Nepal. Knowing Uncle J's love of photography, he'd still be fascinated with my photos.

Everything creative in life fascinated and captivated Uncle J – it was his default setting. It was also why, despite his neurodiversity, he was so hugely successful in the advertising industry.

Although the garden surrounding the cottage was a little wild and untamed, it felt inviting, its energy welcoming. The garden around the main house, though recently attended to, wasn't inviting; its energy didn't welcome at all.

I found this perplexing; surely nature is nature. Places, they say, hold the energy of the people who spend time there.

As I snapped away the last shots of this uninviting garden, I saw the remains of a dead magpie. I hoped Albert had not been the instigator of its demise.

With a shudder, this little black and white bird's presence was enough to send me back to my temporary home.

When I arrived back at Ruth's Cottage, I noticed that

Albert was scratching at something that was wedged between the floorboards of the veranda. He seemed very intent to get whatever he saw out, so in true servant-master fashion, I knelt down next to him to see what his little cat mind was caught on.

Turns out it wasn't his imagination – there was a piece of paper wedged tightly between the floorboards, a very tiny edge visible. I knew he'd have no hope of dislodging this himself, so I kindly offered to help, saying, 'Hang on, Albert, you'll rip it to shreds. Let me help you. I'll grab some tweezers.'

Of course, all Albert heard was 'Blah, blah, blah, Albert, blah, blah blah.'

I tried unsuccessfully to dislodge the piece of paper from the deck. I don't give up easily, so not to be beaten – and to placate and please Albert, who was scratching at the paper again – I looked to see if there was enough space for me to crawl under the decking to retrieve the paper. There was, just.

Underneath the floorboards was dark, dusty and full of cobwebs. As I clawed my way closer to the paper, years of dust fell through the floorboards and into my face and eyes. I made very slow progress in the small crawl space, hoping like hell I didn't wedge myself beneath the cottage. That wouldn't be the best way to meet David Walton.

After much puffing and panting, I finally reached the wedged piece of paper. I gently prised it from between the boards, and, so as not to tear it, placed it down my top, and made my way back to the sunlight.

After I'd spat the dust from my mouth and brushed the cobwebs from my hair and eyelashes, I bent down and let

Albert sniff the paper. He seemed enraptured with it – like sniffing catnip. I gently took it away from his enthusiastic scent-marking efforts, and to distract him, made an offer he couldn't refuse. 'Are you hungry? Come on, I'll feed you early.'

Albert obligingly followed me inside. I knew he was still more interested in what I held in my hand than in any food on offer, so once inside, I put down his meal then put the piece of paper in the desk drawer and away from him. I then had a quick sponge-down to remove the dirt and grime.

Once I'd finished, I put the kettle on; when my tea was made, I retrieved the page from the desk drawer, sat down and unfolded it to see what Albert had been so interested in.

What I saw took my interest immediately. It was a page that had been torn from what appeared to be a diary. I recognised the handwriting from the bookplates of the books that lined the shelves of Ruth's Cottage, which all read: '*ex libris Ruth Richards*' – it was definitely the same handwriting, Ruth's.

When I started to read what was left of Ruth's words – age and weather had faded most – I felt voyeuristic, like I was betraying Ruth by reading her private thoughts.

At first the writing was neat, then it seemed she was writing in a much more hurried manner. It would take me a long time to decipher what was left of her diary entry. Perhaps once I did, I would understand why the page had been torn out.

Frustrated by the deteriorated condition of the page, I decided to put it away until morning, and have a relaxing bath instead. All Albert wanted to do was jump up on the table and rub his little face against it, so I made sure he couldn't find it.

I put the page into the outside pocket of my overnight case, and put it on top of the wardrobe so it would be safe from Albert's attention. I then ran myself a bath, lit some candles and my lavender burner, and immersed myself in the comforting embrace of the old tub.

I was lying there, taking deep breaths, working through my relaxation technique while of course my monkey brain was chattering about the diary page and what it could mean. I mulled over Ruth's words in my mind, trying to fathom their meaning. They didn't sound like the words of the Ruth I had envisaged; the Ruth Uncle J had assured me had been my grandmother's friend and who had left her beautiful energy in this cottage.

Soon the warmth of the water, my deep breaths and the lavender oil calmed me and I closed my eyes to savour the moment, momentarily forgetting the mysterious page. When I opened my eyes and looked into the mirror, I wasn't sure what I was seeing.

It wasn't Grandma Ella this time; it was an indistinct, small oblong shape. It didn't make sense, but I was determined not to flinch from what the mirror had to tell me, if in fact it had anything at all to say.

I shut my eyes, and when I opened them again there was nothing but my own perplexed face reflected back at me. Uncle J was right, I didn't have the same skill and experience with mirror gazing that Grandma Ella had. A huge part of me was relieved.

Once out of the bath, I decided to call John and tell him

what I'd found. As they always screen their calls, at first it went onto their answer machine. Their message said, '*Hi, you've called John, Max and Leroy; leave a message and we might get back to you.*'

I started leaving a message, hoping he'd pick up: 'Hi, John and Max; meow, Leroy. It's Pip …'

As soon as John heard my voice, he did what I'd hoped, picking up and saying, 'Hello, beautiful, great to hear from you. Thought you'd forgotten us. We've missed you. How's it going?'

I loved hearing he'd missed me, and with matching enthusiasm responded. 'Glad you're home. I've missed you, and Max and Leroy of course. It's been very relaxing, with the exception of the psychotic and unpredictable cat in residence. I can't believe I've only got four more days here. The owner gets home day after tomorrow. I'm not sure I'm looking forward to having company. It's been bliss being able to be myself totally, no filters.'

Not missing an opportunity to have a dig, John said casually, 'How dare he come home and ruin your retreat from civilisation. Come on, be honest, don't you think it could be fun to have someone other than a cantankerous cat for company?'

I put him straight, saying, 'For your information, smart arse, I've had plenty of human company. The people at the local shops have gotten to know me. They've been very friendly and forthcoming with information about Albert, Ruth Richards and David Walton.'

I had his attention now. Trying to act disinterested, he said, 'Who's David Walton?'

John is my best friend, but he has a habit of not listening. With mock sarcasm I said, 'Really, John, you know he's the owner of this place. Stop cutting me off and let me finish please. I've got so much to tell you.'

'Trust you to find lots out,' he said mockingly. 'You're like the Spanish Inquisition: people always spill their guts to you. I'm all ears. Tell me every minute detail and don't hold anything back. I want all the goss.'

I'd missed him so much, and to satisfy his curiosity and to keep him on the phone I did just that. I started theatrically. 'Well, the other day, I was getting Albert some meat, and I went to the local vet to get him some Revolution. I don't think he's been wormed for a while … anyway, I digress … I asked the vet nurse if she had any idea who Albert belonged to. She did.'

John interjected, asking, 'Really, who does he belong to? I hope for their sake they're some completely doddery old fart, because that is the only excuse for treating an animal like Albert's been treated. Those photos you texted me of him are heartbreaking; he's so thin.'

I let him vent for a while, then cut back in with, 'Let me finish. She told me Albert was the much-loved cat of Ruth, who, Uncle J assures me, was a friend of Grandma Ella's.'

John gave a fascinated sigh, and I smugly continued. 'I know – freaky, right! Uncle J told me that on the phone on the way here, sorry I forgot to mention it to you. It gets better; he also said I've been to this cottage before, with Grandma Ella, when I was around eight.'

I knew I'd shocked him, again. I was thoroughly enjoying

myself. We often have this banter between ourselves, trying to out-astound one another.

John was becoming more intrigued by the moment, and in a surprised tone he said, 'You've got to be joking! What are the odds of that? Do you remember the place? That is truly bizarre, if you have been there. Come on: what else did she say? Where's Ruth now?'

In a less excited tone I told him, 'Well, that is the really sad bit. It seems she disappeared around three years ago, never to be seen again. Imagine that – disappeared. Apparently, they found her car several kilometres away. The police at the time determined she must have taken her life by suicide. I don't know though, John. I found something today which ...'

To stop my rabbiting on, he steered me back on track, saying, 'Oh, Pip, you're joking? This was supposed to be a relaxing holiday, but it sounds like you've stumbled into a soap opera. This could only happen to you. What did you find today that makes you think the police got it wrong?'

I took a deep breath and, with as much honesty as I could muster, told John everything I could remember. 'So much has happened. First, there's Albert. I can't understand why there isn't anyone who has offered to take care of him, unless of course the owner of this place is supposed to.

'Then there's the way Albert keeps going back to the same rose bush. Did you know they plant rose bushes at the head of every grapevine? According to Google it's because there is a certain type of fungus that attacks grapevines and it affects roses first, so they're planted as an early warning sign of ...'

John quickly cut me off. 'Okay, enough lectures about rose bushes and grapevines. Get back to the interesting bit. What else did the locals have to say about the owner? Did he buy the property after this Ruth disappeared?'

'Well, no, that's the interesting bit. Although they have different surnames, he's her nephew. Oh my God, I've just realised something Uncle J said on the phone on the way here. He thinks I'd met Ruth's nephew when I was little. That's only just dawned on me.'

John had done a great job so far in our conversation of ignoring the elephant in the room – my genetic traits. I was over-excited and feeling safe and comfortable with him; I felt no need to hide my unique genetic expressions. He's used to them, and takes them as an intrinsic part of who I am. How can I best describe those innate traits of mine?

Okay, here goes. The closest I can get is to describe one trait as a squeal. I'd also been throat clearing savagely throughout the call, and my not-often-used and annoying cough made up the trifecta. Lucky John had all three going on in one call.

So now it's time for you to know my genetic secret. I've got mild Tourette's syndrome (TS for short), and my Uncle J, well, he has a severe form of Tourette's. The vocal noises, the tics that manifest, can increase with tiredness, excitement, anxiety and stress.

John knew I was getting overstimulated and he also knew why. True to form, he'd done his best to ignore my tics in our call. John never judged me; he was never cruel about them; he only ever showed great love, concern, compassion and understanding, and he was also very protective of me. Tonight was no exception.

On hearing my tics were escalating, John took control gently but firmly, saying, 'Baby, maybe you should call it a night and finish your story another day. I can hear you have a pressure cooker of tics building up. Can you go for a walk, or get some fresh air at least? You can tell me about the diary entry and your theory about Ruth's suicide tomorrow, okay, hon?'

I knew he was right. Fighting my overwhelming urge to continue my story – make that mega-overwhelming – instead I gratefully responded. 'Yeah, you're right. I am tired, and it's been a day full of surprises. Let's touch base after Walton has returned and I can give you a first-hand opinion of him.'

To lighten the mood before we hung up, he said, 'Great. In the meantime, text me if you think of anything else. That'll give your vocal cords and my ears a rest.'

Wanting the last dig before I hung up, I said, 'Droll, very droll. Why don't you admit it: I'm the most intriguing person you know. I know you're dying to hear more; stay tuned for further developments. Love to Max and Leroy. Bye.'

Clunk, I hung up.

CHAPTER 7

As I hung up, I smiled to myself. I had that warm and wonderful feeling you get when you know someone understands you with all your flaws, yet still wants you in their life.

John has never made me feel broken.

It was still light enough to get some fresh air, so I took a short stroll around the garden to help reset my brain. Nature always restores my equilibrium. How could it not?

When I finally came inside, I set about lighting the fire. Fires take a lot of effort and after a while the novelty wears off; even so, I was determined to have one lit every night.

Once the fire was blazing and Albert fed, I set about making my own dinner. I'd bought a tender T-bone steak and some oyster mushrooms. I served it with a potato with sour cream, peas and carrots.

I'd also bought Albert some steak, knowing he'd love that as a treat. I didn't realise how much he'd love it until I fed it to him. I was his favourite human after that. After I'd finished my dinner, my little ginger friend actually jumped up onto my lap, walking around, kneading my legs until he made himself comfortable, then he lay down and started to purr loudly.

It was the most relaxed and contented I'd seen him since I'd arrived. I didn't dare disturb him from his sleep. Thankfully, I had all I needed already on the coffee table next to the chair.

As I sat reading, I disappeared into the world of the characters in my book and lost track of time. Albert lay asleep on my lap for at least two hours, his little legs softly twitching as he had his cat dreams. Without warning I felt a spiking sensation as he sprang out of my lap, clawing my legs as he used them as a springboard. He jumped so far, he hit the front door.

I knew he'd had a very bad dream. Reassuringly, I approached him as he sat trembling and terrified next to the bookcase beside the door. It broke my heart to see how genuinely upset he was. It must have been some dream.

I tried to placate him, saying, 'Oh, baby, are you okay? Did you have a bad dream?'

As I went to pick him up, he snarled at me; once he realised it was me, he seemed sorry. I did the only thing I could think of to calm him. I got him some fresh meat, diced into tiny little pieces. It seemed to work, but as he gulped it down, he kept looking around the room in fear.

I cooed on, saying, 'It's okay, baby boy. There's no one here who can hurt you. I wouldn't let them even if there was. Come on, let me pick you up and give you a cuddle.'

From my past experiences with Albert, this was a bold move, but I hated to see him so afraid, so I gingerly – no pun intended – bent down and picked him up and cradled him in my arms.

The most surprising thing was that he let me hold and get close to him. After a while, I placed him back on the chair, covered him with a throw, gently kissed his head – yeah, I know, brave woman – turned off the lights and went to bed.

Finally, round three: Pip.

I was unceremoniously woken around 4:30 a.m. by my crepuscular companion. At first, I couldn't work out where the hell the noise was coming from. Finally, I saw him; he was on top of the wardrobe worrying at my overnight case, which soon came crashing to the ground with a deafening sound.

I jumped out of bed, muttering expletives to myself, expecting Albert to fly out of the room in embarrassment – cats hate doing stupid things – but no, Albert was still staring at the ceiling, displaying predator-prey behaviour. I thought perhaps he'd spotted a gecko, but there was no sign of one.

I tried coaxing him down. He wasn't in a mood to follow orders. He continued staring at the ceiling, the only indication that he'd heard a word I said an annoyed flick of his tail, which very clearly said, *'Leave me alone.'*

So I did. Now wide awake, I went and had a shower instead.

By the time I'd finished, he'd come down from the top of the wardrobe and was giving me his 'feed me' noise. Being a good servant, I fed him.

Having a long day ahead thanks to my feline alarm clock,

after breakfast I decided to turn a negative into a positive. I rugged up in my Icebreaker, favourite wool scarf, hat and gloves, and put on my walking boots for a long walk.

Albert, now fed, watched my preparations with bored disdain. He yawned, turned his back on me, jumped up onto his favourite chair and did what most cats do best – he slept.

As I walked away from the cottage, my soul instantly felt nourished by what I saw around me. Begrudgingly I thanked Albert for waking me so early.

Everything was covered in a blanket of misty mauve-grey fog. The leaves on the vines and trees were drooping as a heavy morning condensation weighed them down with fresh droplets of water.

Bright, pearl-like dewdrops clung to fragile cobwebs. Entranced, I snapped away with my camera, hoping to retain glimpses of this early morning magnificence. I'd have photos of something wonderful to show Uncle J after all.

I soon found myself at my favourite spot by the little dam, where I hovered for a long time, captivated. The trees around this body of water shimmered with fog-drip, their reflections visible on the surface of the water.

An old, once-useful fence showed a perfect example of artistic perspective as it disappeared into the water. I took lots of photos of this scene, knowing that when time permitted and inspiration prevailed, I'd paint a watercolour from the pictures, which themselves already had a watercolour feel.

I was finally doing what I'd wanted to do since coming to Ruth's Cottage, making the most of each and every day, on my terms. With only two more days before company arrived – the owner, David Walton – I was determined to enjoy the last of my solitude. It surprised me how much I'd enjoyed my own company so far.

Okay, I know John was right, it was Walton's property, but that didn't stop me feeling a twinge of sadness that my time alone, or rather my time with Albert, was fast coming to an end.

The fog soon lifted, and a brilliance of sunlight and greenery took its place. For a change I'd remembered to bring my mobile with me, and as I sat soaking in the beauty around me, my mobile pinged.

It was Uncle J. His text read: *'Princess, I'm having an amazing time in this incredibly spiritual country. Lumbini, birthplace of Buddha, moved me beyond words. Temples everywhere; the people are profoundly spiritual and very accepting. No doubt their long history of invasion made finding peace a priority. Can't wait to share all of this rich history with you. To this end, I'm keeping a journal, so I don't forget anything. I know your time away is coming to an end. How's it going? Any more mirror magic? I love and miss you. Uncle J.'*

With tears in my eyes – I'm emotional and proud of it – I responded, saying, *'Uncle J, only you could make me feel like I'm there with you. I can't wait to share your journey journal; I don't want to miss a thing. As for me, I now understand the difference between loneliness and solitude. Maybe one more mirror magic moment; not sure. Talk to you about it when you return. I love you more. Pip.'*

I wasn't holding back; I really hadn't been sure what the hell to make of my quick and hazy vision of the small oblong shape in the mirror. If I'm honest, I'm also reluctant to own up to any scrying skill.

Besides, Uncle J's journey through Nepal was hugely important to him, and I wanted my focus to be on that. Just thinking of his bravery in taking such a trip on his own, I was overcome with love, pride and admiration. Two weeks alone in the Hunter is hardly a rich comparison.

My own townhouse had a bathtub. Once I got home, I planned to set up a mirror at the end of it. That would tell me for certain if I'd inherited the family 'gift' from Grandma Ella. Until I worked that out and understood it, the mirror glimpses would be my secret, shared only with Uncle J.

There was also a text from John; he was concerned about our call last night. It read, '*Bestie, hope you slept well? Max and I are going to the Blue Mountains for the weekend. Want to join us? Love, Me.*'

I knew he'd asked me out of kindness, and though I still had another week off, I responded, '*Bestie, slept well, thanks. Took your sage advice and walked in the garden. Thanks for your kind offer, but I'm kind of into solitude at the moment. I might start painting the front bedroom instead. If I don't see you before you head off, have fun. Love, P.*'

My stomach was soon rumbling, so I made my way back to the cottage for some lunch. I loved not having to move to the beat of someone else's drum, but of course I was forgetting Albert.

He was still asleep in the chair, and when he heard my entry, he stretched, yawned, jumped down and went straight to the fridge. I felt a tinge of regret that he'd miss my lunchtime meat treats after I'd gone; he might even miss food in general.

After I'd fed us both, I drove down to the shops to buy enough food to last me for the remainder of my time here. To my surprise I was recognised and welcomed by the locals, which pleased me despite my newfound love of solitude. But I realised I was also looking forward to getting back to my life in Sydney, to my home, to my friends.

When I arrived back at the cottage, I ran myself a bath, set about the ritual of lighting the candles and burner, and eased myself into oblivion; only this time Albert joined me, perching on the chair next to the bath.

Most animals are attuned to energy and emotions, so I took Albert's presence as a sign that he felt drawn to the vibrations in the room.

I now considered this daily ritual as sacred, while also extremely relaxing. I hoped I'd be able to replicate such a time and space at home, making it a regular part of my life.

Albert was soon asleep, purring gently. His purring helped to relax me even further; cats are beneficial in so many ways. As Albert's gentle rumbling lulled me, I closed my eyes, and, much faster and with more depth than last time, slipped into a meditative mini-sleep.

As my eyelids become heavy, I saw a brilliant flash of violet light. I remembered reading somewhere that this meant my 'third eye' was opening, the eye that connects you to a higher consciousness. Funny how you remember these things when you have to.

When I opened my eyes, I looked directly at the reflection of the wick of the candle in front of the mirror. I'm not sure how long I watched, mesmerised by the reflection of the flame, but something flashed into view – the letter A.

That was all.

Not staggeringly interesting, I know. Did A stand for Albert or something else? I had no idea, and it's fair to say that the one thing I'm short on – except when it comes to children, the elderly, animals and the frail – is patience. It seemed that if scrying could teach me nothing else, it would teach me the art of patience.

I was starting to look like a prune from soaking in the tub, so I clambered out. When I'd finally dressed and turned to look at the clock on the bedside table, I was stunned to realise I'd been soaking for nearly two hours.

As I'd done with all my feeble attempts at scrying in the past – Grandma Ella had encouraged me on a few occasions – I wrote down what I'd seen and how the vision had unfolded. Grandma Ella had told me often that what she saw while scrying didn't always make sense immediately. I made sure to add that Albert's purring had helped me to relax more deeply.

Don't get me wrong; I had no intention of making scrying a daily event in my life back in Sydney. To be honest, though, there was a teeny-weeny part of me that felt intrigued to see how far I could make it go.

Tourettic people are known for having enquiring and open minds, for looking outside the norm and having divergent or, if you like, neurodivergent opinions. At any rate, the Tourettic people I know are like that. I'm no expert on the way most people think, because I don't have any experience with what it feels to be neurotypical; I'm wired differently. Hey, who knows! Maybe it's the extra dopamine, or maybe it's having different wiring that makes us more open to different ways of looking at life – or, in my case, ways of connecting to other realms.

Even so, I'd had enough for one night, and with only one night left before David Walton returned home, I decided to put out a plate of nibbles (my favourite way to eat is grazing), pour a glass of wine, put on some music, and dance the night away. Believe me, I love to dance anytime, anywhere, and I don't care who's watching.

Tomorrow was the last day I'd have to myself. Tomorrow was also the last day I'd have to spend with Albert. I resolved to spend the entire day in his company. I'd also start my packing.

That's another thing about me: when I'm ready to go home, I'm ready to go home. Wanting to pack my suitcases early was a sure sign that I'd had enough.

CHAPTER 8

When I woke, it was 4:44 a.m. – for some reason I wake at that exact moment fairly regularly. I was lying on my back, Albert sleeping stretched out along my body. I felt both moved and sad. A few more days here and I was sure we'd become firm friends. As I gently began to stroke his ginger fur, his whole body vibrated with purring.

Not wanting to break the magic, I stayed in bed a lot longer than I'd anticipated. Eventually I gently prised him off and, to make up for breaking the bond we'd finally forged, I fed him immediately. I made myself some toast and a cup of tea, ate, then quickly jumped into the shower.

Once out of the shower, I did a bit of tidying up with Albert anxiously following me around. As I was cleaning off the kitchen bench, I heard footsteps on the gravel outside, then a knock at the front door. I was even more surprised when I opened the door to an extremely handsome man. 'Can I help you?'

He flashed a disarming smile and said, 'Hi, Philippa. I'm David Walton. I own this place. I'm sorry if I startled you. I've come home a day early, and I wanted to see how you're enjoying your stay?'

I'd been taught to be polite, so, despite being annoyed at his early return, I put my hand out to shake his and said as pleasantly as I could, 'Nice to meet you, David. Um, would you like a cup of coffee? The kettle has just boiled.'

I hoped he'd say no. To my relief he answered politely, 'Thanks, Philippa, but I've got to unpack then throw on some washing. You know what it's like when you first get home.'

It was then he saw Albert. Seeing the look on his face, I instantly knew he wasn't a cat lover. Confirming this, Walton said sternly, 'I'm sorry, has that cat been annoying you? It belonged to my aunt. I'll take it out if you want me to.'

As the man made a sudden move to pick him up, Albert hissed and bolted. Seeing Walton's attitude toward cats, I'd have run off hissing also. I'm used to ailurophobes – people who fear or even hate cats – as Zac was one. While we'd lived together, our home had remained a cat-free zone.

I soon found myself defending Albert, with, 'No, really; Albert has been great company and no bother at all. He's a dear little cat.'

This response seemed to bring David Walton back into his default mode – obsequiously charming. Through laughter he said, 'Really, I'd call Albert lots of things, but "dear little cat" isn't one of them. Are you sure we're talking about the same cat?'

Not wanting to escalate the situation, and because I could

feel my tics screaming to explode, I gave a short mirthless laugh to lighten the mood. Being a chameleon comes naturally to me. Quickly and with some disingenuousness I said, 'Well, yeah, I know what you mean; at first I had to hold up cushions for protection when I walked past.'

I immediately felt guilty for betraying Albert. However, Walton took it to mean that a bond had formed between him and myself, and he continued his verbal attack on Albert by unkindly and authoritatively giving me a lesson on cat vs human etiquette: 'I usually find that picking him up by the scruff of the neck and booting him out the door works. You've got to show them who's boss.'

The smile on his smug, handsome face was at odds with his words; the hairs on my arms soon prickled, and I tried to hide the tremor that followed.

With his looks, I was sure he was used to affecting women this way. Like most conceited people, he felt he'd amused and charmed me, if his answering smile to my visible bodily reaction was any indication.

He didn't understand that my response was aversion, not attraction. Wanting to end our conversation as quickly as possible, I said, 'Thank you so much for dropping by, David. I'll let you get back to your unpacking. I'll see you over the next day or so, no doubt.'

He left, and as I shut and locked the door – yes, checking it three times – I pressed my body against it and let out a long sigh. I immediately went out the back door to look for Albert. Not surprisingly, he was nowhere to be seen.

This interaction with Walton made me more determined than ever to finish my packing. It was Thursday. I rationalised that if I headed home tomorrow instead of Saturday, I could see John and Max before they'd left for the Blue Mountains. I'd also offer to look after Leroy, their dear old cat, and hopefully this would help me not to miss and think about Albert so much.

Mind made up, I packed most of my belongings before lunchtime, and put the suitcases in the boot of my car. I left what I'd need for the remainder of my stay in my overnight bag. After that I decided to walk around the property in the hope of finding Albert.

I saw Albert in the distance digging under his favourite rose bush. I was about to bring him back for a cuddle when I was given a masterclass in human versus cat – a.k.a. human dominates cat.

As I watched, Walton walked up to Albert, picked him up by the scruff of his neck and threw him away from the rose bush into some shrubs.

As my blood went cold and my temper flared, I ran toward Walton, my filters off and my TS threatening to explode. With some measure of control, I shouted, 'Hey, was that really necessary? He's just a poor defenceless little animal!'

He hadn't realised I was there, and was momentarily stunned by my sudden appearance and interjection. Then yet again I saw anger on his face – it had transformed him – but that face and his irritation didn't scare me one bit. I was still enraged at what he'd done to Albert.

Seeing my look of contempt, and no doubt trying to regain control of his own temper and the situation – bullies hate to be found out – he tried to placate me. 'I'm sorry you had to see that,' he said. 'He's forever digging around all the rose bushes.'

All I could think to say was, 'Yeah, right, and I still believe in the tooth fairy.'

I knew this situation could only escalate. To avoid that, but in what could only be described as a voice full of contempt – screw civility – I said, 'I'm sorry, but that's no excuse to treat him like that. I don't think your aunt would approve of such behaviour.'

To my astonishment and delight, he turned bright red; I wasn't sure if this was through embarrassment or anger.

By this stage I didn't care. Without giving a rat's arse, I continued. 'I've decided to check out tomorrow instead of Saturday. I'll drop the key back to you on my way.'

This seemed to throw him; you could tell he wasn't a man used to being dismissed. To give him his due, he kept his calm, and with a syrupy tone said, 'I'm sorry if what you witnessed has made you want to leave early. I can assure you, I usually have a much better relationship with the cat. It's hard keeping this place running on my own.'

I didn't believe a word. His performance left me wondering how the hell anyone ever fell for that sort of person. Hearing his insincerity and smooth delivery caused me to shiver again, which he no doubt misread as my falling for his charm.

To end the conversation, I said, 'Yes, I'm sure it's a full-time job. I'd better finish my packing and have some lunch. I'll see you when I drop the key off tomorrow.'

Back in control, he turned to me and with a practiced smile and appeasing tone said, 'Fine; I'll see you tomorrow. I'm sorry your stay had to end like this. I hope you don't put anything negative on Trip Advisor. What you witnessed really isn't who I am.' Then he turned hurriedly and walked off. I thought, *Like hell it isn't.*

Once he'd gone, I hunted everywhere, calling Albert's name. He was nowhere to be found. Eventually I gave up and made my way back to the cottage to finish tidying up.

To my great relief, I found Albert inside. He was sitting in front of the unlit fire, licking himself all over. As soon as I saw him, my heart lifted, but just as swiftly fell. I realised he'd come here because he felt safe with me, and tomorrow I'd have to leave him alone to defend himself.

I went to him, bent down slowly and with real emotion said, 'Hello, darling boy; are you okay? Let me look at you.'

Albert, initially startled, jumped high into the air. Then he seemed to realise it was me. With a look of pure trust on his little face, he allowed me to pick him up.

It didn't seem he had any injuries. Due to their innate righting reflexes, cats always land on their feet. Being tossed into some shrubs hadn't harmed him.

I fed Albert, and half-heartedly made myself some lunch. I had enough left over for both dinner and a quick breakfast before I headed off in the morning.

So that Albert and I could enjoy our last night together, I got the fire going, then ran my last bath in the cottage, going through the ritual of lighting the candles and the oil burner.

After my exposure to Walton, I wasn't expecting this to be quite as relaxing as my other bath experiences had been, but hey, I could always try. I figured it might even help to settle down my tics, which were firing off in my brain like a pressure cooker letting off steam.

Albert looked at me in an inquisitive way; the noises I was making must have seemed odd to him. I wouldn't have blamed him if he'd left me to my own devices, but instead he followed me into the bathroom, jumped onto the chair and looked at me as if to say, *'I'm here for you, like you were here for me.'* That's what I wanted him to have thought, anyway. Besides I was grateful to have company; he soothed and calmed me, and I needed that right now.

It took me much longer than usual to slip into a calm and centred state – imagine trying to meditate on a small boat in a wild storm. My monkey brain was in chatter overload and my thoughts were scatty like the wind, which, by the way, had started up again outside courtesy of another freak storm. I felt nature was responding to the reappearance of Walton. To be fair, weather forecasts had warned of possible turbulence.

As I lay there, I began ticcing – both movement tics and vocal tics this time. On a roll now, my TS had decided to add my nose-scrunching tic as well – think 'cute demented bunny'.

As I was letting my vocal tics fly and muttering away to myself, mainly derogatory comments about Walton that can't be repeated, Albert sat listening. His little head was on an angle, as if by watching me from that angle he could understand this side of me, this untamed side, the constant companion that I try very hard to keep in its place.

It's not a good idea to try to forcibly stop tics or venting all the time. TS has a will of its own that must be obeyed. From what I've read, tics fall within the spectrum of hyperkinetic movement disorders. Sure, you can control it for hours if you need to, but that only delays a more severe outburst of symptoms later on.

Here's an analogy I once read: it's like having your car stuck in a ditch. You continually spin your wheels, but without traction you can't get out of that ditch. However, with focus and dogged determination you can get out; so, too, finally I'd get myself out of a deep Tourettic ditch.

Eventually my Tourettic brain was satisfied to have let off steam, and my tics slowly subsided, leaving me feeling a sense of relief mixed with sheer exhaustion. The low light, warm bath and lavender – a perfect calming trilogy for a person with TS; well, this person with TS anyway – had finally performed their magic.

Albert had also stopped staring, which was a relief, as it can be quite unsettling to have a cat stare at you.

Sensing my now calm state of being, he'd started purring and was soon asleep beside me, all thoughts of my odd behaviour no doubt a distant memory. If only we humans were as forgiving.

With the help of the calming trilogy and Albert's purring presence, I finally slipped into a very relaxed state, then a blissful sleep.

As I opened my eyes, I looked again into the mirror. This time I saw a rose, and despite the already pervasive scent of lavender in the room, I smelled an overpowering musky scent of roses. I closed my eyes to refocus, and when I opened them again, I saw something that made even less sense – a tongue-and-groove panel. That vision made no sense whatsoever.

Finally I realised that Albert had left the room, so, fed up with my final attempt at mirror scrying, I stepped out of the bath, pulled the plug for the last time, dried and dressed myself and went looking for him.

You'll never guess where Albert was. If you said on his favourite chair, you'd be wrong. He was back on top of the wardrobe, staring at a spot on the ceiling; only this time he was trying to worry at the boards with his claws. I realised the pattern of boards on the ceiling was tongue-and-groove.

CHAPTER 9

A shiver of recognition wracked my body as I realised that the spot Albert was pawing was the same as the image I'd just seen in the mirror. The cat was seemingly directing me to it.

Beyond curious, I grabbed a stool from the kitchen and climbed up to see what held so much interest for him. He was persistent, a cat on a mission, scratching away at this one area of timber.

I followed his lead, and touched the timbers he'd been pawing. At first nothing happened. Being persistent myself, I touched a little harder. To my astonishment I heard a click, and a hinged panel in the ceiling opened downwards with an eerie squeak and a shower of fine dust. I jumped down, grabbed my mobile, turned on the torch app, then climbed back up.

When I looked inside the space, the compartment was empty except for dust. But within that dust was a shape where something had stood – something oblong.

I'd had enough for one night, so after I'd taken a photo of this secret opening with my phone, I closed the compartment gently. As I jumped down to wipe the dust off the bed, I caught a fleeting glimpse of movement outside, as if someone had darted away from the bedroom window.

To reassure myself, I went outside to see if there was someone lurking near the cottage. I saw no one, and put it down to imagination.

Back inside, I checked to make sure that the diary page I'd found earlier with Albert's help was still in the side zip pocket of my overnight bag. It was. To make sure it was safe, I folded it and put it into an inside pocket of my handbag. I also made sure all the windows and both the doors of the cottage were locked – three times.

With the rituals that my OCD had to satisfy out of the way, I set about feeding Albert one last dinner. I dispiritedly served myself up what remained of my food. I had half a bottle of wine left which I fully intended to drink. After two glasses, I tipped the rest down the drain.

Once we were both fed, I sat in our favourite chair and Albert jumped straight onto my lap. He seemed somewhat subdued, but definitely content now that we were together and alone. I hated the thought of saying goodbye to him tomorrow, and tried to push it out of my mind.

As I sat there, stroking Albert, I thought about Walton and wondered if he was Ruth's nephew whom I'd met all those years ago, the one Uncle J had mentioned. I couldn't be objective about it – people change so much from childhood to adulthood.

Walton was a very handsome man, but personally I've always been attracted to men with character rather than beauty. Zac had been attractive, physically at least, but he'd never been what you'd call handsome.

Zac kept coming into my mind; not in an 'I miss you' type of way, more of an 'I want you out of my system' way.

Witnessing Walton's behaviour toward Albert had helped to reinforce my feelings that I'd dodged a bullet getting out of my relationship with Zac.

I didn't want the night to end, yet I couldn't wait to escape back to the security of my home, my usual routines. I hoped that Albert would find someone who might look after him better than Walton did. Thinking about it was making me heartsore.

Eventually I couldn't put off the inevitable, and I made my way to bed, leaving Albert warm and cosy on our favourite chair. Sleep took a while to come. The wind picked up again, and every time I heard a branch scrape against the cottage wall, it grated on my nerves like a thumbnail down an obsolete blackboard.

Around 2 a.m., the wind was joined by torrential rain. It made a deafening sound as it lashed against the old galvanised iron rainwater tank, which was soon noisily overflowing.

The full effect was a cacophony, with the white noise made by the wind and rain masking all other sounds. If I had an unwelcome visitor, which I truly doubted in that sort of weather, I'd have no hope of hearing them arrive.

Finally the wind and the rain settled, and I slipped into

an exhausted sleep. True to Tourettic style, it was full of vivid, colourful and perplexing dreams. The noise had greatly disturbed Albert, and for most of the night he hid under the covers next to me, too terrified to poke his head out. This both surprised me and endeared him to me even more. When I found him there during the night, I realised he wasn't the Hannibal Lecter of cats after all.

When I finally woke, it was still intermittently raining. I couldn't help connecting the violent weather yet again to the reappearance of Walton. Several times during the night, I got up to make sure no one was around. I'll be honest: that fleeting glimpse of what I'd felt to be a person's shape at the bedroom window as I'd investigated the secret spot in the ceiling had unnerved me.

Ruth's presence was palpable, yet despite feeling this presence, her residual positive energy, I felt a new uneasiness. Again I thought of her disappearance, and this time I wondered if the energies of the house might be pointing toward something sinister. I wanted to leave the cottage, despite my guilt about leaving Albert behind. In my heart I knew that Albert was the reason why Ruth's presence was so potent; but what could I do? I couldn't abduct him.

I had a quick shower, which helped clear my head. I got dressed, had some breakfast and coffee, and, as there was a break in the weather, I packed the rest of my stuff into the boot of my car. It was all done by 7 a.m.

I checked to see where Albert was so I could say goodbye to him. I couldn't find him. There was a part of me that was sad about this. I wanted to feed and hug him one last time. The coward in me was relieved. I didn't want to see the look of abandonment on his face as I drove off and out of his life.

Car packed, the cottage tidied and the leftover food binned, I did what I always do when leaving anywhere I'm staying: I checked it again for anything left behind – three times.

OCD is exhausting on so many levels, but it's who I am. To satisfy my brain's need for control, I always complete these rituals to my brain's satisfaction. It used to piss Zac off no end; but then again, eventually everything about me pissed him off.

I have another ritual I always undertake when I leave a temporary place – I thank it for keeping me safe and allowing me to live within its walls. It doesn't matter if it's a dump or five-star. I'm always genuinely grateful and thank every place I stay in. I believe every place you visit has its own energy; every place teaches you something. Gratitude is important; it's a positive emotion and a positive energy.

Just before I left the cottage, I checked my bedroom – Ruth's bedroom – one last time, including under the bed in case Albert was there. He wasn't.

As I was leaving the room, I looked up at the seamless secret compartment in the ceiling, imagining once again what it had contained when Ruth had been alive and living here.

As I had this thought, my body's response was to send a sudden shudder down my spine and goosebumps up both arms. I couldn't help wondering if Ruth was trying to tell me something important about this compartment. Alas, what could it be? With one last look around, I left the room.

I found it incredibly painful to jump into my car without saying goodbye to Albert. I was hoping like hell Walton would still be asleep, and in preparation for that, I'd grabbed an envelope from the desk in the cottage and had written a quick note about my early departure, saying I'd phone him soon.

There was no sign of him, so as quietly as I could, I dropped the envelope containing the keys and my note through the slot in the door and drove off. I was relieved I didn't have to speak to him and that I was leaving his negative energy behind.

As I drove out of the property, thinking of Albert, I turned over the past two weeks in my head and began to tic in earnest. Now that I was totally on my own and safe in my car, I let loose.

As I drove along, unheard and unobserved, I let my brain have free rein. I was throat-clearing with a vengeance – thank God I'm not a professional singer – and repeating any words that took my fancy.

I began doing a great pantomime of Walton and his cruel lesson on cats. I had his mannerisms down pat. No doubt, if he could see me now, he'd feel so much more superior, because there was no way that man would ever understand the real me, just as I'd never like or understand the real him.

Driving and ticcing away contentedly – there's a certain amount of contentment and definitely relief in uninterrupted ticcing – I turned over in my head my time in Ruth's Cottage.

What had I come away with, apart from a huge guilt complex about leaving Albert behind? I swapped tics for ticks as I went through a list of what I'd learned.

I'd relaxed for most of my time away – ✓

I'd worked out the difference between solitude and loneliness – ✓

I'd met Albert and made up my mind I'd adopt a kitten soon – ✓

I got in touch with the psychic side of my being, scrying with some success – ✓

I'd met some nice people – ✓

I'd taken some great photos – ✓

I'd got back into sketching – ✓

I'd slept well, most nights – ✓

I'd finally exorcised Zac from my soul – ✓

I think you'd agree that's not a bad tick list for a two-week period.

As I drove away from this wonderful wine valley, the logical part of my brain took over and I speculated as to what, if anything, I could make of Ruth and her disappearance.

What had I found and seen, really? A scrappy, weather-beaten, hard-to-decipher page torn from a diary, and some vague and misty visions in an old mirror. I had nothing concrete or worth repeating, let alone reporting, to the police.

Besides, if what the locals had told me was correct, the police had put Ruth's disappearance down to suspected suicide. Who was I to question that finding?

I sometimes wish I didn't have such an enquiring mind, a mind that always wants answers and won't rest until it gets them. Now I was deliberating how I could find out when

Ruth had disappeared and whether it had been in the local papers.

What could I tell the police, anyway? That I had an extremely vague – and here's the important bit – paranormal sense that something not quite right had taken place in Ruth's Cottage?

I'd spent most of my adult life denying that side of my genetic inheritance, so why the hell was I delving into it now? More to the point, why would I want to share this delving with anyone, except perhaps Uncle J and maybe John?

To satisfy my curiosity, I decided I'd scan and magnify the diary page and see if I could make any sense of what Ruth had written. If it was just a diary entry from an ordinary day in her life, I really didn't have any right to hold onto to it.

If that turned out to be the case, I'd post it back to Walton, in case he genuinely missed and cared about his aunt.

If I did find something concerning in her diary entry, then maybe, just maybe, I'd have something concrete as opposed to something esoteric to take to the police.

Before long, I was turning into my street. I'd never been so pleased to be home. Firstly, I carried what was on the back seat inside and opened up my townhouse to let in some fresh air. Then I headed back to the carport to unpack the boot.

I was taking the last of my things from the boot when I discovered – you guessed it – Albert. He'd secreted himself into the very back of the boot when I wasn't looking. I had mixed feelings: first elation, then trepidation at having to explain to Walton why I had Ruth's cat.

With conflicting emotions about my little stowaway, though I couldn't help admiring his ingenuity, I said, 'Albert, you clever little Houdini. What are you doing in there?'

His response was to roll onto his back and show me his tummy. How can anyone resist such a tactic, manipulative or not?

I couldn't resist it, so I scooped him into my arms and said, 'Well, come on then, let's get you inside so you can inspect your new home.'

In that moment, I realised I'd left out the word 'temporary'. Then I realised it wasn't an accident that I'd left it out. After the way I'd seen Walton treat Albert, he wasn't getting him back; not if I could help it.

As I carried him inside, his purr was big in sound and vibration. He was one very contented cat, and I was one very delighted human.

Checking out every room, Albert seemed to love what he saw and smelled straight away. He proceeded to rub his scent on the mats, doorways and furniture.

The eleven townhouses in my block are unique. The complex was built in the late '60s, and *The Australian Home Beautiful* did an article on their design in 1968. This article described them as innovative and timeless. They were all that, and more.

They were also a very safe environment for any animal, particularly one like Albert, now a fugitive in hiding.

Each townhouse had its own identity and personality, with an internal courtyard space completely encircled by the blank walls of the two-storey buildings around them. These high walls provided a high degree of privacy, both visually and acoustically. Welcome home, Albert!

After I'd unpacked and thrown my washing into the laundry, I made a list of what I'd need for my new housemate: litter tray, bowls, dry and wet food, a bed – the list went on. I'd be able to help Albert settle in over the next week, and hopefully I could explain his absence to Walton only if I needed to.

I had another list besides what Albert needed: I planned to drop into *God's Artefacts* in Crows Nest and buy some special things to set up my guest bathroom.

Before I headed for the shops to stock up for myself and Albert, I checked the answering machine. There was one message from John, welcoming me home.

I decided to visit John, Max and Leroy, who lived in the same complex as me, after the shops and before they headed off for their weekend in the Blue Mountains.

If they needed me to, I'd offer to look after Leroy. But before Max got home from work and they headed off for their weekend away, John and I had a lot to talk about.

CHAPTER 10

After putting the shopping away, I went to see John. He was surprised to see me home early. John's an architect, and more often than not he works from home. When he opened the door, in true John fashion he said, 'Darling, love your hair, it's fabulous; Zac would hate it. You're home early. Did the weather chase you away? Come in; Max is still at work, and naturally I'm left with all the packing.'

With a smile in my voice I responded, 'You always get stuck with the packing, John, because you're so good at it. No, the weather didn't chase me off, I, um … well, I wanted to get home and –'

Sensing more intrigue, John cut in, saying, 'Come on, now, what's happened since I last spoke to you? You never did get back to me about what Walton was like. Packing can wait; I'll put the kettle on and you can tell me all about it. Leroy, Aunty Pip is home; give her a cuddle.'

I picked dear old Leroy up, letting him crawl onto my

shoulder. He's Burmese and vocal, so he greeted me enthusiastically. It was good to be home.

We chatted about life in general, then with coffee pot, mugs and cake on a tray, we headed out into the courtyard.

Pouring coffee, John fired the first question. 'Okay, what was he like?'

I leaned against the chair, shook my head with a smile, and put him out of his misery. 'Very handsome, if you like movie star looks.'

'So, is he George Clooney handsome or Kevin Bacon handsome?' said John eagerly.

I smiled, blowing on my coffee to cool it; I was making him wait and enjoying the moment. When his patience had expired, I said, 'Um, more George Clooney; though having seen a taste of Walton's personality, that's a huge insult to George.' Picking up a piece of cake, I continued. 'His hair is thick and dark brown, with just a shadow of grey at the temples; his perfect teeth are impossibly white; sensual lips; I think his eyes were a hazel-green, but don't quote me.'

John and I've always had a shorthand communication, which is a polite way of saying we cut one another off; true to form, mid-sentence he cut in, saying, 'So if he looks that good, he must have had a pretty horrible personality to make you dislike him in such a short time. Out with it, what did he do to piss you off?'

John has a way of compressing what I'm trying to say. Over the years he'd become used to my Tourettic verbal diarrhoea or blurting – the technical term sometimes used is disinhibition.

I only ever show that side of myself to family and people I trust. John and I have been best friends since Grade 9 – two outsiders together. He'd become adept at guiding me to get to the point without insulting me.

For a while I sat drinking my coffee and eating the toffee walnut cake he'd made, giving myself time to think about how to continue. Then I said, 'Well, let's say he's one of those men who aren't exactly kind to animals.'

A shadow of distaste crossed John's face. He picked Leroy up from his lap, gently stroked him and kissed his head. Voice dripping with controlled disgust, he finally said, 'Okay; now I understand why you're home early. Remind you too much of Zac?'

That took me back. It's safe to say John was very pleased when we'd split up. Defensively I responded, 'Ouch, bitchy, but yeah, upon reflection you're right; he reminded me of Zac in that respect.'

With a satisfied look on his face that his Zac comment had hit the spot – I'd missed our banter – he continued. 'What a pity you had to leave Albert – was that his name?'

It was time to surprise him. With satisfaction, I said, 'Well, that's the thing, you see, when I emptied the boot, I found out I had a stowaway and ...'

John instantly jumped to the wrong conclusion; a conclusion I felt sure Walton would also jump to. His voice sounded ecstatic. 'Pip, you didn't? Did you kid, I mean, catnap him? If so, I've never been prouder of you.'

Our conversation went along these lines for some time, with me assuring John that I hadn't catnapped Albert, that he'd made that decision entirely on his own. Naturally John wanted to meet Albert straight away, so we headed back to my townhouse.

At first Albert was wary – men weren't his favourite humans. Soon, though, John had Albert if not sitting on his lap then at least eating out of his hand. Like me, he used treats to bribe his way into Albert's affections.

John gladly took up my offer to feed Leroy while he was away. This would let Elsa in Unit 9 off the hook.

Elsa was in her eighties, a real eccentric and a loveable woman. Although she loved Leroy, she was forgetful – especially when she became absorbed in one of her large landscape paintings.

As he left, John said breezily, 'Well, darling heart, I need to finish the packing and you need a long hot soak in the bath. Heat up that curry I gave you for dinner so you can concentrate on settling Albert in. Thanks for looking after Leroy. Talk to you when we get back.'

After he left, I was way too overstimulated to jump straight into a bath, so I did what a lot of Tourettic people do – I nested. I checked that everything was in order and in its own place, and I tidied, dusted and rearranged. I go through rare stages where I am so messy I've taken photos to remind myself how untidy I can be, then at other times I'm anal.

Being anal isn't something I'm proud of or want mentioned at my funeral – 'she kept a tidy house'. A true translation of how I am would be, 'On the surface she seemed tidy, but by God were her thoughts disordered!'

Eventually, to gain my attention and get me to spend time with him, Albert gently nipped me on the ankle.

Humans nest and cats rest – I'll leave it to you to determine who's right.

Life isn't perfect and neither am I. I took his meaning – he needed reassurance, love and attention – and I sat down to give him all three. From my point of view, cats have the right attitude. Playfully I said to Albert, 'I can learn a lot from your cattitude, darling boy.'

His response was to gracefully jump into my lap, lick the skin on my forearm, then commence to walk around my lap in small cat-circles, kneading my legs, until finally he gently lowered himself into the sleeping position and began to purr.

Once Albert felt safe and secure, I gently eased him off my lap. He wasn't impressed, but hey, he was living under my house rules now.

Yeah, right – like I believed that.

Once down, he gave me a half-hearted hiss to let me know he wasn't impressed, to which I responded, 'Oh, Hannibal, glad to see you back – *not*. I'm hyperactive and the sooner you understand that and deal with it the better. I've got work to do.'

I got my toolkit out – every woman needs one – and soon had my new mirror hung at the end of the bath in the guest bathroom. It looked very old, with a light-coloured wooden frame and an Indonesian design intricately carved into the wood.

Once hung, I stood back admiring my handiwork. The mirror looked like it had always been there; it filled the void on that wall perfectly and gave the room a much warmer and more expansive feeling.

I placed several different-coloured candles around the room: two at each end of the tub and four on the built-in shelving beside the bath. I put my oil burner, lavender oil and safety matches within reach.

I love the sound a striking match makes – it reminds me of special times, like lighting the gas for a kettle, wood fires and candles.

I'd bought a low wooden Balinese stool in natural teak and a chartreuse cushion. It fitted perfectly into the new theme of the room and would be a comfortable place for Albert to sit should he wish to join me. I was hoping he would.

To finish, I put out my chartreuse towels and bathmats. Chartreuse is my favourite colour in a world full of beautiful colours. It always lifts me up.

I'd come back from the Hunter with a new appreciation for life, feeling that every day should be a special occasion.

My efforts had transformed the guest bathroom into a place of reflection and relaxation. I hoped it would also be a place of expansion – into other realms. If not, my efforts weren't lost; it now looked warm and inviting even if nothing else changed.

Following John's suggestion, I ran a deep bath. I slowly immersed myself into the water, and before long I heard my little stowaway downstairs meowing incessantly. It was a concerned cat noise, as if he was saying, '*Where are you? I can't find you.*'

'Albert,' I yelled, 'I'm up here. Don't panic! I'm still here; come upstairs.'

I'd love to know if animals, on some level, understand what we say, or whether they just pick up on nuances of tone. Whatever the case, Albert followed the sound of my voice and, as casually as he could, jumped up onto the stool.

Then he looked at me and yawned as if to say, '*Who, me? Panic?*'

Once on his stool, he sniffed my arm, then the water, and then the air. It seemed all the smells met with his approval. Once the room had passed the sniff test, he kneaded my new cushion and began to walk in circles – three times, bless him; already we were simpatico. Then he settled into a cat curl, tucked his head under his front paws and gently started his hypnotic purring, which instantly relaxed and centred me.

I wasn't sure if my new set-up would have the same scrying receptivity as Ruth's bathroom, but with deep breaths and walking my brain through the relaxation steps from head to toe, eventually I began to relax deeply, especially with my feline muse adding a soothing and magical background vibrato.

I instantly felt connected to his purrs, to his energy; we were one.

When I opened my eyes and looked into the mirror, there was nothing to see. I was disappointed yet philosophical about this – perhaps it was Ruth's Cottage that had held the magic after all.

Then I remembered that Grandma Ella had said that things of an esoteric nature cannot be forced; they take time, effort, patience and focus. As I matured into my post-Zac life, I decided to look more closely at things of an extrasensory nature. I knew I'd have to find patience if I was to be even marginally as successful as Grandma Ella had been.

I'm not alone in my interests. According to Uncle J, governments around the world are also investigating ESP. Uncle J had recently told me about a book he'd been reading, by American journalist Annie Jacobsen. It's called *Phenomena: The Secret History of the U.S. Government's Investigations into Extrasensory Perception.*

We'd had a long conversation about this book during one of our calls. Apparently, the CIA and DOD have been undertaking research into things of this nature for decades, ever since data came to light that the Nazis had been working on it.

At the end of WWII, half of this found data went to the USSR and the other half to the USA. As neither side wanted to be outdone by the other, they have both spent billions on the study of ESP and other phenomena. Jacobsen was quoted as saying that this situation was the origin of the psychic arms race.

I digress; another of my Tourettic traits. Back to why I was now interested in that side of my being.

In fact, I wasn't really sure. I could see that maybe it was losing Grandma Ella then both my parents so close together. I knew being Zac-free had helped point me in this direction, but apart from these major and dramatic changes in my life, I wasn't sure why my mind was now an open channel. I gave up questioning why, even though I felt both excited and nervous;

perhaps my stay in Ruth's Cottage had been the catalyst. Then again, perhaps it was just time for me to explore.

Despite my lack of scrying success, the bath did make me feel better, rejuvenated in fact. Eventually I pulled the plug, blew out the candles and dried myself. As I looked around at my afternoon's handiwork, I felt very pleased.

Most of my life, I'd relied on the opinions of others to make me feel good about myself. Now I was more concerned with my own opinion of myself – self-love is so important.

I pulled on my favourite dress, went downstairs, put my iPod onto shuffle, heated up John's chicken curry and made myself a pot of herbal tea.

After dinner, with Albert firmly ensconced on my lap in front of the gas pot-belly fire – all the fun without the work – I looked up scrying on Wikipedia.

There was a lot of scepticism from the scientific community – let's face it, we rely on them to be sceptical. None of us want to feel like sheep, following any particular doctrine without questioning, without understanding.

I wasn't put off by the scientific community's take on things; I just tucked it away for future reference. We're all entitled to our own opinion. Sometimes you just know when things are right for you. I hoped that by looking into my as-yet undeveloped abilities, I'd find out who I really was.

With this in mind, I continued reading.

I read that the scrying medium you choose – mine being a mirror and candles – initially serves to focus attention, removing unwanted thoughts in much the same way as the repetition of a mantra or concentration on a mandala induces relaxation.

As I read this, I laughed, thinking, *Yeah right, good luck with my brain.* I had a lot to learn; taking things slowly and practicing patience was at the forefront. Practice might make perfect, but I've always learned best by rote.

After a while, my head started spinning – no, not Exorcist-style; just overloaded. I'd read enough, so I closed my phone, put it on charge and headed upstairs to bed, Albert trailing me all the way.

Perhaps John was right when he'd said that it may be my inherited imagination – shared with Uncle J – rather than inherited paranormal abilities from Grandma Ella that had me seeing mysterious things. Uncle J was renowned for his incredible imagination; it was why he'd excelled in the advertising industry.

As I lay in bed, trying to quieten my mind, I remembered a long-ago conversation I'd overheard between my father and Uncle J.

I used to love to listen to them banter, so I'd crept downstairs one night to listen outside the study door, fascinated to hear them debate their different takes on life. I remember Uncle J saying to my father once, 'For heaven's sake, Geoffrey, use your imagination. Even Einstein once said: "I am enough of the artist to draw freely upon my imagination. Imagination is more important than knowledge. Knowledge is limited. Imagination encircles the world."'

I hoped John was wrong about this being imagination. My time in Ruth's Cottage and my exposure to my first unplanned and feeble attempts at scrying had made me feel very close on another level to Grandma Ella.

I did want to explore if I was like her. I didn't want to hide my authentic self any more. After having this epiphany, a sense of serenity came over me; soon I slipped into a deep and dreamless sleep.

I woke, a shaft of sunlight gently caressing my face. For a short time, I felt blissfully calm – not a state my brain often allows me to feel, but one that I treasure. I also felt that there was a cat asleep across my legs.

I eased my way out of bed, trying not to disturb Albert, then dressed hastily into my jogging clothes. On the way downstairs, I had another peek at my newly styled bathroom.

Okay, I'm a baby about things like that. I appreciate and enjoy the little things in life, the small changes you can make that mix things up and completely change the feeling of a room, the feeling of a home.

Albert was soon by my side. He was curious to know what I was looking at, but seeing nothing of interest – no food – he stretched, yawned, and nearly knocked me over with enthusiastic leg cuddles. I took his point and said, 'Come on then, time to feed you.'

He understood my words, nearly knocking me down the stairs in his rush to beat me to the food room – the kitchen. He'd settled very well and quickly into his new home, and I'd settled very well into my new role as adoring servant. It had only taken Albert, oh, let's see, two days to train me. Life was looking promising with both of us knowing our place.

CHAPTER 11

After feeding Albert then myself, I informed him I was going for what humans call a jog. 'Now Albert, as you know, we humans do silly things a cat wouldn't dream of doing. I like exercise – it's my happy pill – so I'm going to do some right now. But don't fret, I'll be back within the hour.'

Albert's response was to yawn, turn around, slink into the courtyard, plonk down on a chair in the sun, and proceed to do what cats do best – sleep. I couldn't help thinking that if he could speak, he'd have said, '*Whatever!*'

I headed off down Shirley Road toward Berry Island Reserve. It wasn't long till my calf muscles let me know I'd lost some condition; I needed to get back to gym. I was soon in my stride, enjoying the sense of control that exercise always gives me, and enjoying it immensely.

I can't speak for other Tourettic people, but exercise is paramount to both my physical and mental health. The renowned neurologist Oliver Sacks has suggested that extraordinarily quick reflexes may be a beneficial core feature of TS. Obsessiveness, repetition and high energy can come in handy if you know how to channel them.

As I approached Berry Island Reserve, there was the usual Saturday crowd out and about enjoying the benefits of exercise, sun and relatively fresh air. It feels nice to belong, even on the periphery. I saw a few regulars, and we waved and exchanged pleasantries.

By the time I got home, I felt invigorated in the way that only exercise and eight hours' quality sleep can do for me. I felt calm and focussed. I decided to shower, change, and head to Bunnings to buy some sample pots of paint to try on the feature wall of my art room.

Before I left, I patted Albert, then went around to John's house and fed and reassured Leroy that Aunty Pip was on the job.

Home from Bunnings, I painted the three sample paint colours on the wall, and pretty much straight away decided to use a fabulous shade of deep green – Picturebook Green – as the colour for a feature wall. It was a bold statement, but it was my art room and now I only had to please myself.

I was about to text Uncle J to make sure things were good, then go on Google to see if I could find any old articles on Ruth's disappearance, when I heard a ping on my mobile.

You guessed it – Uncle J.

His text read, '*Guess who? Sorry I haven't been in touch. I've had an upset tummy, both ends. Lost 7 kgs. Don't worry, too sick to take photos. I'm good now. Are you home? Do you have anything of an esoteric nature to share with me? Miss you and love you. Uncle J xxx.'*

My mood lifted immediately, despite his over-sharing, or perhaps because of it. His reference to taking photos was an in-joke between us. We'd both been accused of being a nuisance with a camera. Uncle J's view was that we were simply social historians with an eye for capturing the beauty of any given moment. I liked his version better.

Ignoring his second question, I responded evasively, *'You've done it again – I was just about to text you. Sorry you've been unwell; all part of the travel experience right! Yes, I'm home. You'll never guess who I found in the boot of my car? Albert, the cat! I'm keeping him. Apart from that, not much else really. Love you and miss you too. Pip xxx.'*

I knew what his second question meant: had I progressed with my scrying?

The thing is, I wasn't sure I had, and I also wasn't ready to accept and admit that both he and Grandma Ella may have been right all these years.

I'd spent most of my adult life trying to avoid acknowledging that I might have inherited any of her skills. This was mainly to please my parents, who'd both been scientists; you can imagine their take on it.

The other factor was that I already had enough that was different about me without throwing ESP into the mix. So far, I was passing for normal and flying under the radar. But was I being authentic?

After responding to his text, I set about googling to see if there were any newspaper articles about Ruth Richards' disappearance. The locals had told me that there had been several articles in the *Hunter Valley Age* at the time. I decided to start there.

With determination, and Albert by my side, I began my search.

At first I found nothing, but I didn't give up, putting several different words into the search box. Eventually I found some archived articles on Ruth's disappearance. The stories were heartbreaking, with many of the locals expressing how sad they were about Ruth vanishing. Some were quoted as saying it was totally out of character.

After a while, I decided to call it a night. Sleep and I have a fractious relationship – basically I get it if and when I can, which is another side-effect of my Tourette's. I hoped tonight would be a good night sleep-wise, because, as we all know, when you sleep well everything seems better.

I had an easy night's sleep, dreaming about some long-forgotten memories of special occasions in my childhood. I dream most nights, in colour; and, as I mentioned earlier, I keep a dream diary.

I stretched, pushed Albert off my legs and went downstairs to feed him. I then went around to feed Leroy and to reassure him that he hadn't been abandoned entirely, that he still had one staff member on roster.

Once my servant duties had been attended to, I quickly threw down a protein bar, changed into my jogging gear and headed out the door. I was determined to make the most of what remained of my time off.

After my jog, I showered and went back to Bunnings to buy a large tin of paint before I chickened out. When I arrived home, I made brunch and sat in the courtyard to spend some time with Albert.

I couldn't believe how quickly I'd become so attached to him, and vice versa. He was a dear little cat. Now that he was living in a safe and loving environment, the Hannibal side of his nature had disappeared – at least for now.

As I was sitting in the sun eating my brunch – avocado, smoked trout, tomatoes with fresh basil, and sourdough bread with olive oil and balsamic dip – I remembered that I needed to scan and enlarge the page from Ruth's diary to see if that would help me to decipher what she'd written.

I pulled the page out from the inside pocket of my handbag, took it into my office, scanned and increased its size, then printed off the pages. Using the magnifying glass that came with my world globe, I set about trying to make sense of the words that remained.

The diary entry seemed to start out being fairly ordinary. Further down the page, as if something disturbing had taken place, the words became more like a message to someone rather than a personal diary entry. It wasn't much to go by, but this is what I could decipher:

Fri July 1, 2016
Woke to a perfect day. Albert kitten-like wants to play. He continues …

The next several words were indistinct, either faded or washed from the page. Then:

He has given me a reason to … Thomas has gone. He is such a bright little button. I'm sure Thomas …

Not much to go on, I know, but I had enough trouble working out even those words. Further down, Ruth's handwriting had deteriorated, and so had her tone. It read:

He really is a huge disappointment … I must have been … cannot believe he'd be involved with something so …

More unreadable words had faded from the page. The two remaining sentences also made no sense:

… overheard him on the phone …
To meet BOC, I must change … too late …

I read and re-read this enhanced image of Ruth's dairy page. With the exception of the references to Thomas, Ruth's husband, and Albert, it didn't make much sense. I had no idea who she'd overheard on the phone, what they'd said or who BOC was, much less why Ruth would want to meet.

Out of sheer frustration, I put the pages into a folder, took them inside and locked them in my filing cabinet. I had no idea why I chose to lock them in the cabinet; it just felt like the right thing to do.

I went back to the courtyard to make the most of what remained of the sun and hopefully forget what I'd read.

When I sat back down, Albert jumped into my lap, as if he sensed I needed his reassurance. As animals quite often are, he was right: I did.

For some inexplicable reason, I'd felt uneasy reading Ruth's words. I'd also felt a fear I couldn't make sense of, a foreboding that reminded me of my first premonition all those years ago.

This feeling clung about me like a mist. I shook my head, trying to dismiss it. When I couldn't, I knew I needed a distraction.

That's another frustrating thing about Tourette's – not being able to let things go. Some call it compulsivity; others call it tenacity. Either way, when it takes hold it's exhausting.

When a compulsion grips me, I try to find something to channel it into, something positive to distract me from my recurring thoughts. I now settled on two distractions.

Distraction number one: I'd read that for better scrying results, you should remove the glass from the mirror's frame and paint the back of it black.

I carefully did that. Once the mirror glass was dry, I replaced it in its wooden frame and hung it back at the end of the bath.

Distraction number two: I turned my attention to the art room.

I thought I'd at least knock over the hardest part, the cutting in. It's a good distraction, cutting in, especially with dark green paint.

CHAPTER 12

I woke up to a foggy, overcast Monday morning, my arms, shoulders and legs aching. I'd overdone the painting: as well as doing the cutting in, I'd painted the entire first coat. I was right, it had been the distraction I'd needed. My aching muscles confirmed it.

As I pushed Albert off my lap and rolled over to get up, I groaned. Albert made a little concerned cat noise. To put his mind at rest I said, 'I'm okay, little man, I just overdid things yesterday. After breakfast, I'll go for a long walk to iron things out. When I get home, maybe I'll take a long soak in the tub. First things first: how about some breakfast?'

Albert's response was to yawn, stretch and make what I'd come to know as his happy sound. As I headed downstairs, I had a look at my art room, hoping I wouldn't regret my colour choice.

Thankfully, even in the dim light I was pleased with the result. Once I'd applied a second coat, it would be an even deeper and more luxuriant shade of green. I'd use what remained of my time off to rearrange and reorganise my art room.

As I was preparing our first meal of the day, I heard my mobile ping. It was John. '*Hi, pussycat. We're home. Thanks for looking after Leroy. Fabulous weekend. You'll have to come next time. Max is heading off for work in WA for over a week. Let's catch up while you're off. I can tell you all about the amazing food we ate. Hope your stowaway has settled well? Big hugs, John xx.*'

I responded straight away with, '*Hi, handsome. Glad you had a wonderful weekend. Yum, can't wait to hear about the food. Hope you took photos? Albert has settled in like he's always lived here. How about we meet up mid-week? You could come here for dinner. I'll cook; Thai okay? Love, P xx.*'

Before my aching body changed my mind, I headed out the door for a long, muscle-stretching walk. At first it hurt like hell, but after a while I slowly ironed out some of my aches and pains.

I adore walking in the fog. I love the way it envelops the everyday things we take for granted, the way it mutes the world and offers instead shadows and shades of grey. Walking in fog gives me the same comfortable feeling as sitting in a favourite room: it makes me feel safe and secure. I also enjoy watching the little cloud of mist my own hot breath forms as it hits the cold air.

By the time I'd finished my walk, the fog had lifted; as often happens after a foggy start to the day, the weather was pristine and the sky so blue and cloudless it felt unreal.

I made myself a coffee and took it into the courtyard. Not able to avoid it any longer, I sat thinking about what, if anything, I'd do about Ruth's diary entry.

Still thinking, I poured a second cup of coffee and headed to my study to look up the Hunter Valley Local Area Command. I hoped to find numbers for local police stations. Fairly quickly I settled on Cessnock Police Station as the one to phone. It seemed the closest to Ruth's Cottage.

I'd come up with a plan of how to approach investigating Ruth's disappearance. First, I'd phone the local police and tell them I was a freelance journalist working on a story about unsolved disappearances. I wasn't a good liar, I knew that; however, I was about to find out if I was a good actor. If I got nowhere with my cover story, I figured I'd let the whole thing drop.

Twice I dialled the Cessnock Police Station, only to hang up before it was answered. I decided to take a bath to not only ease my muscles but maybe, if my scrying was successful, give me some direction on whether to even make the call. In other words, I began avoiding the phone call.

I ran the bath, lit candles and the lavender burner, and with Albert by my side, slowly eased my aching body into the deep, hot, soothing bathwater.

I went through the usual ritual – deep breaths, relaxing my muscles from head to toes – and succumbed very quickly and deeply. I put a washer over my eyes and breathed in the scent of the lavender and the steam from the aromatic bath salts.

I wasn't even thinking about scrying now; I was way too

relaxed for that. When I finally took the washer from my eyes, I was astounded at what I saw.

In the mirror I saw a misty, veiled image of a woman. I soon recognised her as Ruth. She had a rose in her hand and looked incredibly sad. Then she nodded her head and mouthed one word – 'yes.'

I shook my head and looked back into the mirror, expecting – and, if I'm honest, hoping – that the vision would be gone. Instead, Ruth's presence seemed to mist from within the mirror into the room, then drift back into the mirror again.

I might have put this down to imagination, or even steam rising from the hot bath, except that Albert had sat bolt upright with eyes as wide as saucers. I lay, watching, waiting to see what Albert would do next.

Slowly he stood, stretched and walked along the edge of the bath up to the mirror. Then he balanced himself on his hind legs and gently placed his forepaws on the surface of the mirror, all the time purring loudly.

As I gasped, a vision of Ruth misted out from the mirror and seemed to wrap Albert in an embrace, albeit a spiritual one.

Albert began to make very contented cat-sounds, his little head cocked to one side. He was acting just like the little kitten he would have been when Ruth had disappeared. It was both heart-warming and heartbreaking to see.

I felt overwhelmingly touched, witnessing this connection between Albert and his much-loved Ruth; I'm not ashamed to say that tears flowed freely down my cheeks and mingled with the bathwater.

I stayed in the bath for a very long time after this display of pure love between Ruth and Albert. I felt I had a lot of work to do to show Albert that I could and would love him as much as Ruth had.

With the apparition gone, Albert began to paw helplessly at the mirror, trying to find Ruth. He'd need a great deal of love, comfort and understanding to get through this. He was grieving because again his Ruth had disappeared.

As I pulled the plug, I wrapped myself in a towel then gently disengaged Albert from his mission to find Ruth. As gently as I could, I picked him up from his sentinel position. 'Oh, darling boy, I can see that you and Ruth loved one another very much. I promise I'll try to make you feel as loved as she made you feel.'

Tears spilled from my eyes, dropping onto Albert's coat. Sensing my distress, he seemed to forget about his own, and he began licking the tears I'd shed.

I knew then that we'd get through this together.

One thing I knew for sure – painting the back of the mirror black had certainly helped its connectivity to other realms. Now all I had to do was make sense of what I'd seen, and what Albert had seen or sensed.

After I'd dressed, I fed Albert to take his mind off Ruth. It worked – Albert was always going to have a love affair with food, just like his new mum.

Once Albert had settled and I'd composed myself, I did what Ruth's apparition had wanted me to do – I took a deep breath and sat at the desk, preparing to make the call.

Still stalling for time, I googled 'paranormal', and found thousands of references, including this definition: *In common English usage, occult refers to 'knowledge of the paranormal', as opposed to 'knowledge of the measurable', usually referred to as science.*

From what I read, there are many open-minded and seemingly intelligent people who believe in 'knowledge of the paranormal' as well as 'knowledge of the measurable'. So if I was losing my mind, I had plenty of company.

What I was doing, of course, was putting off the inevitable call to Cessnock police. I made myself a quick sandwich, and after lunch I found the courage to phone. But again, I hung up on the first ring, before anyone had answered.

Remembering Ruth's apparition, I told myself to grow up, and called again. After three rings, the phone was answered by a young female constable. 'Cessnock Police Station, Constable Jackson speaking.'

There was no way out now. I took a deep breath and said: 'Hello, Constable. My name is Philippa Mason. I'm wondering if you can help me.' Too late to turn back; I hoped like hell I could bluff my way through.

'I'll do my best. How can I help?'

'I'm a freelance journalist,' I said evasively. 'I'm currently working on an article about unsolved disappearances. One of the cases I'm looking into involved a woman by the name of Ruth Richards. She disappeared around three years ago in the Hunter Valley region. Are you aware of her case?'

It was done; I hoped I'd lied convincingly. My heart was

pounding, my hands sweating. Lying doesn't come naturally to me. Thankfully I didn't have to wait long for an answer.

To my amazement, she didn't question my credentials or cover story. She did, however, hesitate while thinking; then she responded, 'I've only been at this station for eighteen months. My sergeant is also relatively new and wasn't working at the station at the time. There are a couple of detectives who would have been here then.' She seemed to be thinking for a while again. Then she continued. 'I'll be seeing an officer who is currently on leave at a morning tea on Wednesday. He was here at the time, so I'll see if he can help you. But I can't promise anything.'

I didn't know if she was being polite or trying to get me off the phone, but I didn't care; gratefully I accepted her offer.

She ended our call by saying that sometimes stories like mine can prompt someone's memory and help reopen and solve cases. I thanked her for her time, gave her my contact details and hung up. It was that simple – all I'd had to do was lie. And maybe, just maybe, someone would return my call.

After I'd hung up, I wiped my sweaty palms on my jeans. Stomach still churning, I took a few deep breaths to slow my pulse. I'd done what Ruth's apparition had wanted me to do. I might never hear back, but at least I could relax and put it out of my mind.

I had one more call to make, and I wanted to enjoy what remained of my holiday without it hanging over my head. This was the much-dreaded call to David Walton. I was hoping his answering machine would come on; no such luck. He answered on the fourth ring. 'David Walton.'

Hearing his cultured voice instantly pushed me into nervous mode. If I hadn't met him, I might have been fooled by his dulcet tones.

Before I could lose my nerve, I launched in. 'Hi, David, it's Philippa Mason. I'm phoning to make sure you got the keys I put through the door slot?'

In a curt tone he responded, 'Yes, thank you, I did. I hope your drive home was uneventful?'

Like he gave a rat's arse. It was obvious he was as disinterested in talking to me as I was in talking to him. Matching his tone, and with no compunction, I said, 'Yes, thank you; very uneventful.'

He wasn't going to hear from me about my surprise stowaway. I needn't have been concerned; he obviously had no interest whatsoever in the fact that Albert wasn't around.

'Well, that's good. Now, if you'll excuse me, I have bookings I need to attend to.'

I could tell he was lying even though he was good at it. I willingly took his cue and said, 'Yes, of course; I won't hold you up. Goodbye.'

I hung up the phone so fast and hard I hoped his ears were ringing. He'd brought my mood so low that I needed another walk. As I left the house, I said to Albert, 'Sorry, baby, but I need a cleansing walk after that call. I promise I won't be long.'

As I rushed out the door, the last thing I saw was Albert with his head resting on his front paws. He looked at me with soulful eyes as if to say, *'Don't you leave me too!'*

That look wasn't enough to stop me from going. I needed to do something positive to expel thoughts about my conversation with Walton. I also wanted to ensure that sleep would come easily tonight.

After a fast walk, which helped dispel the unwanted energy, I came home to one very happy and vociferous cat. His welcome was both heart-warming and guilt-inducing.

Cats have a great handle on guilt. It seems effortless for them to put you on a guilt trip, especially if you're the right human.

To make it up to him – he obviously had abandonment issues – I attended to his evening meal then set about making up my own. Albert and I had one very important thing in common: our love of food. I made a simple carbonara, but the fragrance made him eager to sit near me.

After dinner, I flicked through my favourite television programs on SBS, ABC, and UKTV, with Albert happily ensconced on my lap, just like any happy couple.

As I was watching *Lewis*, which was one of Uncle J's favourites, I heard my phone ping. With Uncle J away, I kept it constantly by my side. I'd been thinking of him all afternoon and in answer to the energy I'd put out, he'd responded with, '*Princess, princess, princess. It's me. How are you and Albert? I've had disturbing feelings all day, and well, I just wanted to make sure you were both fine, xx.*'

Yet again he'd picked up on my thoughts and feelings. I was sick of hiding the truth from him, so as honestly as I could, I texted back, '*You've done it again; I was about to text you. I've had a very interesting day. I decided to paint the back of my scrying mirror black. It is now much more receptive – either that or I am. Rather wait till you're home to talk about it, if that's okay? How are you? Any more tummy bugs? Can't wait until you're home so we can talk in person. I love you, Uncle J, and I miss you. It's not a guilt trip – just the truth. Pip xx.'*

I instantly hoped I'd not done an Albert on him and placed him on a guilt trip. As soon as I thought this, I knew he'd never take it that way – it wasn't in his nature to misunderstand me; after all, we shared the same genes.

Not to disappoint – he must have been awake at some ungodly hour – he soon responded. *'I miss you too. I've had an astounding time, but to be honest, I'd like to be home soon – think overstimulation on a grand Tourettic scale. I want to speak to you one-on-one about this path you've finally decided to embark upon. Grandma Ella is happy you have, by the way, in case you're wondering. Love you, princess … Night-night; give Albert a kiss from his Great-Uncle J.'*

Shit! I was emotional today; as I read his words, tears began to flow, and hard as I tried, I couldn't stop them. Albert seemed to understand that his new mum was upset. First he licked my arm, then he started to knead my stomach and make soothing purring sounds.

When I looked down, I saw his dear little face looking up at me as if to say, *'What's wrong? I hate to see you this way.'*

CHAPTER 13

Wednesday evening soon arrived, and along with it, John. I'd spent a busy and enjoyable afternoon preparing a Thai banquet. By the time John arrived, I'd finished my preparations and put the whole fish with ginger in the oven. I'd also prepared prawn tom yum goong and panang nua, or panang beef balls, which I'd serve with rice.

John had a key, so he let himself in. I didn't hear him arrive with the overhead exhaust fan going and being distracted checking the fish in the oven.

As I stood up, he gently kissed me on the back of the neck; believe me, neither of us was expecting my reaction – make that overreaction.

I screamed; John screamed; Albert flew into the kitchen, hackles up, hissing and snarling. Anyone who'd had the couple of weeks I'd had would have been startled; throw Tourette's into the mix and you could say I had an enhanced startle response. It was spectacular even by my standards.

A hand still over his pulsating heart, John said, 'Shit, Pip, you almost gave me a heart attack.'

'Ditto!' I rounded on him. 'You scared the shit out of me.'

Always a man with an answer, John said, 'I think we could both use a drink. Red or white?'

As I leaned on the kitchen bench, regaining my composure, he poured us both a wine. When he'd handed a glass to me, he said, 'So what's made you more jumpy than normal? We have all night, so fill me in on all the details and don't leave anything out or jump ahead using that Tourettic code you use with Uncle J.' Then he pointed to himself, saying, 'Remember – neurotypical. Please be patient, structured and logical in the way you deliver the information.'

It's great to have a best friend like John. He knows me almost as well as Uncle J; he can point out my shortcomings yet still remain non-judgemental and loving in the process. He was spot on, of course: when I'm excited, I speak fast and loud.

My initial reaction was to play with him, but I quickly realised he was genuine in both his concern and interest. I bit my tongue and got a grip on my brain. Instead of spitting out what my Tourettic brain wanted me to say – 'Well, screw you. How about you try keeping up!' – I took a deep calming breath and answered, 'Okay. I can't promise, but I'll do my best.'

I loved his next reaction even more than if I'd said what I wanted to say. He frowned, tilting his head, then said quietly, 'Is it okay to start recounting your time in the Hunter in full now, or would you prefer to wait till we've sat down to dinner?'

I hate people in the kitchen when I'm cooking, with the

exception of John if I'm in the mood for it, and Uncle J anytime. Now I was touched that he was sensitive enough to make this suggestion.

I decided to floor him further, calmly saying, 'No, I'm under control meal-wise, at least. I've been preparing all afternoon. I'd really love your company.'

As I heated the soup and cooked the meatballs, John kept an eye on the fish and boiled the rice. As we worked, I began to recount my time in the Hunter more fully. 'Refresh my memory; where did I get up to last week? I don't want to repeat myself.'

Not missing a beat, John shot back, 'Well, tonight really is full of surprises – you not repeating yourself.'

John wasn't being unnecessarily cruel – I do repeat myself often, which I'm sure is really annoying and at times seems condescending, as though I'm saying, 'Durr, hello idiot, did you get that?'

I'm not sure if this annoying habit is caused by my Tourette's. In truth, Tourette's is an enigmatic phenomenon; I try my very best to control it if and when I can. Now, taking the moral high road, I continued. 'Very funny; but where did I get to?'

John scratched his head and thought for a while. 'Go back to our last phone call from the Hunter rather than our conversation on Friday. I think the last thing you said was that Uncle J felt you'd met Ruth and her nephew before. Does that ring a bell?'

It did. I remembered that Uncle J had used those same words.

John placed his hand on my arm. 'Have I said something wrong? You look stymied; take your time. This has obviously been an ordeal for you.'

I appreciated his patience. I had to compose my thoughts. Finally, I continued. 'Yes, it was quite an ordeal. When you said, "Does that ring a bell?", it reminded me of my conversation with Uncle J on the way to Ruth's Cottage. I used similar words, when he said I'd been there before. His response was, "I hope it's not alarm bells." You see, Uncle J said that's where I had my, um, my first premonition.'

As I said this, I looked at John to gauge his reaction. I was surprised to see him looking pensive rather than dismissive. I felt encouraged by this look, hoping he'd be open to exploring things esoteric tonight.

John could be a devil's advocate on the negative side, and Uncle J could advocate on the positive side. I couldn't think of a better situation than to have them both help me objectively explore and expand my burgeoning paranormal journey. As Uncle J would say, 'Ella would be pleased.'

Dishing up the tom yum goong, I thought again about how to proceed. Once we'd settled and were sipping our soup, I continued. 'Okay, so Uncle J did say that he felt I'd met Ruth and her nephew. David Walton may well have been the young teenager I met nearly thirty years ago. That's what sent me into full blown tics on the phone the other night. Thanks for understanding and terminating the conversation, by the way.'

John, blowing to cool a spoonful of soup, looked at me and, choosing his words carefully, said, 'I knew that some deep emotion was at the bottom of your tics. What premonition was Uncle J talking about?'

Over the next two courses, I tried to explain as succinctly as I could about that premonition.

John sat digesting what I told him. Giving himself time to think about what to say, he became evasive. 'Um, by the way, this food is stunning – you can cook Thai any time. What else did Uncle J have to say?'

I was grateful for this diversion and very pleased with his compliment. 'Thank you. I'm pleased you're enjoying it. I did get annoyed with Uncle J for bringing up the premonition. You know how resistant I've been about travelling down that road. I'm afraid I was a real bitch to him.'

Seeing how sad admitting this made me feel, John reassuringly said, 'Knowing Uncle J, he would have forgiven you instantly, so don't obsess about that – and stop trying to change the subject. Did he have any other valuable information about your first visit to Ruth's Cottage?'

John could see right through me: I was trying to skirt around getting to the crux of it. 'Well, thankfully, as I was apologising for being such a narky bitch, the storm hit. It gave me the perfect segue out of the conversation. I was grateful for that, but I still hung up feeling like a total cow. What our conversation did do, though, is take me back to that time, in my memories.'

John leaned forward. 'Go on. What memories?'

With John as a captive audience, I told him. When I finished, a shiver shook my body. Sensing that the conversation was an uncomfortable one, John leaned back in his chair, rubbed his stomach and came to the rescue again, saying, 'That was absolutely divine. Let's clear these dishes and move into the lounge. We can continue our conversation there.'

I was truly grateful for his empathy and for understanding that this was a conversation we had to have. If I was to be truly authentic with my best friend, I needed to share this difficult and complex story. I knew there was no turning back, no changing the subject.

When seated in front of the fire, to steer the conversation John looked me straight in the eye and said, 'Okay, enough avoiding the subject. What can you remember about that afternoon all those years ago?'

I sighed, took a deep breath and told him about my first time staying in Ruth's Cottage, and my first premonition.

When I'd finished, I went quiet. John said tenderly, 'That must have been a really special yet confronting memory to have. I take it the premonition you had spoiled an idyllic time for you? Explain to me what it was about.'

With the memory of that premonition, my mouth went dry. I took a long drink of water, carefully put the glass down, looked up at my friend and, as honestly and openly as I could, I tried to tell it all.

Sharing the memory felt strange even to my ears. I'd hidden it from my parents, and from everyone except Grandma Ella and Uncle J for so long. Recounting it now, I felt uneasy. It felt as though I was opening a hornet's nest and walking into dangerous ground.

As I was becoming more stressed, I started my least favourite tic, a cross between a squeal and a squeak. Even among family and close friends it's hard to feel comfortable sounding like a pig. A throat-clearing tic can be explained away in so many ways, but a squeak is high pitched, annoying and so much harder to disguise. The topic of conversation had kicked my brain into overdrive.

I needed time out to settle my inner pig down.

As I was about to get up and stack the dishwasher, John stood, grabbed my arm and said, 'Hey, how about I turn on some relaxing music? I'll even rub your neck if you like. Sound good?'

Now I don't know about you, but I never knock back the offer of a neck rub. After John had put on some music, he pointed to my chair and said, 'Sit, before I change my mind.'

I did so, without hesitation. As I sat, listening to relaxing music, my best friend rubbing my neck and shoulders, I could feel a sense of control come back. After a few minutes, he said, 'I want you to stay here and relax while I stack the dishwasher. When I'm done, if you feel you'd like to continue, I'd love you to finish telling me what else has been happening. Is that okay?'

I went to stand and help with the tidying – always wired, always hyper – but John put his hands on my shoulders and eased me back into the chair. He then wheeled the ottoman over and gently lifted my legs onto it.

I took his meaning and the kindness behind it, rested my head on the back of the chair, closed my eyes and said, 'Okay, you win. Try not to make too much noise cleaning up and I'll try to relax.'

I soon took control of my inner beast, my constant companion. As I sat, eyes closed, listening to music, I could hear John quietly working in the background. I knew he'd do an exceptional job cleaning up – my least favourite thing about cooking.

Whilst he was tidying, I slipped upstairs and found the page from Ruth's diary. Sometimes physical evidence makes explaining the unexplainable easier. It's like props used in a play, the mere fact of their physical presence helping to take the audience on a journey with the actors into the plot.

I hoped that seeing the page from Ruth's diary would have that effect on John. It would at least show him that all that I'd experienced was not in my imagination. Seeing the page in Ruth's neat, stylish handwriting would make what I was about to share with him more authentic.

I had briefly entertained the idea of speaking to my GP, Ilona, about it. I couldn't for the life of me think of a way I could broach the subject with her, without her thinking I'd lost the plot.

She's a brilliant GP, intelligent and open minded, and I respect her opinion. Let's face it, most people would feel uncomfortable speaking about things esoteric to even the most opened-minded GP.

I digress again – back to the point.

The physical presence of the diary page would give me something to focus on, and hopefully keep my mind on track. Concentration can, sometimes, distract you from ticcing.

What I was about to share with John, in my mind, was very real indeed. I realised that there was no way I could not confide in him; I needed not only his reassurance but his opinion on how to proceed.

When John came back into the room, wiping his hands on a towel, I had both the diary page and some notes I'd written.

Without missing a beat, he saw them right away, and held out his hand to take them, saying, 'Well, that's all done. What have you got there? Been keeping notes again, have we?'

I was grateful for that smooth segue, and immediately responded, 'You know me, John, always keeping notes. When I got home, I wrote down what I could remember about what had happened, right from the wild drive up. First, read this; it's as good a place as any to continue.'

As he sat down, I handed him both the original page from Ruth's diary and the blown-up version. He switched on the lamp beside his chair and began to read.

As he read, I could see conflicting emotions pass across his face. His brows knitted as he cast over and over the page. I didn't interject or interrupt his reading or his train of thought.

The longer he continued to re-read, the more concerned I became. I wasn't sure if he was disturbed by what he was reading, or if he didn't know what to say.

Eventually he put the pages on his lap, turned to me and said, 'I honestly don't know what to make of this, if anything. For a start, some of the words have disappeared. It's near impossible to make any real sense. What are your thoughts about it?'

I had my answer, and he'd thrown it back at me. He wanted

me to extrapolate. I took a deep breath and began to tell him about my own conclusions, saying, 'John, I'm going to try to be as authentic as I possibly can tonight.'

Misunderstanding, he put his hand up to say something. I didn't want to lose my train of thought, so raised my own hand and said, 'Let me finish. When I say authentic, I'm referring to the esoteric, not the Tourettic, side of my being. There are things I need to share with you that I've only ever shared with Grandma and Uncle J. Please, keep an open mind.'

John squinted as if he was trying to summon up the right words. After several seconds he answered, 'In the past, we've always had fun skirting around the paranormal subject. I know tonight is not the time to be glib about it. So, fire away. I'll try not to interrupt or make sarcastic remarks. Again, what do you make of that diary note? Why do you think it's so important?'

I wished that Uncle J was here to support me. I knew it was time for me to show the courage of my convictions – even relatively new convictions.

I spent the next two hours, till well after midnight, telling John every minute detail about my time at Ruth's Cottage. I was proud of him; he didn't interject often, just sat there nodding his head, asking the occasional question – what's mirror scrying, how did it work and so forth.

The more I recounted what had happened in the Hunter, the more I felt a weight lifted from my shoulders. I'm used to keeping secrets about who I am. Tourette's is difficult for most people to understand – can't you control your tics, can't you relax, can't you take some medication to control it?

Tonight I realised it was easier to tell people I had Tourette's than it was to tell them I was attuned to things paranormal – a hell of a lot easier. Most people can accept the explainable, like a neurological disorder, but find it very hard to accept the unexplainable, like a psychic ability.

Tonight I understood that Tourette's wasn't the only thing about myself I'd tried most of my life to hide.

The model for life that people like Grandma Ella, Ruth, Uncle J and I live by is very different to the one most people live by. For a start, we are super-responders. We're energetically sensitive. We filter our world through intuition, and the thing that scares people the most is that we see things that are hidden. Coupled with my Tourette's, I'm a double curiosity.

I'd talked myself out and had been extremely candid with John. By the time I'd finished, we were both tired and yawning.

Finally, to put an end to the evening, I said, 'Bet you're sorry you asked now?'

John's response was to throw a cushion at me and say, 'For your information, smarty pants, I'm not sorry I asked. I wanted to know and now I do.'

My reaction to this – silent tears. Tears of relief, mainly, but tears just the same. Seeing my emotional state, John moved and sat next to me, wrapped his arms around me and said, 'I feel honoured that you've shared all this with me. I also have to be authentic, though, and say that I'm having trouble understanding the supernatural stuff. I do believe you; I just don't get it. I'm making things worse. I think I'll shut up.'

To reassure him, I jumped in with my usual change-the-topic

response. 'No, darling heart, you aren't making things worse. I know it's a lot to take in. We're going around in circles now, so let's call it a night. Leroy will be wondering where you are. Do you want to take some leftovers home?'

'Hang on, not so fast. Do you think it would be a good idea to have a talk to Ilona about this?'

Ilona is John's GP also; and I had my answer. He obviously thought speaking to her about this was a good idea, which tactfully translated to, '*You might need help.*'

Now that I'd come out of the paranormal closet, I wasn't in the mood to be put back in, or even to be told that who I was didn't make sense because it wasn't mainstream.

Stifling a yawn, in a bored and disinterested voice I said, 'Ah … I've already considered seeing her, but how would I broach this with her? She's a wonderful doctor whom I respect greatly, but I'm not sure she'd be open to speaking about "things paranormal". Besides, I'm not in the mood to have someone suggest more counselling.'

John stood, yawned again, and with a concerned look said, 'I had to suggest it. I'm worried about you. Sleep on it. Now, I'd better get home to Leroy. I will take some leftovers, thanks.'

On that note, having boxed up some of the meal, I saw John out. As he was about to leave, he hugged me and said, 'You know that I love you? I know it took courage to tell me all this tonight and I feel privileged you did. Sleep well; talk tomorrow.'

After I'd shut the gate, I felt two things – relief that I'd finally fully shared my other secret with someone outside my family; and complete and utter exhaustion. The telling of my time in Ruth's Cottage had exhausted me on many levels.

I went back inside, turned off all the lamps and shut down the gas fire. Little Albert, who'd sat in his basket in front of the fire the entire evening listening to our conversation, silently followed me upstairs.

I washed my face, flossed and cleaned my teeth, changed into my PJs and fell into bed – literally. I was soon joined by my little ginger friend. His presence was comforting on many levels, but mainly because he both understood and believed all that I'd shared with John.

To show his love and support, he moved as close to my face as he could, and lay down on my chest as if to say, *'I'm here, I believe you.'*

CHAPTER 14

The rest of my time off work flew by. I managed to get my art room sorted, but not much else. By Monday morning, I was pleased to go back to work, back to a routine; routine soothes.

It was good to see my friends and colleagues in the editorial department. They're an eclectic bunch of people, some warm and funny, all intelligent and hard working. As I walked in on the second level, they were all sitting around our communal glass table, eating breakfast or drinking tea or coffee, getting ready for their work day to commence.

A warm feeling of belonging enveloped me. A few co-workers jumped up to give me a welcome-back hug. It was good to be back among my work tribe.

As the week progressed, I began to forget what had taken place at Ruth's Cottage. Wednesday evening was there before I knew it. John came around to check on me and to see if I'd booked an appointment with Ilona – I hadn't.

As we were catching up on our weeks – John was working from home on a client brief, Max still in WA on business – the phone rang, picked up by the answering machine.

We both heard, 'Hello, Philippa? My name's Bill Browne. I was given your name at a morning tea today. I believe you had some questions about the disappearance of a woman named Ruth Richards around three years ago?'

I don't know who was more shocked, John or I. As I ran to pick up the phone, John looked at me with a face that clearly said, '*What have you done?*'

I snatched up the phone, waved at John with the back of my hand, and he walked out the door, shaking his head in disbelief.

'Bill, is it?' I said into the phone. 'Thanks very much for calling back.'

With reserve in his deep voice, he said, 'That's okay. I believe you're writing an article on various disappearances. A work colleague mentioned you're interested in the disappearance of Ruth Richards? Is that right?' He got straight to the point. Good: I like that in a man, particularly when my cover story is a lie. However, his tone and response told me he had reservations when he said, 'Do you mind telling me what you are trying to achieve with this article?'

I repeated my cover story, this time adding that as part of my research I'd stayed in Ruth's Cottage. I hated lying, but Ruth's apparition had seemed to want me to tell someone who might help. Sometimes the end justifies the means.

Lying has never come naturally to me; in fact, I'm terrible at it. I was glad this conversation wasn't face to face, because he would have known right away I was full of shit. I needed to get him on side.

Nevertheless, I chickened out of telling him about my burgeoning psychic abilities. If I ever got to meet him, I could test the waters.

What I was being honest about was that there was more to the disappearance of Ruth Richards than met the eye. Unfortunately, when I'm nervous I waffle. Tonight was no exception.

The more I talked, the more I felt his interest slipping. I had to do something to retain it, and I took a gamble saying, 'I know this is a big ask, but would you be free to meet up for a coffee sometime soon so we could discuss this in person?'

He hesitated, and I fully expected him to politely decline. He didn't. 'As it turns out, I could spare some time this Friday. Where do you work?'

I plunged in. 'Great. I work in St Leonards, but I can meet you anywhere near the train line. What time and where would suit you?'

We agreed to meet on Friday at Roseville railway station at twelve fifteen. Before we hung up, we each gave a description of ourselves.

I'd done it; there was no turning back. To soothe my mind, I had a long hot shower and got ready for bed. As I was about to start reading a book, the phone pinged.

It was John. His text read, '*What have you done? How did that call go?*' He finished it off with a little emoji face with its hands on its hips.

I responded with an emoji pulling a face, and, '*Very well, thanks. His name's Bill Browne. He was working at Cessnock Police Station when Ruth Richards disappeared, on the case in fact. I told him I was doing an article on various unsolved disappearances. We're meeting at Roseville Station on Friday to talk about it in person.*'

After sending, I held my breath waiting for his response. It wasn't long coming. '*Well, I hope that after you make a fool of yourself, you can let this drop?*'

Don't get me wrong, he wasn't mad; just concerned. Realising this, I responded, '*Yep, once I see how this goes, I'll have done what was asked and can let it drop.*'

It was a feeble attempt to put his mind at rest, but I wasn't in the mood for a lecture at that time of night.

He texted, '*Glad to hear that. Night-night, bestie. Love you.*'

I flipped back, '*Night-night – love you too.*'

Thursday disappeared in a swirl of editorial deadlines and a huge workload. By the end of the day, I was exhausted and happy to be heading home. As I stood waiting for my train at St Leonards railway station, I had an uneasy feeling that someone was watching me.

Furtively I looked around the platform and saw two men who quickly looked away. My built-in women's radar made me shiver. One, just over my height, was junkie-thin with a faded rock-star look about him. He had a receding hairline at the front, and long hair pulled back in a ponytail. I didn't get a good a look at the other one. He was much taller, with a protruding gut, but as he turned away quickly, I didn't see his face. His hair from the back looked crew cut, ends gleaming under the station lights.

The shorter one had stared brazenly at me before he turned away. I couldn't forget the sneering look on his rat-like face. Harsh, maybe, but it was what I saw. His look seemed a mixture of derision and sexual interest.

When a northbound train arrived, they both hopped aboard. I felt more comfortable with them gone. I tried to push the uneasy feeling into the back of my mind, but I was wary and nervous on my dark walk up the lane to my townhouse.

When I got inside, I checked that the courtyard gate was locked – three times – and hurried inside to the warmth and safety of home.

I was welcomed indoors by a vocal and hungry Albert. As I put his meal out, I thought about those two men again. I usually try not to stereotype people, but I hadn't liked the look or feel of them, and I was sure I wouldn't be alone in thinking that way.

Just in case, I wrote in my trusty notebook what I could remember of their appearance – you never know. It gave me the creeps to think about them. I'd been very pleased to see them board the northbound train. Once I'd written their description in my notebook, I tried to push them out of my mind and enjoy my evening with Albert.

Unsettled, I texted John to share my encounter. His quick response surprised and touched me as he responded, *'Make sure you check all the doors and windows. I'm here if you need me. Try to sleep well.'*

I felt safer at once. Before long, I forgot about them entirely. A problem shared is a problem halved, especially when the person you shared it with lives in the same complex and would do anything to protect you. I went to bed feeling much more secure.

When I awoke on Friday morning, I took extra care with my make-up and appearance, hoping that if I wore the right outfit for my lunch meeting with Bill Browne, I'd be able to pull off my deception. I hoped so, but I wasn't confident.

When I looked into the mirror, despite the care I'd taken, I looked pale and tense. I had a hollow feeling it was all going to go pear-shaped once we sat down in Roseville to talk. I felt defeated before I got there.

The morning passed by quickly and soon I was at Roseville station. I saw the man straight away. He'd given an excellent description of himself. I'll paint you a picture.

He was maybe six feet tall, fit-looking, with well-defined muscles. He had a shaved head – which I personally find attractive – and kind, intelligent blue eyes that had a mischievous twinkle to them, even when unsmiling. He had a moustache and a cleft in his chin. It was hard to know how old he was – maybe late forties.

After checking him out, as he turned my way, I said, 'Excuse me, are you Bill?'

I wasn't expecting how his face and eyes would light up when he smiled, and as he did, I felt myself blush. I hoped he didn't notice.

He held his hand out to shake mine, and in a deep voice said, 'Yes, I am. You must be Philippa. Pleased to meet you.'

As he shook my hand, I thought, *Good, a firm handshake; so far so good.* Now all I had to do was lie convincingly to him – either that, or risk telling him the entire truth. Thinking this, I felt myself blush again.

Introductions done, we made our way to the coffee shop. Once seated, we small-talked and ordered our meals and drinks. After the waitress had taken our orders, Bill turned to me and said, 'I know the Ruth Richards disappearance case well. I worked on it with my partner for a time. Can you explain to me who you're doing the article for and what the article is about?'

His direct approach took me back, leaving me lost as to how to respond. I could feel a nervous stutter, sometimes a precursor to tics, coming on. Lying to this man wasn't going to be as simple as I'd imagined or hoped.

I had two options – I could try to bluff my way through, sticking to the cover story I'd given on the phone, or I could tell the truth.

I opted for the latter. With as much dignity as I could muster – great meeting you, and oh, by the way, I lied to get you here – I took a deep breath and nervously said, 'I know this isn't going to give you a very good first impression of me, and believe me I hate lying. The story I gave the young constable on the phone wasn't exactly the truth.'

I stopped, waiting for him to respond – he didn't. Nervously I continued. 'If you allow me to, I'll endeavour to tell you as truthfully and factually as possible the reason why I've become involved with Ruth Richards' disappearance. I'll do this as succinctly as I can. I am truly sorry for the deception used to get you here, but I believe the information I have to share with you justifies my subterfuge.'

In case you hadn't noticed, I was suffering a bad case of verbal diarrhoea.

For a time he sat and looked at me, a look that said, '*I don't believe this.*' Face red with emotion, he eventually shrugged. 'That's not the best start, but as you've admitted your subterfuge and we're here, I'll give you until the end of this lunch. I'll put it on record: I'm not pleased or impressed to have been lured here under false pretences.'

Ouch, right between the eyes. I couldn't blame him, though; I wouldn't have been pleased either.

I tried to muster as much dignity as possible. 'I understand how you feel. I'd feel the same way; I'm truly sorry. What I have to share with you I couldn't have said when I first phoned the station, not without sounding like a total nut-job. I feel very strongly that I have some important information to give you that may help reopen the investigation. Thank you for giving me till the end of our lunch to try to do so.'

As I said this, I felt my tics escalating, and started my throat-clearing. Credit where it's due: he seemed to feel sorry for me, and to ease the tension he said, not unkindly, 'Apology accepted; now facts first. I take it you aren't a journalist doing a story on unsolved disappearances. So why are you so interested in Ruth Richards? In fact, how are you even aware of it?'

Finally: something I could work with. Pushing my tics into the background, I told the truth. 'In the past two weeks, I've been holidaying at Ruth's Cottage. Coincidentally, it turns out she was a friend of my grandmother's, and when I was about eight, I stayed there one school holiday.'

I stopped, rubbing my face, uncertain how to proceed. He sat and patiently waited for me to continue.

More hesitantly I said, 'This is quite a complex story with twists and turns, so I'm not sure where to start. I've brought something with me for you to read. It is a page torn from Ruth Richards' diary, which I found during my stay. Perhaps we could start there.'

As I said this, I handed the blown-up diary page to him, happy that his gaze had left my face and was now concentrating on what was in his hands. I watched as he read over Ruth's diary page.

Eventually he looked up. 'Where did you find this?'

'While I was staying there, Ruth's cat, um, Albert, anyway, he was scratching at it. It was wedged between floorboards on the deck. He seemed insistent about getting it out, so I, um, I crawled under the cottage and dislodged it.'

He looked at me, apparently uncertain how to respond.

Before I lost him, I said, 'There is more to this story, and you did say you'd give me till the end of the lunch. There's only one way; I need to tell you all about my stay at Ruth's Cottage.'

As our meals were being served, I did just that. He didn't say much as I recounted my time at Ruth's Cottage. I more-or-less told him the same story I'd told John. I had this one chance to try to reopen Ruth's case.

As I picked at my meal and he ate his, I continued. I didn't concern myself with how I sounded or what he might think of me or my fanciful story. I jumped in, boots and all, because I'd rather be thought of as an eccentric than a liar.

I'd had the perfect rehearsal with John, and I was again telling my truth; if he put it down to my being a nutter, so be it. At least I'd done what I felt Ruth's apparition had wanted me to do. Once done, I could let it go and move on with my life, knowing I'd tried my best.

Nearly thirty minutes later, Bill Browne had finished his meal. I'd half-heartedly picked at mine as I'd concentrated on telling as much of my story as I felt he needed to hear.

I was exhausted when I'd finished, and I slumped in my chair, sighed and said, 'Well, there you have it – the truth. *My* truth. I don't know what you'll make of it; I only know I had to tell someone. Now you might understand why I lied to get someone to listen. You're the poor sucker who put his hand up to come, and for that I'm truly sorry and grateful.'

As my energy petered out, my tics exploded. Somehow he ignored them. For a while he seemed to contemplate what I'd told him.

Then, with a kindness I neither deserved nor expected, he said, 'That story would have taken a lot of courage to tell. I appreciate you telling it, even if I find a lot of what you said hard to digest or, if I'm honest, hard to believe.'

I felt relieved to have finished telling my unbelievable story, and grateful that he was trying to be objective. But I couldn't leave it at that. 'I know lying on my initial call hasn't given you a good impression. I honestly couldn't think of any other way to approach this. In my defence, it did get you here to meet me, and that was my objective; I could have let the whole bloody thing drop. Oh God, I'm making things worse, aren't I?'

I was getting more agitated by the moment, and, desperate to get some control back, I excused myself and went to the ladies' room.

When I returned, Bill said, 'I don't want to make you feel more uncomfortable than you already do. Let's exchange numbers. I'll go away and think about what you've told me. I'll be honest, I may or may not get back to you, but I will give it some thought. How does that sound?'

I wrote my phone numbers on my card and handed it to him. Then I said, sincerely, 'Thank you for allowing me to keep some dignity. I reiterate that I do believe what I've shared with you needs to be investigated. I also believe there would be some merit in reopening the case. You can keep that copy of the diary page. If you decide to walk away, I'll understand. Thanks for your time.'

Lunch bill paid, phone numbers exchanged, Bill Browne, a true gentleman, walked me to the station and waited on the platform till my train arrived. As it approached, he shook my hand and thanked me again for telling him my story. Turning to wave goodbye, I felt sure that would be the one and only time I'd meet Bill Browne or, for that matter, hear any more about the case.

As the train made its way toward St Leonards, I mulled over in my mind what I could have done differently to convince him that my story had some credibility. I dissected the entire conversation. By the time my train had reached St Leonards I'd come to the conclusion there was nothing else I could have said or done – except maybe not lying in the first place – that would have changed either the outcome of our meeting or his opinion of me and my story. I also promised myself to let it go.

CHAPTER 15

Back at my desk, I was grateful for a busy afternoon. I needed distraction to stop me rehashing the lunch. That's another frustration of having an obsessive nature – over-analysing.

I'm not sure what I'd expected Bill Browne to make of what I'd told him. I'd wanted him to be open-minded and to hear me out. He'd done the latter, if not the former.

Another thought kept cropping into my head about what an attractive man he was. Pity I wouldn't get to see him again.

Before I knew it, it was six thirty. Being Friday evening, most of my colleagues had already taken off to enjoy their weekends. I packed up my desk, put on my coat – it was cold, windy and drizzling outside – and headed for the station.

As I waited for my train, I felt another surge of anxiety about the men who'd been looking at me on Wednesday evening. I glanced around, but couldn't see anyone remotely like the two men. Still, I couldn't wait to get inside the carriage and in the anonymous company of my fellow passengers.

By the time the train arrived at Wollstonecraft, it had started to rain heavily. I made a quick dash up Shirley Lane, and as I was fumbling with my keys to open my courtyard door, I had another sensation that I was being watched. I looked around and saw no one except the shadows of trees waving in the wind.

Once inside, I turned on some lamps, lit the gas fire, and then fed Albert. I'm not ashamed to say that, after checking out upstairs – confirming that Albert and I were home alone – I also checked to make sure the three doors that lead into my courtyard were tightly locked.

I then put a call through to John to tell how my lunch had gone. His answering machine clicked on, and I remembered that, with Max still away on business, he'd arranged to meet up with friends in Kings Cross. Our post-mortem of my lunch with Bill Browne would have to wait.

I had a hot shower, put on my tracky dacks and came down-stairs to heat up some leftovers for dinner. As I ate dinner on my lap with Albert purring at my side, I distractedly watched some Netflix.

As the night wore on, the storm became more intense. After a while, the rain was so loud on the roof that I could hardly hear the television. I decided to call it a night, checking the doors again before I went upstairs. I made sure I had a torch ready in case we lost power, and had my mobile charged next to me. I'd had enough of storms to last me a while, and this one didn't look like abating any time soon.

I lay reading, the shutters in my bedroom tightly closed. Before long I fell asleep, my e-book still in my lap. It had been an exhausting day on many levels, and I was grateful to slide into a numbing sleep that helped me forget my humiliation for a short time.

I was awoken abruptly by a jarring noise. At first, I thought it was the storm still raging outside; then I saw how Albert was reacting. He was letting out a low, doglike growl, and the fur on his back had risen. I tried to soothe him so I could listen more intently. Then I heard a sound that confirmed I was in trouble – a door being rattled; a door being forced.

My first thought was to phone John, then, remembering he was out, I put through a call to 000. The operator answered quickly, asking what service – police – and that line in turn was quickly answered. Hoping they'd believe me more than Bill Browne had, I explained that someone was trying to break into my home. In a hissing voice I gave my address. I also mentioned the two men who'd unnerved me on Wednesday at the station and said I felt I'd been followed from the station that evening. They reassured me there would be someone there soon.

After I hung up, I phoned John, only to get his answer machine again. I left him a quick and almost inaudible message. 'Hi, John, it's me. I think someone's trying to break in. I've called the police. They should be here soon.'

Of course, after the embarrassment of my lunch today I was afraid that I may have mistaken storm noises for someone breaking in. Pushing these doubts aside, I threw on my dressing-gown, grabbed the torch and made my way onto the landing, locking Albert in the bedroom and out of harm's way.

At the top of the stairs, I took a very deep breath. As I was about to make my way down the stairs, I heard Albert scratching loudly at the bedroom door.

Beginning my descent, my heart was pounding so hard that I could hardly hear my own footsteps, let alone whether someone was actually inside. I'd begun to perspire as fear prepared me for fight or flight.

I reached the bottom of the stairs, moving slowly. At that point someone jumped out, grabbed me by the shoulders and forced a hand over my mouth.

Fear did something else to me, almost forcing my bowels to loosen. My blood froze as I smelled his hand over my mouth and under my nose. I recognised the smell, a pungent clove-like smell that reminded me of the *bidi* cigarettes Zac's uncle sometimes smoked. I filed that away, just in case I survived to tell anyone.

In a flash of lightning, I saw he wasn't alone. Crouched near the dining room table was a second man. I couldn't see his face clearly with only the occasional flash of lightening highlighting his features. As he stood up, I noticed he was taller than the one who had me pinned.

The first man was hurting me, his hand tight across my mouth, his other arm wrapped firmly around my waist, making it hard to breathe. As he invaded my body with his hands, he assaulted my psyche with his voice, chillingly saying, 'Listen up, bitch. I've got a message for you. Stop looking into Ruth Richards. This time it's a warning; next time won't be. Understood?'

I'd have agreed to anything to make them leave. I could only nod vigorously in response. With this action, I saw he had a tattoo on his forearm: a playing card, an ace of spades with a skull in the middle.

I don't know whether it was lack of oxygen or that my brain was protecting me from my fear, but the next moments aren't clear to me. I was soon shocked back to my senses when I heard John say, 'The police are on their way; let her go!'

Taken by surprise, the one holding me threw me viciously against the wall, winding me badly. As I gasped for breath, I saw one shove John savagely as they rushed out the door.

When I came back to my senses again, I saw John slumped in a heap. He had a gash in his head that was bleeding heavily. As I squatted and took John in my arms, through tears I said, 'Oh, John, I'm so sorry, I shouldn't have called you …'

True to style, John cut me off with, 'Bit of a drastic way to prove a point, pussycat, but now I believe you …'

As he said this, two policemen rushed in the front door. Seeing that someone had been injured, one quickly put through a call for an ambulance.

What happened next I saw through a veil of mist, which I suppose was shock. One of the policemen asked me to step aside so they could assess John. He led me into the dining room. Then he began to question me about what had happened.

I couldn't concentrate; all I could think of was being with John. Sensing this, the officer, not unkindly, said, 'I know you're concerned about your, um – husband, is it?'

Through my tears, I smiled at this misreading of the

situation. Unfortunately, my smile was misunderstood, and a stern look crossed his face. I said, 'I'm sorry, I only smiled because, well, he's not my husband; he's my best friend.'

As I said this, tears began to flow down my cheeks. Seeing them, his face showed another emotion: a long-suffering look I'm sure a lot of officers get in these circumstances as they realise they've got yet another bloody crier.

To lighten the moment, I popped my head around the corner, thinking to tell John about the misunderstanding. What I saw shocked me to the core. The other officer was giving John CPR. As I went to rush to his side, I was held back by the young policeman who'd been questioning me.

As he gripped my arm he said, 'Stay here, please. You'll only get in the way. The ambos have just arrived; they'll take over and look after him. He's in good hands.'

Sitting back down, I could feel the colour drain from my face. No doubt used to these situations, the officer went to the kitchen and came back with a glass of water. When I took the glass, I saw my hands were trembling.

Before long, the ambos had John on a stretcher and on his way to North Shore Hospital. As I watched them taking him out, still working on him, my heart broke into tiny pieces. Why had I called him? Why had I involved my friend?

After they'd gone, the two officers began to question me in earnest about the break-in while it was fresh in my mind. I spent a good hour trying as best I could to tell them what had happened. I also told them of my conversation that day with their colleague from the Hunter Valley police.

I could tell immediately they weren't interested in what had been said at my lunch with Bill Browne. They were firmly focussed on what had transpired tonight. They were compartmentalising; who could blame them?

The cynical looks they shot one another as I gave them a synopsis of what I'd told Bill showed they didn't want to get involved. I half expected them to drug test me. Police wear their cynicism as a protective suit of armour.

Their cynicism made me realise how extraordinary it was that Bill Browne had been both accepting and non-judgemental. As I thought this, the tears again began to flow, and as shock sank in, I began to shake.

Seeing how upset I'd become, the gentler of the two officers made me a hot, sweet cup of tea, and wrapped a throw from the lounge around my shoulders. He again reassured me that John was in good hands. I felt grateful for his gentle and caring attitude.

After the usual photos, fingerprint dusting and so forth, they said they would be in touch. They seemed confident that what had taken place was a robbery gone wrong, a home invasion robbery with violence. As they were packing to leave, the gentler officer, knowing I was too distressed to drive, offered me a lift to the hospital. I gratefully accepted.

I went upstairs to change, and took some dry food up for Albert. Once I'd thrown on some fresh clothes and washed my face and hands, I gently reassured Albert I'd be home soon and again locked him in the bedroom. Downstairs was a mess; I'd clean up as soon as I could.

By the time I arrived at the hospital's emergency department, John had not regained consciousness. I knew I couldn't put off the inevitable call to Max, and John's parents, any longer, so with no good news to reassure them, I made those heartbreaking calls.

I phoned Max first, waking him. It took him a while to comprehend what I was telling him. Once he realised the gravity of the situation, he said he'd be home as soon as he could get flights.

I then phoned John's parents. Thankfully, Cathy, John's sister, answered the phone and saved me the heartache of having to tell their parents that their son was gravely ill. Through her tears, she thanked me and said they'd be there soon.

After my calls, I tried to find out some concrete information about John's condition. I was told that as I wasn't a relative, they were unable to give me any details.

The fact that John's family lived close to the hospital meant they didn't take long to arrive. As they walked solemnly and quickly into emergency, their tearstained faces looked pale and distraught. They saw me and one by one hugged me, offering me words of reassurance; despite their best intentions, it made me feel worse.

We were soon told that John'd had a CT scan of his head, and was soon to be taken into surgery to relieve some pressure on his brain. We were also told it was going to be a long wait.

After sitting with them a while, John's father said I should go home and get some sleep. Although I didn't want to leave,

I knew they at least had each other. With the stress, I'd also started ticcing furiously; that was the last thing they needed to see and hear while they were waiting for news.

As I said my goodbyes, they reassured me that as soon as they had information, they'd phone. I headed outside to the cab rank for the short journey home. As I left, I asked them to tell John I loved him and would see him tomorrow.

I jumped into the first cab on the rank. Sitting in the back seat, I began to softly sob. The driver, hearing my distress, kindly asked if I was okay. All I could manage was to squeak, 'Yes, thank you.' But I was far from okay.

When I opened my front door, I was assailed by the sight and smell of John's blood. A shudder went through my body, but I was brought back to earth by Albert's plaintive cries from upstairs.

I skirted around the blood, grabbed a towel from the laundry and threw it across the now drying pool. Then I ran upstairs and opened the door to my bedroom. As I opened it, Albert flew past at speed and fled downstairs to his litter tray – he'd held on all that time.

I followed him downstairs, hearing a ping on my mobile. I shuddered, thinking it was a call from the hospital. It wasn't; it was a text from Uncle J. He'd done it again – it read, *'Are you okay? I'm feeling stuff I don't like. Please let me know you're fine. Love you, J.'*

As I read his text, I broke down completely. Once I'd stopped sobbing, to reassure him, I texted back, *'I'm fine, really. Been a break-in here. John's been taken to hospital. Can't tell you much about his condition yet. I'm sorry you've been worried. I'm so sorry. I love you. P.'*

What I really wanted to say was, *'I wish you were here, please come home.'* I couldn't dump that on him, not when he was so far away. There was no need to; reading my mind, he soon texted back, *'I'll change my flights as soon as I can. Want to be there for you, darling girl. Keep me in the loop. Give John my love. Glad you're okay. I love you. Uncle J.'*

Unable to put off the inevitable, I began to clean John's blood from the tiles and the wall, as well as the dusting powder from the furniture and doors. As I meticulously cleaned up my friend's blood, I was softly crying.

My tears were gradually replaced by anger, an anger fed by my overstimulated Tourettic brain. At times of stress, my untamed beast takes over.

As I scrubbed, I began to rant about the intruders and what they'd done to John. I try very hard to keep my outbursts private, for good reason. Once a Tourettic outpouring starts – think of a child wound up on red lolly frogs and soft drink, or someone who has imbibed too many cans of Red Bull – they will not be stopped until they've run their course. Well, that's my experience in stressful times, anyway. Want a tip? Telling someone in a full Tourettic rant to 'calm down' is not a good move.

I also vehemently chastised myself for the danger I'd put John in. I was wild and angry with the intruders, but most of all with myself. That anger kept me going, kept my clean-up on track, but by God it exhausted me.

After a clean-up that I never want to repeat, I had a long hot cleansing shower, then, completely spent, I lay down to rest for a while and, against all the odds, I fell into a deep sleep.

I'd like to say it was a restorative sleep; it wasn't. It was a sleep full of a chaotic and fractured dream. *I was near the ocean; I could smell the salt water and feel the sea breeze against my face. Soon I became horribly lost, until I stumbled across a derelict old house.*

There was someone inside the house; someone I had to hide from. As I looked around for a place to hide, I saw a bright blue boatshed.

Hurrying toward the shed, I tripped on a tree root. As I picked myself up and looked at the shed, I saw it had chartreuse green window shutters. For a time I was mesmerised by their beautiful colour, then suddenly the shutters seemed to shine and pulsate, making me feel both enraptured and afraid.

When I edged closer to the door of the shed, it was locked by several different padlocks. I became more frantic when, as I unlocked each one, it relocked itself. I knew I needed to get inside this shed not only to hide, but for some other reason.

I was jolted awake as Albert jumped onto my bed and nudged me with his head. It was feeding time, and I was very grateful that it was – grateful to leave that chaotic dream behind.

CHAPTER 16

Once showered and dressed, I phoned the hospital to see if there was any change in John's condition. He was still in ICU, so I phoned Max for an update.

As it rang, I could feel a knot in the pit of my stomach and another in my heart. Finally, on the fifth ring, Max answered in a raspy, sleep-deprived voice. 'Pip, I'm on my way to the airport. How are you?'

Those last three kind words nearly undid me. At a time like this he was thinking about me. Tears silently flowing down my face, I took a deep breath and said, 'Max, don't worry about me; I'm fine. Have you heard how John is?'

He could easily sense the anxiety in my voice. 'The operation went really well. They relieved the pressure on his brain. They're only holding him in ICU for another twenty-four hours, then transferring him to a ward upstairs. He's doing well, Pip, really well. Cathy said he asked after you.'

Despite my best efforts to hold it in, on hearing he'd asked after me I lost my self-control. Barely composing myself, I managed to squeeze out an apology of sorts, saying, 'Oh, did he, that's … Max, I'm so very sorry for putting John in danger. I'm so angry with …'

Max gently cut my feeble attempt at an apology short with further reassurance. 'Pip, don't, honey. Don't do this to yourself. You know John loves you; I love you too. It would break his heart if he knew you were putting yourself through this. It wasn't your fault. I know it's going to be hard, but stop blaming yourself. Why don't you go for a jog or go to the gym and let some steam off?'

Though I knew sleep would have served me better, I stuttered, 'That, that sounds like a great idea, and something John would suggest. I'll do that.'

Encouragingly he said, 'That's our girl. Take your phone with you. I'll let you know if they transfer him to a ward earlier. I have to go, I'm at the airport. I'm so glad you're okay, Pip; I mean that.'

The love kept coming. Before I hung up, I thanked Max, told him I loved him and reassured him I'd keep my mobile charged and with me at all times.

As I changed into my jogging clothes, the phone rang. Thinking it was Max, I answered quickly, saying, 'Is everything okay?'

It was Bill Browne, a man I thought I'd never hear from again. In a concerned tone, he got straight to the point. 'Philippa, it's Bill Browne. Are you okay?'

As he was the last person I was expecting to hear from, I

hesitated. 'Oh, um, Bill. I'm sorry; I was expecting to hear from someone else.'

'I had a call just now from a colleague in Sydney. He told me what happened at your place last night. How's your friend – John, isn't it?'

The surprises kept coming – first Max's love and total forgiveness, now a man I'd only met once phoning to see how I was, how John was. Trying to keep a lid on my emotions – think tics – I answered openly. 'I've spoken to Max, his partner. Max says he's out of danger. Max is still on his way from WA. Seems they may transfer John out of ICU in the next day or so. Once they do, I can go up and visit him.' I hesitated to clear my throat. Regaining composure, I continued. 'You say you've just had a call. I'm surprised. Last night, it seemed they'd put the break-in down to a home invasion and wanted to leave it at that.'

Bill cleared his own throat. 'I've worked briefly with the colleague who phoned. He was very concerned about you last night. This might sound presumptuous, particularly after what you've been through, but are you up to catching up to talk about what happened last night in person? I can come to your place, if it helps. I'll bring some lunch.'

I hesitated, wondering how I could get out of this. I had a lot to achieve today. Then with a sigh I said, 'I'm going to be quite busy today, Bill. I need to organise some security for my townhouse. I really appreciate your kind offer, but …'

'I might be able to help you there. I have some friends in the security business in Sydney. I could call them and explain your situation, if you'd like me to?'

By this stage, my head was spinning and I was feeling completely overwhelmed. His kind offer to help organise security was very tempting. Finally, realising I didn't want to tackle this on my own, I accepted. 'Bill, that's very kind of you. Yes, thank you, I'd appreciate you getting in touch with your security contacts and coming around to talk about last night. Lunch would be great; I'm pretty hungry. I'll fix you up for it when you get here. Do you want my address?'

It was that easy – all I had to do was accept his kind offer and I wouldn't have to do this all on my own. After I'd given him my address and hung up, I needed exercise to help me relax and centre my scattered thoughts before he arrived.

I was too upset to go to the gym, so I went for a jog instead. After the jog I had a shower, changed and threw on a little make-up. As I sat digesting what had happened, Albert on my lap, the front doorbell rang.

I opened the door, my hair still wet from the shower. Within seconds of seeing Bill standing there, the chemicals in my body were at work. I was definitely attracted to him.

I'd thought he was good looking yesterday. Today he looked even more attractive, in a blue chambray shirt, jeans and RM Williams boots. His impossibly blue eyes looked even more incredible today; maybe it was the blue shirt, or maybe it was the obvious concern they showed. Trying to push my attraction toward him into the background, I inanely said, 'Oh, Bill, thanks for coming. Come in, please. I've boiled the kettle. Would you like a tea or a coffee?'

As he came in, he took in the chaos: the broken dining room

door; signs of the scuffle that had taken place in the entrance; and, I'm afraid, a few spots of blood I'd missed. As I watched him take it all in, I couldn't help but shudder at the memory.

Seeing my reaction, he touched my arm. 'This must have been some ordeal, Philippa. I'm sorry you had to go through this. How's your friend?'

I felt myself blush. To hide my embarrassment, I walked quickly off toward the kitchen. In my ready-to-explode style, over my shoulder I prattled, 'Oh, John's much better, thanks. I may even be able to visit him later on today. Don't know about you, but I'm starving. I'll make a pot of coffee and you can put our lunches on those plates. How much do I owe you, by the way? It's very kind of you to come all this way. I really appreciate …'

Realising I was heading into a meltdown, Bill took control of the situation, kindly cutting in with, 'It's my treat. How about we sit outside in the courtyard and eat while you fill me in on last night? By the way, I called my friends about your security issues. They'll be here within the next hour. If your windows and doors are standard size, they might even be able to have the security screens fitted today, if not tomorrow. Hope that's okay, money-wise?'

A wave of relief flooded my body. Until that moment, I hadn't realised how concerned I'd felt about my own safety.

The next emotion I felt was anger, mainly for what they'd done to John, but also for violating my home. Tears pricking my eyes, I gratefully responded. 'Thank you. I can't tell you what that means to me. I'm so wound up; I had no idea who to contact or where to start. Money-wise I'm fine. I've been left some recently, so it isn't a problem.'

Soon, with all the pent-up emotions – the fear, the anger, the worry – and no doubt having this virtual stranger being so kind to me, I started my throat-clearing tic. I wasn't in the mood to camouflage my tics by passing them off as a side-effect of all the crying I'd been indulging in. I was in the mood to be authentic.

Giving me time to contain my emotions, he thoughtfully stepped in again, saying, 'You need tissues. Where are they? I'll grab them.'

He was soon back, a box of tissues and a glass of water in his hands. He placed both in front of me. I've always been attached to calm people. I guess we all love what we lack in ourselves. At that moment, Bill Browne was like human Valium. His very presence had a calming effect, his kind gestures even more so.

After I'd blown my nose and sipped some water, I found the strength to say, 'Well, I guess you want to hear first-hand what happened last night?'

'If you're up to it, yes please, I'd like to hear. Take your time.'

As calmly as my overstimulated state would allow, I tried to give him the facts without emotion clouding the story. He sat there and patiently let me go over what had happened in the night.

When I got to the part about the officer doing CPR on John, I lost it completely and began to sob and tic furiously – an attractive combination, as you can imagine.

I was about to explain my Tourette's, but was saved by the bell – literally. The front gate buzzer sounded, and with it I shot nearly three feet in the air. The security people were here. Bill asked if it was okay for him to let them in. I agreed, saying I'd duck upstairs to wash my face.

When I got there, I saw I looked a fright, with red-rimmed eyes and nose. I washed my face, re-applied mascara, put some foundation around my red nose, then tried to contain myself before I headed down to have a conversation about my security needs.

By the time I got downstairs, Bill had obviously explained the gravity of the situation to the two men. One of them gave me an unexpected hug and said kindly, 'Gee, love, sorry about what those mongrels did to you last night. I have a daughter your age. If it's okay, we'll do some measurements and then have a talk.'

This unexpected kindness, again from a stranger, undid me and I began to cry again. Through tears, I hiccupped back, 'Thank … thank you, I'd appreciate that.'

My response under the circumstances was inadequate, but that was all I could manage. Embarrassed silence followed – men feel impotent, I'm sure, in the face of women's tears. A moment later the phone rang. As I excused myself to answer the call, I heard them, together, start coming up with solutions to my immediate problem – my safety.

That is one of the many things men do best – they come up with solutions to problems, and they do that best together, sharing ideas.

The phone call was from Cathy, and she sounded more upbeat than I'd heard her since that first call. Ecstatically she said, 'Hi, Pip! John's insisted I call you. He's improved so much that sometime tomorrow he's being transferred back to a ward on Level 7. He's very tired, but wanted you to know that you're the person, after Max, he most wants to see. He's asleep now, but before he dozed off his exact words were, "Make sure you tell Pip that I love her and that she isn't to blame herself."'

Filled with the joy of relief, I thanked Cathy and said I'd hopefully see her tomorrow.

As I hung up, for the first time since the break-in I felt a sense that things were going to be all right. My best friend was going to be fine.

By the time I'd returned to the courtyard, the 'boys' had very satisfied looks on their faces. The owner of the company beamed me a smile and said, 'Well, young lady, we've got good news. Your windows and doors are of standard size, so today we should be able to have security screens on all downstairs openings. The upstairs we can do either tomorrow or Monday. How's that sound?'

It sounded bloody brilliant, and I told them so. They headed off, saying they'd be back before the end of the day. I was incredibly grateful, especially to Bill, for being able to organise such a quick solution. With a bit of luck, I might get some sleep tonight.

After they'd left, I shared my phone call with Bill, saying, 'That was Cathy, John's sister, with good news: tomorrow John's being transferred to a ward. He's asleep now but I can see him tomorrow. I can't tell you how relieved I am.'

With true enthusiasm, he responded, 'That's great news. I can understand how relieved you must be. The boys will secure your townhouse, so I hope that's another pressure off your mind?'

I'd lucked out meeting this man. He seemed genuinely pleased that John was recovering well, and he'd also been able to achieve the impossible by helping to secure my home. I felt an overwhelming urge to hug him.

Instead, I said, 'I can't tell you how much what you've done for me means. I'm grateful that right from our lunch – God, was it only yesterday? – you've been so open-minded about what I've told you. If the break-in has achieved one positive thing, it's given credence to my unbelievable tale … and I …' Lost for both words and energy, I allowed silence to take over, which believe me isn't something I'm renowned for.

Bill didn't seem to feel the need to fill that silence. For a time, he sat thinking about what I'd said. Eventually he turned my way, and with a look of gentleness on his face said, 'Since our lunch yesterday, I've given some thought to what we spoke about. I'll be honest with you: although I know that in the past the department has used the services of a well-known local psychic, I've not had much exposure personally to such methods. But I've heard second-hand of some success using these methods, particularly with cold cases.'

Then he stopped and looked at me, as if waiting for me to continue the conversation.

Not wanting to disappoint, I cut in. 'Thanks for telling me that. I'm sorry; I'm exhausted. Can you tell me where we go from here?'

It was unfair of me to throw the ball back into his court, but I really was fading fast. I also had the start of a headache, which threatened to knock me out of action any time soon.

He was about to respond when the front gate buzzer rang anew. I'd never heard the buzzer rung so much in the entire time I'd been here. I was overwhelmed with emotion when I opened the gate to see a delivery man with a glorious and colourful bunch of flowers.

As I read the card, my heart lifted; they were from Uncle J. His card read: *'Princess, these should only just beat me. As you read this, I'm winging my way home to you. Stay brave. I love you. Uncle J.'*

More tears flowed, and my tics found new heights of dramatic expression – my squeal accompanied by my nose-scrunching. As I finished reading the card, Bill said, 'Not bad news, I hope?'

'No, they're from my Uncle J … um, Jim. He's been over-seas and, well, when he heard about the break-in, he cut his trip short. He's on the way home now; these beat him.'

I put the flowers down on the entry sideboard. Turning to Bill, I forced myself to be brave. 'I have to explain some-thing to you – no more lies, no more subterfuge. I've got mild Tourette's, hence my, um, well, my tics. Do you know what I'm talking about?'

He looked at me with those sexy, sensitive eyes and said,

'As a matter of fact, I do know what Tourette's is. I wondered the other day at our lunch if that was what I was seeing. Thanks for telling me, Philippa.'

I felt a weight lift off me. 'Great – one more thing about myself I don't need to hide. Psychic abilities and Tourette's syndrome; now you know my other secret.'

I was also tired and grumpy, and sick of him calling me Philippa, and ungraciously said, 'Do you think you could call me Pip, please? Every time you call me Philippa, I feel like you're mad at me. It's a childhood thing.'

Realising I was overemotional and in full Tourettic flight, with a disarming charm he gave me one of his adorable lopsided smiles, a quick salute, and cheekily answered, 'Yes ma'am, of course I can call you Pip, if that's what you'd prefer. Hate to make you feel any more uncomfortable. So, does anything in particular help calm your tics down?'

I couldn't believe it – the man was a marvel.

Albert had joined us in the courtyard; to my great surprise he'd walked right over to Bill and given him a leg cuddle. Bill acknowledged Albert by slowly bending down to tickle him behind one ear. Round one had gone to Bill, and despite my grumpy demeanour, I liked him even more.

Just as I was about to officially introduce Albert to Bill, the front gate buzzer sounded again and Albert again flew under the courtyard decking. Meeting one new human at a time was all my little ginger friend could deal with.

The security boys were back with screens for my downstairs windows and doors. They went about installing them without a single complaint about having their schedule thrown into chaos.

I was grateful to them not only for making my home secure, but for the manner in which they carried out the task. After a few hours they called it a day, saying they'd be back first thing Monday morning to finish the upstairs windows and door. Bill stayed and occasionally gave them a hand.

By the time they left, I must have looked beyond exhausted. Bill said, 'Tell you what, now I know you're secure, I think you need some down-time. I'll head off so you can catch up with yourself. Are you feeling safe now that the boys have put in the screens?'

As I looked around my home, the enormity of what he had helped me achieve struck me. Gratitude filled me. 'Bill, I honestly don't know what to say to you, except thank you so very much. Yes, I do feel a lot safer, and yes, I would like to get some rest if I can, please. I want to go up first thing tomorrow to see John. Again, thank you for everything. Honestly, words fail me.'

He smiled that sexy, crooked smile again, but his tone was modest. 'I'm glad I've been able to help. How about I put some more thought into where we go from here and give you a call tomorrow? Sound okay?'

I assured this generous man that yes, that did sound okay. As I walked him to the courtyard gate, I thanked him again, and we wished one another a good night's sleep before talking again tomorrow.

After he'd left, I felt relief to finally be on my own – fully expressing tics while on your own is so satisfying – yet also sad that he'd left. I understood the former but not the latter. I'd know this man for only two days, so why was I missing him?

To take my mind off him I decided to see if I could do sketches of the two men who'd broken into my home. It took a few attempts. Eventually I was both pleased and unnerved with the sketches.

I was now sure I'd seen them both twice – once at St Leonards station, and again on the night of the break-in. Looking at my sketches gave me the creeps, so I threw them in my writing bureau drawer and locked them safely out of sight.

<h1 style="text-align:center">CHAPTER 17</h1>

All things considered, I didn't have a bad night's sleep. It was dream free, and by the time I woke I'd slept at least seven hours. I went for a short jog; exercise helps reduce tics and the other co-morbid stuff, like depression and anxiety.

I wanted to see John as soon as possible, but I also wanted to be Zen when I did. After my jog, I showered, dressed, did my make-up and headed straight up to North Shore Hospital.

I arrived fifteen minutes before official visiting hours. I was prepared to sit and wait. I had no idea what to expect when I saw John, and that frightened me. One of the nurses saw me sitting outside the ward and suggested I go straight in.

Nervous, I went to the loo first, reapplied my lipstick, then made my way to Bed 19. As I stood watching from the door, I was heartened to see his interaction with a nurse attending him.

His sweet face looked a little haggard from lack of sleep, his sandy blond hair dishevelled. One thing that hadn't changed was his mischievous hazel eyes; they sparkled as he joked with the nurse.

Eventually they noticed I was there, alerted no doubt by a grunting tic that had escaped. I've lost count of the number of times I've been doing my throat-clearing tic in public and people thought I was trying to get their attention to move over. I must admit it has helped on occasion if I'm in a hurry, which I usually am.

I digress – another feature of Tourette's. On hearing the tic, they turned toward me, and as the nurse left the room, she gave me a kind and reassuring smile.

Thankfully John had a room to himself, because despite our best efforts, when we were finally alone we both became emotional.

John held his arms open toward me. 'About bloody time you got here. I've been awake since six. Come and give me a hug.'

As I flew into his arms, the first words out of my mouth pissed him off. 'Oh God, John, I'm so sorry for what they did to you, I'm so very relieved to see you looking so well after …'

In a mock-angry tone my dearest friend cut me off with, 'Stop, enough! Did you not get my message via Max? I don't blame you for very good reason – it wasn't your fault! Stop crying, you're getting mascara all over my sheets.'

As he said this, he gently tilted my head up. 'Let me look at you. No, doesn't look like they did any physical damage, at least. How are you coping emotionally? If those arseholes had harmed a hair on your head, I'd have … I'd have …'

It was John's turn to be emotional, lost for words. Knowing

it would be bad for him to upset himself, I rubbed his arm and said soothingly, 'Sweetie, please don't think about that. I'm fine physically and emotionally, especially now I know you're okay. Please put them out of your mind. You need to put all your energy into getting better so you can go home.'

As I said this, Max arrived. Seeing I was finally visiting, in a jocular tone he said, 'Well, thank heavens you're here. All I kept getting yesterday was, "Pip this, Pip that, when's Pip coming?" Talk about feeling like second prize.'

Seeing Max for the first time since the break-in broke my heart, again. Max is one of those sexy, swarthy men who by the end of the day have a five o'clock shadow. This morning the shadows under his concerned, deep brown eyes matched his unshaven face.

He looked sleep deprived and deeply concerned. To compose myself, and to give them time to connect, I refilled the water jug and poured John a fresh glass.

As I did, Max hugged and kissed his man and said, 'You're looking better today, handsome. Here: I've followed your instructions to the letter of the law. You've got three pair of clean jammies, all new and washed; undies; toiletries; shaver; and a photo of Leroy, who, by the way, sends his love and wants to know when his dad will be home. Oh, my parents phoned again and send their love. Now, where do you want me to put them?'

As Max put John's things away, I sat next to his bed, holding his hand and trying to talk about anything but what had happened. He needed peace so he could regain his health, get home and get on with his life. Conversationally I said, 'Oh, guess who phoned me yesterday, then came around? Give up? You may as well, because in a million years I'd never have guessed, so you won't ...'

I knew my best friend was recovering because he rolled his eyes, put his hands in the air and cut me off with, 'Enough with the guessing game! Who phoned and who came around?'

With a smile on my face – and one in my heart – I told John and Max about my unexpected visitor. They listened, rapt, especially about what Bill had been able to achieve security-wise in such a short time. They were both lost for words, which is rare.

John soon looked tired. Despite their protests I left them alone, promising I'd visit again soon.

In the doorway I paused and said, 'Oh, Uncle J sends his love. He's on his way home as we speak. He's dropping off in Sydney on his way back to Tassie so he can see you. Expect a visit from him in the next day or two.'

They not only loved Uncle J, they *got* him. As I left the room, I blew them both a kiss and made my way out of the ward with a much-eased soul.

Relieved, I decided to treat myself to a takeaway meal – Thai fish cakes and chicken pad Thai. While waiting for my order, I picked up a few delicacies from the deli in preparation for Uncle J's stay, and some fresh meat for Albert.

When I got home, there was a message on my answering machine. I was surprised when I played the message to find that it said, *'Hi, Philippa – sorry, Pip – it's Bill. Can you call me, please? I've got something to discuss with you. Talk then. Bye.'*

I phoned him back straight away. He picked up on the third ring. 'Pip, thanks for calling back. How'd you sleep? How was John this morning?'

He was asking all the right questions, so I assumed he'd forgiven my dishonest behaviour at the start. In my elated mood, I had a brain-spit, babbling, 'Yes, thanks to you I slept well. John's great. It was so good to see him and Max. I'm feeling so much better having seen him. Oh, and my Uncle J arrives tomorrow for a few days. He's going to visit John and he's staying with me. I can't wait. Sorry, I'm a bit over-excited. You said you had something to talk to me about?'

I could hear the smile in his voice at my obvious relief and excitement when he spoke. 'Well, that's all great news. Hope I get to meet Uncle J one day. I know this is pretty short notice, but are you free to go for a drive this afternoon? There's someone I want you to meet. If so, can you bring that brochure for Ruth's Cottage that you showed me yesterday?'

That threw me; he must have had something specific to achieve if he wanted me to bring the brochure on the cottage. After what he'd done for me yesterday, I knew I had no option. With an effort I said, 'Well, yeah, sure I can. I didn't have too much planned. Um, did you want me to meet you somewhere?'

After I'd hung up, I put my takeaway in the fridge, grabbed the brochure, and got an apple to eat on the way. Albert, with a full stomach, was in cat heaven, sunning himself in the courtyard and way too distracted to notice I was leaving him again – or so I hoped.

When I arrived at the café in St Leonards, Bill was already there. We chatted, then ordered lunch and coffee. With that out of the way, Bill turned to me with a pensive look on his face and said, 'Thanks for agreeing to meet me at such short notice. How are you feeling today?'

I answered him cheerfully. 'Great, thanks, especially now John's out of danger. I managed to sleep really well last night, no dreams. Not like the night before. I had a very disturbing and strange dream that night.'

'What did you dream about – the break-in?'

I recounted most of it – leaving out the boatshed's pulsating shutters; I didn't know him that well.

Sipping his coffee, Bill patiently let me finish, then kindly said, 'When someone has been through something as traumatic as you have, the subconscious has a way of dealing with the fallout. Vivid dreams, I believe, are sometimes a way of making sense of things.'

I appreciated his kindness at trying to explain my chaotic dream. Nodding, I said, 'Yes, my grandmother taught me that dreams are important. I wrote down what I dreamed in my dream journal. Enough about all that; you have something important to tell me?'

Bill sipped his coffee, then looked up at me with those sexy eyes and said, 'I've been mulling things over. It's a long story, but I'll summarise.' He took a breath. 'At the time of Ruth's disappearance, there was a rumour we heard from a friend of Ruth's of a new will having been made. This new will was never found, and Brendan O'Connor, Ruth's solicitor and the one who was to make the changes, apparently left the area, or else just disappeared. At any rate, he hasn't been heard from.'

I felt perplexed as to how I could help. 'That's interesting, but I'm not sure how I can help you with that.'

He cocked his head, and with the ghost of a smile brought the conversation back on track by calmly saying, 'I'm getting to that. Ruth had a best friend, Muriel. Through a contact, I've found that she's now living in a nursing home. Muriel is the person I'd like you to come with me to meet and speak to.'

We finished lunch and drove in Bill's car directly to the nursing home. The nurse who let us in made a comment that alarmed us, as she said, 'This is strange. Muriel hasn't had so many visitors for a long time. You're the second lot in the past week. Can you make it a quick visit, please? After the visit last week, she was agitated for days and it took us some time to calm her down.'

Bill and I looked at one another and he raised a questioning eyebrow.

I began to feel guilty that we were here at all, involving yet another innocent person. Did an old lady deserve this disruption to her life?

But Bill had a policeman's training. 'Do you know who the visitor was who upset her?'

Her response chilled me to the bone. 'I have no idea. He was good looking, though. All I know is Muriel was very agitated for days afterwards. Please keep your visit short, and try not to overstimulate her.'

We agreed to keep our visit short; we couldn't promise to keep her second request.

We found Muriel's room, thankful that it wasn't easy to get into either the ward or her room. As she was showing some initial signs of dementia, wandering at times, Muriel was in a locked ward, the only access being via a security door with a visual intercom answered by a staff member on duty. Her room was also very secure.

The first thing Bill did when we arrived in Muriel's room was give her the flowers he'd bought. He then checked the sliding door from her room to the courtyard to make sure it was locked – it was. He would later check with the staff to make sure it was always locked. After what had happened to John, we couldn't be too careful about Muriel's safety.

Muriel had no idea who the hell we were. We sat and patiently tried to build some trust, talking about innocuous things: the flowers, the weather, the nursing home.

As we tried to put her at ease, I felt such tenderness toward her that my eyes misted. That emotion was for her looming decline, but it was also because I knew we were about to ask her questions that might distress her.

Bill gently turned the conversation around to her friend Ruth. Did she remember Ruth? No response. He asked me to show Muriel the brochure with the picture of Ruth's Cottage.

I hesitated, then with Bill's encouragement and a deep breath I took the brochure out of my bag and showed it to her. 'Muriel, darling, do you recognise this lovely cottage?'

There was no reaction at all; then Bill saw her glasses on the bookshelf. He stood up and handed them to her. Once she had them on, I showed her the brochure again and repeated my question.

Her reaction was to beam a beatific smile. Her lovely little face lit up and she said, 'That's Ruth's Cottage.' With a gleeful expression, she snatched the brochure from my hands and eagerly looked through it.

Bill and I sat, patiently waiting and wondering what she would do next.

When she got to the back page, there was a photo of the office in the main house, with David Walton standing next to the desk. On the desk was a beautiful inlaid box.

First, she seemed to study the inlaid box. As she did so her face lit up again and she said, 'That's Ruth's box. It was a family heirloom. She used to keep her secret things in it. She even had a hiding place to keep it in.'

Without saying a word, Bill and I looked at one another. She kept her secret things in that box – what secret things? Perhaps this box was the reason Ruth had disappeared?

Then Muriel saw who was standing near the box and her face froze with fear. Her lips and hands began to tremble, and her mouth opened and shut like a fish out of water.

Realising she was upset at seeing who was standing near the box, I quickly took the brochure out of her hands, folded it, put it back into my handbag and tried to change the subject.

Bill, however, was determined to find out where her reaction was coming from. Keeping the conversation on track, he said,

'It's okay, Muriel. He can't hurt you. He can't get into the ward or your room. You are safe, always safe.'

His words must have soothed her. With his reassurance, a glimpse of what must have been the old Muriel came to the surface as she nodded her head in understanding and pursed her lips into a knowing smile.

As gently as he could, Bill continued. 'So, Muriel, was that the man who visited you last week? The man the nurses said upset you?'

She looked from Bill to me and back to Bill. After a considered silence, she nodded her head and in a quiet voice said, 'Yes. I don't like him; never have. He asked me a question, which I pretended I didn't understand. He asked me if anyone had visited me, asking questions about Ruth. I didn't say one word and he gave up. As he left, he said to me, "Just as well you're senile, you old bitch, or you'd end up like her."'

I let out a gasp, shocked and horrified by what Muriel was saying. To stop from interjecting I put my hand physically over my mouth.

With a gesture, Bill motioned for me to remain quiet and allow Muriel to continue. Although upset, she continued, with a proud tilt of her head and a smile. 'I let him think I was totally gaga.'

At this unexpected admission from Muriel, all three of us burst out laughing.

Bill finally said, 'Well done, Muriel, that was very clever; you did the right thing. He won't come back now.'

This seemed to please Muriel. Bill had come for a reason,

and after a few minutes of harmless conversation he asked Muriel one last confronting and difficult question. 'Muriel, I'm a policeman and I once worked on Ruth's case. Do you think that Ruth took her own life?' He paused. 'Do you know why she had made those comments in her diary?'

I couldn't believe he'd hit her so brutally with these blunt questions, and I shot him a look to let him know how I felt. Unfazed, he looked away from me and back to Muriel, patiently waiting for her to respond.

Muriel had become agitated, immediate and precise. You could see the old Muriel, the fire that once would have been in her eyes, when she answered, 'Ruth would never have done that. She was sad because Thomas died, but she would never leave Albert. My friend did not kill herself. The police asked me about her diary and I told them that what she wrote was a premonition, not what she was planning. I tried to tell the police this, but … they … they … I told the one who tried to arrest Ruth and me at the demonstration about the mines, but he…' Distressed, Muriel stopped mid-sentence.

I'm pleased to say that this time Bill didn't push her. To pacify her, he said, 'Muriel, it's okay. We believe you. Remember you're very safe here. We've had a word to the staff, and they've assured us they won't let that man in again.'

His words were confident and reassuring and seemed to do the trick. As we were about to leave, we thanked Muriel for speaking to us and said that we would visit her again.

On the way out, Bill spoke to the shift supervisor. She knew Bill and remembered he was a policeman; she also trusted and liked him. He confided in her that Muriel had told us that she didn't like or feel safe with the young man who'd visited her. He asked if they'd make sure he was not admitted again, supposing he turned up.

After taking a copy of his photo from the brochure, she agreed, saying she'd bring it up at the next staff meeting.

We left, feeling a little more confident that no harm would come to Muriel; we hoped it wouldn't, anyway. On the drive back to pick up my car, we talked about Bill's futile attempts so far to track down Ruth's solicitor. It seemed he'd left the area suddenly, and no one knew where he'd gone.

Suddenly a chill passed down my spine as I realised what part of Ruth's diary note meant.

As I let out a gasp of realisation, Bill turned to me and said, 'What's wrong? You look like you've seen a ghost.'

With considerable effort, I responded. 'I know what the BOC in the torn-out page of Ruth's diary means. BOC stands for Brendan O'Connor.'

Bill's response was to shake his head and reflectively say, 'I think you're right.'

After that, we drove in silence, each with our own thoughts.

CHAPTER 18

Bill dropped me back at my car then followed me home. He came inside to make sure I had no unwelcome visitors. With my home security not yet complete, I was glad for his caution.

I'd organised with my boss, Amanda, to take a few days off. She was shocked to hear what had happened and said if I needed more time I was only to ask.

Over a cup of tea, Bill surprised me again by how caring and concerned he was. 'Pip,' he said, 'I don't mean to alarm you, but after speaking to Muriel today, I'm concerned that you haven't seen the last of your visitors. After your uncle has gone home, do you have anywhere else you could stay for a while?'

His question confronted me. I knew one thing for sure: I wouldn't risk anyone else I loved. With a confidence I wasn't feeling, I answered, 'Not really. Uncle J lives in Tasmania, so that won't work. I don't want to involve anyone else or risk loved ones being hurt. I guess I'm going to have to be very careful and rely on the great security that's been installed.'

Even to my own ears, I knew my words sounded hollow.

Bill reflected. After a moment, he said, 'I have a cottage on my property, which you're welcome to stay in until things settle down. My mate Pat lived there while his own place was renovated. It's all set up. You could conceivably even work from home, if you needed to.'

I was surprised by his kind offer, and now acutely aware that, since our meeting with Muriel, it wasn't only my own radar that was on alert for danger.

As I was considering his kind offer, I came up with another problem. Over our first lunch Bill had said he owned a dog. Thinking out loud, I said, 'I really appreciate your offer, Bill, but I couldn't leave Albert at home or in a cattery. I'm not sure how Burt – is that his name? – would react to Albert, and vice versa.'

He shrugged lightly. 'We'll cross that bridge when we come to it. We'd just have to keep them apart, and introduce them slowly.'

By this stage, my head was spinning. All I could come up with was, 'Well, thank you for that very kind offer. Uncle J will be here tomorrow. I'll speak to him about it. Hopefully it won't be necessary to, um, put you out; but I do appreciate having your cottage as backup, thank you.'

Bill looked determined, and had the final word. 'Good, I'm glad you'll think about it. I don't feel we've seen the end of your visitors. Anyway, I'd better head off; you've got to get ready for your uncle. So, the boys are finishing the security tomorrow morning first thing, right?'

I loved his practical way of thinking; I loved his common sense. Both made me feel safe. As he was heading to the front door I said, 'Yes, they'll be here around seven. I'm taking the next couple of days off so I can spend time with Uncle J and John; I'm not back at work till Wednesday. I will give some consideration to your very generous offer, Bill; thank you.'

As he left, again I felt a sense of loss. What the hell was happening to me? I'm not normally attracted to someone so quickly.

To keep busy, I made up the guest bedroom for Uncle J, putting out fresh fluffy towels and – of course, as Uncle J is as OCD about germs as I am; think Howard Hughes – fresh cakes of soap.

I even changed the bulbs in the bedside lamps to a lower wattage in deference to his photosensitivity. Trust me, Uncle J is worth every effort I put into making his stay comfortable – he always pays back a thousandfold.

I didn't get much sleep; I felt like a bunny in the headlights. Finally, from sheer exhaustion, around 2:30 a.m. I fell into a disturbed sleep.

I was jarred awake by the front gate buzzer repeatedly sounding and Albert hissing. I'd overslept. It was the security guys, and they were on time. I quickly threw on my dressing-gown, bolted downstairs, opened the gate and immediately began to apologise profusely.

My apologies were good-naturedly accepted, and after I'd

made them a cup of coffee, they got on with the job of installing the rest of my security. As they did, I silently thanked Bill Browne for organising such a seamless transition from feeling vulnerable to feeling safe.

As the boys worked, I showered, dressed and got myself ready to collect Uncle J. I was pleased with John's improvement and excited about Uncle J's imminent arrival.

Okay; you're about to learn something else about my form of Tourette's. I was happily ticcing away – whistling – in anticipation of seeing my favourite person on the planet, my Uncle J. When simpatico Tourettic people get together, they can encourage one another to be authentic. I imagine this authenticity might appear to some neurotypical people to be disruptive and incorrigible. Our behaviour may even look attention-seeking at times; but nothing could be further from the truth – we're overjoyed that someone gets us as much as we get them.

Uncle J and I don't have these misunderstandings when we're together; we get one another. Like Uncle J, I've always been a chameleon, changing to fit my environment. Now all I wanted to do was live authentically and honestly.

When I'm with open-minded people, I feel most at home. When I'm with closed-minded people, I feel most alone.

As I did my make-up, whistling away, there was a knock at my bedroom door. With my frayed nerves, post break-in, I let out a yelp – yes, a yelp – which I hoped was masked by the music I was playing.

The boys had finished the installation. As I was inspecting

their handiwork, I thanked them effusively. I'm not sure if I'm typical of all Tourettic people, but I don't tend to do things by half, particularly when showing gratitude. They seemed genuinely pleased with my response, and as they left, grinning broadly, they assured me that immediate payment wasn't necessary; they'd email an invoice to me.

In the excitement, I'd forgotten to feed Albert, and in no uncertain terms he let me know. To make it up to him, I fed him tiny morsels of fresh meat. Suitably pacified – for the time being, anyway – he sauntered into the courtyard to take up his favourite position on the cane chair in the sun, a chair which quite obviously now had his name on it. Mind you, every chair and bed in my townhouse now had his fur and his name on it.

As I was locking up – checking three times – I glanced at myself in the hall mirror. Uncle J hadn't seen my new, short hairstyle, and I was a bit nervous about his response. Townhouse securely locked, I went over to kiss Albert goodbye. As I did, I said eagerly to my somnolent roomie, 'Albert, darling, I'm about to pick up the most awesome human you'll ever have the pleasure of meeting, my Uncle J. He's going to love you, and I know you're going to love him. Look after the house and we'll see you soon.'

Albert's response was to yawn, stand, stretch, circle and lay back down with his back toward me. My heart warmed at this display of arrogant indifference; it showed me he felt secure.

I adore all animals, cats in particular. I admire the way they manipulate their humans. As I reversed out of my carport – another area I'd need to secure – I was chuckling at Albert's cat-like dismissal. With my iPod playing my favourite music, I drove to Mascot airport.

Despite the underlying reason for this diversion to Sydney, I was very excited about seeing Uncle J. The thing about Tourette's is that it's not only the stressful times in life that over-stimulate you, causing tics to cascade; it's the happy and exciting times as well.

With the trek through Nepal, hearing the news about my break-in and John's hospitalisation, Uncle J was bound to be overstimulated and actively ticcing.

Thinking about the looks that would be both overtly and surreptitiously sent his way, and sent our way if I couldn't keep a lid on my own tics, my protective instincts toward Uncle J were kicking in.

He wasn't the first to walk out. When I saw him my heart instantly lifted, and I felt warm and safe. He's tall, dark and very good looking, with a square jawline, perfect white teeth, and kind light grey eyes fringed with thick dark lashes – eyes that truly are a window into his charismatic soul.

He's a much younger and better-looking version of my father, only neurologically different. Looks-wise, he's the full package, and if he didn't have Tourette's, you'd probably think he'd be conceited.

His captivating looks attract people's attention – we all like to look at beautiful people and things. I love to sit and watch the looks of appreciation when people first see him. Then when he does something, some action which to them seems bizarre but to him seems natural, their faces change and they soon look away.

As he saw me, he beamed his magnificent smile and said something to one of the Qantas stewardesses near him, who looked my way, smiled and waved.

She seemed as absorbed with him as he was with her. There was a spark between them, especially when he gave her a peck on the cheek and squeezed her arm.

I watched him bend down to pick up his backpack. As he stands, it's like watching an elegant and fluid giraffe. His graceful movements, a true dichotomy in contrast to his sometimes disruptive and twitchy Tourettic tics.

As he reached me, he threw down his backpack, lifted me off the ground and hugged me fiercely. When he put me back down, he noticed my short haircut and, by this stage in his overstimulated state, he began to gently tug at my hair.

Emotionally he said, 'Oh, princess, it's so good to see you. I love your hair. You look more like your beautiful mother every day. You've got her cheekbones, and those green eyes of yours positively shine, just like hers did. Turn around, show me the back.'

As I turned around, he continued to tug at my hair. A little boy walking past with his mother innocently said, 'Mummy, that man's naughty. He's pulling her hair.'

Without losing a beat, Uncle J turned to this direct little man – you have to love the purity and honesty of children – and said, 'Yes, young man, you're right. Promise you won't pull anyone's hair.'

As the little bloke was about to answer my uncle, his mother, embarrassed by his innocent and candid comment, quickly stopped his response, picking him up and rushing off, which was a shame – we were both keen to see what he had to say next.

Disappointed – he loved to interact with children – Uncle J looked at me and pulled one of his malleable rubber faces. It's fascinating how pulling a face can transform a good-looking face. We call this his Martian impersonation; on seeing it, I cracked up. It was so good to have him home.

In the car, I decided to ask him about the very attractive Qantas stewardess. I wasn't subtle. 'So, what is it with you and that terribly attractive stewardess? I can see you have a connection with her. What's the story?'

He hesitated a little longer than necessary, trying to find the right words. Eventually he said, 'Trust you to pick up on that. We do have a certain connection. Its early days and …'

Excitedly, I cut him off. 'Early days? Do you mean you're seeing one another?'

I know, that's a very personal question to ask your uncle, but you have to understand, Uncle J and I are more than related – we're twin souls.

He smiled, looked at me and said sheepishly, 'Despite my baggage, I do have the ability to attract members of the opposite –'

I couldn't help myself, and cut him off again with, 'Oh, Uncle J, I realise that. She's got good taste. I couldn't be happier for you. So, what's her name? What's she like?'

He grinned, the type of self-satisfied grin people get when thinking about someone important, and shyly continued. 'Her name's Sam, or Samantha. From the little I know about her, she's special, truly remarkable, and not because of her looks and personality but because of her acceptance of my uniqueness. We haven't had a real date yet, some in-flight flirting and a coffee at the airport once. I really hope something will come of it. Satisfied? Now, stop avoiding the topic. Tell me about this break-in and John. I want all the details.'

With that smooth segue, so smooth, in fact, that I almost didn't realise what he was doing – almost – he changed the subject to speaking about my nightmare. I'd have preferred to grill him about his new relationship, but there was plenty of time for that.

If I'm nothing else, I'm pragmatic. I knew I had to tell Uncle J the entire story, but I was lost for words.

As I thought about where to start, my tics kicked in. Seeing this, he put his hand on my shoulder and squeezed. This loving gesture undid me and I burst into tears. He suggested I pull over at the next available spot so he could drive the rest of the way home.

I did.

He'd flown home early to support me, to be with me – well, maybe Sam might have played a part – but still, what he deserved and what he wanted was the truth, as painful as it was.

After taking a deep breath, I said, 'It's a long story, Uncle J, but I'll start with Ruth's Cottage. You were right, by the way;

I had been there, I had met Ruth and her nephew … David.'

Sensing my hesitation and that I was about to lose it again, he said, 'Princess, I'm here for three days. Take your time. Just explain to me if you can how the break-in came about and how John got hurt. How is he, by the way?'

With another deep breath, I told him. 'He's so much better. I'm so relieved. I don't know what I've have done if he'd …'

To stop my thoughts from heading down that road he said, 'Pip, he didn't die. He's alive and doing well. If it isn't too difficult to continue, tell me about the night of the break-in. You can fill me in on the Hunter Valley stuff over the next few days.'

On the way home, between tics, I tried as best I could to give him the uncensored version of events. I must have shocked him into silence, as not one tic – copy or otherwise – escaped from his being.

He drove in silence, occasionally looking my way, shaking his head in disbelief. I knew that by the time I'd finished my story he'd be trying to supress his own escalating tics.

When we arrived home to my sanctuary, which now looked a tad like a prison, he knew the gist of what had taken place that night.

As we drove into my carport and turned off the engine, I exhaled, turned to him and said, 'I'm so sorry to welcome you home with a tale like that, especially as you would have been so excited to see Sam. I'm so sorry, Uncle J, that you had to cut your trip short, but I'm really pleased you're here.'

His response was so Uncle J; he said, 'I wouldn't want to be any place else except with you. Now let's get inside. I'm hungry, need a shower and a pee, and I have a cat to meet – not necessarily in that order.'

As we got to the carport door, we could hear Albert on the other side meowing. He was both glad to hear I was home and pissed off I'd been out. As we opened the door, when he saw Uncle J was with me, he turned and walked around in circles.

I introduced them, saying, 'Mummy is sorry to have been out so long. I'd like you to meet your Great Uncle J.'

As I said this, I picked Albert up and handed him into the outstretched arms of my uncle, his great uncle.

When Uncle J took the cat, he looked at him and said, 'Oh my goodness, Albert, your mother hasn't done you justice. You are without a doubt the most handsome ginger tabby I've ever seen; those eyes are as green as your mothers. I'm so very pleased to finally meet you.'

And guess what? For Albert it was instant reciprocal love. Children and animals know how to pick good people; my Albert is no exception to that rule.

As I went through the process of opening the security screen then the front door, Uncle J looked around my townhouse courtyard, at the windows and the doors, and tongue-in-cheek said, 'Um, rocking the Pentridge look, princess; very Melbourne.'

Once inside, I punched the code into the security keypad, and in the same spirit he had intended I casually responded, 'Thank you, Uncle J. That's exactly the look I was aiming for. So glad you approve.'

As Uncle J took a long shower, I prepared dinner. I had

some pea and ham soup in the freezer. It wasn't cordon bleu, but it was home-cooked, hearty and delicious, and, as the night outside had turned cold and windy, the perfect meal. I put some Turkish bread smothered in olive oil in the oven to accompany it.

I lit some candles and lavender oil in my burner. Like me, Uncle J hates bright lights – photophobia is prevalent with Tourette's – and as we sat with trays on our laps and rugs over our legs in front of the fire, we ate our soup in companionable silence, Albert sitting adoringly at Uncle J's feet.

After we'd finished two bowls and mopped up with toasted Turkish bread, I got up to remove our dishes and make us some peppermint tea. As I stood with both bowls in hand, Uncle J tentatively said, 'So, princess, you've talked about what happened, but not about how it's affected you. How are you feeling about it all? I detect that this policeman, Bill, has made quite an impression on you. Am I right?'

It was payback time for my pumping him about Sam. When he mentioned Bill's name, I felt myself blush, and of course he didn't miss this.

Before I had a chance to answer, he said gleefully, 'Oh, look at you blush. I think this might be more serious than I thought. Interesting! How long have you known this man?'

He was making me squirm and enjoying himself immensely. I knew he was doing this so that I'd drop my questions about Sam. He was also genuinely concerned about how it had all affected me. To protect myself from having to tell him how terrified I'd been and still was, I went down the Bill road first, evasively replying, 'Bill, yes, like Sam, has made an impression. He's been very kind, helpful and open minded. I like those qualities in a man.'

Having a brain-spit, without thinking he quickly shot back, 'After Zac, I'm not surprised.'

He'd spoken his deepest thoughts about Zac out loud; seeing the hurt look on my face and regretting his words, he swiftly said, 'I'm sorry; that was uncalled for. He's in the past. Tell me about Bill.'

I did, and we spent the rest of the evening talking about Bill. I also told him how I was feeling about my own safety, that the night of the break-in had been a living nightmare, and I feared it was not yet over.

Soon enough jet-lag kicked in, and despite wanting to stay up and talk, Uncle J stood, stretched and through a stifled yawn said, 'Well, princess, I'm failing quickly. I'm going to head up to bed now. We can take up where we left off tomorrow. You haven't talked about how you're going with mirror scrying.'

I thought I'd dodged that particular bullet; wrong. Despite my conversation about the break-in and John, we'd still managed to have a special evening, even catching up on some of the highlights of his trip, so to please – if not encourage – him I said, 'I wondered when you were going to ask. You would have noticed I've got your bathroom set up for scrying. I'm happy to talk to you about it over the next couple of days. Don't get too excited, though; I'm not as gifted at it as Grandma Ella was.'

He stretched, yawned again, then looked at me with a

knowing smile and said, 'Give it time, princess; give it time. Night-night.'

To my delight, Albert stretched, yawned and dutifully followed his great uncle upstairs, leaving me behind to tidy up, turn off the lamps and blow out the candles. I had some competition for his affection, which gave me nothing but joy.

With the comfort of having Uncle J here, I was soon asleep. I'd like to say it was dream free – it wasn't.

I dreamed I was in a long box; no, not a coffin. It was dark, cramped and claustrophobic. I was terrified, knowing that some hidden danger surrounded me.

I must have cried out in my sleep. Soon Uncle J was at my side, gently shaking me awake and saying, 'Princess, wake up. You're having a bad dream.'

As I sat, seeing the terrified look on my face, he soothingly said, 'Oh, Pip, it's times like this I wish mum were still alive. Come on, get your dream journal out. This one might be important.'

When I'd settled and explained my dream, he went back to his room, and, I presume, back to sleep.

CHAPTER 19

We were both up early, another thing we share in common – we're intermittent insomniacs who still love mornings despite lack of sleep. Extra dopamine can come in handy.

Uncle J had set the table and had breakfast under way – crispy bacon, poached eggs, grilled tomato and crisp, well-toasted bread. And guess who was at his side – my roomie, Albert. I'd woken expecting him to be asleep beside me. Seems he'd found a better offer.

When I got downstairs, Albert was ensconced on Uncle J's lap, purring contentedly.

In jest I said to Albert, 'I wondered where you were this morning. I see you've found someone else to adore. Don't forget I'm the one who rescued you.'

'Your mother's right,' said Uncle J, knowing I was joking. 'Jump down and give her a morning leg cuddle.'

Bugger me if he didn't do just that! Springing from his lap

onto the floor, Albert proceeded to weave his way around my legs, and back into my good books.

After we'd finished breakfast and cleaned up, we set out to visit John. As I was about to jump into the driver's seat, Uncle J surprised me by saying, 'Princess, do you mind if I drive? I'm seriously thinking about getting a car.'

Mouth open in amazement, I handed him the keys.

Uncle J's an excellent driver with extremely fast reflexes. However, for many years he hasn't owned a car, saying he didn't need one. As his at times spectacular tics have on occasion freaked out fellow drivers, passengers and the odd policeman, he'd made the executive decision to abstain from driving.

Now he wanted to get back behind the wheel. Sensing more to this than his being kind to me in my fragile state, I cheekily asked, 'So does this urge to get behind a wheel again have anything to do with …'

At his Tourettic best, lightning-fast he cut in with, 'You really won't let it go, will you. If I told you I don't want to jinx it, would you stop with the questions, please?'

He looked so genuinely concerned when he said this I agreed straight away.

'Why didn't you say so? Of course I'll back off. I'd hate you to think I'd jinxed it even before it had a chance to get off the ground. Promise me that as soon as you know it's a viable proposition, I'll be the first to know?'

As he pulled up at a set of lights, he looked over at me, smiled broadly, then proceeded to tap me on the right temple; with each tap he repeated, 'Up here for brains, up here for brains, up here for brains. Of course you'll be the first, princess.'

He had to repeat the first three taps, then count out loud, then another three taps, to satisfy his Tourettic urge. Think of it as how you feel when you have an itch you need to scratch.

The woman in the car next to us at the lights was watching this with an open mouth, spellbound and no doubt horrified.

Seeing her fascination, Uncle J waved effusively and gave her one of his most engaging smiles. When he smiles, he lights up his already eye-catching face. In light of what she'd witnessed, her response was to grimace back a smile of her own.

As the lights changed, eyebrows knitted in a perplexed frown, she drove off shaking her head dismissively – and lifted her middle finger.

The thing is, if he hadn't been displaying these motor tics, she'd have thought all her dreams had come true when he'd smiled at her.

The thing I admire most about Uncle J is his self-acceptance. In the past, he'd had three long-term relationships; sadly, all three of the women had wanted him to medicate.

Sure, they'd liked the packaging, but they hadn't liked what was inside – his constant companion. After a while, he'd realised that he'd rather be himself on his own than not be himself and be medicated in a relationship.

Uncle J doesn't take rude gestures personally – well, most of the time. Today was no exception. He was too excited about being with me and visiting John, whom he loved like a son.

To ease any built-up tension due to her uneducated gesture, I tapped him gently on the head and said, 'Well, screw her, Uncle J. You're right: it's "up here for brains".'

He looked at me, smiled and said, 'Her, princess? She should be so lucky.'

By the time we arrived at North Shore Hospital, Uncle J had begun to tic forcefully. The last time he'd been at this hospital was when his brother, my father, had passed away. It was painfully obvious that these memories had surfaced and kicked him into overdrive.

I could have made some sort of gesture, some attempt to calm him down, but for him, and for all of us with Tourette's, sometimes we don't want to be calmed down; sometimes we just want to be.

So that's what I did – I let him be.

When we arrived at the room, John was alone. When he saw us, his angelic face lit up. By the time the nurse arrived to do John's observations, there wasn't a dry eye in the room.

Once she'd left, John turned to Uncle J. Emotionally he said, 'I can't tell you how good it is to see you.' In a more jovial tone he added, 'Mind you, under the circumstances I'm pleased to see anybody.'

Uncle J bent down and gave John one of his incredibly uplifting hugs. 'Young man, nothing would have stopped me from diverting here to see you and this one here. I was mortified when I, when Pip ...' Lost on how to finish – another thing I like about my Uncle J: his authenticity – he said, 'Oh shit, I promised myself I was going to keep a lid on things, but who cares …' He tapped John on the sternum, saying, 'Good to see you, good to see you, good to see you.'

From the look of deep affection in John's eyes, we knew the feeling was mutual.

Right on time, Max arrived. I was gratified to see his handsome face looking much more relaxed, his dark circles almost gone, his perfect smile back in place. Seeing us both, he dropped what he had in his hands and said, 'Uncle J, Pip, great to see you both. How was your trip?'

I love moments like that, moments where uncomfortable situations can be turned around in a single sentence. Uncle J swivelled to Max and gave him another one of his special hugs – I defy anyone with a heart to not love Uncle J's hugs – and said, 'How are you holding up, Max? You must've been beside yourself with worry.'

Max went to John, kissed him soundly on the mouth, then turned to both of us and, deeply moved, said, 'You know what? I'll never take him for granted again, so I guess you could say something positive has come from all this. Now enough about dramas: tell us about your trip.'

To our delight, that's exactly what Uncle J did; uncensored and in full tic flight, he delighted us with tales of his trip to Nepal.

After spending too much time there – who can resist spending time with your tribe? – we finally went home. As we pulled up, Uncle J's phone pinged. Once he had my car parked, he took it out to see who it had been. It was so special to see the look of joy on his face. As I'd promised not to push the Sam situation, instead of saying what I wanted to say – 'Is it from Sam?' – I said, 'I don't know about you, but I'm starving. Want to walk up to Crows Nest and do Italian at Peter Pan's? Sound okay to you?'

It sounded very okay to Uncle J, so after we'd fed Albert we grabbed a bottle of wine and headed up Shirley Lane.

For the first time since he'd arrived, I felt ill at ease. As we walked up Shirley Lane, I had an eerie sensation that we were being followed, or at the very least watched. I tried to push it out of my mind until Uncle J said, 'Pip, I don't mean to alarm you, but did you see two men back there in that laneway? They seemed very interested in us.'

His observation was enough for me; we'd definitely take an Uber home. It wasn't my imagination; Uncle J had also seen them lurking in the shadows.

We tried to push this out of our minds while we ate, but it wasn't easy. After trying to skirt around what was really on his mind, and on mine, with a look of concern on his handsome, troubled face, he finally said, 'What we saw back there really concerns me, Philippa. I don't like the fact that, in two days, I'm flying back home. You mentioned Bill had offered for you to stay in his cottage for a while. Do me a favour: seriously consider this, please. If you do, you'll take a great load off my mind.'

I was about to make light of his concerns, but knowing he was very serious – he only called me Philippa when he was – I knew this wasn't the time for levity.

Instead I responded, 'Oh, Uncle J, I can't believe I've got

myself into this mess. Why the hell couldn't I have left it alone and got on with my relatively boring life?'

With my honest disclosure, he reached over and took my hand in his. 'My darling niece, there has never been, nor will there ever be, anything remotely boring about you or your life. You did what people with your abilities do; you followed your instinct and your ethics. You're a very principled person, Pip; it's not in your make-up to walk away from something because it doesn't feel right or might inconvenience you.'

As I sat there, tears streaming down his face, he continued. 'For some reason, you were meant to experience this. Maybe it was sent to you as a way to get you in touch with your abilities. I honestly don't know; all I know is I want you to stop beating yourself up, and I want you to be safe.'

As he said this, for the first time in days, I felt a peace come over me. Only Uncle J could help me to understand that the unscheduled path I had taken may have been predestined and sent to help me explore my inherited abilities.

After taking time to digest all this, I kissed him on the cheek – he hates that, so he turned the other cheek, which I kissed as well to even things up. I said, 'Thank you, Uncle J. You always know the right thing to say when my compass is off. I'll phone Bill and see if his very generous offer stands. Will that ease your mind?'

He let out a huge sigh, then let his tense shoulders drop back into a more comfortable position. Tears glistened in his eyes. 'Thank you, Pip; that'll ease my mind greatly. Let's pay the bill and call an Uber.'

When we got home it was just before nine. Unless it's an emergency, I never phone people after that time of night. But I thought that, under the circumstances, Bill would be okay about the time I was phoning.

He answered on the fourth ring. 'Pip, hi. Is everything okay?'

My response was to look toward Uncle J and give him the thumbs-up then let out a sigh. 'Sorry to phone you so late, Bill. I hope I'm not disturbing you?'

He quickly put my mind at rest. 'Of course not. Pat's here; we're watching the Swans versus Lions game. Hang on, I'll mute the sound. So, tell me, what's up?'

Uncle J nodded in a go-ahead gesture. I did, saying, 'Uncle J and I walked up to Crowie for a meal, and well, I felt we were being watched, if not followed. Uncle J confirmed this; he saw a couple of men watching us. I'm a bit embarrassed to ask, but is your generous offer to stay in your cottage for a few weeks still open?'

He didn't hesitate. 'It certainly is. You can come up whenever you want. Promise me you won't walk anywhere for a while, please.'

With another huge sigh of relief and a catch in my voice, I said gratefully, 'Thank you so much, Bill, from both Uncle J and me. I can't tell you how relieved we both are. Oh, hang on, Uncle J is gesturing for me to hand him the phone.'

As I did this, Uncle J winked in a conspiratorial way then introduced himself. 'Hello, hello, hello – a tic – Jim Mason here. I want to thank you for everything you've done for my niece.

She's very important to me, and I can't thank you enough.'

To give him some privacy on this important conversation with Bill, I went to the toilet, leaving him alone to say whatever he needed to say.

As I came back into the room, he was finishing his conversation with Bill. One of his loud pig-squealing tics escaped. He looked my way and raised his shoulders, then pulled a face about his tic. I had to stifle a giggle.

As I watched him listening to Bill's response, a smile lit up his sensitive and relieved face as he said, 'Thank you, Bill. Unfortunately, I fly back to Tasmania Wednesday. Business is bringing me back up to Sydney soon, so I'll look forward to meeting you in person then. Hang on, I'll put Pip back on. Thanks again.'

As he handed me the phone, his tics escalated into a crescendo of vocal noises. To avoid possibly embarrassing me further – not that he would have – he left the room.

When I took the phone back, I said, 'So, um, Uncle J is here for another day. He flies home Wednesday afternoon. I'll speak to my boss tomorrow morning and arrange to work from home via remote desktop. I'll drop into the office and collect what I need work-wise and speak to IT. Um, I'm assuming you have Wi-Fi?'

The timbre of his deep, sexy voice sent pleasant chills down my spine. 'Yes, I have NBN connected. I need to do some dusting and clean out the fridge in the cottage; when and what time do you think you'll arrive?'

My head was spinning; this was really happening. With

a calmness I didn't feel I said, 'How does Thursday morning around ten o'clock sound?'

'Perfect. It'll give me a chance to put some linen on the bed and do a bit of a tidying up. I'll buy you the staples for the fridge. Are you okay about being there on your own on Wednesday night?'

As he said this, I felt the colour drain from my face. Having come back into the room, a concerned look passed over Uncle J's face. I held up my hand to stop him from interrupting, and answered Bill honestly, saying, 'I hadn't thought that far ahead. Max is still not back at work, so I'm sure Albert and I could stay with him.'

His response was immediate and definitive. 'I think that's a very good idea. If they're still hanging around, they may have something planned. Seeing your uncle there has scared them off for now, but you can't be too careful. I'll text you my address. Do you have a sat nav?'

After reassuring him I did, I finished the call with, 'I can't thank you enough. I promise you won't even know I'm there. I'll pay you rent and cover electricity, of course.'

He objected at once. 'You'll do no such thing. It's a couple of weeks, Pip. Now I'll get back to the game; it's a hundred and three to eighty-one in favour of the Brisbane Lions. Enjoy the rest of your time with your Uncle Jim. I'll see you and Albert around ten on Thursday.'

As I hung up, I let out another deep sigh. It was a relief knowing that for a few weeks, at least, I'd be safe; the bonus, of course, was seeing Bill again.

Matter-of-factly Uncle J said, 'He seems nice. It's a shame he probably thinks I was making my squealing pig noise because he's a policeman.'

That thought hadn't entered my mind. When he said this, we both burst out laughing. After I'd finally contained myself – isn't it wonderful how humour can disarm a ticking bomb? – through my own pig-like snorts of laughter I said, 'I honestly hadn't thought of that, Uncle J. That is hysterical. I'll have to explain it to him again.'

After watching UKTV together, with Albert ensconced on my lap for a change – he'd seen Uncle J pack his bags and was not amused – finally we made our ways upstairs to bed.

With the reassurance that I'd soon be safe at Bill's place, I fell asleep very quickly. I was abruptly woken by the sound of crashing glass. Heart pounding, I threw on my dressing-gown and rushed out of my bedroom, colliding heavily with Uncle J in the hallway.

Once we'd regained our balance, Uncle J whispered, 'You stay here, Pip; I'll go and see what's going on.'

'I'm coming with you, Uncle J. Two's better than one.'

As we made our way downstairs, Uncle J grabbed a broomstick from behind the kitchen door. With that in hand – it wouldn't do much damage – we opened the front door and together went out into the courtyard.

Torch in hand, we saw that someone had thrown a bottle over my courtyard gate.

Finding no one in the courtyard, Uncle J bravely opened the gate and looked up and down the laneway outside, with me close behind him and Albert sitting just inside the gate as backup.

Reassured that whoever had thrown the bottle had left, we closed and locked the gate and went inside to get a dustpan to sweep up the broken glass.

As I swept, Uncle J tried to reassure me. 'I was still awake when the bottle was thrown over. I heard a car roar away. I'd say they've left the area. How about I pour us a nip of Scotch and we sit in front of the fire?'

We did. With the frightening sound of the glass shattering still ringing in my ears, it would be a long time before sleep came.

As we sat sipping our drinks, my tics escalating, I shared with him my feelings about being watched. 'I've felt it for a while now. I can't explain it, it's not my imagination. I've thought I'm being watched ever since I saw those two men at the railway station ...'

I stopped, unable to continue. My supportive uncle reassured me, saying, 'I don't think for a moment that you're imaging this. I watched a TED talk by Rupert Sheldrake, and in it he talks about the sense of being stared at. He says knowledge of being stared at is extremely common. He also says that recent experimental research suggests it's real. Trust your instincts, Philippa; those instincts may keep you safe.'

CHAPTER 20

Uncle J came with me to the publishing house where I work. When my colleagues saw him, their faces showed genuine elation. I left Uncle J entertaining them with his quick repartee and, door closed, sat in Amanda's office.

As I updated her, Amanda's face became more concerned.

When she'd finished shaking her head in disbelief, she said, 'Wow; intense. Take as much time off as you need. I'll square it with Chris and Steve. You need to speak to Robert in IT and organise a laptop and remote desktop access. While you're with IT, I'll sort out some work for you to do over the next few weeks. Drop back here when you're finished.'

Her immediate support and understanding of my situation brought me close to tears again. When I'd contained my emotions, I got up, hugged her and said, 'Thank you so much, Amanda. Your support means more than I can express.'

By the time I'd finished setting up what I'd need to work via remote desktop, Uncle J was sitting in Amanda's office with the door closed. I knocked, then entered.

When I saw the look on both their faces, I realised Uncle J had filled her in on the bits I hadn't shared. Uncle J, having only my interests at heart, wanted her to realise the full gravity of the situation.

As I left her office, she hugged me tightly, telling me to be careful. My colleagues did the same, hugging both of us. I'd miss them – they're my work tribe.

When we got home, we sat in the courtyard and ate the Japanese takeaway we'd picked up from the restaurant next to work. As we ate our meal, the sun caressed our backs and soothed our frazzled nerves.

Uncle J turned to me with a look of anguish. 'Princess, I'm so sorry I'm leaving you. I've got this major account which I need to concentrate on. As soon as I can knock that over, I'll be back here.'

Uncle J's neurodiversity helped give him the edge needed in the extremely competitive advertising industry. He always thought outside the box.

He'd once lamented he'd forever be back-of-house with no client contact, no account executive roles on his CV. But creative advertising types are by their very nature more accepting of difference, and so are some of their clients. This major corporate client wanted only Uncle J working on their account.

When we finished lunch, we both became pensive as a melancholy mood descended. We both knew why – I'd soon be taking him to the airport so he could fly back to Tasmania.

As we were about to leave for the airport, he bent down, picked Albert up and said, 'Well, little man, I've so enjoyed meeting you. Now you're the man of the house, so you have to look after your mum. See you next time I visit.'

Before he put him down, he kissed the top of his little ginger head. He looked around my townhouse, taking it all in, especially the new security, then said, 'Princess, now you live in Fort Knox, you're going to be safe, especially when all this mess is over. Promise me you'll text me as soon as you arrive at Bill's?'

I hugged him firmly – he's so tall I fit under his armpits – and through my tears said, 'Please don't worry about me, Uncle J. I'll sleep at Max's and John's place tonight and tomorrow morning I'm driving up to the Hunter first thing. I promise I'll call you when I arrive.'

With that promise, he took his luggage out to the car while I locked up. On the drive to the airport we made plans for his next visit.

I was extremely surprised when he said, 'I've been thinking about this for a while. I love my place in Tassie, but having a place in Sydney would make sense, as most of my clients operate from here. Could you look out for a unit or townhouse for me, when life settles?'

I turned to him, surprise on my face, then with delight responded, 'Really; are you serious? I'd love it if you had a place here. Would you want one or two bedrooms? What area? What price range?'

He began to laugh and, putting both hands open wide with joy, said, 'Such enthusiasm – love it. My criteria is at least two, preferably three, bedrooms and two bathrooms. Something around this area would be nice. Price range is flexible as I've had a few wins with bonuses lately. I'd probably keep my Tassie place as well. Glad to have you on the job, princess. You know my taste and I don't mind if it needs fixing up.'

As soon as I heard 'preferably three bedrooms and two bathrooms', my imagination kicked in. I knew I wasn't the only reason he'd consider buying a place in Sydney. Sam was also factored into this decision.

Never one to sit on my own enthusiasm, I continued. 'I can see where this is going. You're thinking about any future you and Sam might have. Hey, maybe she and I should meet up and she could come with me …'

With a smile – he understands impetuosity – he cut me off. 'Pip, I think there's enough about me that might scare Sam off without having my niece ask her to help choose a Sydney pad for me. Just leave it at you looking, and maybe John with his architect's eye if he has time.'

He was right, I'd instantly become carried away. 'I take your point. I'll do the leg work, and then run them past John before I send you any property details.'

We were soon at the airport. After I'd parked, we walked arm in arm down to the departures lounge, both feeling sad about parting.

After he was gone, I drove home feeling deflated. I had to pack for my stay in the Hunter Valley, and hoped this would take my mind off missing him. I'm not good about leaving home, but this time I felt okay about it.

I'm a list person, so before packing, I typed up a list of what I'd need. I packed my clothes, shoes, toiletries, jewellery, phone, camera, e-book and chargers, a few books and the things I'd need work-wise. I threw in my sketching pad and pencils in case I felt inspired.

Next, I turned to Albert's needs – bed, litter tray, litter, food, brush, bowls and his carry cage, which I left next to the front door.

Seeing me packing, he immediately became agitated and clingy. It made me sad to see his demeanour change.

As I was finishing up, the phone rang. It was Max. He was upbeat as John was coming home in the next few days. 'Hi, Pip. Are you still coming over here to sleep? I'm looking forward to company. I've made chilli con carne, which I'll serve with rice, avocado and sour cream. Sound okay?'

Max knew it was one of my favourite comfort foods. I responded, 'Are you kidding? I love it. Do you want me to bring anything?'

With a smile in his voice he said, 'Great; just bring yourself – oh, and Albert, of course. It'll be fun to introduce Albert to Leroy. We'll do it slowly, in case there's some territorial stuff.'

I smiled as he said this. Poor old Leroy is so ancient, he doesn't even realise who he is, let alone where he is, half the time.

I played along with him by saying, 'Oh, you're right! Leroy might object. I'll leave Albert in his cage for a few minutes then introduce them slowly. I'm nearly done packing. Is seven thirty too late to arrive?'

Sounding relieved, Max came back with, 'No, that's perfect. I still need to make up your bed and put out some towels. I'll see you then.' Before I had a chance to respond, with real concern in his voice he said, 'Don't forget to lock up securely when you leave.'

'Don't worry; I'll make sure it's locked down tight. I'll bring a copy of the new keys around. See you soon. Thanks again for this.'

In the end, Max and I had an emotional evening – talking about John and how well he was doing – mixed with fun, making light of life in general, including taking the piss out of ourselves.

It was really pleasant spending time alone with Max. It's usually John, Max and I. As John and I are always bantering on, Max doesn't always get a look in.

Without John there, the dynamic between Max and I was different, surprisingly comfortable and easy. In fact, it felt like we'd forged a bond that hadn't previously been there. We had one thing in common: our love for John. Since the accident we had become closer over our mutual concern.

This new bond with Max, and meeting Bill Browne, were two unexpected gifts from the whole nightmare. Every cloud has a silver lining; it's important to see something positive amid the negativity.

I slept well, and next morning, after Max headed off to work, with Leroy and Albert now firm friends, I left the two cats together and headed home to pick up our luggage. As I got to my townhouse, I couldn't believe how nervous I was.

Realising this, I got really pissed off, took a deep breath, and as I fumbled to open the courtyard gate, mumbled to myself, 'You are not going to make me afraid to enter my own home. Screw you.'

When I got inside, my mobile pinged; it was a text from Uncle J. *'Hope you and Max had fun last night. Remember to pack your scrying paraphernalia. I've a feeling you might need your tools. If you've had success with the mirror, it's a powerful metaphysical tool, so treat it well. Ring or text me when you arrive in the Hunter. Love you. Talk soon.'*

I responded with, *'Yes, had a lovely night – very special. Max cooked chilli con carne. Not sure if there's a bath in the cottage, so might not get a chance to scry. Talk soon. Love you.'*

I was being deliberately obtuse in my response. I know you can scry without being in a bathtub full of water, because memories of Grandma Ella's scrying were surfacing regularly. I'd also done a ton of research online.

Not to be put off, Uncle J came back quickly – even by his standards – with, *'Really – that's the best you can come up with? You know very well you do not need a bath full of water. Set it up in the bathroom, the steam from a shower may help, along with candles and incense. Remember, scrying can simply serve to focus your attention and remove unwanted thoughts from your mind, a bit the same way a mantra does. Don't overcomplicate it; experiment and see where it takes you. I've attached a few links for you to mull over. I still have Ella's mirror. Next time I'm in Sydney, it's yours.'*

I was duly chastened. He was right; I was putting on an act of not understanding and he'd called me out on my transparent behaviour. I felt embarrassed; then I heard another ping as another text arrived. *'I understand your hesitation, especially after recent events. You must understand, though, your mirror scrying did not make this happen. I want you to explore your abilities fully. The family skills skipped a generation with your father and to a certain extent me. Like it or not, you are a medium, Philippa. I'm proud of you, and want you to carry on the family tradition; in fact, Ella wants me to encourage you. Love you.'*

He'd picked up that I was hurt; before I had a chance to hit back, he'd said the right thing. He'd called me Philippa, so I knew he was serious.

Humbled, I responded, *'I know, Uncle J. Thanks for encouraging me and being proud of me. It is daunting, especially with all that's happened. I'll do my best. Glad Grandma is in touch with you and in favour of me exploring. That's so good to know. Love you too.'*

His final text said, *'Glad that's sorted — my thumbs are killing me. I've texted instead of phoning on purpose. It breaks my heart to hear the objection in your voice. Drive safely, princess. J, xx.'*

Having him remind me to pack my scrying mirror was like having Grandma Ella around; it felt right and reassuring.

He was absolutely right about one thing: with all that had gone on since my last attempt, I'd been understandably afraid to try again.

I grabbed some bubble wrap, took my mirror down from the wall, wrapped it carefully and placed it in the largest zipper compartment of my suitcase. I also packed candles, matches, incense, oil burner and lavender oil.

I didn't know if Bill's cottage had a bathtub. If it didn't, I'd set things up and hope for the best. Even if it was only used as a tool to remove unwanted thoughts so I could tap more readily into other realms, it could be helpful, as Uncle J had suggested.

As I was about to lock up and carry my bags to the car – Bill would think I was moving in permanently – my OCD kicked in, and I was soon unpacking and rechecking what I'd packed. Repacking always reassures me. Hey, if it works for me, it works for me – I don't fight it any more.

Bags repacked, along with Albert's things, I took it all out to the car. I then commenced the ritual of securing my home. I was bad enough before the break-in; now, well, let's say I was in OCD overdrive.

Everything finally locked to my OCD monster's satisfaction, I was headed for my car when I remembered two more things: the sketches I'd done from memory of the two intruders, and my talisman.

After unlocking and punching in the security code, first I grabbed the sketches from the bureau in my study, then I ran upstairs to grab my talisman, which always sat on my bedside table.

My talisman was my father's favourite childhood book, the classic children's novel *Tom's Midnight Garden* written by Philippa Pearce – my namesake.

My grandmother, knowing that my father, her eldest son, hadn't inherited the family predisposition for psychic abilities or an open mind about such abilities, had bought him this book in the hope it might broaden his imagination, if not his mind, about things paranormal.

Good try, but she'd never achieved her goal. Until the day he died, along with my mother, he believed it was all nonsense. Even so, he'd loved that book his entire life.

I always kept it close to me. It reminded me of the little boy who'd read it in wonder; it had become not only my talisman but my connection, as tenuous as it was, to my father. I never liked to leave home without it.

When I'd relocked and rechecked, I headed for the car. By this stage, my tics had furiously bubbled to the surface. Before backing out of my carport, I set my iPod on shuffle, and then drove around the corner to collect Albert.

He seemed to sense that we weren't going back to our safe place, which, to me now no longer seemed quite so safe. Eventually I got him into the cage, said goodbye to Leroy, and securely belted the cage onto the passenger seat.

As I drove, I gave free rein to my tics, with the music blaring and Albert trembling in the cage on the seat next to me. Once on the freeway and out of city traffic, mesmerised by the smooth drive and music, and knowing that I was leaving the stress of the break-in behind me, I relaxed.

Sensing my energy shift, Albert began to chirrup, making a trilling sound as if to say he was pleased that I was feeling more Zen.

CHAPTER 21

Sat nav is a blessing. I'd keyed in Bill's address before leaving Wollstonecraft. Before long, my computerised helper was telling me, 'You have reached your destination'.

I looked at Albert, now peacefully resting in his cage. By way of apology I said, 'Okay, little man, we're here. You're about to see Bill again and meet his dog, Burt. I know he's a dog, but it'd be really nice if you two could get along.'

Albert's response was to yawn and make a cat noise that in my mind suggested two things: *'Where's the litter tray?'* and *'Feed me!'*

As I sat trying to compose myself, I looked around. Bill had a pleasant setup on five acres outside Cessnock. The house was a low-set Federation, which had been faithfully restored. It was surrounded by a lovingly-cared-for garden and lots of trees.

My first thought was, *Oh no, low-set, and lots of trees for people to hide behind; easier to break in without being seen.* Ah, the joys of an overactive mind.

I heard a brilliant line in the movie *Thanks for Sharing* – 'worry is meditation on shit'. I sure had a lot of shit to meditate on.

Hearing our arrival, Bill was heading toward my car with the biggest dog I've ever seen bounding next to him. Seeing Bill again gave my heart a jolt; he looked more handsome every time I saw him. I found him ridiculously attractive, yet he was not my usual type. With my track record, that was probably just as well.

I was jolted back to reality when Burt jumped onto my car door, barking energetically. It wasn't a ferocious bark, more an *I'm on patrol; who are you?* bark.

Seeing Burt's protective stance with Bill at his side, a sense of calm came over me. You may have noticed I'm not internally calm myself. I've always been attracted to calm people – with the exception of Zac, a lapse of taste there.

Bill settled Burt with a stern, 'Burt, get down.' Burt did, and I jumped out of my car and slammed the door before the dog saw Albert.

With a hand gesture toward a now calm dog, Bill said, 'Pip, I'd like to formally introduce you to Burt. Just let him smell your hand and he'll be fine.'

I put my hand down and allowed the largest Rottweiler I'd ever met sniff and slobber all over it. He had a huge head, and the most sensitive and soulful eyes I'd ever seen. Despite his threatening size and boisterous welcome, I instantly liked him. I'm pleased to say the feeling seemed mutual.

When he'd finished, Burt gave a loud welcoming woof and bounded off, tail wagging, toward the house. He then circled back, barking more gently now, turned and headed toward the house again – three times, I kid you not. I'd passed the approval test and he'd satisfied my OCD need for things in threes.

Burt was definitely excited to meet and welcome me into his domain. It would be interesting to see if he felt the same about Albert.

Bill stood, watching his beloved Burt's enthusiasm with a lopsided smile, his eyes twinkling with amusement. Relief obvious in his voice, he said, 'Looks like you've passed the test. Now all we have to do is sneak Albert inside. Can I help you with your luggage?'

Embarrassed by how much I'd brought, I said apologetically, 'Bill, you're going to think I'm moving in permanently. There's so much stuff. I've, um, I've packed too much, and of course there's all my work stuff and Albert's things. I promise I only plan on staying a week or two.'

To my utter relief, Bill laughed and said, 'Pip, I've got two sisters; trust me, they don't travel lightly. Open the boot and we'll start taking your things inside. My best friend Pat's still here, he's staying for dinner. I'll introduce you to him first, then show you the cottage.'

What can I say? I've said this before: Bill was like human Valium to me. His comment about his sisters reassured me that my baggage wouldn't freak him out – the baggage in my boot, at least.

Always the gentleman: I presume Bill had arranged for Pat to be here so I'd feel more comfortable when I arrived and while he showed me through the cottage.

I was immediately nervous about meeting Pat. I'm not always at my best when meeting new people. But I'd had enough of the mercurial me, so I was determined to play the calm me instead.

As we entered the main house, Pat stood with a welcoming smile on his face and said, 'Here, let me help you with that.'

Despite my initial hesitation, I liked him instantly. I was on a roll, feeling well received first by Burt, now by Pat.

As he took my overnight case from my hand, with a broad smile Bill turned and said, 'Pip, I'd like you to meet Pat Cawley. Pat, this is Pip. As I mentioned, she's staying in the cottage for a few weeks until things have settled in her life.'

At Bill's understated comment about things settling in my life, I looked down, blushing furiously.

In a gentle voice, Pat said, 'Pip, don't be embarrassed. Bill's told me what's been going on. You've definitely made the right decision taking him up on his offer to stay in the cottage. I lived in it for nearly six months while my place was being done up. It's very comfortable and safe. Bill, show Pip the cottage so she can see for herself.'

I could have hugged him; instead I reined myself in and said, 'Thanks, Pat. I'm extremely grateful to Bill and very pleased to be here. I'm pleased to meet you also. As you've lived in the cottage, maybe you could show me the ropes?'

I know that was a hackneyed thing to say, but when I'm nervous I tend to prattle and say the first thing that pops into my head. I was also desperate to not start ticcing. Talking helps me let off steam and can help delay my tics, at least for a time.

Taking Pat's suggestion, Bill, looking at Pat appreciatively, said, 'Good idea. Come on, we'll show you the cottage together, then get Albert inside before Burt gets wind of him.'

The cottage was bigger than I'd imagined, attached to the main house by a covered walkway. Although a new build, it had been faithfully recreated to match the original house.

As I walked inside, I felt pleasantly surprised and at home. I believe places have their own energy. I liked the energy of this cottage. Whoever had decorated it had an eye for putting together a welcoming mix through the furniture and colours.

It was open plan in design, with a lounge and dining room in an L shape, and a small kitchenette. There were shutters on most of the narrow floor-to-ceiling windows, and a pot-bellied stove in the lounge room. The bedroom and en suite were in two separate rooms at the back.

Pat gave me a few tips, first about the heating – the pot-bellied stove ran on gas – and how to operate the television, DVD player and so forth; then we headed back to my car for the rest of my stuff.

Realising Albert was inside the car, Burt began half-heartedly barking at the window, tail wagging. Pat had a dog lead in his hand; as we walked toward my car, he whistled to Burt, who immediately ran to him, knowing a walk was on offer. Terrorising the cat could wait.

As we stood watching Pat try to clip the lead on Burt's collar, I knew Pat was someone I'd like to get to know; his gentleness with Burt told me so.

Pat's age – late sixties maybe – was hard to determine. He was wiry with a full head of thick salt and pepper hair and deep brown eyes. They say the eyes are the windows to the soul; if so, it seemed Pat had a soul that had been deeply scarred.

Despite the haunted look in his eyes, Pat had a true calmness as he patiently tried to clip the leash to an over-enthusiastic Burt's collar. The way people treat children and animals is usually indicative of who they are.

Eventually, lead on, Burt was dragging Pat away, eager to explore.

Pat turned toward us with a cheeky grin and said, 'Burt's taking me for a walk. It'll get him away from the car so you can get the cat inside. You're on your own once he's in the cottage.'

Once Burt had dragged Pat out of sight, I opened the passenger door and began to coo soothing words to Albert. 'Oh, darling boy, that was Burt. I'm afraid you two will have to learn to live together for the next couple of weeks.'

Albert's response was to growl and hiss his disapproval and dissent. It did sound fierce, even to my ears – I understand cats and love all their traits.

Beside me, Bill said cautiously, 'Someone doesn't sound too happy. Here: let me carry him in for you.'

He did, Albert hissing and snarling all the way. It wasn't the best start to our stay, but when he'd settled down, Bill would get to know the real Albert – and like him, I hoped.

Once inside, I did what all good slaves do: I set up his litter tray, his food and water bowl, and put his bed next to mine.

As I did all this, Bill leaned against the wall watching, a huge grin on his face.

I stopped my fussing. 'I know what you're thinking: dogs have masters; cats have slaves. In his defence, he did have a long drive here, and cats aren't like dogs –they love their homes as much as their humans.'

As I said this, I realised I'd made the first justification for Albert's presence in Bill's home. Realising this, again, I blushed.

Not unkindly, Bill said, 'My sisters are cat lovers; your behaviour isn't new to me. Puzzling maybe, but not new. I'll leave you to settle in, unpack and set the desk up for work. I've got a tender piece of brisket cooking in the slow cooker. Pat's staying for dinner; we hope you can join us.'

I eagerly accepted Bill's offer. After he'd left, I continued to placate Albert and settle us both into the cottage that would be our home for the next few weeks.

Albert wasn't having a bar of my feeble attempts to pacify him; in fact, he was acting downright catty. I knew my best course of action was to completely ignore him and get on with my unpacking.

So I did.

First, I hung up my clothes and put my toiletries in the en suite. In case you're wondering, there wasn't a bathtub, so Uncle J's scrying ideas would come in handy.

Then I turned my attention to setting up my work station. The desk was set up in the middle of a bay window with built in seats, with great lighting and stunning views of the tree-lined driveway. It sure beat the view from the window in my corner office in St Leonards – a brick wall.

I'd soon successfully set up my laptop to work via VPN. The speeds weren't as fast, but at least I knew it was secure. As far as any hacker would know, I was working from my office in St Leonards.

I was so engrossed with setting up, I didn't sense Albert's presence until he jumped up onto the desk and walked across my keyboard. Anyone who understands cats knows that that's a sure sign your cat does not like being ignored.

I was happy that Albert felt settled enough to display these behaviours, and soothingly said to him, 'Hello, baby. Can I take this to mean you've forgiven me for dragging you back to the scene of so much angst in your life?'

As soon as the words were out of my mouth, I felt both regret and sadness that I'd taken Albert back to the same valley where all his best and worst times had taken place.

My first thought was to crawl back to him with food. It worked; he was soon scoffing it down, purring loudly. As he ate, I realised it was getting darker, and went around the room turning on all the lamps and lighting the gas fire.

Soon Albert was sitting on a throw on my lap in front of the fire. I dozed off and woke when my mobile rang. It was Uncle J.

Instantly remorseful that I hadn't phoned him, I answered apologetically. 'Uncle J, I've been so busy trying to placate Albert and settle in that I completely forgot to phone you. I'm sorry; please forgive me.'

I was surprised by his unconcerned response as he said airily, 'It's okay, princess. Bill and I exchanged phone numbers the other night. He's already phoned to let me know you'd arrived safely. Now you're there, I can put all my energy into concentrating on my client's brief. If I don't call as often, that's why. We can text one another, though. How's Albert settling in? What's the cottage like?'

I filled him in on Albert's very cat-like behaviour; he thought it hilarious. As I did, I simultaneously thought how life was full of surprises.

Uncle J can take a while to feel comfortable with new people, and vice versa. This isn't because of anything lacking in him; it's because he's a truly unique individual. Some never get him; others find his uniqueness an acquired taste that takes time to understand. Once they get to know him, they realise he's worth their patience.

I was pleased that Bill had already worked that out. I admit I was surprised they'd exchanged phone numbers – surprised, but pleasantly so.

That night, Bill, Pat and I spent a very pleasant evening together. Pat and Bill had an easy camaraderie, and during the course of the evening, I saw how much they liked and respected one other.

I also noticed they both tried their best to talk about a variety of topics – anything except the predicament I currently found myself in. I was touched and grateful for this.

It had been a very full day, and around nine o'clock I found myself trying to stifle a yawn. Noticing this, Pat generously said, 'It's been a big day for you, young lady. I'm heading off. No doubt you're keen to hit the sack.'

I was definitely ready to hit the sack. I was also keen to see how Albert was coping all alone in a strange place.

Not wanting to be an ungracious guest, by the time Bill came back from seeing Pat off, I'd cleared most of the table.

Seeing this, Bill nudged my wrist to stop me. 'Pip, leave that please. You've got work tomorrow; I haven't. Why don't you call it a night? Let me know if there's anything else you need. Sleep well and I'll see you tomorrow. Are you okay to walk to the cottage on your own?'

Ready to take back some control, with a bravery I wasn't feeling, I sleepily responded, 'Thanks, I'll be fine. I am feeling very tired. Thanks for a great evening. Pat's a really nice man and good company. I'd better see how Albert is settling in. I'll see you in the morning. Thanks again for everything. I don't know how I can repay you.'

Embarrassed by my thanks, Bill tilted his head. 'In a way, you've already repaid me. It never sat well with me not finding out what happened to Ruth Richards. I've been mulling things over, and have discussed some ideas with Pat. Once you've settled, maybe Friday night, I'd like to talk to you about a plan I've come up with. In the meantime, settle into the cottage and work. Now, you need to sleep. I'll see you tomorrow.'

CHAPTER 22

The first two days staying in Bill's cottage went well. I was sleeping well, and despite Burt's presence, Albert seemed happy, content to sit with me as I worked.

Bill was busy around his property. I saw him occasionally, when he invited me in for a cuppa. He'd asked me to drinks at six followed by dinner on Friday evening to discuss the plan he had percolating.

I finished work early on Friday afternoon, and drove down to Pokolbin to buy a bottle of wine, some chocolate and berries to take to dinner. Once home, I fed Albert, then dressed with a little more care than usual.

As I approached the open kitchen door, I could see Bill stirring something on the stove. I took a deep breath of the aromas wafting from the pot Bill was stirring.

I said, 'Knock, knock! Can I come in? Um … dinner smells amazing. Here you go: I bought a bottle of wine, some chocolate and berries. Is there anything I can do to help?'

Turning, he beamed me a good-natured smile. 'Hope you like spaghetti Bolognese? I've made a garden salad to go with it.' He pointed toward the sideboard. 'I need to set the table. The plates and cutlery are there if you want to do that. I thought we'd eat in the kitchen tonight, if that's okay?'

I did want to help and assured him it was okay; the kitchen was a warm, inviting room. When I'm nervous – I was – I like to keep myself busy.

As I set the table, Bill, the consummate host, asked, 'What would you like to drink? I've got a Hunter semillon, a Clare riesling and a Coonawarra cabernet. Which would you prefer?'

I'd bought an aged Hunter Valley semillon. Pointing to it, I said, 'Why don't we open the wine I've brought?'

Dinner simmering on the stove, Bill suggested we sit in front of the fire in the front room. We sat quietly, sipping our drinks, warmed by the heat, mesmerised by the flames. Neither of us wanted to break the spell, but we knew we needed to discuss my situation and whatever plan he had in mind.

As I looked around the comfortable room, I saw a police cap hanging on the hat rack. To delay the inevitable conversation, I stood, walked over to the rack and took the cap down. 'Is this yours?'

Bill came to stand next to me. I could smell his aftershave and felt myself respond to his closeness.

Softly he said, 'No, it's my father's cap. He was in the service for most of his adult life.'

His nostalgia was obvious. I said, 'So it's a family tradition, then.'

His only response was to nod.

To change the subject, I read the badge motto. "*Culpam poena premit comes*". What does that mean?'

Bill moved even closer, took the cap from my hand and answered pensively. 'Punishment swiftly follows crime. For Ruth Richards, I've got a suspicion that wasn't the case.'

So much for avoiding the subject. After he'd hung his father's cap back on the rack, I moved away, plonked myself back into my chair and with a sigh said, 'Oh, well, from what I've learnt so far, I can understand why you'd feel that way.' Hesitating for effect, after a sigh I continued. 'So, what's your plan?'

Bill looked at me but, deciding it could wait, said, 'How about we eat dinner? Once we've finished, I'll tell you.'

Sounded good to me. 'Perfect. I'm in total agreement to not spoil either of our appetites. Let's eat.'

Over our meal, we did what new friends do: find out about one another. It started with my asking, 'So your dad was in the force and you have two sisters; you're the only boy in the family?'

I seemed to be asking all the wrong questions tonight. A shadow passed over Bill's lovely face, and pain filled his voice. 'I had an older brother, Dave. He was killed in a car accident many years ago.'

Horror filled me. 'Oh, Bill, I'm so sorry. That must have devastated your family, especially your parents.'

He didn't answer at first. Instead he went to the sink, filled a jug with water and brought it back to table.

As he sat back down, he became candid. 'After all these

years, it still makes me emotional to think about him. We lived in a small two-cop country town. Dad was called out to the scene of the accident. You can imagine the effect that had on him. Mum tried her best to recover, but it changed her.' Realising the mood had deflated, he generously changed the subject. 'Enough about me; you're an only child; is that right?'

With an eagerness I didn't feel, I responded, 'I sure am. I was a surprise, coming along late in my parent's lives. With the family genetics, I don't think they wanted to take the chance of having a child like Uncle J.'

Saying this felt disloyal to Uncle J and to my parents. To cover my feelings, I lifted my hands, pulled a face and said flippantly, 'Anyway, here I am!'

Bill obviously sensed my discomfort. 'I'm sure your parents were absolutely thrilled when you came along. I like the sound of your Uncle Jim. Tell me about him.'

After our shaky start – lying my arse off pretending to be a journalist doing a story – I was determined to portray Uncle J honestly. I wanted Bill to understand him as well as like him.

After a sip of water, I looked up at the ceiling to gather my thoughts. 'You would have noticed on the phone the other night that Uncle J also has Tourette's,' I began. 'Where mine is mild, his is quite severe. He doesn't have coprolalia, which is what most people think of when they hear the word Tourette's. I'm over movie makers making fun of people with it; they wouldn't dare make fun of any other neurological disorder.'

A perplexed look crossed Bill's face, and I thought I'd said too much. 'Sorry,' I said. 'I didn't mean to preach.' He shook his head reassuringly, allowing me to continue. 'Coprolalia is the medical term for involuntary outbursts of obscene words or socially inappropriate or derogatory remarks. Anyway, he doesn't have it, but he does have some pretty spectacular motor and vocal tics. Apart from that, he's without a doubt the most amazing person I know. He's kind, funny, intelligent and brave. It isn't easy living his life but he does it with grace and dignity. I'm exceptionally proud of him.'

When I'd finally finished, Bill sat, sipping water and digesting what I'd told him. 'Thanks for telling me about your uncle,' he said finally. 'I can understand why you're proud of him. He sounds like a man anyone would be proud to be related to. I'm looking forward to meeting him in person. Your grandmother sounded like an amazing woman. Tell me about her.'

At the mention of her name, my soul lifted. 'Grandma Ella was without a doubt the most incredible and amazing woman. She had astonishing psychic abilities which she used wisely and sparingly. She could see a troubled soul as soon as one walked into the room.'

I stopped, wondering how I could explain her energy. 'She had the most amazing energy. Even people who didn't understand her abilities noticed. She was kind, intelligent, loving and wise; I could continue but I'd run out of superlatives. She loved me and I loved her.'

I looked up at Bill and said quietly, 'I'm sorry you won't get a chance to meet her. I miss her so much it hurts.' At that, I felt my face crumple, my eyes misting over.

Bill was adept at changing the subject exactly when needed.

'She sounds amazing; I'm truly sorry I won't get the chance to meet her. Now, I've made apple crumble for dessert; can I interest you in some?'

How could I resist? His apple crumble was buttery and moist. After dessert, we moved back in front of the fire.

Bill held up a bottle of Scotch, saying, 'I need a stiff drink before I discuss my plan. Will you join me?'

My stomach churned at the mention of the plan. 'Count me in. By the sounds of what's coming, make it a big one.'

As I watched Bill pour our drinks over ice, I grabbed a cushion that was sitting on the lounge and hugged it. I've always been a cushion hugger, particularly when situations in life turn ominous.

Handing me the glass, he pulled his chair a little closer and with a deep sigh launched in. 'Right, well, as I mentioned, I've been mulling over a plan. Pat and I discussed it at length the other night. Although he thinks it's a bit risky, he understands and supports me doing it.' He took a large sip of his drink.

With a confidence I wasn't feeling, I said, 'Okay, that's good. I'm sure Pat wouldn't let you do anything too dangerous. Tell me what you have in mind.'

At that moment, Burt, who'd been outside sniffing around the cottage, began to scratch at the door. Bill got up. 'I'd better let him in. You don't mind if he sits in with us, do you?'

'No, of course not. I'd love to have him inside.'

Smiling, Bill went to the door and let an enthusiastic Burt into the warm room. The Rottweiler went straight to the fire and plonked himself on the rug with a doggy sigh.

After he'd settled, Bill continued. 'Burt has a few abuse-related issues. Pat talked me into getting him after … after my wife, Laura, passed away.'

I'd wondered when he would bring Laura up. Over dinner with Pat, they'd referred to her a few times – both lighting up when they did. I was keen to know more, but knew better than to intrude on his thoughts.

But he didn't seem to want to continue talking about Laura. 'He was a rescue puppy and some low-life had badly mistreated him. I don't understand how anyone could harm children or animals.'

As he said this, I felt bad that we'd left Albert – who had his own issues – alone in the cottage.

Cautiously I said, 'Before you talk about your plan, now that Burt's settled, is it okay if I get Albert from the cottage? I'll leave him in his cage to start with, and then we can slowly introduce them.'

From the look of alarm on Bill's face, I knew what he thought. Still, he generously said, 'What a great idea. I'll come with you, if you like.'

We went together, bundling a growling Albert into his carry cage, stepping out into the cold night's air then into the warmth of Bill's house, back into a room that contained a very large and damaged rescue dog named Burt.

After an initial snarl and hiss from Albert and a half-hearted bark from Burt, I left Albert in his cage to give them both time to get used to one another.

Bill got back to our subject. 'Where was I? Okay, so this is my plan. I want to find out if David Walton has any connection with those thugs who broke into your place.'

I could feel the tension building within my body. Not wanting my tics to take control, I reached down and lifted Albert out of his temporary prison and onto my lap. Stroking him calmed me and him, but as I did this, Albert looked Burt's way and let out a half-hearted hiss. Burt's response was to roll over, showing his back to us. So far so good; they were agreeing to be in the same room.

With Albert on my lap, and my emotions placated, I asked, 'So, how are you going to find out if there's a connection between Walton and the thugs?'

Bill took a deep breath. 'I've been doing some asking around, and I've found out that Walton is away this weekend, attending a wine exhibition in Western Australia. He won't be back till Tuesday morning.'

I was lost; I couldn't understand how this would help us. Shaking my head, I said, 'Okay, great, but how does that help us? I'm sorry; you've lost me.'

Bill raised his hand. With a patience I wish I possessed, he said, 'Hang on, Pip, I'm getting to that. I've got a few friends in the security business here in the Hunter. One in particular is a good mate. He told me that Walton is due to have his home security system serviced. He also told me how to disarm that system and get into the house undetected.'

He was really scaring me now. Instead of showing my fear, I tried to stay casual. 'I'm intrigued. Why would you need to get into Walton's house?'

He took another sip of his Scotch. 'My plan is to plant a bug in his office, which will hopefully pick up the whole house. My mate can take it out next time he does a service. Walton is spooked, and when people like him get spooked, they get sloppy and make mistakes.'

The lid was finally off. Not caring what he thought, I shot back, 'Shit, you are kidding, right? That's way too dangerous and way too serious. You're a policeman, for heaven's sake. Surely it's against the law?'

The more anxious I became, the calmer he seemed. 'Trust me, Pip, it's been done before, and successfully. I owe it to Ruth Richards to clear this up. The other bonus will be seeing that you're out of danger. Let me worry about the ramifications.'

I knew he was putting a positive spin on what he planned to do. I also felt he'd already made up his mind, regardless of my objections. Resignedly I said, 'Seems you're determined. How are you going to achieve this, and how can I help?'

With a look of surprised relief, he continued. 'Yes, I have made up my mind. I've still got paperwork from when Ruth Richards disappeared, including plans of the house Walton lives in. I plan to break in while he's away and plant the bug, then sit back, listen and watch him implicate himself.'

I grimaced. 'You make it sound so easy. Again, what can I do to help? I need to do something, Bill, as I'm the reason you're involved.'

He stood, walked over to the old oak sideboard, lifted the Scotch bottle up toward me – I said yes; it had been some night – then as he topped up both our glasses and handed mine back, he said, 'Okay, I'd prefer to do this on my own, but if you really want to be involved, you can come with me and be a lookout. How does that sound?'

It sounded terrifying and exhilarating – mainly terrifying, but I wasn't going to own up to that. We sat in front of the fire for the next two hours, honing the plan.

With Albert on my lap, Burt soon crept closer and was now sitting half on Bill's feet. He didn't want any cat sitting closer to his master than he was; after all, it was his home.

Soon the chiming clock on Bill's mantle struck one. We both realised that, with tomorrow night looming, we needed sleep. We'd spent the time going over what Bill had planned and had reached the stage where nothing more needed to be said.

I stood, stretching and yawning, and put Albert back into his cage. 'Dinner was stunning, thank you very much. And thanks for telling me about your plans, but especially for allowing me to be a part of tomorrow night. I promise I'll do my best not to let you down.'

Bill pushed Burt off his feet, stood up and said graciously, 'It was my pleasure. I enjoyed your company.'

Then, stroking Albert with two fingers he poked through the cage door, he said, 'I'm impressed by the way you've behaved tonight, little man; well done.'

Burt's response to the person he loved most in the world touching a cat was a disheartened bark, and he slumped back onto his spot in front of the fire.

Bill, always the gentleman, walked Albert and I back to the

cottage and waited until we were inside and I'd locked the door.

I watched him walk away through the window in the door, and felt my heart clench as I thought about him not only wanting to solve the mystery of Ruth's disappearance but also to see that I was out of danger.

There's only one way to repay that sort of gift, that sort of friendship offered: I would repay Bill by being with him all the way tomorrow evening.

As I prepared for bed, I hoped that I'd find the courage I'd need to do just that. Sensing my disquiet, when I slipped under the covers, Albert snuggled as close as he could to my face without smothering me, and commenced to lick my hand.

Some might be repulsed by a cat licking them. I take it as a great honour – a true sign of affection.

CHAPTER 23

I woke at 11:11 a.m. with a hungry ginger cat sitting on my chest, staring me in the face. I'd slept surprisingly well, considering.

Gently pushing him off, I jumped out of bed. 'All right, all right; mummy slept in. Hang on while I get your breakfast.'

After feeding Albert, I had a shower and dressed. I was hoping like hell that Bill had changed his mind overnight.

I found him in his kitchen poring over paper plans of Walton's house, which he'd visited numerous times after Ruth had disappeared.

As he was engrossed, I had time to study him. I could see lines of worry etched into his face.

Knocking on the kitchen door – I was an invited guest, after all – I casually said, 'Morning – glorious day. How'd you sleep?'

Bill looked up. 'Morning. I slept well, as always. How about you?'

I was happy to respond for a change with, 'I slept remarkably well. Looks like you've been busy. Anything you'd like to share?'

He motioned for me to sit, then got up himself. 'I've made damper. How'd you like some with butter and syrup and a pot of tea? Sound good?'

I nodded eagerly; I love damper. As Bill put the damper, butter, syrup, berries, a segmented grapefruit and a pot of tea onto a tray, I furtively looked at the plans he'd laid out. As he came back to the table, stomach rumbling, I said, 'Yum, thanks.'

After I'd buttered the warm damper, I waved my hand over the plans. 'I'm assuming these are of Walton's place? Still going ahead with it tonight?'

For some unfathomable reason, I was feeling invincible and brave this morning. Amazing what a good night's sleep can do. It wasn't only quality sleep, though, that made me feel this way. I'm going to use a word I've always disliked – I had a premonition that things would go well.

With a mouth full of damper, which he washed down with tea, he took a moment to answer. 'Spot on. I'm familiarising myself with tonight's operation. Are you sure you're still up for it? If not, I'll totally understand. I'm happy to do it on my own. It might help put a niggle in my mind at rest.'

I felt intrigued and a little annoyed at this last comment. I'm afraid a touch tersely I shot back, 'Niggle? What niggle? I'm perfectly capable of being a lookout. I can contain my, um, my energy when I need to.'

With one of his melt-your-heart crooked smiles, hands in the air in surrender, he disarmed me. 'Woo, woo, easy; I've already worked out that you're perfectly capable of assisting me tonight. It's my male pride wanting to protect you, okay. Are we good?'

My hackles went down at once. 'Well, good, because I hate to be misunderstood.'

I could have waxed lyrical about underestimating neurodiverse people, but, realising Bill was being sincere, I chose not to. Besides, I'd done enough preaching last night.

Bill smoothly changed the subject, holding up the tea pot and saying, 'Let's finish breakfast first, so we don't get indigestion. Want another cup?'

I nodded, smiling. 'Yes please, kind sir. I'd love another cup of tea.'

As we sat finishing our breakfast – well, at this hour, brunch – Burt hovered outside the door, watching us through the kitchen window.

I turned to the Rottweiler and not-so-subtly said, 'How are you this morning, Burt? Would you like us to finish our breakfast outside with you?'

Bill took my point. 'I don't like Burt in the kitchen, particularly when we're eating. It's a bad habit to get him into, but I can see you want to include him. Let's finish our cuppa outside.'

You've never seen a happier, more excited dog. As we sat down, instead of plonking himself at Bill's feet, he sat at mine. My heart lifted at this gesture of acceptance, especially from a dog who'd been so ill-treated he'd had to learn to trust humans again. This human was extremely touched that he'd chosen to trust her as well.

As we drank our tea, Burt at our feet, Bill took time to elaborate on the plan he'd concocted. 'Okay, down to the nitty-gritty. I mentioned my contact in the local security business. Well, through him I've been able to obtain some hopefully undetectable bugging equipment to put in Walton's house.'

Not letting him finish – another annoying habit of mine – I jumped in with, 'Yeah, well that sounds easier said than done …'

He raised a hand to stop me. 'Pip, I know you're anxious about all this, and so am I, but please, let me finish.'

Suitably censured, I pursed my lips and made a zipping movement.

He continued. 'So, my mate, um, contact, no questions asked, told me how to disarm the sophisticated security system Walton has installed. Once it's dark we'll head over to his property, disarm the system, gain access through a window that doesn't lock, plant the bug, and get the hell out of there, pardon the language.'

When he said 'pardon the language', I smiled. He didn't know me well enough yet to know I'd find the word 'hell' very tame.

Mistaking my smile as a sign I was pleased with his plan, he said cheerily, 'So you like the sound of it so far, I see.'

I didn't, but with my good feeling – my premonition – boosting my confidence, I responded, 'Yep, I do. I have good feelings about tonight. Now tell me: how are you going to disarm the security system?'

Bill hesitated slightly. 'The system is in a locked box at the rear of the house. I've got a key to unlock it. Once I've disarmed the system, I'll open a window, slip inside, plant the bug, climb back out, rearm the system then relock the box – job done.'

I screwed my face up. 'Seriously, that doesn't sound sophisticated to me. Who's stupid enough to have their security system accessible? He may as well put an ad in the local paper inviting …'

Hand in the air, Bill again cut me off mid-sentence – not unlike how John does – saying, 'I agree, but it's just as well it is, otherwise it would make tonight a lot less straightforward.'

I inhaled deeply. 'You're right. So, once the bug is in and the systems turned back on, what then?'

Bill gave an adorable grimace. 'We get the hell out of there as fast as we can, before anyone sees us or in case his cohorts are keeping an eye on the place.'

The thought of his cohorts pushed the tension in my body up a notch or seven. I must have gone pale.

With an encouraging smile, Bill said, 'Why don't we do something to distract ourselves? How about we take Burt for a walk? Then we can have an early dinner and get ready for our task tonight. Sound good?'

The walk and the food sounded good; the task I could do without. Matching his upbeat tone with a smile, I said, 'Great idea. I'll change into my walking shoes and see you back here.'

When I got to the cottage, an unhappy Albert greeted me at the door, vocally reminding me that I'd left him on his own for nearly four hours again. Worse, I was about to head out without him – again.

As I bent down to stroke him and apologise, he disdainfully turned his back on me and sauntered slowly away, stretching every couple of steps.

Not in the mood for a guilt trip, I idiotically said, 'That's how it is. Well, you don't fool me. I know you've been asleep the entire time I've been out – drop the guilt trip.'

I turned my back on him, changed into my walking shoes and, as I was about to leave, I felt a twinge of regret. 'I desperately need a walk to unwind, Albert. If you were a dog you could come with us. Tell you what: I'll get a harness for you, and the next walk we go on you can come, okay?'

Yeah, right. Taking a cat for a walk in a harness is like taking a brick for a walk, but saying this eased my conscience.

We had an exhilarating and enlightening time on our walk. I hadn't realised how magnificent his property was. Soon we were at a man-made pond, complete with pontoon.

The pond was surrounded by a grove of trees. It was a truly idyllic spot, a place for deep reflection. Once we'd sat, Bill let Burt off the lead, and, tail wagging, he headed straight for the water.

As we sat on the grass watching Burt wade around the pond and smiling at his antics, I told Bill what I thought about his property. 'This is stunning, Bill. I can see you've put a lot of effort into the place. It must have taken you a long time?'

He seemed pleased with my compliment, but as usual he was fair. 'I can't take all the credit. Pat helped me; we did it together.'

I heard in his voice that there was more to this special place. Giving him time to sit with his thoughts, eventually I said, 'I imagine Laura loved it here?'

He turned, looked at me, and with real emotion said, 'Sadly she didn't get to see it finished, but you're right: she loved it here.'

I could see it was time to change the subject. 'Pat's a really good friend. How did you meet him?'

His mood lifted. With a tilt of his head and a sheepish grin he told me, 'Well, I'm sure Pat won't mind my telling you. I met him initially through my line of work. Before Pat gave up drinking, he, um, well, he used to be a regular guest at our local watch-house.'

Aware that speaking about his friend in this way was difficult, I said, 'I noticed that Pat has soulful, almost troubled eyes. I wondered if he'd had a lot of pain in his life.'

Bill's tone turned soft and sensitive. 'You picked that right. Pat's like a lot of Vietnam vets; he came back from the war damaged, a changed man. I'm proud of the way he's turned his life around. I'm also very pleased he's my best friend. I don't know what I'd have done without him and my sisters when Laura died.'

As Bill spoke about Laura's passing, he looked toward the pond and became silent again.

To ease his discomfort, I said, 'I can only imagine what you must have gone through losing Laura. If you don't mind my asking, how did she die?'

Bill turned to me, his eyes glistening with tears. 'Not long after we moved up from Sydney, Laura was diagnosed with a brain tumour. We thought we could beat it, but sadly that wasn't the case. She's been gone nearly two years now.'

He sat quietly with his thoughts for a time, and I with mine, then with true feeling he said, 'The three of them – my sisters, Charlotte and Julie, and Pat in particular – got me through a tough time. He loved Laura and she loved him. He'd sit with her toward the end, to give me time to do things around here. He'd cook meals and bring them around.'

Perhaps embarrassed that he'd been speaking about Laura, he stopped, looked at me, and to change the subject, raised his shoulders and said, 'Anyway, if you get Pat on the subject of how we met, he has his own memory of our initial meetings, I'm sure.'

I liked that he hadn't judged Pat, that he'd defended him. I sensed Bill felt that continuing to elaborate about Pat would feel like a betrayal of his friend. Loyalty is a commendable quality.

With the light fading, Bill whistled Burt out of the water. When he got to us, he did what all wet dogs do – he shook the water from his coat, spraying us both in the process, then rolled around in the long grass to dry off. After our conversation, it was timely and uplifting to watch.

We walked back, neither of us feeling the urge to talk. We had our own thoughts to reflect upon. I don't take people's trust lightly. I was touched that Bill had trusted me enough to talk about Laura and his friendship with Pat. It showed that our friendship had moved to the next stage.

When we got back to our respective residences, I said, 'I need a hot shower. What time would you like me over for dinner? Can I bring anything? You've done nothing but look after me since I arrived. Once tonight's over, I'll cook you a meal.'

Bill unclipped Burt's leash, ruffled his huge head and commenced to dry him down with a towel kept on the veranda. Halfway through, he looked up at me and said, 'Is six o'clock okay? That gives you a while to relax and make it up to Albert.'

With a mock grimace, I said, 'Albert still isn't talking to me after being over here this morning. I'll have my shower and try to give him a cuddle, if he'll let me.'

Finished drying Burt, he stood and said ironically, 'Good luck with that; see you soon. I've got lamb shank and lentil soup cooking in the slow cooker for dinner. Sound okay?'

It sounded very okay; over my shoulder, as I walked away, I said so.

To soothe my nerves and prepare for the evening, I lit some candles and burned some lavender oil in the bathroom. The shower was divine, the pressure strong, and the water hot; I soon began to relax under its soothing touch.

As I dried myself, I looked into the fogged-up mirror. I was about to wipe the mirror clean and apply moisturiser to my face when an image appeared. Surprised at first, I shut my eyes and rubbed them. With a deep breath, I slowly opened them again, hoping that what I'd seen would be gone. It was.

As I stood staring, a misty image took its place – this time, Ruth. As she slowly nodded her head, a gentle smile graced her lovely face. I instinctively knew she was reassuring me that all would go well tonight.

The first image I had seen was a rose – no doubt her calling card.

To reassure her that I understood her message, I said, 'Thank you, Ruth; I feel so much better now.'

As I said these words, she smiled, then disappeared from view.

I had my answer. Uncle J was right – a bathtub full of water is not a prerequisite to see visions or perform scrying.

A shiver ran through my body; it wasn't the cold weather that had caused it. I knew I had to keep control of my visions, to not let them control me. They were a tool to help me, to help us out of this whole bloody mess; a tool to find the truth about what had happened to Ruth – for Ruth's sake, for my sake and, I now knew, for Bill's sake too.

Albert, sensing a change in the energy, was scratching at the bathroom door, desperate to get in.

As I opened the door, I lifted him into my arms, and said, 'Albert, what a clever little man; your Ruth was here. Give me a moment to get dressed and I'll feed you your dinner.'

As I put him down, he dejectedly looked around the room and my heart broke for him. He had sensed his Ruth had visited again.

Dressing in black jeans and skivvy, I finished with a deep blue hoodie, believing dark clothes would be best, especially as the moon was full.

After feeding Albert, I sat with him for a time, soothed his back and assured him that I'd make it up to him. He was soon asleep, so I eased him off my lap onto the chair. Then I quietly let myself out and went over to Bill's for dinner.

Bill was stirring something on the stove again. Seeing me coming, he shouted, 'Door's open. I thought we'd eat off trays on our laps in front of the fire in the front room.'

He had two trays set up with bowls for the soup. As he stirred the pot, he said, 'If you can grab the bread basket and butter, I'll bring the soup in soon.'

Before Bill came into the front room with our dinner, I had a chance to take another look around. Like the kitchen, it was a warm and inviting place. It had two three-seater lounges and several mixed-style single chairs spread in an inviting circle around the large fireplace.

I could feel the energy of friends and family who had shared lots of happy times here. The chair nearest the fire, Bill's chair, was very old and comfortable, in a deep mustard shade. The one I'd sat in last night was newer, a lemon green in colour, with a high wingback and a rug thrown across. Both had ottomans nearby.

A mix of paintings and prints on the walls included water-colours of country scenes. On one wall, sketches hung, adding to the feeling that this was a home.

As I looked at the sketches, I saw that the personality of the people and animals in them had been captured well; they seemed to come to life. I wondered who'd sketched them.

While I was examining these, Bill arrived with our dinner on trays. 'Sorry to take so long,' he said. 'Pat rang while I was dishing up. Don't know about you, but I've worked up an appetite. Dig in.'

Food and I have a very healthy relationship. As I ate the first spoonful, Bill looked my way, anticipation on his face. 'What do you think? I've never made it before.'

I tried another spoonful, sighed and said, 'Absolutely delicious. Who taught you to cook like this?'

As I grabbed some fresh bread to soak up my soup, Bill answered breezily, 'Mum did. She taught both us boys as well as the girls. She said men had a responsibility to share in the cooking duties, same as women. My fondest memories of mum are her teaching us all how to cook. Do you like to cook, Pip?'

I tried to be honest. 'Since I've been on my own, I'm starting to enjoy cooking again. John and Max are amazing cooks; their exacting taste has helped me lift my game a bit. I think when you're happy your cooking reflects that.'

I had no idea where that gem had come from, but after swallowing a mouthful, Bill said, 'I couldn't agree more. It's not much fun cooking for one, or for someone who doesn't appreciate your efforts. I assume that Zac – was that his name? – was the latter?'

I was taken aback that Bill knew his name, or that I'd even mentioned it. Once composed, I said, 'You guessed it. He was critical of most things about me, particularly my cooking. I don't miss him or his condescending attitude.'

We finished our meal in comparative silence, preparing ourselves for what lay ahead.

Bill said, 'I'm having a strong coffee and some left-over apple crumble and custard. Want some?'

Naturally I did; well, the apple crumble at least – the strong coffee I definitely did not need.

As the hour of our departure drew closer, Bill kept looking at his watch. Eventually he got up and let Burt in by the fire. 'Pip,' he said, 'can you stay here with Burt? I want to do a quick drive past Walton's place to make sure it's deserted.'

Thinking he was trying to sneak out and do the deed without me, I said quickly, 'Oh, no you don't; I'm coming with you. Burt will be fine on his own.'

As I stood to grab my jacket, he touched my arm – his touch was electric. He said, 'You are so transparent. I'm not trying to leave you out of tonight. I really do need to drive past – on my own – to check this out. If you like, you can tidy up the dishes. I'll be back soon.'

I'd been told.

Just as I'd finished the washing up, I heard Bill's car return and rushed back to my seat.

He came inside, stood in front of the fire warming his hands, then as he causally checked his watch, he said:

'Well, the place looks deserted. It's nine thirty so let's sit and prepare for a while, then head off around ten. Are you good with that?'

My stomach churned as my body prepared for flight-or-fight mode. 'I'm ready,' I said, masking my nerves. 'You're in charge tonight, so what do you want me to do?'

Bill sat down and turned to me, speaking intently. 'What I want you to do is keep a very sharp lookout. Once I'm inside, it will be hard for me to gauge if anyone is around. I need you to stay close to the window I've climbed through, and if you see anything – and I mean anything – that looks suspicious, you're to rap on the glass three times. Apart from that, I'd like you to keep low and out of sight.'

To reassure him and myself, I said earnestly, 'I can do that. Pity we can't leave straight away. The sooner this is over the better.'

Bill thought for a moment. 'Okay, we'll leave at nine forty-five. I'm going to find a cap and some gloves to wear. I'll be right back.'

When he'd left the room, I felt lost and alone without his reassuring presence. Burt, sensing this, came over, put his head on my lap and let out a huge doggy sigh as if to say, *'Don't be scared.'*

Moved by his concern, I bent and kissed his head, saying, 'Beautiful boy; how anyone could have been cruel to you is beyond comprehension. Thank you for being concerned about me, darling.'

I hadn't realised Bill was standing at the door watching us until he said, 'Burt really likes you, Pip. I'm pleased to see that. That's three people he trusts, now: me, Pat and you. He really has come a long way from the terrified little puppy I brought home.'

The emotion in his voice moved me. Turning, I said, 'He's one very lucky dog to have you as his owner.'

Bill walked over to where I was sitting, ruffled Burt's ears and said, 'Yeah, well, after Laura passed, Burt gave me a reason to live, and I guess I helped Burt to trust again. It's been a long road for both of us, but we've come through it together.'

CHAPTER 24

As we approached Walton's driveway, Bill turned off the headlights. He parked a couple of hundred metres away from the house, under cover of trees, and we walked the rest of the way.

With the moon full, as we neared the darkened house I felt like bolting back to the car. Then I saw the look of determination on Bill's face, a look that made me ashamed of my cowardice. I saw a man who not only believed my unbelievable story but was willing to put himself in danger for me, not to mention break the law. There was only one way to repay that sort of chivalry – I took a deep breath and found my courage.

As we slunk to the house, trying to hug the shadows, an outside sensor light automatically came on. Startled out of my wits, I blurted, 'Shit!'

Bill turned to me with his finger to his mouth and an irritated look. I shut my mouth tightly and gave him a sorry look.

Once the light had turned itself off, we continued, covering the rest of the way to the window in a crouch to avoid triggering the sensor.

Bill found the security box, unlocked it and disarmed the system. He then checked his watch, motioned me to stay where I was and moved to the unlocked window.

The window slid up noisily, grating on our already tense nerves. As I crouched in the dark to keep watch, Bill deftly climbed inside, leaving the window open for a quick exit.

My heart was pumping so hard I thought it would explode. Bill seemed to be gone for an eternity. As I sat on my haunches, hyper vigilant for the sound of someone approaching, I regularly checked my watch.

To my huge relief, he climbed back out through the window, closing it gently behind him. Giving me a thumbs-up, he went to the security box, unlocked it, turned the alarm back on, relocked it and then checked his watch.

As we walked quickly back to the car, avoiding the motion sensor this time, I felt a giddy sense of overwhelming relief that he'd achieved his aim.

Lights off, Bill drove back down the long driveway. Once around the corner from Walton's property, he turned them back on.

It was then that he said, 'That was close. I had to get the job finished in under ten minutes, otherwise an alarm would have signalled a power outage and the security company would have sent a car around. I was in and out in eight minutes and fifty-six seconds.'

I turned toward him, a look of amazement no doubt etched on my face. When composed, I said, 'Bloody hell, that was close. Just as well you didn't tell me about the time limit before you went in.'

His understated response was, 'I guessed it wouldn't have been helpful to tell you.'

As we drove back to Bill's home, the adrenaline kicked in. After his last statement, I had no comeback; instead, I burst out laughing. Bill soon joined me. It was nerve-releasing relief laughter, and by the time we got home, we had tears streaming down our faces.

As we got out of the car, I groaned, 'Oh God, my ribs hurt; I haven't laughed this much for ages.'

Bill locked his car, turned to me and said, 'Don't know about you, but I'm on a post-op high. Want to come in for a while?'

'I sure do,' I chimed. 'I'm too wound up to sleep. Be great to do a post-mortem. Do you mind if I grab Albert?'

Bill didn't hesitate. 'Sure; he and Burt can help us celebrate. I'll put a platter of food together. I've worked up a huge appetite. See you soon.'

When I got to the cottage, Albert was waiting by the door, pretending he hadn't been asleep the whole time. I bundled him into his carry case before he could protest and made my way back to Bill's house.

The door was ajar, so with a quick knock I went inside. I found Bill in the kitchen, making up a platter big enough to feed two hungry men – Maggie Beer pâté, Jarlsberg, a Tasmanian cheddar, fresh figs, almonds, a ton of cracker biscuits and some dark chocolate. Relief had given me an appetite as well.

With a wave of his hand, he said graciously, 'Take Albert through to the front lounge, Pip; he and Burt can become properly acquainted.'

I grimaced faintly, but said, 'I'm game if you are. Let me know if you need a hand to bring that platter through.'

I was feeling invincible tonight, so I opened the cage door and headed back into the kitchen, leaving Albert and Burt to sort out their differences themselves.

When we came back into the room, we couldn't believe our eyes. Burt and Albert were sitting on the same rug, in front of the fire. They weren't exactly bonding, but at least they hadn't ripped one another apart.

Tonight, everything was going smoothly.

To celebrate our success, Bill opened a bottle of riesling. He handed me my glass, raised his own, and with enthusiastic zeal announced a toast. 'Cheers! Here's to both of us for a job well done. I haven't felt this good for a very long time. I hadn't realised how much I miss the job.'

After putting some food into his mouth, he continued. 'I'd lost the will to make a difference; that's why I dropped the ball on the Ruth Richards disappearance case. Now I'm feeling confident I can right that wrong.' I had a mouth full of cracker; before I had a chance to respond, he said, 'And it's all down to you. I'm glad you had the nerve to make that first phone call. That took courage.'

Delighted and emboldened, I responded, 'Thank you. I

appreciate you saying that. Oh, I didn't mention this earlier: as well as my own good feelings, I had another vision before we left. It was Ruth, and I interpreted what I saw as her assuring me all would go well.'

I instantly regretted sharing, half expecting him to make a John-like response.

But he surprised me by saying, 'Well, you and Ruth were right.' Then, seeing my shocked expression, he began to laugh.

'Don't look so shocked; I do have an open mind. I've heard of colleagues in the past using the services of a well-respected local clairvoyant. God, you should have seen the look on your face; I wish I'd had a camera handy.'

In fun I poked my tongue at him. 'Excuse me for being shocked. I'm used to people being cynical about my, um, my inherited abilities; I'm reluctant to talk about them.'

Bill chuckled. 'I understand your hesitancy. I wanted you to know that, although I don't understand how it works, I do believe that you have abilities which are quite unique.'

To lighten the mood and change the subject – tonight wasn't the time for a serious discussion about things paranormal, tonight was a time to celebrate – I said in a self-mocking tone, 'Yep, that's me alright. I'm unique, in more ways than one.'

'Well, I'm really pleased you are,' he responded. 'What's the term you used again, neurodiverse?'

Impressed, I gave an acknowledging smile. 'Give the man a gold star. Yes, that's the term. Uncle J and I are neurodiverse, and you're neurotypical – well, as far as I know you are.'

Bill smiled at my last comment. Now we'd come down from

our high, we'd begun gently probing to find out more about each other.

In the spirit in which Bill had asked, I continued. 'How can I explain this? I know, Uncle J says that the best way to explain it is that it's as if TS has an energy all of its own; a powerful energy.'

Realising I wasn't explaining TS well – I wasn't used to people asking me about it – I stopped, looked at Bill and said, 'I'm not making much sense, am I?'

Bill got up to top up our wine, sat back down and said, 'I think that's a great explanation.'

Pleased with his answer, and to change the topic, I raised my glass and said, 'I once read somewhere that neurodiversity is a natural and valuable form of human diversity. I can live with that.'

He raised his glass back to me as he said, 'That makes sense.'

After our dangerous, yet highly successful, venture, and with the help of a few glasses of wine, we were opening up. Our adventure had forged an emotional intimacy; barriers were coming down.

He sat quietly for a time, then, choosing his words carefully, changed off the neurodiverse track back into esoteric realms. 'Police have been known to use psychics, though officially they say they don't. There was a missing person's case in 2005 where a detective engaged the services of a psychic. She helped turn it into a murder case, and the perp was caught.'

By sharing this, I knew Bill was trying to be open-minded, acknowledging who I am. As alien as it seemed, to be accepted by someone other than Uncle J and Grandma Ella felt good, really good.

I truly appreciated his generosity of spirit, and for a time I didn't know how to respond. I had a lump in my throat over being accepted despite my differences not once but twice in one evening.

Finally, I said softly, 'Thank you, Bill. That means more to me than I can explain.'

Sensing the shift in our energy, and to steer our conversation back on track I said, 'Okay, enough about me. Tell me about yourself. When did you join the police force?

My hesitancy to continue to talk about things esoteric or Tourettic hadn't escaped Bill's notice. He respected my need to change the subject, saying, 'Oh God, I was twenty-two when I joined the force. I did my training at the New South Wales Police Academy in Goulburn, well over thirty years ago.'

I was doing the sums in my head, trying to work out his age. As he was so fit looking and quite a hunk, it was difficult to gauge.

'So you followed in your father's footsteps?'

His adorable crooked smile returning, he continued. 'I did. Mum wasn't too happy, but she kept her feelings to herself. I only found out one night when I overheard my parents talking that she wasn't too pleased with my career choice.'

From his tone I knew there was more to what he was saying, so to encourage him to open up I said, 'I imagine it can't be easy for family and partners to have loved ones in any of the community services?'

Bill sipped his wine for a while, looking into the roaring fire. 'You're right,' he said. 'It's not easy in any of the services – police, military, medical or ambos. After Dave's accident, my parents never fully recovered.'

Searching for the right words I said, 'I know from the experience of my good friend Annie, whose brother died young, that when a child dies it can have devastating consequences on family relationships.'

Bill looked at me with a sad grimace, his heart breaking anew. 'That's for sure. After Dave died, Dad was much stricter with Charlotte and Julie, but particularly with me. From an early age, he'd instilled in both Dave and me that as the men in the family, it was our role to protect the women.'

As he said this, I realised that this man who was helping me – a virtual stranger, a woman he hardly knew – stay out of danger, had been moulded from an early age. Knowing this helped me to make sense of what he was prepared to do for me and what he needed to do to right a wrong for another woman he hardly knew – Ruth Richards.

For a time, the memory of his father's harsh exterior and strict ways seemed to leave him deep in thought. Eventually, with a kindness of spirt I would learn was Bill's way, he said, 'Having said that, deep down Dad was a real softy. He adored my mother and the girls, and despite being tough on me, he loved and cared about me. The job can make you become hardened and overprotective if you don't watch out.'

To lighten the mood, I said, 'Tell me about Charlotte and Julie. What are they like?'

His smile could have lit the forecourt of the Sydney Opera House. 'They're amazing, intelligent, funny, and the best sisters a man could wish for. As kids, Charlotte – or Charlie as we called her – was a sweet little girly girl. Julie was a real tomboy. They've grown into two of the nicest women you could wish to know. You'll like them.'

I was pleased he'd said 'You'll like them.' It hinted at a future, one in which I'd get an opportunity to meet them.

'I look forward to that.'

Before either of us could go down an awkward road, I changed the subject again. 'How's Pat doing post Nam? A friend of my father's was in Nam and suffered greatly from PTSD. You don't have to speak about this if it makes you feel disloyal, but has Pat sought any help?'

Again, Bill thought carefully before responding with genuine emotion. 'Pat likes you; I don't think he'd mind if we discuss this. Yes, he has, but it took some time, and sadly it didn't prevent the breakdown of his marriage to a lovely woman, another Julie in fact.'

We sat in silence, allowing him to think how to continue. Eventually he said, 'He's got two children, Mark and Grace. Mark was about eighteen months old and Grace was on the way when his birthdate was pulled out of the barrel. In fact, he missed her birth.'

We were mellowed by the wine and the fire, and as neither of us wanted the night to end I waited for him to continue. He soon did, saying, 'I admire and respect Pat for the way he's turned his life around. He's had huge struggles with PTSD and alcoholism; he's working on both. Sadly, as often happens with these two complex and difficult conditions, his family have been affected as well.'

I didn't want to interrupt, but I wanted to let him know I understood. As I nodded my head, he went on, sounding more fired-up, which showed a side of his nature I'd not yet seen.

'Don't get me started on Vietnam,' he said vehemently. 'Pat's shared some of his experiences with me over the years. I think he felt he could because I was in the police service. One night when he was still drinking, he told me how, as a twenty-year-old, he'd handled his time in Nam. I'll never forget what he said.'

I moved forward in my chair, listening. 'At first Pat said he felt invincible, then he became reckless, and finally he realised he just wanted to survive long enough to get home in one piece.'

Bill stopped, got up and stirred up the fire, which had died down. Reflectively he went on. 'When he got home, everything had changed. The kids didn't recognise him; Julie had to get to know him again.' He paused, patting Burt, who was sitting at his feet. 'He tells me he was very troubled by this stage, self-medicating, having terrible nightmares, and, well, he'd retreated into himself. He had a group of Nam mates who he'd lived through hell with and very occasionally they'd meet. He'd developed a very black sense of humour about both life and death.'

For a time, Bill couldn't continue. I could see he was genuinely saddened, recounting this story to me.

To give him some time to gather his thoughts and continue

if he wanted, I said, 'It must have been horrific, not only for Pat, but for his wife and the kids.'

Having come this far, he continued. 'Yep, it sure was. His problems ended their marriage. Pat says Julie tried her hardest, but she couldn't cope with his moods, his bouts of alternating anxiety and depression and how that affected Mark and Grace. One night she said she was leaving. Pat said she could stay in the house and he moved into a cottage on his parent's hundred-acre property. He continued to self-medicate, trying to obliterate both his memories and his heartache at losing his family.'

By this stage, I could feel tears forming in my own eyes. I didn't want Bill to see them, so as surreptitiously as I could I wiped them from my cheeks.

He continued, with even more passion. 'It was a crap war that we should never have been in in the first place. Those poor bastards witnessed so many atrocities. Pat confided he'd seen innocent Vietnamese people killed, mates carried away in body bags with no formality, no goodbyes. It's hard to understand how any vets stay sane in the insanity that is war.'

By this stage, I couldn't hold back my tears, so, excusing myself to use the toilet, I left the room. In the privacy of the bathroom, I blew my nose and wiped away my tears. Just as well, because I was a total mess; mascara had run all down my face. After a touch-up with some tissues and water, I returned to the room.

I was both grateful and touched that Bill had shared these stories with me. I now understood the sadness I'd seen in Pat's eyes. I also knew that I owed him both my respect and deep admiration and a debt I could never repay.

Upon my return, seeing my red eyes, Bill became jovial. I knew he wasn't feeling it as he said, 'Oh, sorry, that got a bit heavy. Anyway, as I said, I met Pat on a number of occasions when he was in the watch-house sobering up. Since we met, it has been my honour to see him rebuild himself and try to re-establish his relationship with his children. There's still some angst there, but Pat's a much-loved grandfather.'

I added my attempt to turn the tone around, brightly responding, 'Well, that's good. I'm sure through his grandkids he'll be able to win his children back.'

'Spot on. I've noticed that Mark and Grace seem to be seeing a different side to their dad. He's taking his sobriety very seriously. It's ironic he lives in an area renowned for its wine – talk about temptation.'

On that note, Bill looked at his watch, and with a surprised tone said, 'Wow, it's nearly two a.m. You must be tired. I'm sorry for chewing your ear off like that. Promise me that next time we'll talk about you and your life and friends.'

Secretly I was relieved that we'd spent a good part of the evening talking about Bill's family and friends. Deflecting attention away from myself is a habit I've developed over my lifetime. I'm not sure it's a healthy habit, but drawing people out to talk about themselves had worked well for me, at least until now.

Now I wasn't so sure that my habit of a lifetime was either healthy or authentic. I now had an overwhelming urge to be myself, regardless of what people thought.

CHAPTER 25

Bill spent most of Sunday working around his property. He stopped long enough to have lunch, to which I was invited.

As Burt and I took off for a post-lunch walk, I overheard Bill make the first of several phone calls. Although I couldn't make out what he was saying, from his tone I could tell the calls were serious.

Not in the mood to cook, we heated up leftover lamb shank soup, retiring early to our respective abodes.

Monday arrived, and I threw myself into work for a looming deadline, while Bill worked around the property. I couldn't help noticing he checked the windows and doors of both the main house and the cottage.

I finished work a little early and drove down to Pokolbin to buy ingredients for dinner. I'd offered to cook; I was nervous about cooking so had opted for the easy option: roast pork, with hopefully crispy crackling, apple sauce, gravy and loads of vegies.

I put the pork on early, set the table and lit some candles.

Looking around, I felt it looked too contrived, too much like I was setting the scene for a romantic evening. I blew out most of the candles, leaving only three on the kitchen bench. I also lit some lavender oil to sooth my nerves.

After dinner, which to my absolute relief turned out perfectly, particularly the crackling, we both knew we'd skirted around the inevitable conversation: our next course of action.

Bill leaned back in his chair, rubbed his stomach and said, 'That meal was fabulous. Thank you so much, I really needed a home-cooked meal; food always tastes better when someone else cooks it.'

'I'm really pleased you enjoyed it. I'm out of the habit of cooking,' I admitted, 'so I was a bit nervous.' I paused for effect, then, getting straight to the point, I asked, 'So, tell me, what happens now?'

With a napkin he wiped the grease from his chin, neatly folded it and put it back on the table. Calmly he said, 'Now comes the hard part, Pip: we wait and hope Walton makes a few imprudent calls and puts his foot in it.'

Mimicking his actions, I leaned back in my chair, my hands behind my head. 'Well, I hope you're better at waiting than I am. I'm not known for sitting around.'

Soothingly he said, 'I'm very used to the waiting game, Pip. In fact, I'm particularly good at it. That comes from my time working on an undercover job, for which I had good training. You could say it's my forte.'

All I could do was grin, shake my head and say, 'You really are full of surprises. I'm pleased to hear waiting is your forte.'

We both knew we could have days ahead where we'd have to be alert, so after some fruit and cheese, Bill went back home and I prepared for bed and, hopefully, sleep.

When Tuesday arrived, Bill seemed tense and distracted. He was waiting for the first call. It didn't happen till five thirty that evening, when Walton put in his first call, which Bill played for me.

'I'm back. Anything to report?' That was Walton's voice.

'No, I've been sitting outside the bitch's place, and no sign of her. Seems she isn't there; her car's gone. Maybe we scared her off?'

'Possibly, but we still need to be careful. What are you and the other two morons doing on the weekend?'

'Nothing planned, why?'

'We have problems closer to home. We need to move the package.'

'Think that's wise under the circumstances?'

'Got a better idea?'

'No, but … shit, David, this is getting serious.'

'It got serious when you fucking idiots didn't follow my instructions. You were sloppy. I told you to dump it at the colliery. You will fix this, no questions asked.'

'Okay, calm down. I'll get onto the others. I'll call you once I've spoken to them.'

'Good; and once you do, get back to me so we can make plans to shift it Saturday evening. We need that out of the way before the shipment leaves.'

Clunk – he hung up.

As we silently listened, my stomach churned with fear and disgust. Bill had a similar look of disgust on his face.

As a shiver racked my body, I looked at him and weakly asked, 'What now?'

He squared his shoulders. 'Unless it's an act, which I doubt, looks like they're running scared, which is good because that is when they'll make mistakes.'

'What do you mean?'

He sat down and explained to me what he made of the call. Then his demeanour changed, and in a back-to-business tone he said, 'I've got a few calls to make. Be patient, Pip. I'll fill you in once I've phoned people.'

Nearly two hours later, Bill came to the cottage, a neutral look on his face. Despite this, I could tell something was troubling him. I hate being clairsentient at times.

Bill knocked, and when I let him in, he said evasively, 'That's all sorted. I've spoken to my contact at the security company. He'll phone Walton and organise his annual check of the security system. While he's there he'll remove the bug.' He looked out the window, then back to me. 'I've also phoned Ray Harris, my old boss in Sydney. He's going to organise a covert search warrant and make sure it's issued to the local police, who'll meet us there on the night.'

When he said this, I had a foreboding that all wasn't as it should be. No facts about what was wrong, just that gnawing feeling.

Instead of sharing my feeling, I said confidently, 'Thank heavens you knew to do that; it sounds important.'

Looking out the window, not directly at me, which I felt was a sign he had reservations, Bill continued. 'It is, Pip, believe me. Without it we wouldn't have a case or a leg to stand on. You can't enter someone's property without a warrant and have it stand up in court. I had to do some fast talking to convince Ray that we had reasonable grounds for believing evidence would be found on Walton's property that would lead to an arrest. We go way back, and he trusts my judgement.'

He continued, this time looking directly at me. 'I also told him about your input, Pip. He wasn't surprised; somehow word had got back to him about you already.' At this point he stopped, then in a voice tinged with concern said, 'I have an idea how that happened. I'm glad I was up-front about you. I owed it to him to come clean so he wouldn't have any surprises afterwards.'

The more he talked, the more uncomfortable I became. Not wanting to cloud the waters any further, I simply said, 'That must have been an interesting conversation. How did he respond?'

Apparently not wanting to upset me, Bill glossed over that part of the conversation. 'I just told him it was a fait accompli, and although you had to interpret what you saw, your visions, in the end, were quite often correct. I hope you don't mind, I also told him that your input wasn't going to cost the force; he seemed pleased with that.'

As he spoke, he gave me an unsure smile. To put him at ease, I said, 'Good call; I bet he was pleased.'

'Ray is familiar with that case I told you about back in 2005.'

Seeing my crestfallen expression, he kindly continued, saying, 'Pip, most of us know and accept that some people, for reasons unknown, have these, um, abilities. Okay, Ray's a bit of a cynic, but he's seen enough in his time in the force to know that if I took your skills seriously there was good reason.'

I appreciated his efforts to boost my flagging psychic ego, but if I'm honest, I was fast reaching a stage where I was beginning to wonder if my skills were no more than a flash in the pan.

Instead of sharing this, I tried my best to be authentic. 'Thanks for saying that. I'm as perplexed as anyone that I was the vehicle to receive these messages about and from Ruth.' Knowing there was more, I asked, 'Who else did you speak to?'

Hesitating, and looking out the window again, he said, 'Oh, I also spoke to my ex-partner. He's currently working in Scone. He took over the disappearance case when I took leave to look after Laura. I gave him a tip-off that there might be the possibility of solving Ruth Richards' disappearance. I thought maybe he'd like to be there at the end to help the local boys.'

Not really wanting an answer, I asked, 'How did that call go? How did he react?'

He looked me directly in the face and said, 'With interest.'

I knew straight away something was very wrong with both this phone call and Bill's feelings about it.

Not wanting to bring this nameless feeling out into the open, yet not believing a word of what I was about to say, I said, 'That's brilliant. I can't believe this may soon be over.'

Following my cue, Bill answered just as evasively, saying, 'Yep; I'm sure we'll have this solved in no time.'

I sensed he didn't believe a word of what he'd just said, and with his response, I realised something else about Bill, something important: he was a much worse liar than I was. Knowing that made me like him even more.

He didn't sound at all convincing and, more importantly, he couldn't look me in the face. It was as if he had a feeling or a premonition – I know I sure as hell did – and he didn't want to alert or alarm me. No matter how hard Bill tried to hide his concerns about this call, he hadn't succeeded; I'd picked up on his disquiet.

Being clairsentient has advantages and disadvantages. The advantages are that you can prepare yourself for untoward things that may be just around the corner; the disadvantages are that you also have time to dwell on those untoward things.

Pretending to be elated with the outcome of his calls, we spent what was left of the evening trying very hard not to feed one another's sense of doom.

That might sound inauthentic, but what would have been the point of sharing our disquiet with one another? If you give a situation enough bad energy it can only get worse.

Around ten, Bill begged off for the night. As I watched him through my window, I noticed he made sure that Burt was in place on the front porch. Seeing this didn't do anything to reassure me.

As he left, he told me he had one more call to make; to whom, I had no idea.

It would turn out to be a very important and timely call.

As I got ready for bed, I thought, *Well, there goes another good night's sleep.* I crawled into bed fully clothed and waited; for what, I wasn't sure, but I knew this time I would be fully prepared if and when it happened.

Albert couldn't settle, so soothingly I said to him, 'You've got a bad feeling too, baby. Don't be scared, I'll protect you.'

I was still awake an hour later, and instead of staying alone and afraid in the cottage, I packed Albert into his cage and went to knock on Bill's door. The lights were still on, so I knew he was up.

He answered very quickly and agitatedly said, 'What's wrong, Pip; did you hear something? Quick, come inside.'

Inside, I put Albert's cage down and honestly shared my feelings. 'No, Bill, I didn't hear anything, I'm just having a really bad feeling, a premonition if you like. It's just, I'd feel safer here.'

Annoyed with myself, I slapped my forehead and said, 'Oh shit, I forgot Albert's food and litter tray, and a few other things. I'll just duck back and get them.'

Ever the gentleman, Bill put his hand out to take the cage, saying, 'Here, put him in the room first. I'll come and help you grab what you need. Then I need to show you something. It's important.'

When we got back from collecting our things, Bill followed me into the room. I felt embarrassed about coming over so late, and my tics had kicked in – sniffing and throat clearing – and despite my best efforts I couldn't explain myself further.

To save me the effort, Bill said reassuringly, 'It's okay. I'm pleased you're here. I've been having the same feelings, especially after one call, and I'm not used to it like you are.'

Cutting him off inappropriately, I said, 'Ah, claircognizance.'

He looked at me, brows knitted, and left the question hanging.

I dug myself an even deeper hole, explaining, 'It's just a fancy word for clear knowing. Probably comes with your profession.'

He wasn't in the mood for that conversation. Staying focussed, dismissing my comment, he said doggedly, 'I made up the bed earlier in Laura's old art room.'

Once we'd reached that room, he pointed to a collapsed desk, turned to me and earnestly said, 'This is what I wanted to show you.'

Perplexed, I looked at the desk, wondering what the hell he meant. I was too stressed to take his meaning. Instead, I slumped onto the end of the bed with a huge sigh and flippantly said, 'Don't tell me you want me to do some art therapy?'

His reaction told me we were in real danger. Instead of taking my glib comment in the vein in which it was intended – a poor attempt at humour – he turned to me, his face full of annoyance and concern. In a teacher-like voice he said, 'What I want to show you *is* important, so come here and pay attention.'

Duly chastised, I moved closer, keeping my big mouth shut and my overactive brain in line.

Bill began to explain. 'I need to show you something about this desk.'

From what I could see, it was a drafting type table on hinges that had been folded down flat.

Bill put me out of my misery. 'I built this table for Laura. It lifts up on hydraulic hinges. She wanted somewhere out of the way to store her art supplies. Here: look at this.'

As I watched, Bill pulled at the table, which impressively pivoted out and up and with two distinct clicks was now the perfect art table.

Ticcing away, stressed to my eyeballs, I less-than-politely said, 'That's a great set-up, Bill, really cleverly put together, but I ...'

In a tone I hadn't heard him use before, he said, 'Let me finish. If you bend down, can you see the opening here under the desk? At the moment, it's full of boxes of art supplies. I'm going to move a few boxes out later and put them in the garage. But for now, can you see that behind the boxes, there's a space? I want you to climb in there.'

I'd changed my mind about his mood – he wasn't in teacher mood, he was in cop mood.

Following orders, I didn't say a word; I simply climbed into the space and, understanding what he wanted, pulled a box in front of me.

From my hiding place, I heard Bill say, with satisfaction, 'Good, I can't see you.' Then I heard the hinge on the desk creak as he closed it back down. As he did, my hiding space became much darker, and much less a place I'd like to hide. Through the crack in the hinged table, I could still see some of the room.

Stress-induced claustrophobia was starting to kick in. Almost hysterically I asked, 'How long do you want me to stay in here?'

My policeman friend, a little more tersely, responded, 'I haven't finished explaining things yet. Can you slide along left, till you get to the end?'

Knowing he wasn't in any mood for non-compliance, I obligingly shuffled along on my bottom till I'd reached the end, then I meekly said, 'Now what?'

'Okay, good. Now feel above your head. You'll find a catch. Push the catch, and push the lid up.'

I did, and as I pushed the lid open, there was a very loud creak. Hearing the noise, I heard Bill swear profusely.

He wasn't perfect after all.

He continued, saying, 'You should find yourself on the end of the side veranda, close to the shed.'

I was, and as I gingerly stood, the bitterly cold air hit me like a bucket of iced water. Looking around, I could see that this exit from the art room was well hidden behind an established bush.

Then I knew that Bill was not only showing me a hiding place; he was showing me an escape route. Now my dream, when Uncle J had flown back from overseas, made sense.

Shaking my head to remove thoughts of my dream, I wasn't sure whether I should hop back in and slide back into the art room, or use the front door.

I giggled to myself, thinking, *Oh, I could come back in via the front door, walk up behind Bill and say 'tada' – just like a materialising magician's assistant.*

The stress had pushed me into hysterical Tourettic overdrive.

I do have a unique sense of humour; I'm not sure if it's familial or Tourettic or both. I really missed the old fun me; I'd like to find her again and let her out to play. But first things first: I had to stay alive.

Taking the neurotypical path, I decided to go back the way I'd come. Slipping inside, I closed and bolted the veranda opening and slithered back behind the desk, knowing that Bill would let me out from behind it and into the room.

As I returned, in an attempt to distract me from my now-confirmed fears, Bill casually said, 'It was once a firewood box, but it hasn't been used for years. Instead of pulling it out and plastering over the opening, I turned it into a space for Laura's art supplies.'

As he explained this I thought, *That explains the splinters in my bum.* I knew better than to share that gem.

As he helped me out of my dark and dusty hiding place, he added, 'If I tell you to get in there, I want you to do it straight away. Once you're in there, I'll lock the desk in place. They won't know about the space behind it. If by some chance they do work it out, you know the escape hatch. Just take off as fast as you can, okay?'

My stress levels now at their peak, I stifled a highly inappropriate giggle as I thought about a cat in a hat instead of a magician's rabbit. Taking a calming breath, I thought to ask, 'What about Albert? Can I take him in with me?'

Without hesitation, Bill said, 'Not a chance. I'll hide Albert. Trust me: animals, particularly cats, will find their own escape route. It would be too dangerous to take him with you.'

Realising I'd asked only after Albert, I belatedly added, 'What about you and Burt, Bill?'

With a ghost of a smile, he said, 'Trust me, we'll both be all right, especially if I don't have to worry about your safety. Anyway, that's what I wanted to show you.'

He looked at his watch. 'I need to move some boxes, then oil that hinge. I know this isn't going to be easy, but we need some sleep. I'll see you in the morning. Remember, I'm just down the hall if you need me.'

Fully clothed, Albert by my side, against all odds I fell asleep. I was abruptly woken by Albert snarling. I tried in vain to soothe him so I could listen; soon Burt started to frantically growl and bark.

Bill had chained him to his kennel on the veranda. From the sounds of it, he was dragging the kennel along the full length. Good idea chaining Burt to the kennel like that.

Bill was quickly at my bedroom door, finger to his mouth, signalling me to not make a sound. In a whisper he told me there were some men here, but he reassured me they had no idea that Albert and I were here, so if we stayed out of sight we'd be safe.

He motioned for me to climb into the space behind the art desk. I did so immediately. He then gently lifted Albert and hid him in a box at the end of the bed.

From my hiding place, I saw him pull up my bed, making it look unslept in. He then threw my clothes into my overnight bag, zipped it and neatly put it on top of the wardrobe. He was so cool, so calm.

I sat crouched in my hiding place, paralysed with fear, trying to remain calm and breathe softly. As always, when I was stressed, I wanted to pee badly, but I didn't dare think about it. I held on and concentrated on listening. Then I remembered my watch. I'd left it on the bedside table and knew it would give me away. Shit, shit, shit.

I heard a pitiful yelp and knew they'd done something to Burt. I'd kill them with my bare hands if he was badly injured.

At once my hiding place was enveloped by a deep foreboding darkness, no chinks of light now showing. They'd switched off the mains power. Without power, Bill's security system was useless.

To compensate for the lack of visual stimulation, my hearing became acutely sensitive. As I sat trying to calm my breathing, I heard the sounds of splintering timber and shattering glass, and could only imagine they'd forced their way into the house by kicking in the front door.

It was excruciating listening to these sounds and feeling impotent to help.

All I could think was, *Not again, this can't be happening.* As I hid, feeling like the world's biggest coward, I bit my tongue to stop my tics from giving me away – and I prayed.

CHAPTER 26

Before long, someone walked into the room. In a sliver of moonlight, I saw him through the crack of the folded down art desk. He was tall and well-built, had short ginger hair and a neat goatee. I didn't recognise him.

His eyes were the thing that stood out: they were so dark brown they were almost black.

He looked around the room and walked over to the wardrobe, quickly opening the door. Then he turned and lifted the lid of the box where Bill had hidden Albert.

As he opened the lid, Albert flew out, wailing and spitting. I'm proud to say, the man got such a shock that he tripped and fell backward. Albert flew out of the room, and I hoped to safety.

As he was picking himself up, someone else came into the room. I recognised him from my break-in. He had a six pack of beer in one hand.

He said, 'Fuck, what was that noise? Is the bitch here?'

Embarrassed by his fall and glad his friends hadn't seen his reaction to Albert, he spat back, 'Not that I can see. Have you checked the cottage? She's probably there.'

'Nah, the slag isn't there. We've pulled the place apart. What are we going to do with Browne?'

The other man said, 'We've got orders to take him with us. What the fuck have you got those beers for?'

With a smile on his rodent-like face the other responded, 'I thought we'd knock a few back, it's a long way to the colliery.'

With one more look around the room, they were about to leave when the one Albert had scared turned and tried to lift the art desk. I held my breath and closed my eyes, waiting. It wouldn't budge, so he gave up and left the room.

I sat very still, trying to catch my breath, desperate to hear what was being said outside. Soon, the voices stopped and I heard car engines starting up then drive away.

I finally crawled out of my hiding place via the balcony, tiptoeing on my sock-clad feet through broken glass and in through the kicked-in front door.

As I cautiously entered the house, I called Bill's name. There was no response, and my heart sank. Bill was gone, and Albert was missing. I found Burt lying in the front yard, semi-conscious but still alive.

I went back inside and pulled on my shoes and coat, which Bill had thrown into the overnight bag. I looked for my watch, but it was gone. Bill must have scooped that up as well.

I looked around, overwhelmed with concern for Bill. Then

Burt started to stir, and when I ran back to comfort him, I saw that Albert had beaten me to it.

Albert was sitting next to his canine friend, licking his head – rescue animals understand what rescue animals need.

At first Burt growled at us, snarling and snapping. In a soft, low voice I said, 'It's okay, boy, it's okay. I'm sorry the bad men hurt you. You have to help find Bill. Please, Burt; we need you.'

Burt slowly stood and shook his big head, sending slobber everywhere. Groggily he started to sniff the ground. What could I do? If he ran off, I'd never find him, or Bill.

Not thinking, I asked, 'Hey, boy, what do you smell?'

Then I heard a car approaching. I grabbed Albert, whistled Burt and took them back to hide in the safest place where we'd all fit – the kitchen pantry.

As we waited, I sat, mobile in hand, wondering if I dared phone the police. It wasn't fear of being heard. After Bill's oddness about the conversation with his colleague, it occurred to me that not everyone in the force might be trustworthy.

Soon Burt started to growl and bark furiously; Albert tried to match his growl. I tried to stop Burt barking, putting my hand over his mouth; it was useless.

Loud knocking erupted at the kitchen door. Burt's barking escalated to a ferocious level, until a familiar voice on the other side of the door said calmly, 'It's okay, boy, settle down.'

Burt did settle, and started a whimper of welcome, scratching at the pantry door to be let out. This gave me the courage to come out and peak through the window. It was Pat.

After I'd let him in, Pat looked me over. He said, 'Shit, Pip, what a mess. Are you okay? Where's Bill?'

I burst into tears. 'I have no idea; I think they took him with them.' At that moment my cough tic kicked in; I could finally and safely let off some stored tension.

Apologetically Pat said, 'I'm so sorry; I got here as fast as I could after Bill's call. He rang me quickly when he heard Burt barking.'

'It's not your fault Pat,' I said. 'We need to find Bill. How do we do that?'

He took immediate control. 'Grab what you need for you and Albert. I'll sort out Burt. You're all coming to my place. Please, make it quick. We need to find Bill soon.'

Before leaving, I had the longest, most relieving pee, then threw my things into the overnight bag along with Albert's food. I also shoved his litter tray into a plastic bag.

When I got back into the kitchen, Pat was waiting. Impatiently he said, 'Come on, we need to get away from here. Burt's already in the car.' Then he seemed to remember something. He rushed into Bill's office, saying, 'Wait here a minute.' He soon came out again, carrying a bag. With one last look around, he turned off the lights and we left.

CHAPTER 27

As we drove away, I thought about what Bill had said about people not taking Pat seriously, not understanding him the way he did.

Tonight, I'd witnessed a man who, without a thought for his own safety, took control of the situation, giving me courage in the process. Never underestimate a true friend.

Once well away from Bill's place, Pat began to speak. 'I'm sorry if I was terse with you back there. Bill asked me to find you and get you safely away; I was focussed on keeping my word. We'll head to my place, settle these two down then talk. Have a think about what you heard tonight, Pip. Anything at all, no matter how inane, might help us work out where they've taken him.'

It was my turn to be terse. Less-than-gratefully I said, 'Seriously? I have no idea where they took him. You're the local, surely you have some idea; and who are "they", anyway? Did Bill tell you who he thinks is behind this? He seemed stressed after a phone call with a colleague.'

Pat gave me a swift look. Calmly he said, 'He did; fellow cop Scanlan apparently sounded strange when he spoke to him. After the call, Bill seemed to think there was reason to worry about his motives. I guess tonight proves there's something in it.'

By now, in full-flight Tourettic overdrive, I said expressively, 'I have no frigging idea who Scanlan is, Pat; you aren't making sense!'

Pat gave me a look that said, *'Who'd have thought someone like you would use such colourful language?'* With restraint he said, 'He's Bill's old partner; they worked on the disappearance case together. He took over when Bill went on leave to care for Laura. I've never liked him; he's a condescending prick, um … excuse my colourful language. Bill now feels Scanlan is implicated in some way with Ruth Richards' disappearance. He also feels that's the reason her case was never solved.'

All I could think to say was, 'That doesn't sound too good.'

'No, it doesn't,' he said, 'but Bill's given me the names of the cops he trusts. Once we have a talk, we'll need to phone them.'

Despite my stress levels, I felt I owed him an apology. 'I'm sorry for my terseness; I'm really concerned about Bill.'

Generously he said, 'I know, love; me too. We're nearly at my place. For now, sit back and take a few deep breaths.' We drove in through a gate, then he switched off his headlights.

In the dark, I couldn't see much, but I knew Pat's property was private and well protected. I began to relax a little, especially when I saw that Burt knew the place. He immediately ran around, sniffing and looking for Bill.

Despite hating his cage, Albert seemed content to stay safely inside it.

It was painful watching Burt looking for Bill. Eventually he gave up and slumped forlornly at the front door. Albert, finally venturing out of his cage, went and plonked himself closely beside Burt.

Once inside, I saw that Pat's home was comfortable, inviting and cosy. It was scrupulously clean with a diverse mix of lovingly renovated furniture. His brave eclectic style showed he was a man who wasted nothing, a true recycler and restorer of things both beautiful and useful.

There was a pot-belly stove, which he stoked up and soon had roaring, as well as two characterful and comfortable chairs, both set up in front of the fire. Burt immediately slumped in front of one with a forlorn exhalation.

Pat turned to me, a look of despair in his eyes. 'Bill usually sits in that chair.'

My heart squeezed tight at this explanation.

Pat made us a strong cup of tea and put out some banana bread. He also set down some food and water for Burt and Albert.

I couldn't eat, I was too distressed. As we finished our cups of tea at the kitchen table, Pat pointed to a lovely old wooden divan bed, close to the fire. He said, 'Make yourself comfortable; we need to talk.'

I moved to sit on the divan. Looking at Pat, I said, 'I've been wracking my brain; can you give me time, please? I was pretty terrified, and I was in the firewood box the entire time.'

To guide me, Pat gently asked, 'What do you remember hearing tonight?'

I raised my hands and shrugged my shoulders.

Not put off, Pat calmly and pragmatically asked, 'Okay; what did the car sound like? How many voices did you hear? Did Bill say anything that might be important, that might give us a clue?'

I shut my eyes and tried to think. The car, it had sounded loud. The voices, were there two? Three? What had Bill said?

Remembering, I opened my eyes and with new hope said, 'Well, the car sounded loud; I think there were possibly two, no, maybe three, men; when they took Bill outside onto the veranda, I heard him say, "I've been expecting you."'

Pat, keen for me to continue, became a little agitated. 'Come on, Pip, this is important. Did Bill say anything else? His life could depend on you remembering any minor detail.'

Exhausted and tense, I turned my head away and began to cry, silent tears of frustration rolling down my cheeks. Burt noticed, stood close and licked my face.

Though secretly pleased, with a half-hearted reprimand, I said, 'Don't, boy. Stop licking me.' But as Burt licked my face, I remembered something else that Bill had said. I sat up in excitement.

'I remember now; Bill said to someone, "Well, mate, now I know why you were so concerned to take the pressure off me; it all makes sense."'

Pat sat up at this. 'Good girl. That's important and it does make sense to me. Sounds like Scanlan was there. Bill told me on the phone earlier tonight, he thinks he knows why Scanlan wanted to take over the disappearance case. At the time he thought it was to give him space to be with Laura. After something Scanlan said in the call, he thinks that may have been convenience rather than compassion.'

I had no idea what he meant. 'What changed his mind on that call?'

Pat, thinking carefully, said, 'Apparently Scanlan said, "Leave it alone; these aren't people you want to piss off."'

Understanding hit me. 'Shit.'

I knew Pat was Bill's friend for a reason. If Bill trusted Pat, there was good reason. Burt did also, so that was enough for me. I began to relax and to feel that together we could find Bill, hopefully alive.

By this stage my exhaustion was complete. Seeing this, Pat suggested we try to get an hour or two of sleep. He moved a bamboo screen beside the divan for privacy. Though I desperately wanted the escape from my thoughts that sleep could give, I knew it would be next to impossible.

As I crawled under the blanket, Albert curled into the back of my legs. Stress consumed me, and my tics started again. They must have been loud, because from his bedroom down the hall Pat eventually said, 'Love, can you keep the noise down a bit? I need some shuteye.'

I lay there thinking, *Yeah, right, easier said than done*, but aloud I said, 'Sure, Pat, I'll try.'

Before long, Pat was snoring, affording me the luxury of ticcing away to my brain's content.

Tired but wired is a recurring theme for me.

I woke, not knowing where I was, to the smell of bacon cooking. As I jumped out of bed, remembering the urgency of our situation, I quickly put on my boots.

From the kitchen Pat, ever the pragmatist, said, 'Sleep well then? Here, grab one of these rolls. You can pour the tea on the way. We're got work to do.'

He'd made up bacon and egg rolls and a thermos flask of tea.

After I'd washed my face and cleaned my teeth, we headed out the door. On the way, Pat asked me the first of many questions. 'Okay; any idea where they might have taken Bill?'

I wasn't expecting that question – again. Starting the day off badly, I slammed the car door and curtly shot back, 'God, no! Like I said, you're the one with the local knowledge.'

Unperturbed by my curt response, Pat started the engine. 'Well, I've been mulling that over and haven't come up with anything yet. We know Scanlan's involved, so we could start there.'

Sleep deprived, I felt lost. Forgetting our conversation of three hours ago, I asked, 'Scanlan? Who's Scanlan?'

Showing a patience I'd soon grow to love, Pat replied, 'We talked about him last night. Roger Scanlan was Bill's partner; they worked together in Cessnock. He took over the disappearance of Ruth Richards once Bill took leave to look after Laura. Bill talked about the case often over the years; it didn't sit well with him, the way the case was never solved.'

I recalled our conversation. Optimistically I said, 'Where does this Scanlan live? Could Bill have been taken to his place?'

Pat assured me not. 'No, that's highly unlikely. If Scanlan is involved, he'd be too devious to allow that to happen. I think Bill will be someplace no one would think of looking.'

His words sent a shudder through me; stating the obvious, I said, 'Great; that gets us exactly nowhere.'

I'd started to tic again, and I knew that could drive him crazy. 'Bill told you about my Tourette's,' I said. 'I'm sorry; stress exacerbates it, so I could be pretty annoying today.'

Pat surprised me with, 'Well, love, you remind me of a mate in Nam. He had similar mannerisms. He was a great bloke, funniest bugger I ever met, sharp as a tack.' I nodded, interested. He continued. 'Initially we were concerned about going on patrol with him. He used to sniff and clear his throat quite a bit, just like you. We all thought he had a nervous disposition. Some of the blokes used to clear their throats as a greeting to him. He was good-natured about it.'

I rolled my eyes at him, thinking, *Typical*.

Not put off by my gesture, Pat went on. 'We were worried the Viet Cong would hear him. Thing is, it was the other way around: he always heard them well before any of us. He had a sixth sense about danger that we learned never to ignore. Fascinating thing was, when he was concentrating in the field, his habits stopped.'

'That's common,' I explained. 'Concentration can stop tics for a time. The poor bugger probably didn't even know he had Tourette's. There are lots out there who don't, usually putting it down to nervous habit or sinus problems.'

Understandingly Pat nodded. 'You could be right. My point

is, like him, I feel you'll be good to have around in a crisis; kind of a lucky charm.' Getting back on track, he added, 'Right, we need to go over again what was said last night when they took Bill away.'

Frustration boiled in me. 'We've already been over that, Pat; how can it help?'

He changed down a gear as we crested a hill. 'Trust me, love, you were pretty stressed last night. Maybe today you can remember something else. Did any of the others say anything? Anything at all that might be helpful.'

To my surprise, I did remember something. 'One of them said, "What are you doing, dickhead?" The response, I think, was, "Grabbing a few beers for the drive. It's a long way to the colliery."'

Obviously pleased, he responded, 'That's brilliant, Pip. That's what we needed you to remember – good girl. Anything else?'

Pleased and deflated at the same time, I said, 'No, Pat, I honestly can't think of anything. Is that helpful, though?'

Pat reassured me at once. 'It sure is. The Hunter region is a big mining area. There are still a few mines operating, but you can bet they wouldn't take him to an active mine. There are over fifty abandoned mines in the area; now it's a process of elimination. Let's look at who we know is involved so far.'

Lost for ideas, I said, 'So how do we work this out?'

He hesitated. 'We put everything we know down on paper and see what we come up with, then we make a plan.' He pointed to the glovebox. 'In there's a notepad and some pens. You write everything down. We can't waste any more time.'

By the time we'd reached town, we had a list and background of everyone Pat thought was involved.

Eager to give some hope, Pat said encouragingly, 'I've been thinking. A few years back, there was a local mining company run by a bloke called Lindsay Jenkins. He was a nasty, bad tempered, egotistical prick of a man – sorry about the language – who thought he owned the town and everyone in it. There was a bit of an ecological disaster a few years back with one of his mines; something with poisonous sulphuric acid, iron and aluminium leaching into the local creeks.'

I was getting impatient with how long his story was taking, and said, 'Pat, can we cut this short? I don't see how this helps.'

Pat looked at me over the top of his glasses. 'I'm getting to that. He had a son, though I can't remember his name. I was still drinking heavily at the time.'

I interjected, 'How can we find out where this old mine is? We need to find Bill and help him.'

Calm under pressure, ignoring my mounting anxiety, Pat continued. 'The only way I can think to find this old mine is by going into the local newspaper, the *Hunter Valley Age*, and looking up old articles. From memory, there was a lot about it in the papers at the time. The locals were up in arms, with lots of demonstrations. It might give us an idea, anyhow.'

At the mention of demonstrations, I had a shiver, confirming we were onto something. Excitedly I said, 'Oh God, those could be the demonstrations Muriel was talking about!'

Now it was Pat's turn to be perplexed. 'Who the hell's Muriel?'

'It's too long to go into; she was a friend of Ruth's. What time does the office open?'

Looking uncertain, Pat answered. 'From memory, eight a.m. Let's head over there and finish our tea and rolls in the parking lot.'

Once parked, we threw down the rest of the rolls, and right on eight made our way to reception, where we were directed to the second floor. Emily Martin, the librarian who greeted us, was efficient and very helpful.

Pat introduced us and told her roughly what we were looking for. She didn't question why, simply said, 'I know the years you need. I remember Mr Jenkins very well.' Her emphasis had been on the word *very*. 'There was quite a lot of controversy at the time when his mine closed down. Wait here, please; I'll get the microfiche for you.'

As she left, I said disdainfully, 'Really, microfiche? They haven't heard of scanning?'

As she came back with several small white envelopes in her hand, she must have heard my less-than-charitable comment. Laboriously she said, 'I know it seems an antiquated technology, but microfiche is still used widely for media storage. Now, you need to place the microfiche face-down, with the white strip up, and then slide the tray under the lens. Move the tray around to find the right page. You can use this position dial on the right to turn the image for easier reading. Use this dial below the screen to zoom in on the image.'

I shot Pat a look, rolling my eyes, and in response he gave me a stony look that I took to mean, '*Keep quiet.*' I did, and Emily continued. 'Once the image is clear, slide the tray to find the correct page. To print, change the film type button to image. Hit the start button to print your page. Your printing will come from the printer on the right. Please remember to put each microfiche back into its envelope and return it to the basket over there, marked "returned microfiche".'

I could have throttled her for wasting valuable time showing us how to use the bloody equipment.

Pat didn't see it that way, and with a charm I hadn't seen him turn on before he said, 'Thank you very much, Miss Martin. You have been very helpful; we appreciate that. You are a credit to the newspaper.'

Pat's charm worked; she blushed, saying if there was anything else at all she could help him with, just ask. Then she wrote down her direct line and handed it to him.

I was smirking as she left; I knew he'd won a heart. After she'd walked away, reading me like a book, Pat said, 'Young woman, I know what you're thinking, and you have a lot to learn. It pays to keep the unnoticed people in this world on side, as they're the ones with lots of very useful information. She will go away now and rack her brain to come up with any other articles she can think of, you wait and see.'

'I didn't say a word, Pat. I felt you handled her very well.'

With a smile that transformed his face, Pat said, 'It was written all over your face. You can't bullshit a bullshitter. Now, let's get to work. We don't have much time. Here, take these three and I'll do the others. Can you remember how she said to operate these dinosaurs?'

Frustrated and concerned, I shot back, 'Yes, Pat. I can, thank you.'

'Come on, Pip, no time for being a drama queen. We need to work together on this.'

With that sage advice, we sat at separate stations and began the search. Pat knew what we were looking for. I had probably been in high school when this all had happened. After a frustratingly slow forty-five minutes, we had nothing and I could feel the tension building.

At any moment my tics were going to take off in spectacular fashion. We were in the reading room of the newspaper library surrounded by 'Quiet Please' signs. Things could only get worse.

Just try to tell a Tourettic person under pressure to relax, to calm down. Want to know what I want to say when a neurotypical person says that to me? I want to say, 'Tell you what, I'll relax and calm down if you stop breathing. Deal?'

I was soon ticcing fiercely – holding them in is like having an itch that you can't scratch, only worse.

Seeing this, Pat gently said, 'Don't worry, love, we'll find what we need. I promise.'

It was said softly and gently. No wonder he was Bill's best friend. I wanted to weep, or get up and hug him. I did neither, just smiled and thanked him with my eyes. He hadn't told me to keep the noise down. He could have – he'd chosen not to.

I'd love a hundred dollars for every time I've been told to

calm down, relax. An ex-friend once said to me, after not seeing me for years, 'I see you still have that annoying throat-clearing habit.' I found out recently from John that for years this same guy had referred to me behind my back as 'the airhead'.

Charming, right!

Tourettic people can appear to be frivolous at times, hyperactive and disjointed in their communication, their brains spitting out information at a rapid pace. We're far from how we appear, and we should never be underestimated, not ever. Oversupply of energy and quick reactions can be useful in so many ways – we were soon to find this out.

It sometimes happens to me that in the most stressful times, sudden and unexpected calm descends upon me and I have an epiphany – or a premonition, if you like.

In a flash I knew that soon we would have something positive, something concrete to work on.

I must have been smiling at this epiphany, because Pat surprised me by saying, 'So, had one of your premonitions, hey, Pip?'

I was speechless, which is rare for a person with verbal diarrhoea.

Stunned, I stuttered, 'I, um, um ...'

He smiled gently. 'Bill told me about your skills, Pip. You don't have to hide them from me. The best thing about being an old bloke is that life teaches you some lessons, the most important being to have an open mind. I've seen some things in my time that can't be explained logically. So, out with it, what did you see or feel?'

I told him I had a very distinct feeling we'd soon find what we needed.

With matching smiles, we both went back to work. Soon Emily came back with one single microfiche in her hand. She went straight to Pat. I noticed that she'd fixed her hair and put on lipstick. Pat noticed also – she was a very attractive woman and Pat was a very attractive man. He was giving her admiring glances, and I felt the tingle of a spark between them.

With a smile that transformed her looks to beautiful, she said proudly, 'I think this might be helpful. For some reason it had been archived. I was tidying the storeroom last month and came across it. Hope it's what you're looking for.'

With all his charm, Pat thanked Miss Martin. She was obviously pleased, and told him, 'My pleasure; please call me Emily.'

Pat's patience had paid off; be nice to the unnoticed people and they'll go the extra mile.

As she walked away, Pat put the microfiche into the reader. I pulled up a chair and sat next to him. The hairs on the back of my neck stood up in confirmation that soon we'd find the answer.

The article was from a time when a group of locals had been demonstrating regularly against one of the mines in the area. It discussed some problem with poisonous sulphuric acid and other toxins leaching from an abandoned coal mine into local creeks. There was mention of several arrests.

The thing that had us on the edge of our seats and ready to fly out the door was the photograph that accompanied it.

In the photo, a group of local people were demonstrating,

and right at the front of the group stood Ruth and Muriel; younger for sure, but definitely them. Even more interesting were the other people in the photograph.

To one side of the women, the caption underneath told us, were a prominent local mine owner, Mr Lindsay Jenkins, and his young son Brett. Even though it was many years ago, I recognised him right away; he'd been there when they'd taken Bill away. He was the one Albert had scared, with the evil dark brown eyes, the one I'd seen from my hiding place. There was no doubt in my mind it was him.

Another interesting fact in the article was the arresting police officer's name, Roger Scanlan, and more importantly the details of the colliery where the demonstrations took place. The article went on to say that the mine was soon to be shut down and abandoned.

It was all the information we needed.

Hands shaking, Pat printed the article, removed the microfiche and put it back into its sleeve. He wrote a note to Emily and put it back into the return tray with money to cover the printing. I grabbed the printed article from the printer and we headed for the car park. We had some work ahead of us.

We drove back to Pat's property. I was thinking about how we were going to find this colliery and hopefully rescue Bill, if in fact he was still alive. As we drove, I watched Pat's face change as he shook his head, and then a smug expression appeared.

Wanting him to share the reason for the look, I said, 'Okay, Pat, out with it – what is that enigmatic look about?'

He cleared his throat. 'I've remembered something Bill said

to me years back. I know where he met Joe, his friend in the security business. It was at the old colliery where the demos took place. He was on duty at some of the demos and struck up a friendship with one of the security guards.'

Frustrated, I said, 'And that helps us exactly how?'

Pat shook his head slightly. 'Be patient. I'm getting to that. Have a look at that photograph for me, will you.'

I pulled out the pages we'd printed, one of which included the photo. It wasn't the clearest photo, but Pat was right: there in the background was a van with the name of the security company on it.

Elated, I said, 'You're a genius Pat, you truly are.'

His tone grew measured. 'Let's hope it's Joe's business. The name doesn't sound familiar.'

On the way back to Pat's place, we stopped off at Bill's house to collect the monitoring equipment from the pantry, where Bill had told Pat he'd hidden it.

Hoping the name and contact details were on the equipment, Pat quickly pulled out the box, undid the tape and pulled the microphone and recording device out.

The name of the company, Hunter Security, was on the side of the equipment; but something much more important was taped to the bottom of the box.

Bill had sealed the recording of the phone conversation inside an envelope. On the outside he had written: '*To be opened in the event of my disappearance or untimely death*'.

His message sent shivers down both our spines. Inside was a precise note, written in Bill's handwriting.

Dear Joe,

Firstly, I hope things are going well for you, Marg and especially for young Daniel. He's a good kid and I'm sure he'll make you both proud one day.

Thanks for the loan of the equipment, mate. I really appreciate you not asking any questions. A couple of favours – if anything should happen to me, if I should suddenly disappear, can you make sure that this tape is given to Pat Cawley, please?

Also, can you ask Pat to look out for Pip, a friend of mine who has been staying here? Pat knows most of the background story. Pip can fill in the rest.

I owe you an explanation, but I don't want you to be in any danger, so I'll just say it's to do with the disappearance of Ruth Richards. Be very careful who you confide in about this.

Thanks again, Joe. I'm hoping to thank you properly myself over a meal and a few beers soon, mate.

Sincerely,

Bill

Pat and I quickly taped up the box. I put the envelope safely in my backpack. Pat looked at me and said, 'We've got some equipment to return, and a note to hand over.'

As we were about to leave, Pat noticed a message light flashing on Bill's phone. We stood there transfixed, staring at that blinking light, both feeling agitated and apprehensive. Then Pat pushed the play button.

We held our breath and silently listened. The recording went, 'Oh, hi, Bill, it's Brendan O'Connor here. Sorry, I've been away. I got your message. Yes, I did help Ruth Richards change her will. There's more I need to tell you, but not on the phone; um, can you call me, please, so we can arrange to meet?'

He'd left his phone number, which Pat quickly wrote down.

CHAPTER 28

When we arrived at Hunter Security, Joe, a big man, was at his desk. As he stood, Pat introduced me and we shook hands. Joe was very solid in build, with a gut that showed he enjoyed his food. His handshake was extremely firm and his face was pleasant rather than handsome, especially when he smiled.

Pat didn't waste time filling Joe in, and immediately handing him Bill's note said, 'Mate, can you read this please? Bill's missing; we need your help.'

As Joe read the note, his broad face paled with shock. 'What on earth is going on? Bill said he was onto something; this sounds serious.'

We told Joe everything that had happened, right back to my time in Ruth's Cottage. He listened, more concerned with every word.

Joe was another person Bill had helped. When their son Daniel had gone off the rails on drugs, Bill had taken him under his wing and tried to save him from self-destruction.

After hearing the entire story, with a look of determination on his face Joe asked, 'So, how can I help? What do you want me to do?'

Pat responded. 'Firstly, did you remove the bug from Walton's house today?'

A perplexed look on his face, Joe responded, 'No, I didn't; Walton called saying he'd have to put the service off. He said he had a lot on and would get back to me.'

Pat and I looked at one another, and Pat said, 'That's great news.'

Joe shrugged slightly. 'I'm glad to be the bearer of good news. How exactly does that help find Bill?'

'It's a big ask,' said Pat, 'but could you set it up so we can continue to monitor any calls Walton makes?'

Joe's eyes widened. 'Yeah, sure; but if you're going to help Bill, I want to be there. I can ask Marg to listen to any calls. She could text me if she hears anything relevant.'

Pat and I shared a look; we could use Joe's expertise, but we knew that by involving him we could be putting him in danger.

'Before you make up your mind about this,' said Pat, 'I need to return a call. Ruth Richards' solicitor Brendan O'Connor left a message on Bill's machine sometime in the past twenty-four hours. Once I call him, we can make a more informed decision on where to go from here. I'll put him on speaker, but to speed things up, I'll do the talking.'

Joe and I nodded. Pat's call was answered on the fourth ring.

'Brendan O'Connor.'

We could hear children playing in the background.

Pat jumped straight in. 'Hi, Brendan, my name is Pat Cawley. I'm a friend of Bill Browne. I'm here with two other friends of his. We have you on speaker. Bill's gone missing and we're very concerned for his safety.'

I was stunned at first with his blunt approach. But Pat was right; we didn't have time for subtleties.

After a moment, Brendan O'Connor said quietly, 'Hang on a minute, will you? I'm on speaker. I need to go outside.'

When he came back onto the phone, the tension in his voice was palpable. We hoped his wife and children hadn't heard what Pat had said.

Brendan said, 'Sorry; I wanted to get out of earshot of my wife and kids.'

'I'm sorry,' said Pat earnestly. 'I didn't realise you were on speaker.'

'It's okay; they didn't hear. My wife is in the laundry and the kids are watching *Peppa Pig*. Can you tell me what's happened?'

Pat filled him in with as much information as he needed.

We heard the worry in Brendan's voice as he said, 'Bloody hell. I was afraid something like this might happen. These are very dangerous people you're dealing with. I'm trying to keep my family safe from them.'

'We understand, and we don't want you to get involved as such. We just need the information you talked about in your message to Bill, please.'

Brendan thought for a minute, but acquiesced. 'Shit, I'm

sick of hiding out from these mongrels anyway. I've already moved my family to Pittwater to keep them safe. What do you need to know? I'd do anything to get these animals off the street so I could sleep nights.'

We looked at one another, and Pat answered for all three of us. 'Thanks, Brendan; we appreciate the position you're in, but you and your family should be safe living in Pittwater.'

'Yes, my wife's family live here. They know what those scum threatened me with, so they're always on the lookout for people who don't belong. Luckily everyone here notices when blow-ins appear, especially with the only way in and out being by boat.'

Alarmed, Pat asked, 'What did they threaten you with?'

His answer chilled us. 'They said if I ever told anyone about my last conversation with Ruth, I'd find my wife and kids missing, and they'd never be found again – just like Ruth.'

The three of us looked at one another, shaking our heads. Finally, Pat responded, 'That must have been harrowing. Sounds like we need to involve the police. Is there anything else you can tell us that might help us find Bill?'

Brendan paused. 'Not that immediately comes to mind; let me think. Ruth told me on the phone that she'd heard some very disturbing information about her nephew, hence the reason for the will change. She was going to elaborate at our meeting. Unfortunately, she didn't turn up.' He stopped for a while again, thinking. Then he said, 'He had two thugs with him as a back-up when the threats were made. I'll describe them to you.'

As he gave a rundown of the thugs, Pat looked at me and I nodded my head in confirmation. They were surely the same men who'd broken into my townhouse.

Brendan said if we needed him to, he'd speak to the police and gladly go to court when the time came. Pat promised to let Brendan know as soon as we had any news.

We all thanked him in chorus, then reiterated that we'd involve the police. We told him to try not to worry, that soon they would have their lives back – we hoped so, anyway.

After he'd hung up, Pat suggested we listen to the phone calls from Walton's house that Bill had taped. We did so, and one part of call that stood out was, *'Good, and once you do, get back to me so we can make plans to shift it Saturday evening! We need that out of the way before the shipment leaves.'*

We sat for a time, analysing that last sentence, wondering what the shipment was.

Eventually Joe shared a family secret. 'Our son Dannie is heavily into drugs again. Marg and I know he has a local dealer close by in the Hunter. The shipment could be drugs.'

The more we delved, the more we realised we were out of our depth. Our main priority was finding Bill, and finding him soon.

Fact – we knew they were going to a colliery on the night they took Bill. Knowing this, Pat asked, 'Do you have any information on the abandoned Waratah Colliery, the one you did the security detail on where you first met Bill?'

Joe jumped straight up. 'I do! I don't throw anything out, which annoys the hell out of Marg. Give me a while; I'll need to go through some archived boxes I've got in the shed.'

Soon Joe was back, covered in dust but looking much happier; he'd found some plans of the old colliery. Joe put the answering machine on, then locked up, pulling down the shades. 'The plans should come in handy if they're holding Bill there,' he told us.

After looking over these plans, we had our own plan set. We'd drive to the colliery come nightfall, and hopefully find Bill still alive.

Our plan went like this: Pat and I would head to Pat's place, prepare for tonight and have something to eat – not that I felt like eating, but still.

Joe would go home, fill Marg in and get her to keep tabs on Walton's calls, texting us if she heard anything, then Joe would head to Pat's, arriving around four thirty.

We'd drive out to the old colliery in Joe's work van. Joe felt no one would take much notice if they saw his van out there; he regularly patrolled several of the old sites.

Meanwhile he'd have everything we'd need: wire cutters, torches, thermal imaging scopes, and, as he was a licenced security guard, his gun.

As well, we'd have Bill's old Glock 22 service pistol, which Pat had grabbed last night, and the Highlander M85 bolt-action rifle Pat used to shoot foxes. We hoped like hell we wouldn't have to use them.

Once back at Pat's, I packed my backpack with water, food and a first aid kit. If Bill was alive, he'd be thirsty, hungry and he may need medical attention.

I wanted to take Burt along, but Pat wasn't so sure. I won. Burt had his own set of skills; like a lot of Rottweilers, he was exceptional at following a scent.

We were as ready as any ragtag rescue team could be. All I had to do now was wait for Joe, find some courage and focus.

When I was out of the shower and dressed, I walked into the lounge room. Pat looked at me, sniffed loudly, and a little tersely said, 'Pip, is that patchouli oil you've got on?'

Burt wasn't the only one with a good nose.

Perplexed as to why he'd asked I said, 'Yes, it is.'

'Go and scrub it off. They'll smell you coming a mile off.' He was right, of course – why not take a brass band and lights as well?

Apologetically I said, 'Sorry, Pat; I'll do that straight away.'

As I stood in front of the mirror in Pat's bathroom scrubbing off the patchouli, I felt a physical coldness in the room, then a very strong smell of roses. I knew Ruth was with me.

I stopped scrubbing and looked around the room. I found no evidence of her presence, only the deep, redolent smell of roses; tonight that scent was overpowering.

A shiver passed through me, affected by her ethereal presence. I knew she had something very important to tell me, to show me.

As I turned back toward the mirror, within it I saw a misty shape of Ruth that shimmered, then disappeared, then shimmered again and reappeared.

It was as if she stood right in front of me, close enough to touch. I knew intellectually this wasn't possible, but still her presence was tangible.

Then Ruth smiled and nodded her head slowly, acknowledging my presence. Once she'd reassured me, she began what I can only describe as a lesson, instructing me on how to safely open a portal within Pat's bathroom mirror.

I stood there mesmerised, watching her every move. She turned and looked deeply into another mirror within this mirror. She raised her right hand, then, one finger at a time, pressed each finger onto the glass of this inner mirror, at the same time looking over her shoulder to make sure I understood.

When she'd finished the lesson, she turned back, looked me in the eyes and nodded. I felt she was saying, *'Now it's your turn; be brave, be strong.'* Those last four words sent another shiver of fear up my spine and into my heart.

As her image disappeared, I shook my head, took a deep breath, then slowly and tentatively began to follow her instructions. I felt I was moving in slow motion, outside my body. I raised my right hand, then one finger at a time slowly placed each one onto the surface of the mirror. I knew instinctively that once I'd tapped into this portal, I'd witness something important through my third eye. It was time for me to fulfil my role, to become a seeker of the truth.

As my thumb, the last digit to touch the mirror, made contact, my eyes blurred and my head went light as a point in the mirror swirled open. I was looking through a portal into the past, seeing the night of Ruth's demise.

Once my eyes focussed, the first scene was of Ruth, her diary clutched to her chest, asleep in her bed – the same bed I'd slept in. I couldn't take my eyes off her as she lay with a ginger kitten – Albert – by her side.

As I watched, Ruth was woken by a noise. She sat up, looking very afraid, peering out her bedroom window.

I saw a pair of evil faces peering through her bedroom window: the two men who'd broken into my townhouse. Ruth, seeing them, got bravely out of bed.

She was showing me, step by step, what had happened on that night over three years ago. I saw her tear a page from her diary and put the book onto her bedside table. She took a deep breath, threw back her shoulders, tilted her chin and walked toward the door, bravely opening it and stepping onto the veranda.

As she did, one of the men lunged at her, knocking her to the ground. I saw Ruth fumbling, trying to wedge the page she'd torn from her diary between the cracks in the veranda floor.

Someone pulled her to her feet. As he did, she tried to scream, to struggle from his grasp, but her little body failed her. She must have been so terrified by now, this brave woman.

What I saw, heard and smelled will haunt me forever; their brutality was frenzied and savage. When they dragged her down into the vineyard, she was pulled up time and time again by her hair, and despite her desperate muffled screams and pleading, she was stabbed repeatedly in the chest and upper body.

Two of them worked on her, one stabbing, the other kicking her in the stomach, the ribs, wherever he could reach. The amount of blood she lost was staggering; her unheard cries for help broke my heart.

I smelled fear mixed with the metallic scent of blood and desperate last-minute bodily functions. Though terrified, Ruth was brave to the end, and would not give up her struggle to survive.

A third man stood at a distance, passively looking on, a disinterested bystander. He appeared to be in charge though, and I recognised him also; it was Brett Jenkins.

Finally, bored with her struggles to survive, one of the men put a plastic bag over her head and watched as she slowly suffocated. When she finally stopped struggling, she was dragged down further into the vineyard.

As Ruth finally lay dead, I overheard disjointed snippets of conversation between the three men. One, showing a touch of remorse in his voice, said, *'I've got no fucking idea why he wanted to kill the poor old cow. She's his own flesh and blood.'*

A second one, active in the killing, sneeringly responded, *'The silly old bitch overheard him on the phone organising a shipment, and confronted him about it.'*

The third one, pumped up and euphoric on a post-kill high, let out a sinister, chilling and high-pitched laugh. He said, *'That'll teach the old bitch to eavesdrop.'*

Nothing in my life had prepared me for what I'd seen and heard in that vision; it was horrifying. I was so sickened by what I'd witnessed, I was about to be physically ill, then my vision blurred, my head grew light and another set of images appeared.

As the heavens opened, I saw them burying Ruth. I now understood why Albert had been digging at that one particular rose bush when I stayed in Ruth's Cottage.

Once more my vision blurred; as my eyes refocussed I saw one final vision. I saw the man in charge, who'd remained clear of the violence, take his shoes off and walk into the cottage, and into Ruth's bedroom.

He climbed on the bed, and pushed on the secret door in the tongue-and-groove ceiling. It swung open, and he reached in and took down a box from the hiding place. It was the box that now sat in David Walton's office.

I now understood why Ruth had wanted me to see that hiding place when I'd stayed there.

As he was about to leave the cottage, he picked up her diary and quickly flicked through it. Seeming reassured, he laughed, put it back on her bedside table, took one last look around and left.

I stood there for some time with my mouth open, eyes wide with fear, gasping for breath. My pounding heart was the only noise I could hear.

Then I heard Ruth's voice clearly say, '*Turn away from the mirror, turn away – you know the truth, you can now avenge my death. You are safe, Pip, always safe, I will protect you; thank you.*'

As my third eye – or at least the portal to the truth – closed, I slowly began to come back into my body, back to consciousness. I understood now at a cellular level how vigilantes are made. I no longer wondered about where they found their moral certainty; now I had my own. Ruth had given me the courage to not only find Bill but to avenge her death.

Anger thrilled through me like a flame, coupled with an intense desire to find Bill, knowing he was in grave danger. That anger would come in handy, giving me the courage and the strength to face whatever tonight held.

I was brought abruptly back to the present by Pat yelling my name and loudly banging on the bathroom door, asking me to unlock it.

I had no memory of locking that door.

As I sat on Pat's lounge, drinking a strong, sweet cup of tea he'd insisted I drink, he told me Albert had flown into the house like a wild animal, running straight to the bathroom door. He'd growled and wailed loudly, then started madly scratching at the door to get inside, to me, and perhaps to Ruth.

As I recounted the vision to Pat, he sat silently holding my hand. Pat had no words of comfort; there were no words. Albert tried his best to soothe me by jumping onto my lap and trying to lick my face.

As I looked down at Albert's dear little face, I knew we'd need to lock him inside before we left, to keep him safe.

As I thought this, my mind in Tourettic overdrive, a feeling of stress-induced delirium passed over me. I thought that if Albert knew what I was thinking, and he could talk, he'd say to me, *'No you don't; you won't be leaving the cat at home tonight.'*

Thinking this, an odd and unanticipated giggle erupted from me. A look of grave concern passed over Pat's face.

I said, 'Don't worry, Pat. I'm fine – just a bit of stress-induced hysteria.'

He didn't get a chance to answer. Joe had pulled up outside, and Pat went to let him in, giving me time to pull myself together. Ruth's reassurance tonight had helped me feel a peace I shouldn't have felt.

I also felt a new determination, a new urgency to find Bill, and a resolve that had hardened me. We'd find Bill; we'd also get those men for what they'd done to Ruth. Knowing that kept me sane.

CHAPTER 29

When Joe sat, we filled him in. As I recounted my vision, disbelief showed on his perplexed face. With my newfound zeal, I didn't care; I simply told him what I'd seen – we didn't have time to convince him.

With Pat's acceptance of what I'd recounted, Joe soon accepted at least some of what I'd seen. If he had doubts, he kept them to himself. As the gravity of the situation sank in, Joe's usually pleasant face transformed, and he became very angry about what they'd done to Ruth, a woman he'd admired and liked.

My visions, courtesy of Ruth, gave us all the edge we needed – we were very angry and very ready.

At my insistence, we'd put Burt in the van. I'd planned on leaving Albert safely inside, but we couldn't find him; he was nowhere to be found outside or inside. Eventually we gave up looking for him.

Just before we were about to leave, Pat said, 'I'm going to put that call through to the young policeman Bill said he trusted.

I won't be long. I'll go outside; the reception is better.'

It was then I knew Pat was also a very bad liar; there was nothing wrong with the reception. Just as I was about to protest, a text pinged its arrival on my mobile.

It was from Uncle J, and it read, '*What's wrong?*'

Typically, he'd picked up that all was not well with me. I know the old saying – *a problem shared is a problem halved* – but you know what? Sometimes a problem shared is a problem doubled.

I was feeling brave and full of resolve, so I sent him back a very ambiguous text saying, '*Don't worry; never felt more sure, more strong. Trust me; talk tomorrow. Love you.*'

I knew Uncle J wouldn't believe my text, but instead of burdening me with his doubts, he simply texted back, '*Okay, I'll trust your instincts; stay safe. Phone me when you can. Love you more.*'

Pat walked back into the room. Joe was ahead of me in asking questions. 'So, what did he say? Did he believe you? Is he meeting us there?'

Pat, nodding, filled us in on the conversation. 'Yep, he did. He told me if Bill's in danger, he's in. Apparently, Bill once covered his arse when he was a rookie, and he's never forgotten that. He's going to drive out that way and meet us about a kilometre from the colliery. Then he's coming in the van with us. Come on, we need to go.'

Joe breathed a deep sigh of relief. Pat locked up, and we walked to the van. As we went, Joe said, 'That's good news. We need all the help we can get.'

I nodded. Before we piled into the van, I took one last unsuccessful look around for Albert.

It was dark, cold and we were fired up – me in particular. Joe reiterated that no one would take any notice if they saw his van out that way. He assured us that the element of surprise would give us the edge we badly needed.

The drive felt interminable, and soon I was ticcing fiercely. All I could think was, *Give me a break*. No such luck; the closer we got, the worse my tics became.

I knew that once we got there, I'd control them. That's what I've done most of my life, control my urge to tic to save myself embarrassment and others annoyance.

As we drove, I thought about what I'd witnessed tonight. Not for the first time, I wondered if my neurodiversity helped enhance the neural activity in my brain, giving me access to other realms, to things past, things present and things future.

As I was thinking this, my tics subsided. Mistaking my silence for nerves, Pat turned around and reassuringly said, 'You're quiet, Pip. I know you're nervous, we all are. This will go well, especially now we have some police backup.'

I responded honestly. 'I am nervous, Pat; I'd be an idiot not to be. That wasn't why I was quiet though; I was just reflecting on a few things.'

As I said this, the police officer, who'd already arrived at the rendezvous site, flagged us down, jolting us all back to reality as the gravity of the situation sank in.

He'd parked his car out of view. When we pulled up, he quickly jumped into the back of the van and sat next to me and Burt. Nervously he introduced himself, 'Hi, I'm Senior Constable Donovan. Call me Connor.'

Joe didn't waste any time, hitting the accelerator before Connor had his belt on. Pat turned, hand-out to shake his and do the introductions, saying, 'Thanks for coming; I'm Pat Cawley, this is Joe, and the young woman next to you is Philippa, Pip for short. We appreciate you taking this risk, Connor.'

Connor didn't hesitate. 'Trust me, if it wasn't for Bill, I wouldn't have a career to risk. I hope you don't mind. I put my partner on stand-by. I didn't give him too many details, just said if I was to get in touch he was to respond quickly.'

Though Pat's face showed concern, his voice remained calm. 'Bill trusts you and if you trust him, good move. Now you're here, you're in charge. How do you want to handle this?'

For the rest of the ride to the colliery, the men discussed tactics. I sat there listening, with a mounting feeling that I wasn't going to be allowed to contribute.

When we got to the site, Joe cut the engine and lights and coasted to a well-hidden spot behind an embankment and off the road.

Constable Donovan turned to me and, with as much authority as a very nervous, very young Senior Constable could muster, said, 'I'm sorry, Pip; I need you to stay here in the van with the dog. We need to make sure he – um, sorry I don't know his name – doesn't give us away. Keep him quiet, please. Joe, you can lead us to the way in, then I need both of you to follow my lead, okay?'

All I could think was, *Good try, another not-very-good liar.* He'd used Burt as an excuse to keep me, the woman, out of harm's way. I was beyond livid, but what choice did I have?

Seeing how upset I felt now, Pat turned toward me gently, saying, 'The young man's in charge, Pip, and he's right. We don't know what to expect once we get beyond that fence. The last thing we need is for Burt to start barking. Tell you what, if we need you and Burt, I'll give a loud whistle, and you can both come running. Deal?'

I was too pissed off to answer civilly, so I tersely shot back one word: 'Fine!'

As I watched, Joe in the lead, they made their way to a spot in the fence that was easy to climb through. I have to admit, there was a part of me that was relieved to be in the van – just a tiny part.

Wanting a better view, Burt moved over my lap, and tried to squeeze his very large head through the gap in the window, sniffing the air. As I concentrated on keeping him calm, my tics slowly subsided and my stress levels dropped a little. Thank God for animals.

I sat there watching them make their way into the site. Without warning, Burt started a low growl, and I knew something was very wrong. Settling him first, I wound the car window down, wiping the condensation from the glass so I had a better view.

The boys were crawling further in. Meanwhile in my peripheral vision, I spotted someone over to their left. I couldn't warn them; I felt impotent.

In my mind, Ruth said, '*Go in there; distract this man. You'll be safe.*'

So much for feeling relieved. As I securely tied Burt's lead to the steering wheel, I gave him a firm, whispered command: 'Burt, be a good boy and stay here. Be quiet and stay.'

Quickly and silently, I jumped out of the van, reaching over to grab my backpack. Once I had it on, I gently shut the door and made my way into the site.

I'd just reached the fence when guess who flew past me? Give up?

Albert – he'd been in the van the whole time. The first thing I thought was, *I guess, like the woman, the cat didn't want to be left out of the action.* The second thing I thought was that I knew he'd be safe; I knew we'd find him later. Ruth would make sure of that.

As I crept along, now between the stray figure and my friends, my clothes became sodden from the heavy dew. My companions had stopped; I knew they'd seen the man. He was so close to me I could smell him – he'd just finished a cigarette.

As I studied his face in the moonlight, I saw an unkempt beard and a slightly turned eye – not much more. Still, I was certain I'd never seen him before, which could come in handy.

As I was thinking this, Ruth commanded, '*Stand up, now.*' I did.

We collided heavily, leaving us both momentarily winded. He shone a torch in my face, shook his head in relief and disbelief, grabbed my arm roughly and demanded, 'Whoa, what are you doing here?'

Thankfully a certain kind of role-playing comes naturally to me; I'd played a role my entire life. I'd played normal.

To distract him from my friends, in a startled and angry tone and through now-chattering teeth, I spat out the first thing that came to mind. 'Oh, for God's sake, you frightened the crap out of me.'

Twisting my arm further, he said, 'Answer my question. What are you doing here?'

Mouth dry, palms sweating, I said, 'My car broke down. I saw a light, and came here hoping someone could help me. I thought this was a farmhouse.'

I know, it wasn't my best effort, but I was genuinely terrified. He thought for a while, then, sounding unconvinced and unsure, twisted my arm again. 'That sounds like bullshit. You'd better come with me.'

As he dragged me off in the dark, he shone his torch around, making sure I was on my own. I hoped like hell the guys were in hiding. As we walked, I stumbled on the uneven ground, slipping on loose gravel.

Thrown off-guard, he grabbed my elbow to help me up. 'Be careful, the ground's very uneven. It's not much further; once the boss speaks to you, if you really have broken down, we might be able to help.'

Mock indignation filled my voice, 'Of course I've broken down. Why the hell else would I be out here at this time of night?'

I was running out of puff and felt grateful when I saw the shape of a lit shed in the distance. Built of rusty corrugated iron, it was nestled in a gully not visible from the road.

I knew his boss was inside; I hoped Bill was too.

As we reached the door, he rapped on it three times. It was soon opened, and another man I'd never seen before stepped outside.

When he saw me, he said angrily, 'Where was she, Cleary? Was she on her own?'

Cleary responded immediately. 'Boss, she says she's broken down. I didn't see anyone else; I'm pretty sure she's alone.'

Boss-man didn't sound at all impressed. 'You fucking moron. Have a look around and report back to me if you smell a whiff of anything being wrong. Go, and keep that fucking two-way on.'

After he'd finished hauling Cleary over the coals, he grabbed my arm savagely, and with anger in his voice said, 'I know who you are and I know you're looking for Browne. Stop the bullshit and tell me who else is here with you.'

I thought he'd dislocate my shoulder. Through my pain I managed to say, 'Stop, you're hurting me. Pat Cawley was supposed to come with me but he got pissed instead. He's either paralytic drunk or unconscious as we speak.'

Finding this amusing, he burst out laughing, letting go of my arm as he did. It's hard to laugh and break someone's arm at the same time, I guess.

His laugher made me wild. There's nothing like anger to give you extra strength and courage.

After he stopped laughing, he said, 'That sounds like Pat, all right; once a drunk, always a drunk.'

He composed himself and pushed me inside, slamming the

door, then he thrust me along a cold, dark corridor to another door. As he opened it and shoved me heavily inside, he said, 'Look who Cleary found. The dickhead fell for the story her car had broken down.'

As my eyes adjusted to the stronger light in this room, I saw that there were two other men here. To my horror, I recognised them – they were the two thugs who'd killed Ruth, the two who'd broken into my townhouse and hurt John.

At the shock of seeing them, my head went light and I nearly collapsed. I hoped like hell my friends had seen where I'd been taken.

To add fuel to my feelings of total helplessness, one of the thugs picked up a gun and aimed it at me.

Twisting my arm further to show he had control, the one in charge said, 'Relax, dickhead, put that down. I was right; using Browne as bait worked.'

As the other put the gun down, he laughed. It was a harsh, jarring sound that froze my blood. With undisguised glee, he malevolently said, 'Well, if it isn't the fucking bitch that started all this. Where was she, Scanlan? Was she on her own?'

So I had a name now – boss-man was Scanlan.

Tightening his grip and twisting my arm further, Scanlan hissed his response. 'So she says.'

With courage I wasn't feeling I said, 'Ouch! Do you mind? You're hurting me.'

The gun-happy one came toward me, sneering. 'We'll do more than fucking hurt you before the night's out.'

From the look on his face, I could tell he had plans, and I wasn't going to be a willing participant in them. The hairs on the back of my neck stood up as an involuntary shiver passed through my body. Mind racing, trying to decide how to survive this situation, I quickly looked around for any sign of Bill – there was none.

Suggestively grabbing his crotch, the thug's voice was chilling. 'Let her go, Scanlan, so I can have some fun.'

At this, the one with the crew cut spoke up. He had a beer gut, nervous twitch and a voice that sounded like a footballer who'd been hit in the throat a few too many times. He rasped, 'Watch out, mate; that dick of yours is going to get you into trouble one day.'

Scanlan shot them both a withering look. 'He's right. We've got more pressing issues than your dick. Get out there and find out if she's alone. I don't trust that moron Cleary. Put your dick away and concentrate.' He gave the one with the beer gut a cold look. 'Have either of you checked Browne lately? No? Well, for fuck's sake go and bring him back here.'

As they walked past me, the slimy one with plans for me said, 'Later, bitch.'

I couldn't leave it alone. As he passed, I leaned forward and whispered, 'I know what you two cowards did to Ruth Richards. I know the truth.'

Hearing this, he spun around so fast he looked like Linda Blair from *The Exorcist*. He spat at me, 'What did you say, you fucking witch? You just signed your own death warrant.'

As he went to grab me, Scanlan shouted, 'I said go and get

Browne. You can kill the bitch later. I've got some questions to ask her first. Now piss off.'

Thankfully, they were good at taking orders. I hoped like hell I'd stalled them long enough to give the guys time to find Bill.

Once they'd left, Scanlan turned to me, pointed to a folding chair, harshly pushed me into it and said, 'Sit down; we need to talk.'

I did; my options were running out fast.

I hoped the boys would see these two thugs leaving and follow them to where Bill was being held.

To distract Scanlan, I tried to worry him. 'Oh, one thing I forgot to tell you; I phoned the police before I came. They should be here soon.'

His immediate response was to raise his hand as if to slap my face. Instead, he took a hand in the game of chance and said, 'I don't believe you; I'd know if you had.'

All I could think was, *Bugger, he does have someone else on the inside.* I just hoped it wasn't Connor's partner, the one he'd put on standby.

My next ploy was to try to get him talking about himself. Pat had told me Scanlan had once been a brave and decent cop. He'd met a woman who'd wanted more than a policeman's salary could provide. To find the funds to keep her interested, he must have gone astray. The relationship didn't last, but he'd already crossed to the dark side.

Thinking fast, if not cleverly, I tried steering him into what I hoped would be a long and distracting conversation. 'I don't understand how someone like you could be involved with people like them. I've heard you're a good cop, a brave cop even; you rescued that family from their flooded car. Those aren't the actions of a bad man. How come you're involved with these people?'

This seemed to throw him, and a rush of emotions crossed his face. But he was quick to turn patronising. 'You're young. Life hasn't had the time to show you how things really are. You're right, I have been a good cop, and I guess a brave one. It didn't do me any favours, so I've decided to invest some time and energy into my future. These people are scum, but they're going to help me retire comfortably.'

My brain wasn't in the right gear tonight. Carelessly I responded, 'Really, that's it? It's all about greed?'

Those seven little words enraged him.

He was so angry, so wild, that he started to scream at me. First, he grabbed me by the shoulders and began to shake me; then, as he continued to hurl abuse at me, he put his hands around my throat and proceeded to choke the life out of me.

With spittle flying from his mouth all over my face, he ranted, 'You're a smart-arse little bitch. You have no idea, the things I've seen, what I've had to endure in this job. I've seen the likes of them get away with murder; the money they've made from being on the other side of the law. What I'm making on the side here is the least I deserve after a lifetime wasted looking after ungrateful bitches like you, protecting you from vermin like them.' As he continued to choke me, his voice grew self-pitying. 'You'd never understand how hard it's been for me. You don't have the faintest fucking idea.'

I was finding it harder to breathe, struggling with what strength I had to pull his hands away from my throat.

The door flew open. The wind was literally knocked out of me as I hit the ground, Scanlan falling on top of me.

It was Burt who had knocked us to the ground, but it was Bill now trying to pull Burt off Scanlan before he killed him, or in the process me.

In the pandemonium, still gasping for breath, I tried desperately to push myself away from the snarling, slobbering, vicious attack dog darling Burt had turned into.

Bill was trying hard to pull Burt off Scanlan and away from me. Burt had accidentally bitten me several times in the chaos. Eventually I got my breath back, and Bill had Burt under control.

Now I had a chance to look at Bill properly for the first time. He had bruises on his face and neck, and his face looked a little dehydrated. Apart from that he looked amazingly well.

With Scanlan secured and Burt now subdued, Bill came over to me and bent down. Concern filled his voice as he asked tenderly, 'Are you okay, Pip? I'm sorry – Burt didn't mean to hurt you. You were just in his way.'

I tried to reassure him, my voice a croak. 'I'm okay, Bill. How are you? We've been so worried about you.'

My throat was too sore to continue; instead, I pathetically burst into tears.

Sensing I was upset, Burt began to growl ferociously at Scanlan again. Bill called him off; Burt begrudgingly complied.

It was obvious Burt had made a mess of Scanlan, particularly his hands and face. He'd need medical attention for some deep punctures. He'd probably need stitches, a tetanus shot and antibiotics – we'd both need the last two.

Connor, Joe and Pat came into the shed, the other two culprits in tow, their hands cuffed behind their backs. We soon found out their names.

One – Robbo – looked like he had come out of a fight in the ring, with Joe Lewis the winner. The other – Ace – had his face and neck a bloody mess, covered in very nasty and angry scratches. There was no sign of Cleary.

Connor was soon on his two-way calling for backup from his partner.

While we waited for other police to arrive, the men, still in awe, recounted the role Albert had played in helping them successfully detain the scumbags.

After I was pushed into the shed, they'd watched and waited until they saw the two men, on Scanlan's orders, leave.

From their position, Pat, Joe and Connor watched, stunned, as Albert had stealthily followed the two men to the shed where they were holding Bill. While the two men fumbled with the lock in the dark, Albert found his way inside the shed through a broken window.

As they'd rushed into the shed where Bill was being held, Albert had conducted his own surprise sting, flinging himself from a shelf onto Ace's head. Accompanied by horrifying wailing, spitting, scratching and snarling, Albert had proceeded to shred his face.

Horrified and distracted by Albert's attack on his sidekick,

Robbo had failed to see Pat, Joe and Connor enter the shed until it was too late. While Albert made a mess of Ace's face, Connor felled the man with a kick to the back of his knees, jumped on him and cuffed him.

They had then tentatively disengaged Albert from Ace's face and secured him as well. Albert the vigilante cat had helped by using the twin elements of surprise and vengeance. His vengeance, they assured me, had been brutal, swift and thorough.

There is nothing more disturbing than the primal wail of a very angry cat – it comes right from the gut and sends shivers through you. Albert had a score he'd waited years to settle. When a cat was hissing, snarling, wailing, flailing and carrying on like Albert, it was safest to give him some space – and for a time, Pat and the others had.

Finally, Albert had slumped, spent from his vicious altercation and from taking revenge against the man who'd been the cruellest to his Ruth.

All throughout Albert's attack, they told me, Burt – apart from the occasional teeth-baring and growling at the already-subdued Robbo – had mostly stood with his mouth open watching his feline friend. Apparently, they'd all watched in awed silence, marvelling at the ferocity of Albert's long-awaited retribution.

When the boys had finished recounting these incredible events, with dread in my heart, I croaked, 'Oh no. The poor little fellow. Is he okay?'

They looked incredulously at one another, then all four burst out laughing.

Why is it that at times of debilitating stress we humans do that? Freud and his ilk gave it a name – paradoxical laughter. By now I was trying to hold it in myself as I defensively croaked, 'What? What's so funny?'

The others were laughing too much to respond, so, feeling sorry for me Pat said, 'You'd be better off asking how the low-life he attacked is, Pip.'

Between guffaws, Joe jumped in with, 'Yeah, you should take a close look at the face the cat used as a ladder.'

Regaining some composure, Bill added, 'Yeah, remind me never to get on that cat's bad side.'

Connor, tears rolling down his face, added, 'Totally agree, mate; wish he was my partner. The last I saw of him, he was outside de-barking a tree.'

Pat had a final laconic viewpoint. 'We should dub Albert and Burt the "A-Team" – honestly, you should have seen them.'

Their relief, their laughter, was infectious, and soon I had my own tears of laughter and relief running down my face. Every time I took a breath between laughs, my throat and my ribs hurt like hell. The pain and the ecstasy of the relief that Bill was still alive and that I was still alive were a heady mix.

At that moment Albert hurtled sideways into the room, ready for action. I was amused to see that, in unison, Burt and four strong men quickly stepped back from me, giving Albert space.

From his concerned demeanour toward me, I knew that if Albert could have spoken, he would have said, *Are you okay? If those animals – no, that's an insult to animals – if those humans did this to you, I'll rip them apart. I'll, I'll …'*

He was quite obviously still in fight-or-flight mode. To calm him down, I bent forward, cautiously picked him up and put him over my shoulder, saying gently, 'Come here, my little hero. I believe we owe you a huge debt of gratitude. You brave boy. I'm so proud of you.'

As I gently smoothed his fur, cooing endearments, he settled a little.

I couldn't help but smile at the shocked looks on the faces of all the males in the room – Burt included.

Shaking his head, Connor was the first to speak next. 'Shit; you're braver than I am, picking that cat up like that.'

My only response was a proud and enigmatic smile.

As I gently continued to stroke him, Albert calmed down and started to purr loudly.

I'd seen first-hand in my vision in Pat's bathroom the horror of what he'd witnessed, the brutality of what was done to the one person who, in his short life, had shown him true love.

I understood that in losing Ruth, Albert had lost his world, his security, his reason to ever trust again. To reassure him, I gently kissed the top of his head and whispered in his ear, 'Don't worry, my darling, we'll look after one another. I promise you no one will ever hurt either of us again.'

CHAPTER 30

It was then that we heard the car. My immediate reaction was to panic and, still clutching Albert, I jumped up. Connor reassured me, saying he'd put through a call to his partner; it was the local police who'd come to give us a hand.

Relieved, I dropped to a crouch, still clutching Albert. Now that I felt safe, I started to shake. My body flooded with a huge adrenaline dump. Some obscure neurotransmitter deep inside my brain, as old as evolution itself, sent the signal that I was out of danger and could come out of fight-or-flight mode.

Of course, the night wasn't over; there were others to apprehend. Bill quickly spoke to the police, telling them the whole story.

After a look around the old colliery, they found boxes that contained drugs – methamphetamine, to be exact. Scanlan's comments now made sense; along with the others, he was profiting from the sale of illegal drugs.

The police needed to get to Ruth's Cottage fast, before the

other two realised something had gone wrong. The three men now in custody, scoring points, had divulged their plans for the night: they'd intended to meet Walton and Jenkins at the cottage around 1 a.m.

Once there, they'd planned to dig up Ruth's remains and bring them back to the colliery, where they were to be disposed of, along with Bill Browne, down a ventilation shaft, never to be found.

Burt, Albert and I went with Joe in his van. The police had agreed that Bill and Pat should drive Scanlan's car so as not to alert the others that anything was amiss. On the drive there – now that I wasn't concentrating on staying alive – my tics came back in earnest.

Joe turned to me and said kindly, 'You did really well tonight. You're safe now, and so is Bill, thanks to you and the dynamic duo next to you. That's some cat you've inherited.'

Close to tears, I haltingly responded, 'Thanks, Joe; you guys were amazing. I can't take much credit.'

When we arrived at Walton's place, Joe parked behind the local police. We were told to stay near the van and out of harm's way.

As we watched, the local police made their way through the trees toward the cottage, where they'd be waiting in the dark when Bill and Pat arrived in Scanlan's car.

As they made their way to the cottage, Joe and I looked at one another. In a moment of clarity, I shrugged and pointed the way they'd gone.

Joe gave me the thumbs up and whispered, 'Yep, I want to see this.'

I responded, 'Me too; let's go.'

We quietly made our way through the trees, following the same path the police had. We'd worry about the consequences later. Seeing the police crouched ahead of us, we stopped and waited just far enough away for them not to notice us.

In the distance, we saw the silhouette of one person in the headlights of Scanlan's car. Something was wrong – both Walton and Jenkins should have been there.

I whispered to Joe, 'This doesn't look right; there's only one of them.'

Joe, concern in his voice, whispered, 'It doesn't look like Walton; must be Brett Jenkins. What now?'

Stating the obvious, I said, 'Maybe Walton's up at the main house?'

Sensing my intention, Joe said, 'Leave this to the police. They need to play this out and arrest Jenkins.'

As we watched, Bill and Pat, hoodies up, approached Jenkins. We heard him say, 'You bastards took your time getting here. Did you remember to bring the bag for the bones? Walton is furious; he got a phone call and pissed off ages ago, saying he was going to chase you lot up.'

Then he stopped dead, as he realised, too late, that things had gone very wrong.

At that point, it all happened: the local police jumped out of the bushes, guns drawn, yelling, 'This is the police! Put your hands in the air.'

As they called out, Bill and Pat hit the ground fast.

Jenkins gave up without a fight. He dropped the shovel and

put his hands in the air without a single shot being fired. He was used to following orders; the man who usually gave them was gone.

I'd expected a more dramatic end, and if I'm honest, there was a small part of me that wanted that drama for what they'd done to Ruth, to Bill, to John, to all of us.

Once Jenkins had been cuffed, Joe and I came out of the bushes. Two police cars made a dramatic entrance, lights flashing, and took him away.

But where was Walton?

The police officers, guns drawn, made their way to the main house; Bill was visibly furious Walton wasn't in custody.

Me, well, I was having a very strong and very bad feeling that our dealings with David Walton were going to take a new and dangerous twist.

By the time we all got to Walton's house, another two police cars had arrived. Once inside, it quickly became obvious Walton wasn't there. A check of his bedroom showed he'd taken most of his clothes with him. It was obvious he'd been tipped off about tonight. Someone had warned him.

When the house was secured, Bill checked the office for Ruth's box; it was missing. Bill was frustrated, angry and agitated. Walton had escaped, and he blamed himself, wondering where he'd gone wrong.

To ease his mind, I said, 'It's disappointing, but at least you caught the other four. Walton can't hide forever. At some stage he'll be caught and punished.'

Pat added reassuringly, 'Mate, Pip's right. It's not the perfect outcome, but pretty close to it. At least we got the bastards who murdered Ruth.'

Too wild to talk, Bill shook his head and walked off, back toward where Ruth's remains had been dug up.

Pat and I looked at one another, shrugged and quietly followed. The only sound we heard on the walk to her gravesite was the noise of the bats nestled upside down in the surrounding trees.

When we came to the site of Ruth's burial, we heard Burt's frantic barking; he was still locked in Joe's van. Joe immediately hurried to let him out. Returning, he told us Albert wasn't in the van.

As Bill aimed his torch at where they'd been digging, we saw Albert sitting next to Ruth's temporary grave. The muscles of my heart squeezed tight; for a moment, I'm sure, we all forgot about Walton.

We solemnly walked closer to Ruth's grave, and as we looked down, we saw what remained of Ruth.

This wasn't the way I'd wanted to meet her again; this wasn't what I wanted to remember her by.

Her skull was at a strange angle, twisted slightly sideways as if her hastily dug grave wasn't large enough even for her small frame. Her flesh had all but disappeared; most that remained were dry remains: her skull, her bones. There were also scraps of material from her night attire.

It was heart-breaking to see how little was left, and to think she'd waited so long for this moment of truth. Having seen enough, I turned away, overwhelmed by feelings of deep, raw sadness.

Finally, we had proof about the truth of Ruth's disappearance, about her death – people who take their life by suicide can't bury themselves.

Nothing needed to be said, except perhaps an apology that this night had taken so long and that Walton had got away, and maybe a silent prayer to hopefully send her on her way.

Burt slowly walked up to Albert, bent down and gently licked his little head. Like myself, Bill, Pat and Joe were visibly moved by his gesture.

When the time came, I picked Albert up and took him back to the van. I kissed him on the head and placed him on a blanket, and Burt jumped in next to him. I knew they'd be friends for life, and knowing that gave me comfort.

The finding of Ruth's remains and the arrest of Scanlan and the others was a successful outcome; still, there was a general feeling of failure in the air, a disappointment that Walton had been warned and got away. His escape escalated the frustration of the past years, particularly for Bill.

When the forensic team from Sydney arrived, they checked that the local police had the search warrant and that it was in order. Once satisfied, they roped off the property as a crime scene. I was curious why they were interested in a three-year-old murder.

Bill seemed to know one of the men in charge at the scene, and nodded to him in recognition. I wondered if it was his old boss who'd organised the search warrant, and if so, why a man of his rank had travelled all this way?

As I stood back, unnoticed in the turmoil, I watched as

the virile, attractive senior policeman took command and was shown due respect by the other officers working there.

His blue uniform was neatly pressed, his shoes polished. The epaulettes on his shoulder no doubt bore the insignia of a superintendent. His police cap sat just right, his posture erect, his bearing proud. He suited his uniform and his rank.

Eventually Bill introduced me to him. 'Ray, I'd like you to meet the young woman I told you about on the phone, Philippa Mason. Pip, this is Superintendent Ray Harris.'

As he firmly shook my hand, his manner was professional, polite and measured. I felt him sizing me up, trying to work out if I was to be taken seriously. Noticing my battle scars, he asked how I was feeling.

I wasn't concerned about what he thought about me; I was, however, concerned about how involving me would reflect on Bill.

After hearing the full story first from Bill then from me, despite some sceptical looks during the retelling when he saw the irrefutable evidence of Ruth's remains, he seemed to accept that I'd played a part.

The forensic team, all kitted up in their plastic shoes and jumpsuits, set up a tent covering Ruth's grave, making sure the crime scene was not further compromised. They took photographs of her remains in situ. They also took photos of the property and the inside of the cottage.

It was surreal watching them meticulously record a murder scene. I thought I'd feel more jubilant that the truth had finally come out. All I felt was an overwhelming sadness.

Then, as if to comfort me, I again felt Ruth's presence. I knew she was pleased that finally the truth had come out – she hadn't taken her life by suicide, she'd been murdered!

I've no doubt that she was watching, an enigmatic smile on her sweet face, happy that she was finally vindicated. I also felt she was grateful that I'd persevered, that I'd been prepared to face inevitable ridicule about the unorthodox way the truth was found.

Then – I promise this is true – she whispered gently in my ear, saying, '*Thank you, Philippa, for finding out the truth. Please tell Albert I will love him now and forever. Take care of him, please; I will look after you both always. My nephew will be brought to justice.*'

As the whispering ended, the colony of bats that slept nearby woke and flew out of the surrounding trees and over our heads. Their departure was oddly serene, the only sound the fluttering of their wings. It was eerie and breathtaking to see their silhouettes against the backdrop of the moon.

Their flight sent a chill down my spine, and as I looked around, I knew I wasn't alone; all working on the property felt the same way.

From the look on Superintendent Ray Harris's face, I knew the timing of their departure wasn't lost on him, as I saw him visibly shudder at the spectacle of what we all, I'm sure, felt was Ruth's final departure.

Some things are inexplicable.

Moved by the timing of the bats' flight, Bill shot me a look that needed no words. As he turned away, I saw him look over at Pat and Joe's stunned faces, and, wide-eyed, shake his head and turn his back, trying to regain his composure.

Once he had, remaining ever practical, he faced us and began to tell us what would happen next.

Point one – the property was now a crime scene.

Point two – the investigation could take some time. There had to be lots of purposeful documentation taken of the conditions at the scene, including collection of physical evidence, evidence that could hopefully illuminate what had happened, at what point, and who did it.

Point three – there would be an ongoing search for David Walton, the man responsible for organising Ruth's murder.

Point four – Ruth's remains would be packed into boxes and transported to Sydney. A team of forensic pathologists would then take over and start their long and arduous job of determining time of death, cause of death, identification from clothing, dental records and DNA tests – both Ruth's and, hopefully, the murderers.

Point five – the investigating police would work closely with forensic pathologists and the forensic laboratory in a meeting of three specific areas of expertise: science, logic and the law.

That joint effort would determine how Ruth had been murdered, and they would eventually charge and punish those responsible, including Walton.

I wanted to get away from this very sad and depressing scene to go back to Bill's and have a long, hot, cleansing shower.

We headed toward Bill's place in silence, each with our own thoughts. I sat in the back of the van, Burt's head on my lap,

Albert asleep beside him. I tried to reassure Burt that I wasn't mad at him, that he was safe, that we were all safe again – we hoped.

Burt needed a lot of reassurance. Albert, well, he was asleep, exhausted from his rightful anger and deep grief. I'd reassure him when he woke. I'd also give him Ruth's message of love.

I was pleased to get back into the safety of the cottage. I can't remember when I've enjoyed a shower more. I was very sore; the hot water hurt my wounds, but I had to wash away the filth of being around the scum we'd defeated tonight.

I washed my hair, and used my lavender soap to scrub away the smell of fear, the smell of evil. When I went into the bedroom to dress, Albert was still fast asleep; he'd had a big night.

By the time I got back to Bill's place, he had also showered. We both looked human again – almost. Pat had made us some scrambled eggs, toast, sausages and grilled tomato, with large pots of tea and coffee.

He'd also given Burt the largest piece of meat he could find in the fridge, and had a tin of sardines ready for Albert when he finally surfaced.

Ravenous, we all ate in silence. As I swallowed each mouthful, my throat hurt like hell, and I began my pig-squeal tic. You know what? I'd earned it, so I didn't give a rat's arse about trying to contain it.

After a while, Bill spoke up. 'I can't thank you both enough for what you did for me. You not only saved my life, you've helped solve the murder of a very decent woman who can now hopefully rest in peace.'

We both looked at him with tears in our eyes – yep, Pat too – until I croaked, 'Bill, it's me who owes you all the thanks. It's my fault you got involved in this mess. If I'd only kept my big mouth shut, none of this would have happened.'

Pat jumped in, comforting me. 'Yes, you're partly right, Pip; but if you hadn't spoken up and got us involved, those lowlifes would still be out on the street, murdering innocent people, or ruining lives by selling them ice.'

For a time after that Pat seemed lost for words, then he said, 'Ice is without a doubt the vilest drug to hit our streets. Nothing compares to this epidemic. It wreaks havoc on the lives of those addicted, the people who love them and many other innocents. Joe tells me his son Dannie says our area should be renamed Ice Valley.'

Bill turned to me. 'Pat's right. There've been many wrongs righted over the past few days, especially tonight. If you hadn't had the courage to tell your far-fetched story, and I'll be honest, I did have my doubts when I first met you and heard your story, the scum would have won.'

As I listened, I began to tic even more. Give me a break, okay – I was tired, sleep deprived and emotional. I was also feeling shattered, remembering my visions as well as seeing Ruth's remains.

Defensively I said, 'Yeah, well, you've only heard the half of it.'

This was unfair; Bill had yet to hear the story of my horrific vision in Pat's bathroom mirror. Again, in my own defence, seeing what I had would have tipped anyone over the edge.

Knowing that now wasn't the time to recount what I'd witnessed, Pat interjected calmly. 'Bill, there's more to tell you, but we'll fill you in tomorrow, when you've both had some sleep. Suffice to say, Pip had a very intense and disturbing vision at my place tonight, before we left for the colliery.'

As Bill was about to ask what it was, Pat put his hand up and firmly said, 'Not now; tomorrow. The last thing Pip needs at the moment is to recount it all. Let's call it a night. Tomorrow is going to be a huge day; there will be police interviews and you could both do with a visit to a GP. So, come on, off to bed.'

I was about to go when I remembered I had yet to explain to Pat what I'd said about him to Scanlan. I sheepishly turned toward him and said, 'Pat, by the way, if you heard what I said to Scanlan tonight, I hope you realise that I had to tell Scanlan that story about you being pissed? I'm sorry if saying that upset you; it was the only excuse I could come up with quickly to explain why I was supposedly there on my own.'

With a huge smile, Pat graciously said, 'Pip, it was a stroke of genius. When you said it, I looked at Joe, smiled and gave him the thumbs up. Joe thought it was brilliant too. Like Scanlan said, people always think you can never trust a drunk. What he didn't realise was that this ex-drunk owed Bill his life, and tonight I was given the opportunity to pay him back. You did well, pulling that out so fast.'

I felt a rush of relief flood my body; I was clean, well fed and, for the first time in over two weeks, I felt safe with these two men and, of course, Burt and Albert. The only nagging thought circling around in my overactive brain was – how and where Walton would be caught, and by whom?

I rose to make my way to bed, then bent and kissed them both on the cheek. Bill smelt amazing, like soap and talcum powder; I had to hide a shiver of attraction.

Pat gave a little chuckle when I kissed him. Burt came over and pushed his big head against my leg.

I looked at Bill and said, 'I know you don't like him sleeping inside, but do you mind if he sleeps in the cottage with Albert and me tonight? Just one night, please?'

With a ghost of a smile, Bill responded, 'Sure, but just tonight; don't make it a habit or you'll ruin the dog. Dogs aren't like cats, Pip, they need rules; they don't make up their own. Pat's right, tomorrow is going to be huge. Sleep well.'

I woke the next morning and found myself right on the edge of the bed. Don't know if you've ever tried to make a rescue Rottweiler and a cat with attitude, who've both had a very bad night, move over when they're hogging the bed.

No? Well, trust me, you put up with the piece of bed they allow you.

I rolled over and gave Burt a hug; he licked my face, which hurt like hell. Then, as Albert stretched out fully on his back, I blew softly on his tummy. He rolled over, I like to think with a smile on his face, and kept on sleeping.

We could all learn a lot from cats.

It was close to eleven when I surfaced. I showered and made my way over to Bill's. As I walked toward the house,

I could hear sounds of raucous laughter, and my heart lifted.

I love being around happy people; they're infectious, and I always want to catch some of that happiness.

When I walked in through the open kitchen door, Pat, Joe and Bill were all sitting at the table drinking coffee and rehashing last night.

When they saw me, they caressed my soul further with their welcoming smiles.

Bill stood up and breezily said, 'Pip, great to see you. Pull up a chair. I'll get you something to eat; tea or coffee?'

As I sat, overjoyed to be with them, I beamed him a smile and said, 'Tea, please, and anything that's easy food-wise. What were you three laughing about? I could do with a good laugh.'

They all started to giggle again, like three schoolgirls. It was delightful to see, and before I knew it, I'd joined in.

Then to put me out of my misery, Pat said, 'Oh, Pip, we were just going over how bloody awesome Albert was. Burt did a good job of sorting Scanlan out, but Albert! How is the little darling this morning?'

When he said this, the other two incorrigibles burst out laughing again.

I knew they were still getting over both my lack of fear and my concern for Albert last night.

Playing along, I said, 'Well, you know, he kind of likes the name the "A-Team". Naturally he thinks the A stands for Albert; I'm not game to tell him it doesn't, and I'd advise none of you to either. So, tell me again about what happened. I was a bit, um, stressed last night.'

They went through it again, leaving nothing out, telling me what had happened while I was with my new best friend Scanlan.

We were a close band now, sharing an unbreakable bond and not yet tired of retelling our story.

Once they'd finished, Bill pointed to Pat and Joe and, with great emotion, said, 'This pair were perfection. With the help of Connor and the A-Team, they were pivotal in taking those two out of action.'

On a post-operation high, we continued in this vein for some time, talking about the highs – rescuing Bill, the 'A-Team', the four arrests – and the lows – finding Ruth's remains, Cleary and Walton's escape.

Pat and Joe were doing their best to boost and lift Bill after the failure of not arresting Walton in particular.

I couldn't force myself to have a vision or a dream about where Walton was or who had tipped him off. It doesn't work like that.

Soon, sensing an undercurrent of tension, Burt stood and rested his head on his master's knee. With a troubled look on his tired face, Bill distractedly patted his head.

My little Albert, in a tension-breaking moment of his own, was soon at the door, stretching and yawning, with a look that said, *'Can't a cat get some sleep around here! Now I'm awake, where's my breakfast?'*

With his arrival, Pat instantly jumped to his feet, bowed and said, 'Pleased to see you've deigned to give us your presence. You must be hungry after expending so much energy last night.'

We all watched to see what Albert would do as Pat opened a can of sardines, put them into a bowl on the floor, then hammed it up, saying, 'Your Majesty: sardines in spring water, if you please?'

To our amusement, Albert yawned, stretched and did the royal walk past, condescending to give Pat the briefest of leg cuddles. Then he went straight to his food bowl and proceeded to passionately devour his well-earned meal.

His antics had us all laughing again, and for a time the tension lifted.

After he'd finished his well-deserved meal, Albert stretched and majestically sauntered over to where we were sitting.

I was proud to see how warmly and respectfully he was greeted, not only by Burt but by these three brave men – my newfound friends.

As he jumped up onto my lap, he yawned – sardine breath isn't all that majestic – and again I imagined him saying, '*The "A-Team" – I like that!*'

CHAPTER 31

We needed to be at Cessnock Police Station at 1 p.m. to be interviewed by the team from Sydney who'd taken over the case. The same team had been working on closing down an ice lab operating in the Hunter region. Believing the two cases to be connected, they'd taken over the Ruth Richards' case as well.

Before we went to the station, Bill and I saw the local GP to have our respective cuts, bites and bruises seen to. You can imagine the alarm bells that went off when she saw us. She was amazed by our story, and we wouldn't have blamed her if she hadn't believed a word.

By the time we arrived at Cessnock Police Station, it became apparent that Roger Scanlan, David Walton, Brett Jenkins and several others were involved in operating an ice ring.

Jenkins, with the help of his wealthy father's legal counsel, had made a plea bargain for a lesser sentence by giving details about Ruth's murder and the reason for it. As it turned out, the unauthorised and inadmissible bug Bill had put in Walton's house wasn't needed for charges to be laid, which was just as well.

It transpired that Ruth had left her substantial estate to her only living relative, her nephew David Walton, until she'd overheard him talking to members of the drug ring about an ice shipment.

Horrified, she'd confronted her nephew. He'd tried to convince her she was mistaken. Not believing him, that same afternoon she phoned her solicitor, Brendan O'Connor, for an appointment, telling him she wanted to change her will.

Walton had followed her and overheard the call to Brendan. He'd heard her say she'd hand written a draft copy of the changes and would go over them with him.

Toward the end of her call, she'd confided in Brendan that she feared for her own safety, having overheard something very disturbing and having confronted her nephew about it.

She'd never made it to that appointment. Walton's men had taken care of that, and had also made a threatening visit to Brendan O'Connor. The rest was history.

After her call to Brendan, Walton had seen Ruth hide the draft copy of her new will in the oblong box, putting it in the concealed hiding place in her bedroom ceiling.

If you look up the meaning of the word 'greed', it says 'an intense and selfish desire for something, especially wealth and power'.

David Walton's greed was so intense that he was not only prepared to kill his own flesh and blood, he'd also become involved in the manufacture and dealing of ice, a choice that would ruin many lives.

The only person associated with the murder of Ruth who remained at large was David Walton. I knew Bill wouldn't rest until Walton joined the rest of them, where he belonged – in prison.

It's comforting to know it is possible for our world to be changed for the better by the actions and intentions of decent people.

CHAPTER 32

I woke to the sound of birds singing, a warm shaft of sunlight caressing my face. I felt so at peace at that moment that I didn't want to break the spell. But as we all know, life isn't like that, and the next thing I knew, Burt was scratching and barking at the front door of the cottage to be let in.

Who can resist the love, adoration and attention of a dog? I can't. I pushed Albert gently off my lap, got out of bed, pulled on my dressing-gown and went to let him in.

When I opened the door, in his enthusiasm he knocked me down. It made me love him even more.

Seeing his enthusiasm, now out of bed, Albert snarled at Burt. Inanely I chastised Albert, saying, 'Leave Burt alone. Dogs are loving and enthusiastic. I realise to your feline sensibilities it looks obsequious, but drop the superior attitude.'

I then turned my full attention back onto Burt, ruffling his ears and cooing endearments to him.

I soon realised Bill was watching our interaction, grinning from ear to ear. To cover his embarrassment, he said, 'Sorry; we were getting worried. It's twelve thirty. Are you hungry?'

Shocked that I'd slept so long, I gently pushed Burt away, stood up and said, 'You're kidding; is it really that late? I haven't slept in that long in years.'

Bill confirmed the time. 'It is. Have a shower and come out onto the porch for something to eat. Pat's here, and so are Joe, and Marg, his wife. They all want to celebrate how things turned out. Marg is dying to meet you and have some female company. See you soon.'

As I showered and washed my hair, I thought about the past two weeks and what a journey it had been. This time three weeks ago, none of these people had been part of my life, yet already I couldn't imagine not knowing them.

I don't fit easily into new friendships; I take my time. I'm aware that to show my true self puts a lot of pressure on new relationships. I have to choose which of the two sides of me I want to present.

First, there's the person my parents, with the best of intentions, had schooled me to be – a person who passed the test and always had the right conversation at the right moment.

Then there was the other side of me, the untamed side, that I usually only show in the privacy of my own home and around people I trust.

For most of my life, I'd feared that, if my friends truly knew who I was, if they knew about my random rambling Tourettic thoughts, not to mention my burgeoning psychic abilities, they'd walk away. In thinking that, I'd done my friends and myself a disservice.

Since my parents had both passed, a certain pressure had lifted from my life, and for the first time I felt that I could show the world the real me, without filters and possibly without fear of rejection.

I now realise that some people not only accepted the quirky side of me, but felt comfortable and invigorated by my authentic self.

I was blessed – I had the genetic template of Uncle J to explain my Tourettic self, and Grandma Ella to explain my psychic self.

Many people with TS self-diagnose, regardless of whether or not they have that familial guide. That makes sense: if you know there is something wrong – no, something different – about you, you want to know the reason.

I'm sure that many who have psychic abilities and who have no one to guide them on how to use them, how to filter and interpret them, try to either smother or ignore those abilities. They haven't been taught how to use and honour their abilities.

I'm a double curiosity. Let's face it, who wants to be that different in a world that disdains any degree of true individuality?

I have loyal and loving friends who have no problems with who I am. Over the past two weeks, I had added three more to the mix – well, five if you include Albert and Burt.

Now I was about to meet Joe's wife Marg, and found myself wondering how I might have been described to her.

True individuality comes at a price.

Once out of the shower, I looked in the mirror and, despite the bruises and scratches on my neck and arms and Burt's bites, I wasn't unhappy with what I saw, superficially at least.

Once I decided I'd have to do, I said out loud, 'Okay, time to make an entrance and see if your new friendships are strong enough to survive and grow.'

As I was about to walk outside, I hesitated, turning to Albert. 'Wake up, sleepy head. Try not to be such a misanthropist. Come out and have something to eat. We've got sardines in spring water!'

What I really wanted was for him to be with me. I needed his presence, his moral support. I wanted to hold him in my arms and use him as a shield.

To Albert's horror, I picked him up, waking him in the process – shock, horror – and headed out the door, my feline shield in place.

As I looked to where they were sitting, talking and laughing, I felt both an overwhelming tenderness toward them and a fear that, now the crisis was over – well, almost – perhaps they would go on with their lives as they had before, without me; that I wouldn't fit long-term.

As I was thinking this, Bill disrupted my thoughts with, 'Pip, we were worried you'd gone back to sleep.'

They were sitting around a long table laden with all sorts of delights. I soon forgot my reservations as I realised I was ravenous.

With my mouth already watering, I said, 'I'm sorry; I hope you didn't wait for me. You must be starving!'

Pat responded in his usual laconic way, saying, 'Of course we did; you're the star attraction.'

With this, Bill introduced me to Marg, who was a hugger and a lovely warm person, who I instantly liked and felt comfortable with.

I don't know what it is about spontaneous displays of affection, but they always put me at ease and make me feel accepted; I knew my friend count had gone up by one.

Gesturing toward the seat next to him, Pat said, 'Come on, Pip, sit next to me; we're all starving.'

I sat with my feline shield on my lap until, bored with our company and annoyed by our laughter – cats for some reason seem to hate laughter – he jumped down and joined Burt in the shade of a tree.

I can't remember when I've enjoyed an afternoon more. The conversation flowed, the food was sensational, and, with the exception of Pat, we all celebrated with a few glasses of wine. The afternoon would have been perfect, except for one thing – Walton was still at large.

It wasn't long before the conversation turned to what had happened over the past two weeks, and particularly the other night. We talked as only people who've survived something as dangerous as we had talk, at times in truncated sentences.

Soon, frustrated by our conversation, Marg said, 'Slow down, you lot, you're leaving things out. Don't forget I wasn't there, so, as boring as it seems to you, please don't leave anything out. I want to hear every minute detail.'

And so the afternoon went, with us all repeating our own

version of the entire story so that Marg wouldn't feel left out and so we could relive our moments of fame.

Then, sheepishly, Pat said, 'Marg, you didn't hear what Pip said to throw Scanlan off the scent when he asked her who'd come with her.'

In chorus, Pat and Joe proudly told Marg how I'd handled Scanlan. As we went over and over the highlights, I couldn't help feeling a sense of pride about what we'd achieved together.

The subject of Walton was skilfully avoided – no one wanted to bring the afternoon down – but we all knew the dialogue would soon turn that way.

Pat looked at Bill and asked the question on everyone's lips. 'So, what happens now about Walton? He can't have disappeared off the face of the earth. Have the other four given any information about where he might be?'

Bill didn't respond for a while, then with a solemn look he said, 'Not that I know of, not yet anyway. I'm going to get in touch with some contacts in Sydney and see if they have any leads. If I can, I'd like to see this right through to the end. I want to be involved in catching him. I won't feel right about this until that happens.'

We understood.

Bill, seeing the looks on our faces, knew that his frustration was bringing the celebration down. To change the tone, he said, 'Enough about Walton; we're celebrating the other four being caught. Don't mind me; I'm like a dog with a bone about this case.'

When Burt heard the magic word – bone – he began a

gentle insistent woof, as he looked intently into Bill's face, salivating in anticipation.

It was the tension-breaker we needed, and Burt got his bone.

As the afternoon progressed, my mind began to wander as I started to think about going back to my life in Sydney. I felt both a sadness that I would have to leave and a joy that I would soon be home.

I was looking forward to going back to work and some routine; routine soothes and helps to centre me. Explaining how I got my bruises, scratches and bites while still remaining in control was going to take some effort.

Before we knew it, it was time to go our separate ways. Joe and Marg were the first to leave. Once they'd gone, Pat, Bill and I, with the now inseparable Burt and Albert at our feet, had coffee inside.

We talked for a while longer, and when it was time for Pat to leave, I felt the energy change as we faced the prospect of going back to our respective lives.

Then Pat threw in a lifeline, looking at Bill and saying, 'I guess someone will eventually arrange a service for Ruth Richards. It seems only fitting that she be given a decent send-off. Do you have any ideas on when that will be?'

I could have kissed Pat, but I didn't; I shut my mouth and waited for Bill's response.

After a moment's hesitation, he said, 'Not yet. I know she still has a lot of friends in town. I'll go and see Muriel for a start. Pip, will you be able to come back for a service once it's arranged?'

And with that conversation started, I began to relax as I realised that, even if I never worked with Bill in the future, it was still possible to stay in touch.

As Pat left, with a look of satisfaction on his face he said, 'Well, I'll see you before too long, young lady. You look after yourself and Albert till then.'

Then he gave me an unexpected bear hug.

Tears welling in my eyes, I hugged him back. 'You sure will, Pat, you can count on it.'

Jokingly Bill said, 'Okay, you two, break it up; Pip, you've got an early start tomorrow to beat the traffic back to Sydney.'

After Pat had gone, we cleaned up the rest of the dishes, Burt closely following us as we did. Albert, of course, slept. They'd both enjoyed the day; the circle of people they trusted was growing larger.

When it came time for bed, I wasn't sure if I could hug Bill in the same way as I'd hugged Pat. I felt nervous around him, a sure sign that my feelings for him were deepening. I was very attracted to this gentle man.

Eventually, tiredness taking over, I yawned and said, 'I'd better get to bed; Albert is already giving me death stares.'

I bent down to give Burt a gentle kiss on the head. As I looked up, I saw Bill was watching with that irresistible smile.

Then, in his deep and sexy voice, he said, 'Where's my kiss?'

I walked slowly toward him, my heart doing somersaults. Sensing my hesitation, he gently put his arms around me and softly kissed the top of my head.

As he held me, he said, 'I'm so glad nothing happened to you, Pip. I don't think I could have forgiven myself if it had.'

I wanted to kiss him on his soft, sensual mouth; instead, taking his lead, I kissed him on the shoulder and said, 'I wouldn't have forgiven myself, either, if anything had happened to you.'

At that moment, I felt that for me something had changed irrevocably; but I didn't know how Bill felt.

I had to resign myself to the idea that I'd know in time. With another hug and a quick and oh-so-gentle kiss on the lips, we went our separate ways to bed.

As I got ready for bed, I felt an exhilaration I hadn't felt in a very long time; I knew my life had changed forever.

I realised something else: I hadn't had one tic all afternoon. At least, no spectacular ones, just run-of-the-mill throat clearing. I knew why: I was enjoying myself, I felt I belonged and I felt safe around these people – around Bill in particular.

Before I went to sleep, I checked my mobile. There were several texts, mainly from Uncle J and John, but one each from Annie and Phoebe as well.

I texted Uncle J straight away, telling him I was safe and happy. I also let John and Max know the same. I'd contact the girls tomorrow, as exhaustion was taking over, and I soon slipped into a deep and dreamless sleep.

I woke bright and early, feeling surprisingly pleased that I was going back to my old life, which now included Albert. I stripped my bed and took my sheets and towels into the laundry.

I found Bill already up and about in the kitchen. He'd made us a healthy breakfast of Bircher muesli, fruit, hot muffins and a steaming pot of fresh coffee.

We didn't linger over breakfast, avoiding stressful topics. We talked in generalities, like what lay ahead for each of us. In fact, we were both restrained, bordering on uncomfortable, as we sat together over breakfast.

Once we'd finished, Bill helped me pack my car and strap Albert's cage onto the front passenger seat.

Burt seemed distressed at our departure, which was touching to see.

Car packed, we settled on a goodbye hug and a peck on the cheek. As I drove off, I felt a hollow feeling in the pit of my stomach mixed with excitement to be heading home.

Driving down the Pacific Highway and back to my life in Sydney, I felt mixed emotions – elation tinged with despondency.

Uninvited thoughts of Walton surfaced. On my own, with no need to supress, I had freedom to tic to my brain's content, which was both a relief and a release.

As well as Walton, I thought a lot about Bill. Despite the traumatic events of the last several weeks, my thoughts about him were mostly invigorating and uplifting.

I say mostly, because there were other thoughts that were nerve-wracking as I admitted to myself that Bill would not leave Walton's capture to anyone else.

CHAPTER 33

It was incredible to be home. Once inside the courtyard, I let Albert out of his cage straight away, so he could see he was back home and safe. I opened the front door like a kid on Christmas morning; I couldn't wait to get inside.

When the security alarm went off – I'd forgotten about it – Albert and I both jumped. I punched in the pin and turned it off. As I looked around at all my familiar things, I instantly felt safe, and let out a sigh of relief as I was enveloped by the serenity of my haven. It was a place I could live in on my own terms, a place where I could be myself.

Once I'd unpacked and thrown my dirty clothes in the wash, I phoned Amanda to tell her what had happened since I'd seen her last, saying I'd be there that afternoon.

Her response was pure Amanda as she said, 'God no, Pip, are you serious? Come in tomorrow.'

After my call to Amanda, I made it a priority to see if John and Max were home. I wanted to not only reassure myself that

John was okay, but also to know that they weren't angry with me for what had happened.

They were home and overjoyed to see me, both wrapping their arms around me at the door. I immediately started to cry, and through my tears apologised profusely to them both, particularly John – my friend and now my hero.

We spent the next hour catching up on John's progress and what the doctors had said on his discharge from hospital. In turn, they were keen to hear what had happened in my time in the Hunter.

John was quite obviously proud of his bravery that night; Max was just relieved and happy to have his life partner well and back home. They both told me there was nothing to forgive me for, and I left with a healed heart and soul.

Afterward I drove to Crows Nest to buy some food. I dropped into the delicatessen near the car park and bought my favourite things – dolmades, olives, smoked salmon, pâté, avocado, Danish fetta and Turkish bread. I'd dine in style tonight – my reward to myself and, of course, Albert.

When I got home, I put the groceries away and settled into spending some serious nesting and bonding time with Albert. I walked around my townhouse, checking each and every room, feeling relief via the calming energy I always felt in my safe space, my home.

I'd come home with a newfound passion to eat only what I loved; coming so close to not being alive can do that to you. I prepared Albert and myself an early repast, which we ate together sitting on the floor at the coffee table in front of the fire.

All seemed well with our world.

I woke early and dressed for gym, feeding Albert before I left. I was heartened to see he'd put on some condition. I was desperate for a good workout to help clear my mind and prepare me for the inevitable questions from my work colleagues. My gym tribe welcomed me back and I happily got stuck into giving my body the workout it needed, the workout it craved.

Exercise is my way of remaining emotionally healthy. Medication hasn't worked for me – exercise is my happy pill. Gym is the only place outside of my home where I can be my hyperactive self, without anyone telling me to relax. It gives me an opportunity to burn off stored energy.

I like the 6 a.m. slot; all the regular early morning people were there. They are mostly happy and positive, glad to be there. I warmed up on the running machine for ten minutes before doing the circuit of machines.

I don't watch the morning news on the televisions provided, preferring instead to listen to music. I can't see the point of releasing endorphins that trigger positive feelings, then neutralising them by listening to the news. I'd do that tonight.

After gym, I showered and took extra care dressing for work. Being winter, it was easy to cover the scratches, bruises and bites on my arms and legs. It was a little more difficult to hide the finger-marks and the scratches I'd made myself trying to pull Scanlan's hands away from my throat. A strategically tied scarf hid most, but not all.

As I left home again, I reassured Albert that I'd be home

early that evening. His response was to yawn, roll over and turn his back on me.

Sometimes you don't need words to get a point across.

When I arrived at St Leonards, I was nervous about the questions my work colleagues would ask. I don't like being the centre of attention, but I realised that, with the battle scars I wore, this was going to be very hard to avoid – in fact I had a snowball's chance in hell.

Everyone was sitting around the glass table in the centre of Editorial having their caffeine kick start.

As I walked toward the table, someone said, 'Pip, it's so good to have you back! The place isn't the same without you; we missed all the laughs.'

I was home with my work tribe and it felt bloody fantastic. The questions about my absence and the way I looked began, so with as much detail as I was allowed to give with a police investigation going on, I filled them in.

Questions were fired at me; if I didn't feel like answering them, I simply said, 'Sorry; I can't really go into details.'

As I recounted, yet again, what had occurred, I felt an emotional exhaustion descend. It reminded me of the exhaustion I'd felt at the end of an eleven-kilometre fundraising run. As we'd reached the end of the run, we'd been made to do a lap of a sports oval to cross the finish line. Only difference: this morning I wouldn't get a t-shirt and certificate for my efforts.

There had been a small article about the arrests in Monday's *Sydney Morning Herald*. My colleagues made the connection and understood the position I was in.

Thankfully the topic soon changed to work. I was grateful there was a deadline approaching; everyone would soon forget about my Hunter Valley adventure and move on to the reassuringly mundane.

As I got back into the groove of work, I mulled things over in my mind.

One positive outcome: I was now set up to work via VPN. I wasn't sure how things would pan out between Bill and me, but if there was to be a relationship in the future – work or otherwise – I knew I could work remotely.

We all know the pitfalls of long-distance romance. Now that I was in the driver's seat of my life for a change, I wasn't keen to disturb the flow; problem was I couldn't get Bill off my mind.

Who knows? Without the added stress of tracking down murderers, having horrific visions, being kidnapped and people trying to kill us, we might find each other boring. I doubted that; and besides, I knew that all the mayhem wasn't behind us.

I promised myself that I'd let romance take a back seat – I was okay coasting along in neutral. I wanted to spend more time reconnecting with myself, with Uncle J and my friends; I had some making-up to do.

After Zac had an affair with a co-worker, I did have a few trust issues. Even though I hadn't been content for a long time, it had still hurt.

The universe sometimes disguises gifts as punishments.

I wasn't ready yet to jump into a relationship; a fling, maybe, to soothe my wounded ego. I didn't want to turn Bill into the transitional man; he deserved much more.

After living with Zac for a while, Uncle J, sensing my unease, had come around less often, preferring to meet me on my own. I'm ashamed and furious with myself now that I had allowed that wedge to come between us. I will never allow that to happen again.

Before Uncle J moved to Tasmania, he'd spoken to me openly, honestly and without rancour about how he'd felt about my relationship with Zac. He'd held no malice toward Zac, he simply couldn't stand him, his outlook on life or the way he'd treated me. Uncle J once told me Zac wasn't the right person for me to spend my life with.

I'd known at the time that what he was saying was true, but I was young and stupid and, well, not ready to accept the brutal truth – oh, and I'd thought I was in love.

Knowing that Uncle J liked Bill even without meeting him seemed to me to be a very good omen.

CHAPTER 34

Home from work, Albert met me at the door, meowing loudly. He was less than impressed that I'd been out so long, even though he'd probably slept most of the day – think abandonment issues.

I kicked off my shoes, dropped my handbag upstairs, changed into my jogging gear and fed him. With a full tummy, he seemed to relax.

Taking this opportunity to leave for a quick jog, I said to my forlorn feline, 'I'm going for a run. It's a silly thing humans do; I'll see you soon.'

As he looked up at me, I continued guiltily. 'I'm sorry, baby. I really need a run before it gets dark. I'll see you in about thirty minutes. I promise when I get home we can spend the evening together.'

Albert's response was to indifferently turn and walk away, as if to say, '*Yeah, right.*'

I grabbed my keys and took off down Shirley Road, across

the causeway and around Berry Island Reserve. There were still plenty of people about, out walking their dogs or fitting in some exercise.

On my run, I realised what the silent ache in my heart was – I was missing Bill. I missed his calm presence, I missed the smell of him, his essence, I missed being near him. I'd held back phoning or even texting, wanting him to be the first to make the move. Childish, I know – rejection issues.

I decided that when I got home, I'd call Uncle J. I needed to tell him what had happened in the Hunter. I'd also missed him. What I also wanted was to take my mind off missing Bill.

When I got to the front gate, I was pleased to see Albert waiting for me; all was forgiven as he welcomed me back with little chirrups of cat love.

I washed my face and hands and started preparing my dinner. Just as I was about to start cooking, the phone rang – it was Uncle J. He had pre-empted my call and beaten me to it.

I turned off the gas cooker, and elatedly seized the phone. 'You've done it again; I was going to have some dinner then phone you. I'm so glad to hear your voice. How's the client brief going?'

Excited as he was, one of his recent rituals kicked in: repeating things three times. It's nice to see yourself in others sometimes, especially in someone you love and who loves you unconditionally.

He said, 'Too easy; too easy; too easy. How are you, beautiful? I've been having some very weird and scary dreams about you the past few days. What's happened? I want to hear everything.'

Yet again, he'd picked up that something wasn't right in my world.

As he'd finished telling me about the client brief, I spent the next fifty-eight minutes filling him in. As I did, his tics escalated. I felt aggrieved I'd upset him, and told him so.

In a moment that was purely Uncle J, he passionately said, 'Philippa, promise me that, no matter what, you will never hold things back from me again.'

From his tone, I knew he was deadly serious. I wasn't sure I could keep that promise.

I was hesitating to frame my response when Albert provided the perfect circuit-breaker. He jumped onto my lap and began to lick my face, which made me burst out laughing.

Relieved at my laughter, Uncle J said inquisitively, 'What's so funny? Tell me, tell me, tell me.'

It was good not to have to make a promise I couldn't keep. 'Oh, stop it Albert; he's licking my face, Uncle J. He's the most adorable cat when it comes to affection.'

Uncle J wasn't to be put off by my convenient segue into Albert's antics. 'I'm flying up to see you,' he said, 'as soon as I can organise things here. To think that I could have lost you, it ...'

I stopped him finishing that sentence by saying, 'But you didn't. Honestly, I'm fine, and I'd love to see you; I've missed you so much. Please, come and stay for as long as you like. We can look for a place for you together.'

If coming close to death teaches you anything, it's that you need to spend as much time as you can with the people you love, the people who are important to you.

Hearing my enthusiasm at his suggestion, he said, 'Good! I'll get onto Qantas right away and book flights.'

This prompted me to cheekily ask, 'Oh, that reminds me: anything to report on Sam?'

With a smile in his voice he answered, 'A little bit of progress. We've had lots of texts and emails and the odd call. I like to get to know people through correspondence; that really taps into their soul, who they really are. We seem very compatible that way. Let's just say, I'm quietly confident.'

We hung up, both emotionally wrung out. I was pleased I'd be seeing him soon. I hoped that Sam, who was based in Sydney, would feel the same way.

As I was preparing dinner, my thoughts turned to introducing him to Bill.

I'd tried to explain Uncle J's unique behaviour to Bill, his combination of TS and OCD. Explanations aside, to meet him in person is a completely different ball game. Bill wouldn't get the Wikipedia version of Tourette's; he'd get the real deal.

When I'm with Uncle J, I tend to emulate him and his behaviour – another common trait of people with TS is mimicking one's environment. Again, that could be interesting for Bill to see.

Before I knew it, it was nine fifteen and too late to call Bill to say I'd arrived safely. Yep, I was being a coward. Rejection is my Achilles heel.

CHAPTER 35

When I woke, I was pleased to see a text from Uncle J. He was arriving in a week once he'd finished and handed over the brief to his client.

I texted back, saying I'd pick him up at the airport.

I was disappointed to see that Bill hadn't texted, even though I had no right to be. Acting on impulse, I typed a brief and casual text and sent it before I could lose my nerve.

It read, '*Hi, hope you and Burt are good? Any news on Walton? Uncle Jim is coming to stay soon. It will be so good to see him. Thanks again for everything. Pip x.*'

To distract myself, I went for a jog. Exercise always improves my mood. I wasn't ever going to make the drug companies wealthier when I had exercise to kick me back into line.

As I was about to leave for work, I heard a ping on my mobile. I grabbed it while I was walking out the door, reassuring Albert that soon he'd have the company of Uncle J all day long.

When I got on the train, I pulled out my mobile to see if it was a text from Bill. It was, and it intrigued me.

'Hi, Pip; good to hear from you. You've been on my mind. Lots happening; can't go into it. Glad Uncle Jim is coming to stay. It might be a while till I can see you again. I really want to. Hope you want to see me also? Burt's good, but he seems to be missing you or Albert – or both; know how he feels. No news yet on Ruth's funeral. Bill x.'

His response instantly lifted my spirits and made me feel guilty. My moral compass kicked in and I knew I should have texted him as soon as I'd arrived home. My behaviour was childish and churlish, but it was too late to change.

Uneasy that he hadn't answered my question about Walton, I responded, *'I sure do. I'm intrigued and hope things are okay? Don't worry about me. With Uncle Jim coming, I'm going to be busy. Look forward to speaking to you soon. I miss you and Burt too. Pip xx. PS: whatever you're busy with, stay safe.'*

This time I was certain about hitting send.

His almost instant response was, *'Great, that's a load off my mind. I was wondering, when I didn't hear from you. Looking forward to seeing you again, and meeting Uncle Jim. Don't worry about me. Talk soon. Bill xx.'*

My mind at rest – guilt aside – I spent a busy and productive day at work. When I got home, Albert was waiting for me at the gate. I determined then and there to make it up to him by foregoing my jog. I'd spend the night concentrating on Albert and catching up on texts and emails to John, Annie and Phoebe.

I was keeping busy, trying not to fixate on what Bill had meant in his text. I was also avoiding bed in case my dreams were unwelcome and prophetic.

As I prepared for bed, Albert sat at my feet, watching my every move. Once settled in, I patted the doona and said, 'Come on, little man, time for cuddles.' He jumped up right away.

Waiting for sleep, I checked my phone several times for texts from Bill – there were none. As I lay there, overstimulated, I remembered a dream I'd had while on a holiday in Asia.

I'd dreamed about a striking wooden chest of drawers with twenty small drawers, each in different coloured wood. A few days after that dream, I saw that exact same chest of drawers in a street market in Keelung. Seeing it had sent tingles down my spine. I'd wanted to buy it on the spot, but a disinterested Zac had walked on past.

Prophetic or precognitive dreams are a form of extra-sensory perception where you perceive information about places or events, through paranormal means, before they actually happen.

As I recalled this dream, I slipped into a deep sleep, Albert gently snoring beside me with his head resting on my leg.

I soon began to dream a bizarre and disturbing sequence of scenes that made no sense; the dream also felt familiar.

I knew Walton was there, in my dream, waiting for someone. He was in an isolated house near water. He wasn't alone; there were others in the house, though I couldn't see their faces.

I saw a jetty and pontoon where a small boat was moored.

There were tall trees surrounding the house and a lean-to shed at the side.

I knew there was more I needed to see; it was as if I was caught in a *Groundhog Day* sequence of events. For the life of me, I couldn't wake from this dream, I couldn't move past this derelict house.

It was like that dreadful feeling – I'm sure we've all had it – when you know someone is in the room but you can't wake up to protect yourself.

At last I woke, heart pounding, and immediately reached for my dream diary on the bedside table. As I wrote the dream down, I knew I had to tell Bill.

Though not yet 3 a.m., I texted Bill, telling him about my dream. I knew that somehow it related to Walton. Not expecting an immediate response, I rolled over to try to go back to sleep.

Soon, my mobile rang. I answered without thinking. 'Hello, Bill?'

Bill's response was, 'Yes, Pip, it's me. It's good to hear your voice.'

Now my heart was pounding for an entirely different reason; I realised how much I'd missed him.

Past playing games, I responded honestly. 'It's good to hear your voice too. I'm sorry; I didn't mean to wake you.'

'You didn't,' he said. 'I've got a lot on my mind. Tell me about your dream.'

I told him about the derelict house, the jetty, the pontoon, the small boat, and how I felt there was more I'd needed to find out but couldn't, as I'd felt stuck, unable to shift past the derelict house.

When I finished, I said, 'I honestly don't know what to make of it all.'

Without hesitation, he said, 'You've recounted a similar dream to me, Pip. Remember when we met for coffee on the way up to see Muriel? Do you still have the details of that dream?'

I instantly knew he was right and turned to that date in my diary, saying, 'Oh my God, you're right. There was a bright blue boatshed with chartreuse shutters in my first dream. Do you have any idea where it might be, in reality I mean?'

With real trepidation in his voice, he answered, 'Brendan O'Connor and his family live on Pittwater. Maybe that's where your dream is. I hope he hasn't involved them.'

Remembering what Brendan had told us during his call, I agreed. Then, to reassure Bill, I said, 'I didn't sense there were children involved. I know someone else was there, but I couldn't see faces. I'm sorry I can't be more specific than that.'

Bill spoke gently, placating me by saying, 'That's a great help. Once it's a decent hour, I'm going to phone Brendan's mobile and see if I can reach him. I know it's a big ask, but could you drive to Church Point ferry terminal; do you know where that is?'

I didn't hesitate. 'Yes, I can and I do; we used to go there when I was young.'

Bill's tone grew excited. 'A mate and former colleague, Nic, works with the Broken Point water police. I'll try to organise a police boat to meet us there. I'm bringing Pat along; I might need you as well, Pip. You'll recognise the house. Do you feel okay about this?'

I didn't want to say that I'd walk over hot coals to see him again, so instead I said, 'Of course I am. What time do you want me there?'

I heard him pause to check his watch. 'It's nearly four a.m., can we aim for five thirty at the latest? From memory, high tide is around six a.m.'

Just as quickly I agreed, saying, 'I'll be there. I'll charge my mobile; if you're held up, text me.'

I showered and dressed, feeling both nervous and excited. I filled Albert's water and food bowls up, packed my backpack, and texted Amanda saying I wouldn't be in.

Next, I texted John, asking him to look in on Albert tonight in case I was late home – leaving out: in case I didn't make it home.

As I left, I felt a flutter in my stomach, caused by nerves and excitement. The nerves were courtesy of the prospect of what lay ahead, the excitement courtesy of seeing Bill again.

CHAPTER 36

I arrived early, parked off the street close to the ferry terminal, and walked the rest of the way. The coffee shop on the pier was open, so I had a coffee.

As I sat sipping the brew, I looked at the glorious scene; the water was a pristine azure blue, reflecting the cloudless sky. It seemed to mock or contradict my feelings of doom about what lay ahead.

Maybe that was a good omen – good weather, good outcome. It certainly belied the day that probably lay ahead.

From my seat near the window, I watched Bill arrive. He was with Pat and two very large men. I watched the interaction between these men, assuming one was Nic.

The older man was tall, solidly built, with a very strong chin. The younger man, though not as tall or imposing, had similar mannerisms to the older one. He had a softer face, and his jaw, though strong, wasn't as pronounced. Even with these surface differences, I could see an undeniable family resemblance.

They soon disappeared from my line of sight. After a short time, I sensed then smelled Bill standing behind me – the fresh smell of soap and something else, a scent that was quintessentially Bill: pheromones were at work.

My initial desire was to jump up and throw my arms around him; seeing he had his work persona in place, I simply stood and turned toward him, waiting for his lead.

As he reached me, he gently pecked me on the cheek, propriety taking precedence – I sometimes get it right. As he kissed my cheek, I felt the unfamiliar roughness of stubble against my face; he hadn't shaved.

He'd also squeezed my arm, I hoped to privately let me know he was pleased to see me.

When Pat saw me, he had no such qualms; he wasn't here officially. He gave me the biggest hug and a kiss on the cheek, making me feel very accepted.

All businesslike, next Bill introduced me around. 'Pip, I'd like you to meet Nic. This is Nic's son, Luke. They both work in the police force, Nic with Broken Bay Marine Area Command. I called Nic this morning and he insisted on coming along, even though he's on leave.'

With the most infectious smile, Nic reached over, shook my hand firmly and said, 'Pleased to meet you.' Then, with a look of pure pride, he looked over to his son and continued. 'Luke here overheard my call with Bill and insisted on coming along.'

As I looked to the smiling face of his son – the similarities were staggering when they smiled – Luke, reaching to shake my hand, said, 'Pleased to meet you. I'm on leave too. The old man and I were going to do some fishing. Anyway, looks like we'll still be out on the water.'

A man after my own heart, Nic said, 'I've starving; let's see if we can get something quick to eat. The tide this morning is six forty-six, we don't want to miss it.'

I couldn't help thinking about what Napoleon is thought to have said – 'An army marches on it stomach.' Nic was obviously an advocate of this sentiment.

The food arrived quickly – bacon and egg rolls. As we ate, Bill seemed distracted and anxious, looking at his watch and outside often.

To distract him, I asked, 'So did you manage to get onto Brendan O'Connor this morning?'

With the most concerned look on his handsome face, he responded, 'Yes, I did; I phoned his mobile in the car on the way here. He didn't answer, though; his wife, Amelia, did.'

I knew from his voice and demeanour that this wasn't good. Sensing this, we all sat silently, allowing him time to continue.

With a deep sigh, Bill recounted the call, saying that when Amelia had answered the phone, she said quickly, *'Brendan, is that you?'*

Bill told us he'd explained to her who he was. At first, she was hesitant to confide in him. Sensing her hesitancy, and running out of time – rushing to get to Church Point and beat the tides – he'd told her he had backup police on the way, and then he'd recounted my dreams.

As he'd told her about them, Amelia went quiet. Eventually

she'd confided that Walton had contacted Brendan, threatening that, unless he helped him find somewhere to hide, his wife and children would be in danger.

The main reason she'd told him this was because what I had seen in my dream was, without a doubt, her father's old house in Towlers Bay.

She'd offered to go along to show him where the house was – it was tucked away in a small inlet surrounded by trees, and hard to find.

Bill had convinced her that the best place for her was with her children, and by the phone. She hesitantly hung up, agreeing to do just that, with Bill promising to phone her as soon as he had news.

After he finished recounting this call, we sat for a time in silence.

Breaking this silence, Pat mused, 'Wonder how Walton found out where Brendan and his family were living?'

Brow creased, anguish on his face, Bill answered, 'I don't know. I've been trying to work that out myself.'

Nic looked at his watch, urgency in his voice. 'None of that sounds too good. We need to make a move. Those bastards who said they'd meet you here are going to miss the tide. I've got my boat moored nearby. We need to head off now. You can contact Superintendent bloody Harris on the way.'

We did.

As we piled onto Nic's boat, Pat held his hand out to help me on board, and Bill put his hand on the small of my back to steady me. Soon we were moving, on the tide, making our way toward Towlers Bay and hopefully to where Walton and Brendan O'Connor were holed up.

Bill kept trying to contact Superintendent Harris, with no luck. There were no messages from him. Perplexed, he spoke to Nic, who offered to contact one of his workmates to see if they'd been left a message.

After a brief call, he hung up, shaking his head. 'Don't know what's going on, mate. No one seems to know anything about this. I've put them on notice just in case the dickhead has forgotten to contact them. They've promised to let me know if they hear from him. Sorry; can't do much else.'

Bill looked at his friend, perplexed yet grateful, and said, 'Thanks for checking. Maybe he contacted Eden. I assumed he'd phone you guys. I'm really sorry to have involved you like this without official sanction.'

Nic looked at his friend, and with conviction on his face and an irreverent tone responded, 'Let me worry about that. Besides, the son and I are out fishing with friends. What's the harm in that?'

Bill knew Nic was trying to downplay their involvement to ease his concerns – he also knew Nic was putting himself on the line for their friendship.

As I watched this touching scene, I got a flash: it was of us approaching the house, but it was dark.

This didn't make sense, but I knew I had to share it. 'Bill,' I said, 'got a minute? I've just had a small vision. I saw us approaching the house in the dark. It wasn't daytime. It felt safer that way.'

Bill looked at me, perplexed at first, then sanguine. 'Okay; thanks, Pip. I'll talk to Nic and Luke for a bit. Sit back and enjoy the scenery while you can.'

Dismissed.

A demarcation line between us where his work was concerned was obvious. We'd have to sort that out if I was to continue to offer my abilities.

This time, however, I did what he asked, and soaked up the scene around me. If there is one thing I adore, it's being near water. I'd have liked a better reason to be here, though.

Eventually, sick of playing the good girl, I walked over to join their discussion.

As I approached, I heard Pat, ever the voice of reason, say, 'Pip could have a point. Nic, you know this place well, don't you?'

Nic nodded; Pat continued. 'Is there somewhere we could moor then make our way to the house on foot?'

Nic considered this, then quickly smiled, nodded and said, 'There is. Old widow King lives in an inlet just around from the house. She's a dear old thing, deaf as a post and blind as a bat. I'm sure she wouldn't even notice if we moored at her jetty. Even if she does, we can explain our presence as a fishing trip.'

Bill, encouraged by this, asked intently, 'How easy is it to get from there to where we think Walton and hopefully Brendan O'Connor are?'

Nic responded with local knowledge. 'Piss-easy; we could make our way up behind her property, through the bush, then stake out the house from a hill until it gets dark. From up there, we'll have a good view of any arrivals, as well.'

Relief obvious in his voice, Bill said, 'That sounds promising. How hard will it be to get inside unnoticed?'

Again, Nic didn't disappoint. 'I've been to the house on a few occasions. There's a trapdoor underneath for deliveries which could get us inside, hopefully unnoticed. Might get a bit wet doing it; the house sits out over the water, and water laps at the bottom of the stumps when the tide comes in. It should be dark by around four forty-five to five at this time of year; a few hours sitting and waiting won't hurt.'

Bill still seemed concerned. 'Can we approach Widow King's house by boat without passing through Walton's view?'

Giving it some thought, Nic eventually responded. 'Yes, there's a series of creeks that dissect the bay. We could motor up one of those and come to Mrs King's place from the other side. It's a bit shallow, but if we take our time and don't go aground, we should arrive unannounced.'

Pat, laconic and practical as ever, said, 'Well, we have plenty of time, so let's get to Mrs K's. Once we're there, we can eat. I've got insect repellent and sunblock if anyone wants some. Midges love me. We'll also need to sort out what equipment we'll carry with us.'

I felt like kissing Pat, not only for his forethought, but for his calming manner – so I did kiss him. The other three seemed to agree with my sentiment, if not my way of showing my appreciation, and all chorused in with their thanks for his attention to the practicalities of life.

The longer we motored, the more nervous I became. Of course, my constant companion decided to make its presence felt via my throat-clearing tic.

Sensing my embarrassment, Bill said reassuringly, 'Let it go, Pip; don't hold it in. I've explained to Nic and Luke about your Tourette's. They understand.'

As he said this, he briefly rubbed my shoulder. His empathy and gesture reassured and comforted me.

I was having a lot of practice at authenticity. If I didn't watch myself, it could become a habit. It was good, not wasting my energy supressing my tics. Not supressing them now meant that tonight, when I needed to be quiet, I wouldn't have a built-up explosion of tics. That could be handy.

Soon Pat walked up to me and said, 'You'll be right tonight, love. Remember how well we worked together as a team in the Hunter. We all have our own set of skills; yours are just a bit more, um, unique than the rest of us. I have the utmost confidence in you.'

He looked hesitant and uncertain as he said these words, but they touched me deeply.

To reassure him, I quietly said, 'Thank you, Pat. That means so much, coming from you. You just gave my confidence a boost.'

Embarrassed but pleased, knowing I needed a distraction, he said, 'Well, love, I don't say things I don't mean. Now we all need to keep our eyes open, so grab this pole, and if you see the boat coming too close to the bank, gently push it away.'

It seemed to take forever to slowly navigate and motor our

way up the creek. We were all glad that Pat had packed the blockout. Nic had a few caps on board, so our heads were covered as well. I was offered and put on one of Nic's fishing jackets to protect my arms. Pat made sure we drank enough water, and he suggested we eat as well. Every dangerous operation needs a Pat.

Abruptly there came a loud noise, and smoke billowed from the prop area. Nic, the consummate boatman, stopped the engine immediately. Colourfully he said, 'Fuck it … sorry, Pip. I think something's stuck in the propeller. We're going to have to pull it up and have a look.'

With a huge grin, I said, 'Don't worry about using the F word around me, Nic. I've been known to use it myself on occasion.' To shift the focus off his language, I added, 'Will that cause a huge problem, having something stuck in the propeller?'

If I was going to continue to work with the police and have them feel like I was part of the team, they had to know I'm not easily offended by swear words.

Nic shot me a broad smile. 'Good to know. I've got a bit of a reputation for language. With the prop, depends what it is.' Then he turned to Luke with a fatherly smile and volunteered him, saying, 'Son, you're young and fit; jump over and have a look.'

Luke did just that. It turned out that someone's t-shirt had wrapped around the prop. Luke soon had it unravelled and the blades clear again. Luck was on our side – so far.

Seeing his son hold up the offending shirt, Nic said dryly, 'Oh good, might get some money for it on eBay.'

We all laughed, breaking the tension. It was then, as the tension eased, that Ruth came to mind. I hadn't thought about her for a while, but at that moment I realised she was definitely with us; knowing this felt good.

I must have been smiling as I had this realisation, because as I looked up, all four of the men beamed at me. Misunderstanding my smile, Nic said proudly, 'Knew the young bloke could fix it.'

Luke looked particularly pleased with himself. I was about to tell them the reason I was smiling, but when I looked at Luke's proud, beaming face, I couldn't steal his thunder.

Instead, I simply said, 'Well done, Luke. I'd hate to have been stuck out here.'

Nic soon had the boat restarted, and we began to slowly make our way to Widow King's inlet, clear of the creek and back in open waters. Nic made sure he kept the speed down so the noise of our approach wouldn't reach Walton.

When we got to her private jetty, young Luke jumped off and tied up, covering part of the boat in the process. Nic had moored at the furthest end of the jetty, so the boat couldn't be seen easily from the bay.

I was glad to be back on shore because, boy, did I need to pee. As I was looking around for a private place to go, my thoughts were mirrored when Bill said, 'Don't know about the rest of you, but nature calls. Pip, I think that's a good spot for you over behind that shed. Take your time so we blokes can relieve ourselves in privacy.'

As I pulled a pained comical face, they all laughed, and I

quickly ran toward the shed. The simplest things in life can build bonds and break down barriers.

Our common relief was reflected in our mood as a good-natured banter developed between us. Nic had a wicked sense of humour as well as colourful language. Before long, there was an easy camaraderie between us, and a true sense that we were in this together.

Then Bill became serious. He turned to Nic and said, 'Okay, mate, this is your territory. Where to from here?'

Knowing it was time to be serious, Nic responded, 'Well, the first thing we have to do is skirt up past Widow King's house without alarming or alerting her. If we can achieve that, we're assured that news of us being here won't get out.'

Nic proceeded to explain the route we'd take to reach our stakeout. He warned us about ticks – the arachnid type – and snakes. So, snakes, ticks and tics were the trilogy of things we wanted to avoid on our journey to the stakeout, and knowing that the former two existed just added to the possibility of the latter.

We had equipment to carry and enough backpacks to go around. I filled my own backpack with what remained of the food, plenty of water, the blockout, insect repellent – all the comfort stuff – and the binoculars, which were good for both day and night vision.

What was inside the men's backpacks was unknown to me. From the weight of them, it seemed they had come prepared for anything.

Before we left, I handed them the blockout and insect

repellent. After one final adjustment to our shoes and back-packs, with our heads low we followed Nic, making our way quietly up the side of Widow King's house. We hoped to make it to the ridge above before she noticed our presence.

The sun was beating down, the cicadas making a deafening noise as they snapped their wings. The grass was long and at times sharp. The path, such as it was, was very uneven. It was a hot and uncomfortable walk as we slowly made our way up to the ridge and out of sight. Before we reached the halfway point, we were all in a lather of sweat, but we pushed on without stopping. We needed to get out of sight as quickly as possible.

After forty minutes, we finally reached the safety of the trees that lined the ridge. To catch our breath, we sat for a time under the shade of a large tree and thirstily drank some water.

Breath caught, I fished around in my backpack and bought out some by now melted chocolate. Pat had thought to put it in for those who wanted an instant sugar hit.

After we'd scoffed a few sticky pieces down, Nic amusingly said, 'Well, come on ladies; this isn't *Picnic at Hanging Rock*. Follow me.'

As he led us toward the stakeout – and hopefully David Walton and Brendan O'Connor – I could see why Bill had turned to Nic for help. He had a knack of surrounding himself with very capable and loyal friends.

If we thought the slog up the hill to the ridge was bad, we had a lot worse ahead of us. The lantana had taken over on the ridge and we had to find a way around or through it.

Pat gave us a horticultural lecture, saying, 'Lantana is a

bloody curse. Try not to get it on your skin or near your eyes, Pip; it's a bad irritant. Keep away from those green berries in particular. I've seen poor bloody cattle eat the stuff and die in agony when feed is scarce.'

Nic, ever-ready with verbal antics, said in a mock-gruff voice, 'Thanks for that uplifting bit of information, mate. Pip, you follow Pat's instructions; don't eat the lantana.'

Trying to emulate his father, Luke chorused, 'Yeah, Pip, Dad's right, don't eat it.'

As we chuckled, I realised I hadn't ticced since we'd left. I was both concerned with reaching our destination and consumed by the physicality of it all; both were a panacea for stopping my tics. I also realised that I fit in well with these men, and, more importantly, that they accepted me as part of the team.

Finding our way through the lantana became very hard work, and after a while Nic said, 'What mongrel stuff this is. I should have thought to bring a machete.'

Calmly, Bill responded, 'We've got plenty of time, Nic. How far is it to the house? It's only two forty-five, so once we get past this, we can have a rest and wait for dark.'

Nic readily agreed. 'If it wasn't for this mongrel weed, we'd be there by now. As the crow flies, it's about ten minutes around this next bend. We could try to go down the ridge a bit and see if there's a way around, but we'd leave ourselves open to being seen.'

Bill made the decision for us. 'No, I think we should stay on this route. Come on; we're nearly there.'

We were tired, sweaty, thirsty and hungry. With Bill's

encouraging words and some perseverance, we eventually made it through the lantana. We were covered in scratches, but through, nonetheless.

We got down on our hands and knees and crawled to a thicket of trees up ahead. As we looked down, we could clearly see the derelict house and the colourful boatshed, and if we could see them, then Walton could see us. We were relieved when we arrived in the thicket above the cove, where the wait for darkness began.

Once under the cover of the trees, I pulled out my ever-present hand sanitiser – who says OCD doesn't come in handy? – and we attended to our scratches. It stung like hell, but it was better than them becoming infected. We then ate what was left of Pat's food and drank water to rehydrate. It was good to stop, and for a short time we almost forgot why we were there.

Nic, it turned out, was a great storyteller, and for the next hour or so he kept us quietly entertained with his tales. As noise carried clearly from the ridge, we had to stifle our laughter, and eventually Bill unwillingly told him to stop.

With full stomachs and glad to finally be in the right place, those of us who could do it had a nap. My nap was full of vivid dreams. I wasn't sure if they were prophetic or just my subconscious trying to sort and store the day.

I felt unwell from the sun and exertion. I'd packed some sachets of electrolytes, and so I added one to my drink bottle and drank it.

As we all sat quietly together, we took turns to keep a

lookout. Before we knew it, the sun was setting and darkness was upon us.

Bill spoke quietly. 'Okay, I think it's time we made our move. Luke, I'd like you to stay here with Pip and keep a lookout. Nic, Pat and I will make our way down to the house. We'll let you know when to join us.'

Luke and I looked at one another. He held his tongue, but I impetuously blurted, 'No way.'

Tersely, Bill answered, 'That's not a request, it's an order. We need a lookout. Luke, I don't want Pip up here in the dark on her own. This is not negotiable. Here; use this torch if for any reason you need to warn us – but it better be a good reason.'

Even at this early stage, I knew that once Bill had made up his mind there was no way to change it. Begrudgingly we both agreed to his plan.

Just before they left, Bill turned to Pat, handed him a piece of paper and said, 'Mate, I want you to stand guard outside the house. Nic and I will go in, and if you think things have gone pear-shaped, I want you to call the number Nic's given me, a.s.a.p. They will send out a police launch and backup, especially if you mention Nic's name. Make sure Pip and Luke stay safe.'

Then Bill turned to me. 'You have any of your premonitions or visions, Pip, no matter what it is, stay up here. Walton is dangerous, and we don't know who else is involved. The less people around to worry about getting hurt, the better.'

He cocked his head to make sure I was paying attention. I nodded that I was, and he continued. 'We don't know if Walton is there on his own or not; dangerous people do dangerous things. We also have Brendan O'Connor's life to consider. I owe it to him and his family to get him out safely.'

I knew he was coming from a place of caring concern, but it still annoyed the hell out of me. I knew he needed a clear head and didn't want to be concerned about my feelings, so I said, 'Sure, I understand, boss. See you soon.'

He beamed me that beautiful crooked smile and said, 'Yes, see you soon.'

I was pissed at being left behind to be babysat by Luke, but I also understood the reasons for this. It was going to be a long and difficult night.

As we watched these three brave men make their way down in the dark, my heart sank. I wanted them all to be safe and for this night to end well. I said a silent prayer and sent a message to Ruth saying, 'Please look out for them, Ruth; they're doing this for you.'

CHAPTER 37

I felt impotent, perched up high and safe out of harm's way; I'm sure Luke did as well. It was torture watching their slow and arduous descent into whatever mayhem the night had in store. Luke and I took it in turn to watch their progress through the binoculars.

As we lay there in the grass, the almost-full moon shone its light across both our forms. I hoped we didn't stand out from down below. The mozzies had come out in force, so we sprayed on more repellent and shared what was left of the chocolate.

Luke was a kind young man who obviously had a deep love for his family and a close bond with his father. I knew it must be hurting him to be here with me instead of with his dad, so I said, 'I'm sorry you got stuck babysitting, Luke. I realise you'd rather be down there.'

He hesitated for a moment, but responded kindly. 'No, Pip; looking out for you and being a lookout are important jobs. If we see anyone approaching, we can warn them. I'm where I'm supposed to be. In the force, we all know that what the boss says goes, and we all have our roles. No matter how we might feel about the job we're given, they're all important.'

Just as he said this, we saw the lights of a boat off in the distance. It was some way off yet, still out on the bay, but there weren't too many places it could be going – either Widow King's place or the house where Walton and possibly also Brendan were holed up.

It was then that I got a premonition that those on board the boat approaching were not friendly. I let out a gasp, and Luke said, 'Don't be alarmed; there are lots of locals who motor home this time of night. It's not necessarily someone going to the house.'

I shook my head in response as my something-bad-is-about-to-happen radar switched on, every hair on my neck prickling.

Then I felt it – Ruth's presence – and the words she whispered in my ears chilled me to the bone. *'You and this young man need to get down there.'*

As her voice rang in my mind, I shuddered, turned to Luke and said, 'You're going to have to trust me, Luke. We need to get down there, fast. Something is about to happen and it's not good. Please believe me, I'll explain later.'

To my amazement, he didn't hesitate; he simply said, 'Okay, what are we waiting for? Here, give me your hand; it's quite a drop.'

He wasn't wrong; even with his help I landed heavily, twisting my ankle.

Fortunately, I was wearing my high-sided hiking boots;

unfortunately, my filter wasn't on, and I blurted, 'Fuck, that hurt.'

Luke's response was to shake his head, smile and say, 'No wonder you and Dad hit it off so well. Can you walk, Pip?'

'Don't worry about me,' I said tersely. 'We need to get down there and find Pat.'

On the way down, we could tell that the boat we'd seen from the ridge was heading toward the house. Coupled with my premonition, I knew it could only mean trouble.

I think both Luke and I knew now it was the lift out of here that Walton had told Brendan O'Connor he was waiting for. This also meant that taking Walton by surprise was going to be even harder.

In my stressed state, I began to softly tic; it took every ounce of my being to stop. Realising this, Luke gently squeezed my shoulder and said, 'Pip, stop for a minute and compose yourself. We need to approach the house swiftly and quietly.'

'I know, I know, I know.' I crouched in the long grass, took several deep breaths and again asked Ruth for help and some courage. As I did this, I felt a gentle wind caress my neck and face and a surreal calmness descend. I knew Ruth was with us. I nodded to Luke, and then we quietly continued our journey down to the house.

When we were about fifty metres away, Pat jumped out from some bushes, quickly placed his hand over my mouth and pulled me down with him. Luke, seeing it was Pat, followed suit, dropping next to both of us.

Pat took his hand off my mouth and put a finger up to his

lips, then up to his ear. We took his message and listened. The wind was blowing our way; we could hear snippets of conversation coming from the house below.

The boat we'd seen approaching had moored and two men were making their way up to the house. Things were going from bad to worse; my premonition now made sense.

The three of us edged closer to the back of the house; from there we could faintly see the outlines of people inside. The lights they had on couldn't be seen from the bay. We saw Walton let the men in, look around, then quickly shut the door.

It was then that we saw Bill in a back room, standing over someone. It looked like he was trying to untie the person; we hoped it was Brendan O'Connor, and that he was still alive. In answer to our unsaid question, Brendan slowly stood and began to shake his hands and legs, no doubt to help his circulation.

Just as he did that, the door flew open. Bill tried to hide but wasn't fast enough. Next, someone hit him. He immediately fell to the floor. Brendan O'Connor, hands in the air, animatedly talked to the men.

One of them motioned for him to sit back down, seeming to retie him. They then disappeared from view, having obviously secured Bill as well. As they went to leave the room, someone apparently kicked him hard, and I felt my blood run cold and my anger rise.

Pat groaned softly next to me, seeing his best friend being badly treated. Softly and reassuringly, Luke said, 'It doesn't look like they know Dad's there. Maybe he's inside, waiting for a chance to do something.'

Pat and I nodded; we understood and appreciated both his concern for his father and his need to give us hope.

Then Pat remembered what Bill had said about calling for backup. Ducking low, he made the call, explaining that medical assistance was also needed. To give credibility to the call, he handed the phone to Luke, who confirmed the urgency of the situation.

As Luke hung up, he said, 'They'll pull out all stops. I've explained that their approach has to be undetected; Dad trusts these men and they know the area well. Backup and medical assistance will be here soon.'

Taking some control, Pat said, 'Yeah, but in the meantime, we need to do something. Come on, think. What can we do?'

It was then that Ruth said, *'The power, cut the power.'*

Before I could think, I blurted, 'Ruth says to cut the power.'

Pat looked at me in amazement. 'She's a bloody genius.'

Luke glanced from Pat to me in perplexity and was apparently about to ask who the hell Ruth was when Pat said, 'It's a long story, mate; we'll tell you later. By the sound of it the house is on a generator, not mains?'

Luke nodded. 'This old place hasn't been put back onto mains power since a huge storm knocked out the power pole. From memory, Dad said there's a huge generator in the shed over there.'

'Good lad. Pip, you stay here. Luke, come with me, son; we need to stop that generator. Hopefully it will bring at least one of them out to check what's going on. We'll take it from there.'

As I watched, Pat and Luke silently made their way to the

shed to turn off the petrol tap. All I could think about was Bill and how much damage they'd done to him.

Soon, slowly but surely, the noise of the generator that had been subdued by sounds of wind and ocean wound down, sputtered, then stopped. The lights inside the house went out, and I held my breath waiting to see what would happen next.

It was now pitch black in my hiding place. I heard a voice, then saw a torch, first on the back porch, then weaving its way down the steps. One of the men was clearly going to see if the generator had run out of petrol. That left two inside: Walton and one other.

Hopefully Nic knew by now which room Bill and Brendan were being held in. Luke had assured us earlier that his father was very calm under pressure and would wait till the time was right. I hoped this was true.

An almost unbearably long time later, another dark silhouette appeared at the top of the steps, yelling after the first man and swearing under his breath when he got no response. He scuttled back into the dark house, like the lowlife cockroach he was – and I apologise to every cockroach on the planet for that comparison.

He soon reappeared, torch in hand, mumbling under his breath. In the glow I saw it was Walton. I held my breath as he made his way toward the shed, hoping and praying that Pat and Luke were ready for him.

He passed so close to me I could have leaned out and touched him; to get further out of sight I stepped back – an almost fatal mistake.

As I did so, I lost my footing and fell heavily backwards, snapping twigs.

As I was trying to scramble back onto my feet, Walton spun, and with lightening reflexes aimed his torch at me. Before I could stand, he grabbed me, pulling me up roughly.

In an angry, sinister voice, he spat, 'You bitch, I should've known you'd be involved. I'm going to deal with you once and for all. You can join your boyfriend in oblivion.'

True to his word, he began to choke me with a ferocity that stunned me.

As I struggled to get out of his vicelike grip, I wondered why he'd always had his henchmen do his killing for him – he quite obviously had an aptitude for it.

Out of nowhere, Ruth materialised. She was like a vapour at first, then like a hologram.

It was clear that Walton could also see her. With shock on his now not-so-handsome face, he fell back in horror, letting go of my throat.

For a time, we were united in our amazement at seeing Ruth's apparition. Walton glanced at me with eyes full of fear, mouth open, shaking his head – he wanted to make sure I was also seeing Ruth. As she hovered above us, the gentle woman I knew Ruth to be had dissipated; she was enraged.

The air around her seemed to freeze, and each breath I greedily sucked into my oxygen-starved lungs burned. As I exhaled, my hot breath hit the chill air; it was as if I was exhaling fire or fog against that icy coldness.

Ruth's disgust at her nephew's betrayal was so deep, I could feel the pain that emanated from her; I felt the betrayal and the anger at what he'd done. It was raw, it was intense and it was visceral.

Mixed with these strong emotions, I also felt the care and concern she had for me. I knew she wouldn't allow her nephew to do to me what he had done to her. I knew Ruth would protect me, save me.

As I began to regain my breath, I felt a sudden calmness. It's a great feeling to have a spirit protect you so fiercely.

I felt smug, seeing the look of abject terror on his face. Even very handsome people look ugly when they're afraid.

Then Ruth said something to her nephew. The wind swept her words away, but whatever she'd said made him forgot me completely. With a now ashen face, he turned and began to run away from her, away from me, toward what he thought was the safety of the shed.

Tonight was full of surprises for David Walton. What awaited him there instead of sanctuary were Pat and Luke. I watched in awe and satisfaction as he flew into their trap.

I understood his fear; I'd also been horrified by the apparition of Ruth, seeing her rage. For a time, I stood rooted to the spot, grateful to be alive, but also heartsick to see such a kind and beautiful woman transformed by her anger.

Then Ruth disappeared. I saw two men, torches in their hands, come toward me, toward the still-darkened house. Time halted; I couldn't see who the men were. Was it Walton and his accomplice, or Pat and Luke?

As they got closer, in the light of the moon I saw that it was

Pat and Luke, and my heart lifted. When they reached me, I took a deep breath and was about to speak when Pat put his finger to his lips and pointed to the house.

They were going in, and, thanks to Ruth's suggestion about turning off the power and her then scaring her nephew half to death, the odds were even. Pat, seeing the angry marks on my throat, gently touched my neck, then pointed for me to stay out of harm's way in nearby bushes.

I was over staying out of harm's way; once they were inside, I intended to ignore Pat's well-meant direction and follow them in.

As I waited to make my move, I saw Pat and Luke move up the steps onto the porch. They opened the door and slipped inside. I heard raised voices and then a great ringing bang – a gunshot. This was turning into some night.

I took a deep breath and ran up the stairs. I hesitated just outside the door, afraid of what I might find, then threw open the door and stepped into the still-dark house.

Once my eyesight had adjusted, I could see someone lying on the floor in a dark pool, which could only be blood. I hoped it wasn't Luke or Pat. I slid along the wall and further into the darkened room, keeping as far from the body as possible.

A figure came out of the far room where Bill and Brendan were presumably still lying; in his flickering torchlight I saw it was Luke. My presence momentarily startled him, but then he said, 'Pat, Dad and I are okay. We need to get that generator on so we can see how Bill and Brendan are. Here, take the torch, go in and see for yourself. I think I can hear a boat approaching, so backup's here. Everything's going to be okay.'

With these reassuring words, he slipped out the back door and ran toward the shed, presumably to turn the generator back on. I went into the room and found that Brendan was untied, and that Bill lay semiconscious on the floor.

Pat and Nic were crouching by him. They looked up, shone their torches at me and saw the look of concern on my face. Pat said gently, 'He's going to be fine, Pip. His pulse is strong and he's very fit. It sounds like the police launch is here. Can you run outside and get them here as quickly as you can?'

Shaking my head, I looked at Bill almost motionless on the floor, then Nic said, 'He's right, love; take the torch and let the boys know what's happened. Tell them we need to get Bill and the other bloke out there to a hospital a.s.a.p. Do it, Pip – we won't leave him.'

Unwillingly, I did as I was asked. As we re-entered the house, the lights came back on and I saw Nic leaning over whoever was lying in a pool of blood on the floor.

Nic told the arriving officers that, once a doctor had checked the unconscious suspect over, he was to be cuffed, taken on board and kept separate from Walton and the other suspect. Luke then led a couple of police officers out to the shed, where Walton and his offsider had been left securely bound.

With everything in hand, Nic described what had happened. Once the power had gone out, he'd known it was his time to make a move. He'd heard the first man leave, then, when that man didn't return, he heard Walton being ordered to find out what was causing the hold-up. Nic had then patiently waited for either Walton's return or for his son's arrival, desperately hoping it would be the latter.

When he'd looked out the window, he'd been relieved to see his son and Pat together approaching the front door. In the darkened house, he'd silently slipped into the room where the distracted third man was waiting by the window, and then he'd crouched behind a chair, ready to react.

When the door had opened, Nic's first instinct had been to protect his son and Pat, so he'd lifted his gun and shot the third man in the thigh. The man had staggered toward the door before collapsing.

As one doctor assessed first Bill and then Brendan, a second doctor attended to the wounds of the man Nic had shot. They soon had all three suspects cuffed and securely on board the police launch.

I couldn't keep away from Bill any longer, so doctor or no doctor I went back into the room. From the sombre looks on their faces, my heart sank.

Reading my thoughts and feeling my heartache, Ruth gently reassured me: *'He will recover; trust me.'*

With her reassuring words, a sense of calm yet again came over me. As I said, I liked having a crossed-over protector reassuring me – a lot. All the same, her anger as an apparition had terrified even me. I didn't think Walton would get over that visitation from his aunt any time soon – well, I hoped not, anyway.

Despite the reassurance in Ruth's words, I burst into tears.

Concerned, Pat came over to me and said, 'Pip, it's okay,

love. Let the doctors have a look at you. I think the marks on your throat are superficial, but best to make sure. The doctor thinks Bill will be fine; his vitals are good. They're going to hydrate him because of a bit of blood loss, then get him onto the launch. There'll be an ambulance and an escort waiting to take him to Mona Vale Hospital. Once he's there, they'll do a CT scan, just as a precaution.'

Though pleased to hear this news, I said, 'I'm fine, Pat, honestly; I know Bill's going to be okay. Ruth told me.'

Young Luke, by now standing at the door, said in a perplexed tone, 'Are you two going to put me out of my misery and tell me who the hell Ruth is?'

As Pat and I looked at one another, from sheer relief we began to laugh – not quite uncontrollable laughter this time, but we were working our way up to it. The medical staff, having seen this reaction before, took it in their stride.

Luke said, 'I don't get it; what's so funny? I asked a simple question.' He was tired and grumpy, and quite frankly his tone was justified.

Then Bill groaned, and in a heartbeat Pat and I were by his side. He looked at us, gave his crooked smile and in a slurred voice said, 'What's funny?'

Then his eyes closed again, and with a smile on his face he went quiet. The doctor assured us this was a good sign and continued to stabilise him for the trip by launch to the waiting ambulance. The fact that our laughter had roused him momentarily was a good sign that, as Ruth had said, he was going to be okay.

Once Brendan was checked over, he phoned Amelia. We felt we were invading his privacy, but as he didn't leave the room, we all heard him say, 'Em, baby, it's me.' He paused to listen to her response then, gently, trying to calm and reassure her, he said, 'Baby, stop crying; I'm fine, honestly. They got Walton and his mates. We're safe now, all safe … No; I've got to speak to the police, but as soon as I can, I'll be home. I love you too. Give the kids a kiss and a big hug from me. Yes, see you soon … No, the police will drop me off. Okay, bye, love you too.'

As he hung up, the brave face he'd shown his wife in that call dissipated and he began to tremble, tears threatening to spill as he slipped into shock.

The doctor sat him down and placed a Mylar blanket around his shoulders, then asked the police if they could interview Brendan soon so he could get home to his family. Except for marks around his wrists and ankles, and mild dehydration, he was in remarkably good shape – physically, at least.

As I watched all of this, I felt good knowing that, in some small way, I'd helped rescue him. As Brendan was trying to compose himself, he suddenly realised that I was in the room. In an oddly polite tone, as though we were meeting for the first time at a party, he said to me, 'Sorry; I'm Brendan.'

He was in shock, so, just as politely, I responded, 'Yes, I know; I'm Pip.'

A look of recognition flashed across his face. 'Oh, you're the lady who had the dream. I'm sorry; my wife was a bit emotional just now, so I don't know how this fits in, but she wanted me to thank you.'

I felt myself blush with both embarrassment and pride. 'Oh, no; you need to thank Bill and these three men. I was a very small part of this rescue, I ...'

Pat interjected, 'She's being modest, mate. Pip was far from being a small part, believe me. But there's plenty of time to tell you about that. You need to do what you have to do, then get home to your family.'

I was grateful for Pat's speech. I was exhausted, my throat was bloody sore, and I could feel a headache coming on. Now that I wasn't concentrating on staying alive, I could also feel a build-up of tics itching to explode.

They soon had Bill stabilised, on a stretcher and down the front stairs. The hardest part was lifting him down onto the police launch. Once we were all on board, the police launch gave Nic a lift to his own boat so he could take Brendan O'Connor back home to his family.

Once settled on board, Pat and I sat as close to Bill as we could without getting in the way of the medical team.

Sensing my growing feelings for Bill, Pat said, 'Here, Pip, you sit next to Bill. I'm damn sure he'd rather see your face than my ugly mug.'

As I sat there, the doctor, having just checked on Bill, asked if he could look me over, including down my throat, to make sure there was no visible damage. The outside of my throat was still red but fading. God only knew what the inside was like.

In my usual self-deprecating way, I said, 'Don't worry about the inside of my throat. With my Tourette's, I've cleared my throat most of my life. I'm sure it's as tough as old leather down there.'

Not to be deterred, he continued. 'You must understand, being choked is more serious than it feels or sounds. Do you remember how long you couldn't breathe for?'

By this stage I'd had enough and was about to spit out, 'How the hell would I know? I was too concerned with trying to breathe.' Thankfully my rational brain kicked in, and instead I said, 'Not long, though it seemed like an eternity. I'd say no longer than six or seven seconds.'

'Well, just to be safe, when we get to Mona Vale Hospital, I'll organise for you to have an X-ray to make sure. It can take weeks before it's obvious that serious damage has been done. If you feel in any way out-of-sorts over the next several weeks, go straight to hospital. The doctors at Mona Vale will explain all of this to you. Try to relax now, if you can.'

Pat listened intently to all this, then said, 'Don't worry, doctor, I'll keep an eye on her and make sure she looks out for anything unusual.'

This was said firmly, with Pat looking directly at me. His concern moved me to tears, which progressed to air-sucking sobs as I lost it completely.

Pat got up and gently wrapped his arms around my shoulders. 'It's okay, Pip; let it out, let it go. You've been very brave; let it go.'

And I did.

Once we'd dropped Nic, Brendan and another officer off at Nic's boat at Widow King's place, and I'd calmed down,

Luke finally asked, 'Okay – who's Ruth?'

Pat and I looked at one another, then Pat sheepishly said, 'I think I'll leave that explanation to Pip.'

I shot Pat a scathing look that even Albert would have been proud of. Then I took a deep breath and did just that, leaving nothing out. After tonight, Luke deserved the truth, the whole truth and nothing but the truth.

By the time I'd finished, going right back to that first night in the Hunter, I had a very mystified Luke sitting there, mouth wide open, jaw hanging, shaking his head.

To bring Luke back to planet earth and shut his mouth – it wasn't a good look – I gently took two fingers, lifted his jaw to close it, then said, 'So there; ponder on that for a while.'

Leaving Luke shaking his head in disbelief, I walked away chuckling to myself, realising I'd picked up that particular quaint expression from Uncle J.

I'd had my phone charging since we'd embarked, and I soon heard several pings. I retrieved my mobile, and, leaving it plugged in, read my texts.

The first was from John. It read, *'Pip, I hope everything's okay? Where are you?'* He was obviously concerned and I instantly felt guilty.

I quickly texted him back, saying, *'Sorry; I'm okay. Mobile needed a recharge. I'll explain tomorrow. Did you feed Albert? xx.'* I didn't see the sense in alarming him at this late hour.

A little tersely, my best friend texted back, *'Of course I fed him. He's beside himself with separation anxiety. When will you be home?'*

'*It's been quite a day; will explain when I have time; on the way to take Bill to Mona Vale Hospital. P xx.*'

Not to be put off easily, he texted back, '*Mona Vale Hospital? God, Pip, where are you and what have you two been up to this time? Honestly, woman, you exasperate me.*'

My reply was curt. '*Too much happening to explain; need to speak to the police first. P x.*'

Resigned to the fact that he'd get nothing more from me, he responded, '*You are the most infuriating yet strangely intriguing best friend I've ever had. I hope Bill's going to be okay. I'm having palpitations trying to imagine what you've been up to.*'

Guiltily I responded, '*I'm sorry; I didn't mean to upset you. Love you. P xx.*'

He came back, '*Pip, I was joking, kind of. I'll feed Albert tomorrow morning. Fill me in if and when you can. Love you too. J xx.*'

I texted, '*Thank you. Please tell Albert I love him and I'll see him soon. I don't know what I'd do without you. P xx.*'

With one final text for the night, my dearest friend said, '*I'll pass your message on to Albert. I actually believe he'll understand. I might even try bringing the little fella over here, if Leroy doesn't object. Bye, pussycat; love you; take care.*'

His last text brought tears of relief to my eyes, knowing that Albert would have company tonight. I had enough going on without adding guilt about Albert into the mix.

CHAPTER 38

When we finally arrived at the pier, two ambulances were waiting, engines running and lights flashing. There was also a police van waiting to transport Walton and his offsiders to the lock-up.

As they settled Bill in the ambulance, they wheeled the guy Nic had shot in the leg past us. As I saw him under the street light I recoiled, shocked.

I hadn't recognised who he was at first, as he was unshaven, wasn't in uniform, and was wearing a wool beanie. Now the hat was off and I saw him under good light, I realised who he was. As I did, an uncontrollable shiver wracked my body.

Pat, always acutely aware of other people's emotions because of his own post-Vietnam PTSD, gently said to me, 'Pip, it's all over. They can't hurt anyone anymore.'

I looked at Pat, still stunned. 'You don't understand. The man Nic shot is Superintendent Harris. I'm sure. Didn't you recognise him?'

Pat and Luke looked at me in utter disbelief; Pat, uncharacteristically, said, 'Bloody hell! Are you sure?'

I giggled and said, 'Yes, Pat, I'm pretty bloody sure.'

The ambos motioned for us to jump into the ambulance with Bill. Then, accompanied by a police escort, they put Harris in the other ambulance.

Luke rode in a police car; Pat and I went in the ambulance with Bill. Pat sat in the front, allowing me to ride in the back with Bill.

I'm not always comfortable around hospitals or things medical – I'm not squeamish, but I'm like an emotional sponge in that I absorb the energy and pain of people who are unwell.

On this occasion, though, I didn't want to be anywhere else but in this ambulance and on the way to the hospital with Bill.

CHAPTER 39

The staff at the emergency department at Mona Vale Hospital were ready and waiting when the ambulances pulled in. Bill was rushed in first and taken to triage. Nothing makes you feel more impotent than seeing someone you care about rushed away to be assessed and cared for by strangers, albeit caring ones.

As they took Bill inside, Pat and I turned to watch Harris disembark.

As he was wheeled past us, he turned to me, and in an acerbic tone said, 'I knew you were trouble the moment I laid eyes on you.'

Pat was about to respond, but one of the ambos shook his head and said, 'Mate, don't waste your breath; he's not worth it. Go inside and see how your friend is. We'll deal with this one.'

As they wheeled him inside a little too fast over a drainage grid, Harris winced in pain. One of the ambos shot us a smirk as they disappeared into the bowels of the emergency department.

Emergency services work closely together – if you mess with one, you mess with them all – and there are many ways to show solidarity.

Once Pat had given Bill's personal details to the admissions clerk, we found ourselves in a waiting room outside triage. It wasn't long before a doctor appeared, telling us they were taking Bill down to radiology for a CT scan of his head. She was both kind and matter of fact. That mix of professionalism and kindness reassured us.

She suggested we grab a coffee; it was going to be a long night. Immediately I felt hunger pangs, and Pat and I set off on a mission to satisfy both his caffeine craving and my food one.

We had to settle for the biscuits in the relatives' room just off the emergency department. I don't know why packaged plain hospital biscuits always taste so good – they never taste that good at home.

After an interminable time, we were told that Bill's CT scan was clear. To keep a close eye on him, he was being transferred to ICU for the night, then a ward tomorrow. The mention of ICU alarmed us.

Pat suggested that I see a doctor myself to make sure my injuries wouldn't come back to bite me. I was loath to leave; from my own experience of visiting my mother in ICU, I knew they usually preferred relatives to visit two at a time, just like the Ark.

As I was about to leave, Bill's sisters, Charlotte and Julie, who Pat had called, arrived and immediately threw their arms around Pat.

Standing back, I had the chance to observe them. Bill had described their lovely natures, but not their appearance. From his descriptions, I felt I already knew them. I wished I was meeting them under different circumstances.

Like their brother, they were both very attractive, though in different ways. Charlotte was about my height with a mid-length, impossibly shiny auburn bob, symmetrical features, lovely pale skin and her brother's sparkling blue eyes. Julie was taller and slimmer but with similar facial features. She had a trendy blonde concave haircut framing striking hazel eyes and perfectly-shaped eyebrows.

As I watched, I could see that they shared the same mannerisms as their brother. Despite the circumstances, they remained calm.

What I wouldn't give to be like that. Calmness is something I've always admired in others. I guess you're attracted to what you lack.

Pat introduced me to them as someone Bill had become close to. As he said this, I saw a fleeting look pass between the sisters as a ghost of a smile crossed their lips.

This went some way toward soothing my fears that they might think me too young for Bill. Of course, then there were my tics. My Tourette's is an innate part of me; that doesn't mean it's easy to show it to new people.

After introductions, Pat explained that I needed to be

checked out medically. He said he'd take me down to triage and then come back to the waiting area and sit with them.

There's a term used by intensive care staff – 'ICU time'. They try their best to talk to relatives and, as in our case, friends, as soon as possible, but their first priority will always be looking after their patient.

I was grateful to Pat for his insistence. It took my mind off what was happening with Bill and away from the calm but worried looks on both his sisters' lovely faces.

I was seen relatively quickly – again, this was emergency service staff looking after their own, and knowing that they put me in the same category as Bill gave me a sense of belonging to something much bigger than myself.

After hearing the story of what Walton had done, the doctor sent me for a chest X-ray just to be safe. Strangulation, he told me, can cause pulmonary oedema or overload in the lungs, which can last up to two weeks after an assault.

All I could think was, *Thank God Ruth had materialised as quickly as she had.*

Sensing that I already had information overload, he sent me to X-ray saying he'd tell me what else I was to look out for later.

When I returned, true to his word, he continued. He said that over the next several weeks I was to watch for certain tell-tale signs that things weren't right. Strangulation can produce a lot of long-term side effects. Depending on the length of time the strangulation took, cutting off a continuous supply of oxygen can cause brain cells to malfunction and die – some immediately, others weeks later. Even minimal force can cause bleeding and/or swelling inside the neck, leading to vascular disaster. A force as little as two kilograms of pressure can damage the carotid arteries, compromising blood flow to the brain. Blood clots may form inside the artery and block blood flow or break off and travel to the brain.

The list went on: problems sleeping – like I needed more disturbed sleep patterns; vision changes; ringing in the ears; impaired memory and concentration.

I was grateful this doctor took the time to alert me to the dangers of strangulation. None of this information had been given to me by the doctor I saw after Scanlan had tried to strangle the life out of me.

They say ignorance is bliss – ignorance can also be fatal.

After reiterating to me how important it was for me to take his warnings seriously, he let me go. I found a concerned Pat waiting outside.

He stood and, as I walked toward him, said, 'Everything okay, Pip? I was getting worried. You were in there a long time.'

Wanting to reassure him, I said, 'Yep, clean bill of health. The doctor just gave me a list of things to look out for over the next few weeks. The chest X-ray was clear. Let's head back up to see if there's any news on Bill.'

He accepted my glib response. Pat knew when to press for facts and when to let things slide. The more I knew him, the more I understood why he was Bill's best friend.

Bill's sisters had been visited by the unit's social worker, who'd assured them Bill was in ICU as a precaution only, and because beds in other parts of the hospital were full due to the particularly bad flu season. She assured them that once he was settled, they could see him.

We were all hugely relieved.

Both sisters were keen to know what had happened. Having two family members in the police force had prepared them for our censored explanation and the wait ahead.

By the time we'd finished telling them about the night, my tics were screaming to explode. Credit where credit's due: my brain had behaved well most of the day. I knew I'd soon have to excuse myself and find some privacy.

Intellectually, I understood that, if they were related to Bill, my Tourette's would be accepted by them. But I wasn't ready to take that risk just yet, and I quietly told Pat I needed some space.

He nodded and said, 'Good idea Pip; take some time out. Keep your phone on so I can text you when we hear news on Bill.'

I found myself a quiet and, hopefully, safe space and let my tics off their leash. I'd held them in a long time, so my brain was not going to let me off lightly. It was ready to pay me back – bigtime. I was soon drawing attention to myself, and people were staring.

In their defence, I must have looked a sight after the day I'd had, combined with my out-of-control vocal tics – yes, plural: I'd added a not-often-expressed squeaking tic. I must have looked like someone out of control on something of a chemical nature.

In a way, I was out of control on something chemical, but it wasn't a man-made mind-altering drug; it was a self-made chemical, a product of my unique biology, that meant extra dopamine receptors were firing like there was no tomorrow. In a moment of self-preservation, I decided a brisk walk was what I needed.

I left the hospital and walked to the end of Coronation Street toward the ocean. The smell of the salt air and the sound of waves would ease my worried and overtaxed soul. I sat in the park at the end of the street, overlooking the ocean, and silently wept.

These were tears of pent-up fear, frustration and overwhelming anger – not a good combination for anyone.

I sat there for over half an hour, and slowly I felt a sense of control come over me, particularly as I remembered what Ruth had said – that Bill was going to be okay.

With some control back, I stood, took one last look at the sea, and walked up toward the hospital. When I was almost at the front entrance, my phone pinged as a text arrived. I'm not like most people – obsessed with people keeping in touch, keeping them in the loop; phones do my head in – but this time I snatched at it.

The text was from Pat, and it read, '*Bill's settled. He's asked for you and after you.*'

A man of few words at times, our Pat; a man I'd hug as soon as I saw him.

I was about to enter the lift when my phone started to ring. I answered with, 'What did you forget, Pat?'

I was surprised to hear John's voice. 'It's me. I'm just touching base to see how you are and how Bill is?'

Overwhelmingly pleased to hear his voice, and sorry I'd forgotten to phone him, I responded apologetically. 'Oh, John, I'm so sorry! It's been busy and intense since we arrived. I should have phoned you. I'm sorry if you've been concerned.'

My dear friend said, 'I'm not the only one; Uncle J phoned. He's been trying to get onto you. Hope you don't mind – I filled him in, and he got quite excited and kept saying, "I knew something was wrong!" He's brought his trip forward. Max and I are picking him up from the airport this afternoon.'

Hearing this, I was upset that I'd worried them, but very pleased to hear that Uncle J was arriving today. I desperately needed his reassuring presence.

I thanked John profusely, finished our conversation and headed to the lift and the ICU waiting room.

When I reached the waiting area, Bill's sisters had come back, and Pat, next on the tag team, was in seeing Bill. The looks on their faces said more than words could ever express: they were quite obviously very relieved.

When they saw me, they echoed what Pat's text had said – Bill wanted to see me.

Pat soon came back, and in his usual understated manner said, 'Better get in there. He won't be satisfied till he sees for himself you're okay.'

My initial thought was, *Oh no, I must look a mess*. I'm not vain, but it had been some day, and I did want to at least tidy myself up. I turned to the girls for some feminine reassurance, asking, 'How do I look?'

In unison they responded, 'You look beautiful. Just go in.'

Then Charlotte said, 'Here, Pip, borrow my mirror and lip gloss. You don't need it, but it'll make you feel better.'

At her kind gesture, tears came to my eyes. Seeing this, both sisters wrapped their arms around me, hugging me tightly, while Pat stood back watching and grinning like a Cheshire Cat.

I grinned back at him, then – God knows why; relief, immaturity, both – I poked my tongue out at him. To my great pleasure and surprise, he poked his tongue back.

I love to see the child in everyone peep out occasionally.

CHAPTER 40

If you haven't been inside an intensive care unit, it's a bit of a shock, a sensory overload. I'd been inside one when my mother was ill. Having already experienced one doesn't make it any easier – it just prepares you for the onslaught.

Firstly, the units are secure areas, so you have to be let in. The lights are bright and the atmosphere feels sterile because it is and has to be. You can hear alarms as other patients fight to regain their health.

You can't help but feel you're invading their space and intruding on the grief of their relatives. You try not to look at the relatives, and if you do make eye contact, you simply nod slightly to let them know you understand their pain.

As I approached Bill's bed, two nurses were talking to him. I stood back to give them space and to allow time for myself to prepare. Then Bill saw me standing back, and with a smile on his face, that crooked one I'd learnt to love, lifted his hand and motioned for me to come closer. 'Pip, come here: I want to see you really are okay.'

Both nurses turned to look at me, and with a smile on her face one said, 'So, you're the famous Pip we've heard so much about.'

I felt myself blush, moving as close as I could to Bill without getting in their way.

The other said, 'We're nearly finished. He's doing really well. We should transfer him to a ward some time later today or tomorrow morning.'

Despite that bit of uplifting news, I felt tears threatening again. To save Bill the angst, I pulled myself together, and in an attempt to lighten the mood I dryly said, 'Well, you look a bit better than last time I saw you. Honestly, the things some people do to get out of paperwork.'

I was rabbiting to cover my overwhelming sense of relief, my nervousness at being so close to him, and to stop myself from losing it – inappropriate humour raising its head again.

Realising my quandary, he kindly shot back, 'You know how much I hate paperwork. Hopefully Nic's on top of it. Come closer; I want to see you're okay.'

I did move closer; I desperately wanted to be near him, to kiss him. I wasn't sure if it was appropriate given the circumstances. I was feeling cautious and uncertain about taking our relationship to the next level.

To cover, I ran my fingers through my hair and excused my appearance by saying, 'God, I must look an absolute mess after last night.'

He saw my tentativeness, gave me that smile again and said, 'You look wonderful. I'm so glad you're okay.'

Bill wasn't yet aware of what Walton had done to me, and if I had my way he wouldn't be finding out any time soon. To change the subject, I said, 'John phoned before to see how you were. When Uncle J couldn't get onto me, he phoned John and Max. They told him what's been going on, so he brought his trip forward – he arrives tonight.'

Bill seemed genuinely pleased to hear this. 'That's great. I can't wait to meet him.'

As he said this, a nurse came up and gently but authoritatively told me it was time for me to leave, as Bill needed to rest and have his observations taken.

I agreed straight away; he looked tired and pale. As I got up to leave, not knowing how to say goodbye, he motioned with his finger for me to bend down close.

As I did, he whispered, 'I'll see you soon, right?'

A thrill went through my body at his words and being so close to him. With false casualness I said, 'You sure will, but get some rest now.'

Then he unexpectedly kissed me on the mouth. I felt my knees tremble and my heart soar – the man could kiss, even in the state he was in; heaven help me.

When I got outside, his sisters were about to leave to freshen up, and said they were coming back to visit Bill later. Pat needed to get back to the Hunter and had organised for his brother to pick him up.

I let them know that my uncle was flying in and I wouldn't

be here again till tomorrow. Pat assured me that Bill needed rest more than a ton of visitors, and said that once he had Burt sorted, he'd be back again himself.

With this reassurance, and a headache now thumping like a sledgehammer, we said our goodbyes and I headed for the cab rank to make my way back home.

By the time I got into a cab, I got a text from John saying he and Max were out collecting Uncle J from the airport. I couldn't wait to see Albert, realising how much I'd missed the little man.

As we drove, I remembered my car was still parked at the ferry terminal. I knew I'd be way too tired to collect it today. Uncle J and I could hire a car tomorrow morning and drive up together; I'd need my car to visit Bill.

Meanwhile I thought about making it up to Albert. From what John had said, he'd need a ton of reassurance. I also sent Amanda a text. I didn't know how much longer my employers could keep accommodating my new vocation, but I hoped it could be for a bit longer, at least until I could make up my mind if I wanted to be involved in another police case.

The minute I thought this, I knew my answer – I sure as hell did. One thing at a time, though: I had an uncle to make up to and a very pissed off cat to appease.

CHAPTER 41

As the cab pulled up outside my home, I felt an overwhelming joy that I'd soon be safe inside. I was disappointed Albert didn't meet me at the gate. As I unlocked the front door, I could hear him meowing loudly from inside. John had locked his cat door to keep him safe.

That wasn't the only thing John had done. My adorable Albert was wearing an emerald green bowtie, which really complimented his ginger fur.

As I crouched to let him jump onto my lap, I heard him purring loudly, and knew my absence had already been forgotten and forgiven.

I sat on the floor, tears streaming down my face. 'My darling boy, I'm very sorry that you've been so frantic. Please forgive me? Now, let me look at what Uncle John has dressed you in.'

He tucked his head under my chin and put a front paw on each shoulder, and as I stroked him gently, I promised to take the bowtie off once Uncle J had seen the effort John had gone to.

As I sat on the floor, the events of the past days played like a movie on rewind through my head, and everything caught up with me. I began to tremble as silent tears splashed my cheeks.

My little radar-in-a-bowtie sat up, looked at me with his penetratingly beautiful green eyes, then jumped off my lap and walked over to his food bowl. I'm positive he was trying to distract me from my thoughts. It worked – slaves never get a day off or time for morbid reflection.

As he looked back at me, still slumped on the floor, I jumped up and said, 'Okay, Albert, I'm so sorry; you must be starving.'

Albert scoffed his overdue meal, but as he ate, he kept tensely looking over his shoulder, making sure I was still there. I was certain of one thing: I'd soon be cleaning up cat vomit if he didn't slow down.

I was desperate for a long shower, but before going upstairs I said, 'Albert, slow down; you're eating too fast. I need to head upstairs and do some, um, grooming, before Uncle J arrives. See you soon, baby.'

I stood under that glorious stream of piping hot water – ignoring my own two-minute rule and preserving our world's most precious commodity – and it felt so soothing, so calming as it washed away the trauma.

Out of the shower, I carefully applied a little make-up to lift my tired face and chose my brightest and favourite outfit, one I knew Uncle J would like. It's hard to be mediocre around him.

I was just putting on my earrings when I heard the courtyard gate open – John and I have keys to one another's homes.

In unison, Albert and I ran downstairs to greet John, Max and Uncle J. I was overjoyed to see them, these three men I loved and who loved me. Uncle J threw down his cabin luggage, grabbed me in his arms and, lifting me off the ground and hugging me tightly, kept repeating, 'Princess, princess, princess.'

I hugged him back and said, 'Thanks for coming early. I can never explain to you how much that means to me. I love you so much.'

A sigh of relief at seeing I was okay escaped him, and he gently put me down and said, 'I love you, I love you, I love you.'

Knowing Uncle J and sensing that a diffusing of the situation was in order, John said, 'Uncle J, Albert is waiting for some attention.'

I threw my best friend a grateful smile, bent down and picked up my suitably attired Albert. 'Uncle J, Albert's dressed for the occasion. Doesn't he look handsome?'

As John had rightly assumed, Uncle J was utterly captivated by Albert's attire; so captivated, in fact, that he slipped out of his threes phase, took him from my arms, straightened his bowtie and said, 'Why, Albert! You do look handsome. Thank you for dressing for the occasion.'

Albert crawled up and settled himself comfortably over Uncle J left shoulder as if they'd known one another forever – and perhaps they had.

John and Max had organised dinner: green chicken curry, jasmine rice and chickpea dahl with raita and garlic roti. They'd thought of everything, including wine.

Max carried Uncle J's bags up to his room, and soon enough the table was set, the wine was poured, and the four of us were seated around my dining room table sharing our delicious meal, with Albert sitting beside us on his own chair.

Everything seemed right with my world, until I remembered that the one person I'd love to be there was missing. A look must have passed over my face, because John said, 'Pip, as soon as we finish, call the hospital and speak to him.'

I was transparent, obviously. All three men – and, if you can believe it, Albert – were looking at me as I said, 'Do you mind? I've had enough; I'm stuffed to the eyeballs. I'd like to phone him right away.'

When I rang, I learned that Bill had been transferred out of ICU and into a general medical ward. I spoke to the receptionist first, asking could she please give him a message that I'd called and was thinking of him, but she immediately said, 'Hang on, I'll put you through.'

She must have let him know who was phoning. In a moment Bill was on the end of the line, and with real feeling he said, 'Hello, Pip, I'm so glad to hear from you.'

Heart fluttering, I tried to think of something not too gushy to say. 'Bill, how are you? You sound so much better than when I left earlier today. I'm so glad you've been transferred to a ward.'

Cheerfully he responded, 'So am I, believe me. You don't get much sleep in ICU – not that I'm complaining. They looked after me incredibly well. What are you up to? Hang on, is Uncle Jim there?'

With a smile that I couldn't keep out of my voice, I said,

'Yes, he is, and John and Max. We're just finishing off a curry the boys made.' I could have bit my tongue for saying 'just finishing' – Bill said, 'Oh, Pip, go back to your meal. We can talk tomorrow. Give everyone my best. Look, snap, they've just brought my meal, though I doubt it will be up to yours if John and Max are living up to their reputation. Enjoy your evening; we'll talk tomorrow.'

As I hung up, I realised we'd both reverted back to being awkward with one another – danger over, let's not show how much we care.

As I came back to the table, all eyes were on me. John was first to comment, encapsulating what the others must have been thinking: 'That was quick. How is he?'

Uncle J, never missing a beat, said, 'When do I get to meet him?'

They were so subtle. I wasn't sure I wanted to share my feelings about the brevity of our call, so instead I did what I normally do – I rabbited on, trying to change the subject with, 'Woo, slow down, give a woman a chance to relax and finish her meal first! I need to drive up to collect my car. Uncle J, are you up for hiring a car and driving me up to collect it? I also have to square things with work. If I continue to work, um, with the police, I might need to come up with a plan.'

Uncle J had obviously already given this some thought. Rocking forward in his chair, he said, 'Easy-peasy, easy-peasy, easy-peasy. Do what I've done most of my working life: get an ABN and contract for them. Works for you and works for them; they won't want to lose you.'

I knew he was right – it was that simple. I also knew that, although he was acting as if my continuing to work with Bill and the police was fine by him, he had conflicting feelings about it. His lapsing back into threes was a sure sign of this. He wanted me, his only living relative, safe.

I stood, kissed him on the top of the head and said, 'You're a genius, Uncle J. I'll give Amanda a call after we clear up.'

Max jumped in then, saying they'd clear up and I should make my call now.

So I did. As Uncle J had expected, she said she thought we could make that work and that we could discuss it when I came back to work.

After clearing up, the four of us sat in front of the fire talking. Wanting to call it a night, Uncle J started to sing a song he used to sing to me as a child to encourage me to have a shower and go to bed. To the tune of 'Let's Forget About Tomorrow', he started to enthusiastically sing, *'I'm gonna have a Chihuahua, I'm gonna have a Chihuahua, I'm gonna have a Chihuahua cause Chihuahuas they are fun.'*

Of course, in true Tourettic form, I instantly joined in singing this inane song over and over. Fact – get Tourettic people together, and they love to mimic one another. Well, we love to mimic lots of things, really. Uncle J had always had a tendency to turn phrases into songs. It's one of the reasons he's so brilliant and successful in his field – his neurodiverse brain was jingle heaven.

Soon John stood, stretched and yawned – he'd heard this routine before – and with great love said, 'If you two are going to start that routine, we're going home. Besides I need a Chihuahua … great, you've got me doing it now.'

They went home to Leroy, and Uncle J finally had me all to himself. Once they'd gone, we caught up on lost time, particularly the esoteric occurrences of the past twenty-four hours. There's no better feeling than being with your tribe. When it came time to get ready for bed, Uncle J said in a mock-upper-crust British accent that he mimicked so well, 'I don't know about you, Pip, old girl, but I'm stuffed, and we have a long drive tomorrow.'

And as he walked upstairs, Albert lovingly following, all I could think was that I couldn't wait for Bill to meet him.

CHAPTER 42

As I lay in bed thinking about Uncle J, I realised that the advertising industry was one of the few work environments prepared to not only accept but to embrace my uncle's neurodiversity. From what I'd heard, in his working life his Tourettic tics and antics made for some very interesting and 'out there' brainstorming sessions.

Uncle J could out-brainstorm most in the room. The calisthenics that his brain performed in these creative meetings had a flow-on effect; a no-holds-barred approach, if you like. Creative people not only accept difference, they embrace it and thrive on it.

I lay there thinking about what we'd discussed. We'd talked about how well his career was going; how his life in Tasmania meant he missed seeing me; and how he was quietly confident in his new relationship with Sam.

We'd talked about my parents and we'd even wasted a few minutes on Zac, both agreeing he'd taken enough time away from us.

We'd talked about my initial visit to the Hunter, which had pushed me down the esoteric path. We agreed that Grandma Ella and Ruth had probably had a hand in my choosing Ruth's Cottage in the first place. Lastly, we'd talked about Albert and, of course, Bill.

I couldn't remember feeling this content, feeling this alive, for a very long time. Eventually I drifted into a deep and dreamless sleep.

After the best night's sleep I'd had in forever, Uncle J, Albert and I had a huge breakfast. After breakfast I booked a cab to take us to the hire car company.

Albert wasn't impressed that we were going out. To sweeten the bitter pill, I bribed him with treats. As we were leaving, he'd already taken up his favourite spot in the sun in the court-yard. Then the cab arrived in Shirley Lane, the driver tooting three times, pleasing both my uncle and me.

Uncle J, both excited and nervous about meeting Bill, promptly proceeded to mimic this sound – toot, toot, toot; toot, toot, toot; toot, toot, toot. It promised to be an interesting day.

The hire car people were a little, shall I say, concerned that Uncle J would be driving their car. Tourette's misleads people. He's an exceptionally good driver: attentive, careful, and his reactions are lightning fast. Rather than trying to convince them of this, I simply said I'd be driving – if only they knew.

On the way to collect my car, Uncle J eventually got around to asking, 'So, princess, what do you think Bill will make of me?'

It was the very first time I could remember him expressing a concern about what one of my friends would 'make of him'.

Taken aback, I was momentarily lost for words – rare indeed. I wanted to choose my next sentence carefully, to reassure him. Eventually I said, 'You know I don't care what anyone thinks about you. If they don't get you, that's their bad luck …'

'Well, thank you, princess –'

I cut him off. 'No; let me finish. Having said that – and I mean this – Bill will love you; I have no doubt. So will Pat, so promise me you will just be yourself!'

After a long pause – mind you, all pauses seem interminable to the Tourettic brain – and with a smile on his handsome face, he said, 'Okay, okay, okay; I will.'

CHAPTER 43

Once we'd found a park and checked with reception what ward and bed Bill was in, we made our way up to the second floor. I couldn't believe how excited yet nervous I was at seeing Bill again.

Sensing my unease, and forgetting his own, Uncle J wrapped his arm around my shoulder and said, 'You look beautiful, princess. He's probably as nervous as we are at the prospect of seeing us both. Just try to relax, said the pot to the kettle. Come on, you know what I mean.'

As we rounded the corner to the entrance of the ward, we saw Pat, Julie and Charlotte. We were both pleased at their obvious delight in seeing us.

Pat, in his gentle disarming way, introduced himself and the sisters, saying, 'Hi, you must be the famous Uncle Jim. I'd like to introduce Bill's sisters, Julie and Charlotte.'

I felt myself tense, not because I was ever ashamed of Uncle J – I never was and never would be – but because I wanted him to feel comfortable. He felt the same way about hospitals as I did.

I was amazed when he quietly and confidently said, 'Pat, I'm very pleased to meet you; Pip's told me a lot about you – all good things – and ladies, I'm very pleased to meet you both also. You must be so relieved that your brother is doing so well. I know Pip is. I'm so looking forward to meeting him … I … I …'

Okay, like me he waffles on when he's nervous, but I was so proud of him I couldn't wipe the smile off my face.

Pat kindly jumped to the rescue, saying, 'We've all been in to see him, so why don't the two of you go in. We know he's dying to see you, Pip, and to meet you, Jim.'

After saying our goodbyes, since they were about to leave, Pat quietly took me aside and said, 'Pip, Bill looks great. He thinks they might send him home today or tomorrow; they need the bed.'

Gratefully I responded, 'That's fantastic news. Thanks, Pat.'

Pat was full of good news today, and continued. 'Oh, by the way, I bumped into Emily from the *Hunter Valley Age*. She told me Ruth Richards' memorial service will be in the next week or so. She knew Ruth personally, so she's helping put together the service. I'll get her to email you the details. Now get in there and put the poor man out of his misery.'

Even stressed to the eyeballs that day at the newspaper, I'd sensed a connection between Pat and Emily, despite Pat's denials. I hoped so, anyway.

As they left, Uncle J and I made our way to Bed 23. When

we pulled the curtain back, Bill was sitting up reading, and he looked, well, he looked amazing. I felt my heart do a flip.

When he saw us both, his face lit up. His voice sounded a little nervous as he said, 'Pip, I've been waiting for you to turn up. You must be Jim; nice to finally meet you in person. I've heard so many good things about you; it's a real pleasure to meet you.'

The fact that Bill seemed nervous about this meeting made us both instantly want to make him feel better. To my surprise and joy, Uncle J responded with, 'Likewise, Bill, likewise. I'm very pleased to finally meet you also.'

He'd only said 'likewise' twice! We were off to a very good start; well, I thought so, until he reached out and tapped Bill on his right shoulder three times.

Bill didn't disappoint, taking those three taps in his stride. He didn't flinch, he just accepted them as quintessentially Uncle J, and it made me love the man even more.

Excitedly Bill said to me, 'Sounds like they might send me home, either later this afternoon once the doctor has done his rounds, or first thing tomorrow morning. Has Pat told you the memorial service for Ruth is going to take place in the next week or so? Emily has the details.'

I didn't let on that Pat had, saying, 'Oh, Bill, that's great news on both counts. Burt is going to be so happy to see you. No doubt Pat will get Emily to email me the details of when the service is. How are you feeling?'

'I feel great. I just want to get out of here as soon as I can. You don't get much sleep in hospitals. How are you? I get the feeling I haven't been told the full story about the other night. What's being left out?'

There was no way I was going to upset him by telling him that Walton had done a Scanlan on me, or about Ruth's apparition, for that matter. What could I say? 'Oh, yeah, I forgot to mention: Walton tried a Scanlan on me, and this time instead of Burt knocking him over, Ruth scared him half to death, saving my life in the process.'

Nah, that conversation wasn't going to happen just yet.

Uncle J, sensing my reluctance – his radar was working just fine – jumped to the rescue. 'So, Bill, my niece tells me there might be a possibility to use her innate abilities doing some work with the police. Are they going to pay her for her time and skills?'

He could be direct at times, particularly where my best interests were concerned. On this particular occasion I could have kissed him for asking questions I hadn't had the nerve to ask.

If I was going to continue to put myself in harm's way, it was only fair that I should be given some form of recompense, or at the very least have my medical bills covered.

Bill didn't bat an eyelid. In that question he saw a like-minded man, a man who would protect his family no matter what.

Before I could finish saying, 'Uncle J, don't be so …', Bill jumped in.

'Jim's right. I've given this some thought while I've been here. We need to discuss the situation fully. First, do you want to continue to help, and if so, how would you like to structure it? I'd need to speak to those in charge to see if we could formalise this, um, working relationship, so this is a conversation that we'd need to have at some stage.'

I was extremely grateful to Uncle J for kicking this idea into the ballpark, and he knew it, judging by the self-satisfied smile on his face.

Needing to give it some more consideration though, I said, 'Thanks, Bill. I appreciate it, but let's have that conversation when you're home and we have the time to discuss it properly. I don't think a busy public hospital ward is the right time or place.'

It occurred to me that I was avoiding having the conversation because it wasn't something I'd ever thought I'd do for money. I'd need some sort of recompense though, especially if I was going to be losing hours from my publishing job.

First things first, though: neither of us knew if the police department would even be open to using me again. It might end up being a love job.

Once we'd skirted around the conversation we needed to have, the three of us spent a pleasant time getting to know each other better.

Uncle J had an overwhelming urge to keep touching Bill's shoulder three times, but none of us was particularly perturbed by this manifestation or his fascination for Bill's right shoulder.

Eventually, being the sensitive man he was and wanting to give us time alone, Uncle J said, 'Well, I'm going to try to find a decent coffee. I know, tall order in a hospital. Does anyone want one?'

We responded in unison, 'Yes, please.'

Orders taken, and with three departing taps for good measure, he left us alone, or as alone as you can be in a four-bed ward.

Once he'd left, Bill smiled and motioned with his finger for me to come closer. 'Come here; I've been dying to kiss you since you arrived.'

His brush with death had obviously removed a few of his own filters.

I bent down, and we kissed. I don't think I will ever get tired of his kisses. They melt me, they calm me and, okay, they excite me in a way no one else's kisses ever have. I couldn't wait to be held in his arms, away from the sterile and unnatural environment that all hospitals are.

One thing still concerned me, though; if I was to work with Bill in his role with the police, was it possible to have a professional working relationship with someone I felt so attracted to, and who I now knew was attracted to me?

Over the past few days, I'd wondered if our attraction had anything to do with the phenomenon called 'near death attraction'. Throw that into the mix of what was already a very multifaceted situation – age difference, neurodiversity and near-death attraction, three complex bedfellows. I had to wonder if it would work. I guessed time would tell.

CHAPTER 44

Before long, Bill was back in the Hunter. Apparently, Burt was beside himself when Pat first dropped Bill home, even piddling himself in his excitement at seeing the one human being he loved above all others. Sorry, Burt: too much information.

I'd gone back to work, and had what passes for a formal meeting in publishing about my working life with the company. We agreed, in theory, that if I set up an ABN, I could take on work as and when I wanted to, when they had work available. It was a risk, and we agreed to give it a three-month trial both ways to see if it worked for them and for me.

It was more than I could have expected, and I was extremely grateful, in fact quite proud, that they felt enough of me to even consider this new work arrangement.

Uncle J had decided to extend his stay, so he could spend time with me and start looking for somewhere to buy. I hadn't asked him outright, but I was sure that Sam had also been factored into his decision.

Bill and I kept in regular contact. Whenever he phoned, Uncle J would tactfully leave the room. Meanwhile, Emily sent an email with the details of Ruth's memorial service. It was to take place on Ruth's property, and her many friends would attend. With my new contractual working arrangement, it would be easy for me to schedule time off to attend.

I was determined that Albert would go to the memorial service. He needed closure; he also needed to see his canine friend, Burt. Anyway, I felt he did.

Uncle J, Albert and I drove up for the service together. As we entered Bill's property, I could feel the butterflies in my stomach. Those butterflies were for many reasons, and driving back to the Hunter bought it all back to me, especially my stay in Ruth's Cottage, when my life as I knew it had changed completely and irrevocably.

The feeling was excitement at the prospect of introducing Uncle J to all my newfound friends, at Albert seeing Burt again, and, most of all, at my seeing Bill. I was both dreading today because I'd miss her, and pleased that Ruth would finally be at peace.

As we drove up the driveway to Bill's house, Bill and Burt, hearing us coming, were waiting on the front veranda. Burt, recognising my car, began to run up and down the front of the house. Uncle J fell instantly in love with Burt, and Burt took to him on sight, nearly knocking him over in his excitement to meet him.

Animals are better at sensing beautiful people than humans are.

Then Burt realised I was there and jumped up, licking my face, my neck, all over. At last, in what can only be described as a priceless moment, he saw Albert and I have to tell you we were all forgotten as these two friends became reacquainted.

Once inside, we sat in front of the fire and had a cup of tea and some scones, which were fresh from the oven. With Burt and Albert snuggled together at our feet, we discussed how the memorial service would unfold and how healing it would be for everyone concerned.

Bill had put a lot of thought into the sleeping arrangements. Uncle J had the back bedroom in the main house. I had the guest bedroom, next to his. Bill wanted my uncle to be certain that he not only cared about me, he respected me.

After a wonderful roast beef dinner, we prepared to retire early. Uncle J, giving us time to talk and say goodnight in private, was the first to head to bed. Albert and Burt weren't leaving one another's sides, and were sound asleep in front of the fire, which by now was smouldering embers.

When I was finally alone with Bill, I felt quite reticent knowing Uncle J was close by. Bill surprised me by saying that he'd already had a tentative conversation with his superiors in Sydney about the possibility of my working with them in future.

They would, in theory, be open to call upon my services when needed. Discussions would have to continue regarding how, if at all, they could compensate me, budgets in the police force being tight.

After this unexpected conversation, we did spend a very

pleasant time getting reacquainted. Talk about sensual over-load – near death attraction or not.

When the clock struck eleven, knowing we had a very long and emotional day ahead of us and that Uncle J was just down the hall, we reluctantly made our separate ways to bed.

CHAPTER 45

After breakfast, Pat arrived with Emily to discuss the order of Ruth's memorial service. With Emily's help and personal knowledge of Ruth, they'd done an incredible job of putting together a very moving service, with a wonderful photo tribute that they showed us in advance.

There were photos of Ruth with Thomas, her much-loved husband; Ruth with friends; Ruth at community events; Ruth at demonstrations in her younger years; and Ruth acting the fool, living life to the full, not afraid to pull a face for the camera. The ones I loved the most were photos of Ruth with Albert. All of these photos had been carefully collated, lovingly put together to show the vibrant and much-loved person Ruth was.

When I saw the photos, I cried, not only tears of grief, though I knew that was definitely what we all felt, but tears of joy that they had captured her life so well, a life obviously well-lived if not well-ended.

I also felt a real sense of loss that I hadn't known this wonderful, interesting and vibrant woman when she was alive, my only connection with her being unconventional, to say the least – first meeting her briefly as a child, then after her brutal and untimely departure.

The seven of us, including Albert and Burt, set off in a group to send her on her way. The service was to be held on the vineyard of the property she and Thomas had lived and loved. As per her wishes, her remains were to be buried with him in their small private plot.

It was a glorious day, the sun shining and not a cloud in the sky, as if Mother Nature was honouring Ruth by creating the perfect day. When we arrived at the little cemetery on the property, there was already a good crowd of people congregated to say goodbye.

I was moved to see that a couple of policemen from Sydney had taken time to attend the service of a woman they'd never met. They were there to represent the police department and to pay their respects at this overdue send-off.

Nic and Luke had also made the journey to pay their respects to a woman they'd never met. Ruth's true essence as a person had affected many people both in life and in death.

Brendan O'Connor, his lovely wife Amelia, and their two beautiful children were there also. The children, captivated by Albert and Burt, were not aware of the sad reason for the gathering. Children and animals always make the saddest of occasions bearable by the mere fact of their presence.

When Brendan introduced Amelia to the rest of us, she

thanked all the men for what they'd done to rescue and protect Brendan. Then she turned to me, gave me a firm hug and whispered in my ear her thanks for the unorthodox part I'd played in not only helping to save Brendan but in giving her family back their life.

While all of this was going on, Uncle J stood back with the broadest and most endearing smile and a look of pride on his handsome face. Believe me, when Uncle J smiles, you can't help but feel happy.

I was grateful and moved to see that both John and Max had made the journey as well, again to say goodbye to a woman they'd never met but had been touched by. They hadn't told me they were attending, so their surprise presence was comforting and so appreciated.

Of course, Joe and Marg were there, but by far the biggest contingent was Ruth's remaining friends – you know the ones: the older, unnoticed people in society. One thing for sure, they weren't going unnoticed today, not if they had anything to do with it.

Thankfully there was one person missing today, the person who should have loved and cared for Ruth, showing her the same love and care she had given him – her nephew, David Walton. Instead, through his evil greed, he'd been the one responsible for her life coming to such a brutal and untimely end.

He and his cohorts were still in prison, awaiting their respective trials. No one mentioned him, or the tragic way Ruth's life had ended. No one gave him or the brutal circumstances of her death the power to ruin Ruth's farewell; this day was all about her and how much she'd changed lives and made the world better.

As the service unfolded, one by one each person who wanted to pay tribute to Ruth Richards had a turn. There would be no one in the background telling them to hurry up, that the next service was waiting to commence; not today. Ruth had waited a very long time for the truth to come out and to be reunited with Thomas and buried in the place where she wanted to rest – by his side.

There were some very moving eulogies that day, and some very amusing ones, as well. By most accounts, Ruth had a very wicked and quirky sense of humour. That was the main thing that the people who loved her wanted to remember her by; that, and how kind she was.

As is often the case at funerals, mixed in with the laughs there were also tears, especially when Muriel, the bravest of all, got up to have her say. She was having a good day, dementia-wise. Hesitantly, she told everyone just how much their friendship had meant to her. As she spoke, there wasn't a dry eye in the place.

During the service, I held Albert on my lap while Burt sat close by. I knew Albert didn't understand the human need for closure on such a grand scale, but I felt he wanted to be there at the end, to see the woman he loved above all others finally rest in peace.

As the service came to an end, during the silence as Ruth was buried in her chosen resting place with her much-loved

Thomas, Albert jumped down from my lap and went to stand beside the gravesite. I felt my breath catch, and as I gulped, trying to keep my composure, Bill on one side and Uncle J on the other each grabbed and held a hand, giving me support and strength.

As I looked around the eclectic mix of people attending Ruth's service – old friends, local people, hardened and strong police officers, John and Max, Brendan and Amelia, dear Muriel and her carer to name a few, you could see how greatly moved everyone was that Ruth was now finally at peace.

In a private moment between us, I thanked Ruth from the bottom of my heart for all she'd done.

She was the reason why I had reconnected with my clairsentience, my innate esoteric abilities, my true nature and the essence of who I am.

She was the reason I'd met Albert, Burt, Pat and my other new friends.

She was the reason I was now connected on another level with Uncle J.

She was the reason the mystery of her own disappearance and murder had been solved, and for Bill now having a clear conscience, knowing that justice had finally been served.

Finally, she was the reason I'd met Bill, the man who, if the stars remained aligned, I would spend a lot of time with, both professionally and personally.

As the last guest threw an orchid, Ruth's favourite flower, onto her coffin, I silently said my last goodbye; well, at least that's what I thought.

'Rest in peace, dear Ruth; Albert and I are going to miss you terribly.'

Then, as I felt a gentle breeze caress my face and neck, Ruth clearly responded, *'No you won't, my dear; I'm not leaving either of you. Seems you might need me still!'*

ACKNOWLEDGEMENTS

Much of *Ice Valley*, is set in the Hunter Valley region, which is a beautiful and safe place to live and visit. It is home of the Wonnarua people. I'd like to acknowledge the traditional owners.

I want to thank the amazingly talented team at Independent Ink for their hard work, guidance, and professionalism, in helping me on the journey to self-publish *Ice Valley*. They are a superb team of professionals, offering exceptional service. It's been a pleasure working with you all. I've learnt so much from you, and could not have done this without your guidance.

Jennifer Kremmer from Book Anvil worked on the initial manuscripts with me. Working with Jennie was like taking a master class in writing. I want to thank Jennie for being such a great mentor, for her editing skill, patience, encouragement, insight, generosity of spirit, friendship and for helping me to improve my craft. I am forever in your debt.

Many friends over the past five plus years have read at least one of the three manuscript drafts; some read the first and final drafts.

I'd like to thank – Bronny, Cheryl, Jane, Kerry, Margaret and Vik. Thank you for your patience, suggestions and for being such supportive friends. Your feedback and encouragement have meant so much to me.

My niece Natalie designed my author website. Thanks Nat, I am so grateful you did. With your artistic flair and skill as a designer, you nailed it.

Ice Valley started life in 1999 as a short story assignment for a Book Editing and Publishing Course. Years later, I emailed it to my niece Georgie to read. With her encouragement I turned it into my novel *Ice Valley*. Thanks Georgie.

My family have given me their love, support and encouragement, to keep writing, to get *Ice Valley* finished. You've all shown me by example what perseverance is. Thank you one and all. I love you.

Detective Bill Browne is named in honour of my Uncle William Norman Browne, Police Registration Number 3298, who sadly passed away in 1939, aged 30. When he passed, he was with Brisbane CIB, Plain Clothes Staff. Wish I'd known you Uncle Bill.

Last but not least, to my patient, loving and supportive husband Laurie. I could not have done this without you darling. You good-naturedly read all three drafts and gave some very helpful suggestions. I'll never forget when you read the first draft you said: 'I can't believe you wrote this Jill, It's brilliant'. I still laugh when I remember that compliment. You are my best friend and my world. I love you.

If I've forgotten to thank you, I'm sorry. It's been a long and wonderful journey of discovery for me, and I thank you all for being a part of it.